LOVE *at* LAST

LOVE *at* LAST

---❦---

THREE HISTORICAL ROMANCE NOVELLAS
of LOVE *in* DAYS GONE BY

A Search for Refuge · KRISTI ANN HUNTER

Summer of Dreams · ELIZABETH CAMDEN

Up from the Sea · AMANDA DYKES

BETHANYHOUSE

a division of Baker Publishing Group
Minneapolis, Minnesota

A Search for Refuge © 2018 by Kristi Ann Hunter
Summer of Dreams © 2016 by Dorothy Mays
Up from the Sea © 2019 by Amanda Dykes

11400 Hampshire Avenue South
Bloomington, Minnesota 55438
www.bethanyhouse.com

Bethany House Publishers is a division of
Baker Publishing Group, Grand Rapids, Michigan

Printed in the United States of America

Library of Congress Cataloging-in-Publication Data
Names: Hunter, Kristi Ann. Search for refuge. | Camden, Elizabeth. Summer of dreams. | Dykes, Amanda. Up from the sea.
Title: Love at last : three historical romance novellas of love in days gone by.
Description: Bloomington, Minnesota : Bethany House Publishers, [2019]
Identifiers: LCCN 2019002250 | ISBN 9780764234163 (casebound) | ISBN 9780764233425 (trade paper)
Subjects: LCSH: Romance fiction, American—21st century. | Christian fiction, American—21st century. | Historical fiction, American—21st century.
Classification: LCC PS648.L6 L653 2019 | DDC 813/.08508—dc23 LC record available at https://lccn.loc.gov/2019002250

Scripture quotations are from the King James Version of the Bible.

These are works of fiction and/or historical reconstruction. In historical reconstruction, the appearances of certain historical figures are therefore inevitable; all other characters are products of the author's imagination, and any resemblance to actual events or persons, living or dead, is entirely coincidental. In works of fiction, the names, characters, incidents, and dialogues are products of the author's imagination and are not to be construed as real. Any resemblance to actual events or persons, living or dead, is entirely coincidental.

Kristi Ann Hunter is represented by Natasha Kern of the Natasha Kern Literary Agency, Inc.
Amanda Dykes is represented by Books & Such Literary Agency.

Cover design by Brand Navigation

19 20 21 22 23 24 25   7 6 5 4 3 2 1

CONTENTS

A SEARCH
for REFUGE

❦

A
HAVEN MANOR
NOVELLA

KRISTI ANN
HUNTER

1

MARLBOROUGH, ENGLAND
1804

Margaretta had used the word *desperate* many times in her life, but she'd never truly known the meaning until she stood in the open door of a mail coach, clutching an eight-month-old letter and praying that someone in this minuscule market town would know where the writer had gone when she moved on.

And that Margaretta could find that writer before Samuel Albany found her.

Because that writer was Margaretta's last hope. And hope was something Margaretta desperately needed to find. In the truest sense of the word.

"Are you getting out here, miss?"

Margaretta forced her gaze away from the broad stone-cobbled street lined with red-bricked buildings and porticoed storefronts. The man holding the door and growing justifiably impatient wore the red coat of the English mail service and thick layer of travel dust. To him, Margaretta likely appeared a woman without a care in the world compared to his current discomfort.

If he knew she was running for her life, would he still think that?

Not that it mattered. His opinion couldn't matter. No one's could. Margaretta knew the truth, knew what decisions she would be willing to live with, and that was all that could be allowed to matter.

"Yes, I'm getting off." She shoved the letter into the pocket of her bright yellow cloak and wrapped her hand around the worn leather handle of her valise. The heavy bag bumped against her knee as she climbed down, threatening to toss her on top of the dirty mail worker and flatten his nose even more. She jumped instead, jarring her knees as her walking boots hit the ground. It was an unladylike exit from the vehicle to say the least, but far better than landing on the ground on her backside.

Blowing a hard breath out between pursed lips, Margaretta stepped to the side and set her valise at her feet. She adjusted the hood of her cloak so that it shadowed her face. Yes, it made it difficult to see around her, but it also kept people from seeing her. She'd much rather people remember the enormous hood of a ridiculous bright yellow cloak than her face. As a woman traveling alone on the stage, people were going to look at her. It was either wear something memorable and distracting or cover herself in the somber colors of mourning, which she wasn't willing to do. That would be like admitting defeat before she'd even begun.

Lifting her valise, she turned her head to survey the town with a critical eye. It was charming, with a considerable openness she'd never experienced in London, but she didn't have the luxury of standing around, pondering the benefits of fresh air and space. Her time was limited, her funds even more so. If she was going to solve her problems before both of those commodities ran out, she was going to have to be smart. And while she'd tried very hard to always be prudent and practical, clever had never been required of her.

She slid a hand into her pocket and curled it around the already wrinkled paper. Her friend Katherine had always been clever, though, and Margaretta was counting on being able to follow her friend's clever path to make sure everything turned out as it should and everyone stayed safe for at least the next few months.

Hopefully Katherine hadn't been so clever that Margaretta's efforts were entirely futile. This letter was the last connection Margaretta had to her friend, and it held pitifully little information.

Exhaustion crowded Margaretta's mind. She'd been traveling for three days straight, taking mail coach after mail coach on a wide route around London to avoid anyone who might be looking for her. As long as everyone thought her safely tucked away in Margate, sea-bathing with Mrs. Hollybroke and her daughters, she would have time. Time to hide, time to come up with a plan, time to accomplish the impossible task of finding Katherine. Since complete disappearance seemed to be part of Katherine's solution, Margaretta could only hope her letter was the start of a small trail of breadcrumbs.

So the questions was, if Margaretta wanted to find someone who didn't particularly want to be found—where would she start?

Her stomach grumbled and clenched, reminding her that the meat pie she'd consumed at a roadside inn for breakfast had been eaten a very long time ago.

She wasn't going to do anyone any good, particularly not herself, if she collapsed from hunger and weariness in the middle of the street. Food and lodging first, then. Tomorrow she could start her search.

The large three-gabled inn to her right looked promising and comfortable. It also looked like it catered to the expensive tastes of those traveling from London on the stagecoaches. Not only would staying there make her purse dwindle faster than she'd like, it would also put her at risk of running into someone she knew. She couldn't have anyone going back to London with the news that Margaretta was in Marlborough.

So she started walking. Away from the inn and the delightful smells drifting out of it. Away from the coach and the people with whom she'd spent the past several hours sharing a tiny space.

Away from everything she was familiar with.

Travel was something she'd done a great deal of in her life. One didn't have a father in the business of saddles and harnesses without getting a chance or two to test out the leather creations. But never had she wandered alone, away from the areas populated with other travelers like herself.

A deep breath trembled its way into her tight lungs. She could do this. One foot in front of the other. Breathing in for two steps and out for two steps. Absorb the idyllic calm of the wide street that grew quieter the farther she got from the stable. Find something to focus on and just keep moving until a solution presented itself. It was a scary prospect that made her normally pragmatic self shake in her boots, but for the past month and a half it had served her well. Pick a point and move toward it.

Farther down the street, a woman swept the pavement in front of a store. The sign simply read *Lancaster's*, but the array of bundled herbs hanging in the window and the barrels of food beneath indicated the store was likely a grocer. Margaretta's stomach grumbled again. It wouldn't be a gourmet meal, but if she could patch together a meal of fruit and cheese and perhaps other foods not requiring much preparation, she'd spend less than half of what she'd have to spend in an inn's public room.

It was as good as any other option she had at the moment. Her lips flattened into a line of determination as she gathered her strength together and moved toward the grocer, trying to ignore the nervous fear that made her want to glance over her shoulder to see if anyone was following her.

Nash Banfield stepped away from the door to his office and followed the woman down the street.

Given the location of his office just off Marlborough's central street, he'd seen many a person disembark from a variety of carriages. Normally he paid them only mild attention, but the brightness of this woman's cloak had been impossible to miss as she paused in the door of the carriage, a spot of sunshine framed by faded, dusty paint and the thin grey clouds that covered the sky.

Clouds that made it strange that she took time to pull the enormous hood over her head, shielding her dark hair and pale skin from view.

No one had joined her, and she'd claimed none of the trunks and bags being removed from the top of the carriage. Instead she'd taken her lone leather valise and walked with firm strides away from the coach, the inn, and all of the people.

Nash had been a solicitor for many years, and he'd rarely seen anything good come from someone traveling alone, traveling light, and hiding her face.

He'd seen that face for only a few moments before the hood had cast the strong brows and full mouth into deep shadow. From this distance, he couldn't make out the emotion riding her features, but there had been little doubt of the strength with which she felt it. It was evident in the square of her shoulders, the press of her lips, the determination in her pace.

In Nash's experience, strong emotion of any kind had the potential to turn dangerous.

Mr. Tucker, a well-dressed man who owned one of the local cheese factories, passed her, tipping his hat as he went.

The woman didn't acknowledge him, and instead turned away to cross the street. The folds of her yellow cloak swirled around her, revealing a dress of deep blue underneath it.

Nash pressed his lips into a flat line as he clasped his hands together at his lower back and waited, watching to see where she was going. It wasn't that a stranger in town was anything new. Many people dressed as fine as she and considerably finer came through town, viewing it as a humble and rustic resting point between London and Bath.

Most of those people didn't take the mail coach, though.

In a few days, the town would be bursting with people—strangers and locals alike. When the weekly market came to town, Marlborough would explode with people. The wide cobblestoned street would be filled to capacity, if not beyond it, and noise would echo from the tall roofs and narrow side alleys. But right now, the town was quiet.

It was a small community; only two parishes divided the town, and the people who roamed the streets and did their business during the week were close. They'd surrounded Nash after the death of his sister, helped him heal from the final loss of the last person he had held so dear, kept him from retreating into a dark and consuming melancholy that he feared would come for him.

They'd become his family.

Nash's hands dropped to his side, and his natural inquisitive curiosity shifted toward grave concern as it became evident that the woman was walking straight for Mrs. Lancaster's store. The older woman had kept the business after the death of her husband, continuing to provide a place for Marlborough's residents to buy food, spices, and a variety of other items during the week without waiting for the crush of Saturday's market. But the woman was generous to a fault, particularly to young women. She'd befriended many of the ladies who worked in the local poorhouses and replaced more than one little girl's wooden graces hoop without asking for a penny in return.

When Mr. Lancaster had gotten sick, he'd asked Nash to promise to look after his wife. That had been nearly five years ago, but it hadn't taken long for Nash to learn that watching over Mrs. Lancaster wasn't easy, considering the fact that the woman never did anything in a way that could remotely be considered normal. Nash dreaded the day someone took advantage of the old widow's kindness.

Someone like a woman who got off a stage and headed straight for the grocer. Perhaps she knew she'd be able to trade a sad story for gain.

He pushed off from the wall and strolled down the street. The people of Marlborough had saved him eight years ago. This town was the only family he had left. He was ready to protect it if necessary.

❖

Margaretta's eyes widened as she took in the shelves and barrels of foodstuffs, herbs, and a myriad of other things she'd have never thought to find in a grocer. Did they have stores like this in London? She'd never really done the shopping in London, at least not for food. Ribbons and hats and gloves were interesting, but they didn't provide the same visual texture and smells as a room full of culinary potential.

Everywhere she looked she saw something else, something she wanted to remember next time she sat with the housekeeper to dither over the menu, to make slight adjustments in the planned dishes and anticipate how excited her father would be to have something new on the table that evening.

Of course, it would be a long time before she could return to their townhouse in London and while away the morning with a menu and her imagination. Right now, she was more interested in the baskets of late-season apples and nectarines and was giving serious consideration to eating them in a back alley despite the fact that they were raw. She was simply too hungry to care and didn't have a means to cook them anyway.

The woman she'd passed as she entered hummed as she followed Margaretta inside and stored her broom in a nook near the door. The tune was vaguely familiar. A song she'd heard in church, perhaps? It was not a tune that lent itself to dancing so it couldn't have been from a ballroom.

Margaretta's mouth watered as her senses adjusted to the quiet of the grocer after the noise of the traveling coach. She could smell cheese and bread in addition to the various herbs and spices that filled more shelves. It was a welcome change from horses and the unwashed bodies of travelers. The room was dim, forcing her to push her hood back, so she kept her back to the door as the woman approached.

"Well, now, don't get many customers fresh off the stage. What can I get you?" The woman rounded the counter. She was spry, though her right foot drug a bit behind her as she walked. Age rested comfortably on her round face, framed by a few gray-streaked brown curls escaping from the cap on her head.

"Two of each of these, please." Margaretta indicated the fruit baskets as she set her bag on the floor in front of her feet, making sure to drape the edge of her cloak over it. "Perhaps a bit of cheese and a small loaf of that bread."

The lady nodded and began bundling Margaretta's choices in a piece of brown paper while she talked. "This is the best bread in the county, but don't tell Mr. Abbot at the bakery down the street. Still irks him that I sell loaves for Cecily White in my store, but there's nothing he can do about it. You're lucky she was late bringing them in today. I usually sell out by noon."

Margaretta carefully counted coins from her reticule. She couldn't help but smile as the woman prattled on, but her expression turned into an embarrassed frown when her stomach rumbled a loud protest at the delay of food.

Without pausing her sentence, the woman tore off a chunk of the bread and handed it to Margaretta before wrapping the rest of the loaf in the parcel. "Now if you're wanting biscuits, I'll send you down to Mr. Abbot. He sells the best, though his daughter is the one what actually makes them. But we all pretend his wife does it, even though she struggles to even roll out a pie crust. What business that woman had marrying a baker is beyond me."

The woman looked up with a wink. "Oh, hello there, Mr. Banfield. What brings you by today?"

Her eyes cut to Margaretta as she spoke, giving the distinct impression that the older woman believed her customer had been the lure for the gentleman's visit instead of the vast array of foodstuffs.

Margaretta tried to look at the newcomer out of the corner of her eye. All she could see as he doffed his top hat was a mass of dark hair and a simple brown single-caped great coat.

"Good afternoon, Mrs. Lancaster. I'm afraid I ran out of peppermints." He stopped next to Margaretta at the counter.

Mrs. Lancaster gave a half laugh. "Well, come on back here and get them, then. You know where they are since you just purchased a tin two days ago."

The man stepped behind the counter and crossed behind the old shopkeeper. His bright blue eyes focused on Margaretta as he passed, and she tried not to stare back, but was still able to make out a straight, thin nose and strong chin.

"Have you met this lovely young lady yet?" Mrs. Lancaster asked as she took Margaretta's money.

Mr. Banfield turned, a small tin in his hand and a half smile on his lips. "No, I'm afraid I haven't had the pleasure."

"Me either." The woman grinned at him, her face settling

into the lines of a smile with comfortable ease, proving that all the wrinkles in her face weren't put there by age. "We can indulge ourselves together, then, shall we?"

Margaretta swallowed two nibbles of bread down hard as the woman's wide smile beamed in her direction. She wanted to take her food and run, to hold on to her privacy and anonymity, but she was going to have to talk to people if she wanted to find Katherine, and it would be much less suspicious if she talked to everyone. So she did her best to smile back.

"I'm Mrs. Lancaster, dearie. And this here is one of our local solicitors, Mr. Banfield. Seeing as you're new in town, we're probably the best two people to know. I know all the best places to get into trouble, and he knows how to get you out of it."

Her cackling laugh sounded considerably younger than she appeared, with a lilt to it that could take the edge off of any number of potentially offensive statements.

Margaretta had no idea what to say to that and the discomfort caused the heat of a blush to ride high across her cheekbones.

Mr. Banfield stepped forward, his attention finally diverted from Margaretta to the old woman. His smile was indulgent, and it was obvious he cared for the woman. "Mrs. Lancaster, the only time you get into trouble is when you attempt to help others get out of it."

His gaze swung from Mrs. Lancaster to Margaretta, losing the air of loving indulgence as the smile fell into a flat line, and he braced his feet to confront her.

Margaretta straightened her shoulders and stuck her nose in the air, not caring if it made her look haughty. She'd done nothing to earn this man's derision and held his gaze while she answered the shopkeeper in order to prove it. "How nice to meet you, Mrs. Lancaster. I am Mi—" She coughed to cover her hesitation. Who could she possibly say she was? Samuel was sure to be looking for a Mrs. Albany so she couldn't possibly give them her real name.

Being a *Miss* would be the easiest way to throw Samuel off should he come looking, but that would cause a host of other problems for Margaretta if she was still in town in a month or two. She coughed again to buy herself a bit of time and held up the chunk of bread with an apologetic smile.

"I'm Mrs.—" *Name! Name! She needed a name!* "Fortescue."

She nearly groaned. Using her maiden name was nearly as bad as admitting her married name was Albany. If Samuel came to Marlborough, he'd find her for sure.

2

Nash slid the tin of peppermints into his coat pocket and reached beneath the counter to pull out Mrs. Lancaster's log book. He noted the price for the candy on his page of the ledger and then waited for it to dry. If he took twice the time necessary before closing the book, no one knew that but him.

That the woman was married surprised him, especially now that he could see her face up close. What sort of man let such a striking woman traipse about the country by herself on the mail stage? Wherever Mr. Fortescue was, he wasn't doing a very good job.

That, or Mrs. Fortescue was enough trouble to warrant more attention than Nash's mild concern and curiosity.

Mrs. Lancaster, unsurprisingly, didn't seem encumbered by any similar worries as she barreled on, talking as she did with everyone, whether friend or stranger. "And what brings you to Marlborough, Mrs. Fortescue? Have you come to stay for the market this weekend? You're in luck. I hear Mr. and Mrs. Blankenship will be setting up a stall. Finest pendants I've ever seen. Mr. Lancaster saved up for months and bought me a peacock brooch. One of my most treasured possessions."

Nash couldn't help the smile that quirked one side of his

lips. Mrs. Lancaster always seemed to know just how much information to bait a hook with. He was fairly certain she knew everyone in town's personal business, which made Nash very glad that he didn't really have any. He handled the contracts, land agreements, and leases that people in the area needed, and he tried to help where he could, be a caring and friendly part of the town. But at night he went to his rooms alone. He didn't even employ a valet anymore, choosing instead to have one of the local laundresses see to the cleaning and mending of his clothing.

If he had to guess, though, he'd say that Mrs. Fortescue's amount of personal business more than made up for Nash's lack thereof.

The dark-haired woman clutched her paper-wrapped bundle a little tighter and flattened her lips in what was probably supposed to look like a smile, though her dark eyes remained flat and wary. "That sounds lovely, but I don't know if I will still be in town Saturday."

Nash slid the ledger back under the counter with a sigh of relief. If she was just passing through, his instincts were clamoring without reason. Dozens of troublesome people passed through Marlborough every day without causing a problem. Even Mrs. Lancaster couldn't help a person who wasn't there.

"Of course you will. No finer town in England than Marlborough. Now that you're here, you'll want to stay a while." Mrs. Lancaster nodded her head and poked a finger into the air as if her word was law and she expected everyone to obey it.

For the most part, people did. But in this case, Nash had a feeling they would all be better off if she didn't choose this particular lost soul to work her magic on. Was it the way Mrs. Fortescue was standing, guarding her bag and shielding herself from the world? The way she was very obviously hungry but didn't bear the look of someone who knew a lot about living life in such a condition? There was no doubt in Nash's mind that she was running, or at the very least, hiding. Not something Nash would willingly concern himself with, except that she'd looked so determined to bring her plight into Mrs. Lancaster's store.

He angled his head and smiled again at Mrs. Lancaster. "There is a world beyond Marlborough, you know, and some people do have obligations in it."

"I suppose that's true." The already short woman seemed to sink into herself a little bit, making her body appear as round as her face. "If everyone lived in Marlborough, we'd be a bit crowded."

A sigh of laughter sounded from Mrs. Fortescue and for the briefest moment her smile looked a little less forced. The moment was soon gone, and she settled back into a tense silence.

The desire to bring back that brief moment of lightness, to expand it until he was able to hear her laugh and see a true smile on her face hit Nash in the chest. Perhaps Mrs. Lancaster's inclination to save lost souls had worn off on him over the years. He tried to quash any such ambition with a dark frown. His allotment of personal charity was taken up by the members of this town, particularly those who had been taken advantage of and required his services at one point or another.

Mrs. Lancaster had never accepted his attempts to guard and rescue her though, and this moment didn't seem to be the exception. "Where are you off to, then?"

"I, um." The younger woman ran a finger along the seam of the folded paper on her package, revealing scratched and worn light brown gloves that were streaked with road dust. Too much damage and filth for a single day's travel from London.

She cleared her throat. "I'm not entirely sure."

Did she really not know where she was going or had she already reached her destination? Even if he assumed the best, that her seemingly pointed walk straight to Mrs. Lancaster had been coincidental, that didn't mean he could leave Mrs. Lancaster unprotected. The young woman was definitely on the run. What had she done?

Mrs. Lancaster slapped her hands on the counter. "Then there's no need to run off. You can stay here and see the market."

Nash cleared his throat. "Seems a strange part of the country for an exploratory pleasure jaunt. It's not like you'd sell many travel journals about the wonders of the wilds of Wiltshire."

Mrs. Fortescue took a deep breath and made that strange flattened attempt at a smile once more. No one was fooled. At least Nash wasn't. "I'm looking for—er, meeting someone."

Mrs. Lancaster clasped her hands to her chest, her round, lined face tightening into a broad smile. "Oh, people are ever so much more interesting than jewelry. Who are you looking for?"

Mrs. Fortescue darted a look at Nash before turning her dark eyes back to Mrs. Lancaster.

Nash frowned. Was she as wary of him as he was of her? Had she expected to find Mrs. Lancaster alone and vulnerable? Or was she truly a skittish woman in need of assistance? A dull throb took up residence at the base of Nash's neck.

The woman swallowed and straightened her shoulders once more, causing the voluminous yellow cloak to part, showing a simple dark blue gown underneath. He'd caught a glimpse of the skirt when she crossed the street earlier, but he hadn't expected the rest of the dress to be so plain. The neckline was only slightly rounded, not even requiring a chemisette to remain modest. Why would the owner of such a dress choose an eye-catching cloak?

"Just an old friend."

"May I see you to the location where you are meeting your friend?" Nash stepped from around the counter and bowed his head in Mrs. Fortescue's direction. It was the gentlemanly thing to do, offering to escort a lone woman, but it would also allow him to know who she was connected to in his little town.

The color that had begun to fade from her cheeks rushed back, perhaps even brighter than it had been before. She pressed her lips together before wetting them and giving a shaky smile. "Oh, no, that won't be necessary. I'm going to simply find a place to stay tonight and search for—er, meet them in the morning."

Nash's wariness eased, replaced by curiosity and concern, for both of the women in the room. Whoever this young woman was, subterfuge was not her normal style. The slips of speech were too prevalent. He supposed they could be intentional, but anyone with the ability to blush and stammer on command would have aimed for a much higher target than a small-town grocer. In fact, he was beginning to wonder if the unidentified emotion he'd seen earlier wasn't simply fear.

"There's a set of rooms above the shop." Mrs. Lancaster slid around the counter. "Mr. Banfield can take your bag upstairs if you'd like."

Nash swung around to look at Mrs. Lancaster. "You can't just take in a boarder without knowing anything about her," he said at the same time that Mrs. Fortescue piped up, "Oh, I couldn't possibly be such an intrusion."

Chocolate brown eyes narrowed as she frowned at Nash. "What are you implying, sir?"

Nash narrowed his gaze in return at the captivating woman he was more and more convinced by the minute was going to bring havoc into his neatly ordered life. Just because he'd absolved her of any nefarious intentions didn't mean he was ready to trust her. "I'm implying that she doesn't know you from Eve and therefore shouldn't give you free run of her property."

Mrs. Lancaster pushed her way in between them. "She's hardly the first young lady I've helped, Mr. Banfield. Why else do you think I'm always sweeping my steps when the mail comes through? I want to see who the good Lord brought to town for me to bless."

Nash sighed. "That's very noble of you, Mrs. Lancaster."

"Of course it is. That's what the Bible says to do after all, isn't it?" Mrs. Lancaster turned to Mrs. Fortescue. "Why don't you tell me about your friend? I might have helped her, too."

Mrs. Fortescue smiled at the older woman, a genuine smile even if the rest of the expression looked a little sad. "I'm afraid Katherine would have come through here quite a few months ago."

"Traveling alone, like you?" Nash asked, earning himself another frown from the woman. He snapped his teeth together with a click and turned his attention to look at whatever graced the nearest counter. He'd probably learn a lot more if he let Mrs. Lancaster do the talking. As long as he stayed nearby he could prevent the old woman from doing anything potentially detrimental to herself. But he couldn't stop himself from asking, "Where is your husband?"

Her eyebrows lifted. "Laid to rest in a field outside London. One can only hope he found his way to Heaven from there."

Margaretta lifted her chin and put every scrap of energy she had left into not dropping her gaze. Over and over again she reminded herself that she had nothing to be ashamed of. She'd done nothing wrong, and there was nothing this man could do to her.

Unless he knew her brother-in-law. Was there any chance Samuel would have enlisted the help of professional men around the country to look for her? It seemed a bit too organized and thorough for him, but Margaretta wasn't about to assume anything. It would be almost as bad if the man knew her father, but Mr. Banfield had had no reaction to the name Fortescue.

The next breath slid into her lungs with a little more ease than the last. For right now, at least, everything seemed to be as it should be.

She turned her best smile on the older woman, hoping her fear didn't show on her face. The chance that she could afford a set of rooms when she could barely afford to stay at an inn was slim, but here would be a much better place to hide if she could. "How much to use the rooms above?"

Mrs. Lancaster waved an arm about. "Dust and sweep the store and we'll consider it a trade. Not today, of course. You can start tomorrow."

"Mrs. Lancaster," the man nearly growled through gritted teeth.

The grocer frowned. "She just got off the stage, Mr. Banfield. Only a heartless termagant would put her to work right now, and we've already established I've more heart than you like."

Another bubble of mirth broke through Margaretta's tension, and she lifted a hand to cover the small chuckle that threatened to escape. But the stench of travel clinging to the glove reminded her exactly what her situation was and threw a wet blanket over any vestiges of humor. A smelly, wet, dust-covered blanket.

No one—not her father, not Samuel, not anyone she'd ever met in her entire life—would expect to find her sweeping floors in a simple shop with humble rooms above it. Mostly because she would never have dreamed of placing herself in such a situation, but right now, it was ideal. Her money would last longer, and maybe she'd have a chance to talk with Mrs. Lancaster alone. If anyone was going to remember Katherine, it was probably the nosy but endearing old woman.

Right now that sweet old woman was jabbing an elbow into Mr. Banfield's side. "Take her bag up and let her get settled. I've customers to tend to."

Mr. Banfield ran a hand along the back of his neck, stabbing his fingers through the hair at the back of his head. It was obviously not the first time today he'd done such a thing, either.

Any style his hair had held today had been lost, ruined by too many encounters that called for similar gestures of frustration.

The man needed to learn to relax.

Not that Margaretta had any real claim to such ability at the moment, but he could hardly claim a dire predicament as the reason for his tension.

The last thing she wanted, though, was such a tense and suspicious man taking her bag. Custom-made for her by her leather-working father, there wasn't another satchel like it anywhere. Father was known for making the most exquisite saddles in England, but the valise had been a special project just for her. She couldn't let Mr. Banfield get a close enough look at it to see the Fortescue Saddlery medallion on the clasp.

Margaretta cleared her throat as she scooped up her valise handle in one hand while the other clutched her bundle of food. "Please do not trouble yourself. The building is not very large, and there are only so many places the stairs can be located. I shall have no trouble seeing myself up."

His eyebrows lifted as his head jerked back a bit. "I'm sure you wouldn't. Nevertheless, I'd hate to disappoint Mrs. Lancaster. May I take your bag?"

Her grip tightened instinctively. She swallowed. If she were going to keep him from being too curious about her, she had to put him off guard. Until now, he'd been the one suspicious of her. What would he think if she turned the tables on him?

With more bravado than actual indignation, she stuck her nose into the air. "No, thank you. You've made no secret that you find my presence here unsettling. I'll not have you running off with my bag in an attempt to make me leave."

His hand went to his neck again, but this time it didn't push into his already disheveled hair as he dropped his gaze to stare in the vicinity of his toes and his shoulders slumped inward. A deep breath expanded his chest before he dropped his hand and straightened once more, a considerably softer look on his face. "My apologies. I assure I will keep all of my efforts to protect Mrs. Lancaster as honest as possible. I would never resort to anything so underhanded."

Not quite the apology she'd been hoping for, but she could work with it. "Nevertheless, I intend to hold on to my belongings for the time being as I have no one to protect *me* aside from myself."

A more heartbreakingly true sentence had never been uttered.

He tilted his head to the side and watched her for a moment before gesturing toward the back of the store. "The stairs are this way."

As they walked farther into the depths of the store, Margaretta marveled at the variety of goods around her. Since when did a grocer need a shelf displaying porcelain teacups and embroidered reticules?

"A sampling of wares from some of the people who will have stalls at Saturday's market," Mr. Banfield explained, noticing her gaze. "So many of the town's inhabitants spend the whole day selling that they've no time to peruse the other stalls. Mrs. Lancaster keeps a few select items on hand to sell during the week." He cleared his throat as he pushed open a door at the back of the shop that opened into a narrow alley. "I'm afraid the dusting and sweeping you agreed to is probably a bigger job than you thought."

Especially given that she'd never dusted or swept a thing in her life, unless one counted scooping a hand of cards off the table surface as dusting. She blinked a few times, hoping to clear her head from worry and the encroaching weariness so she could say something that convinced him she knew what she was doing. "I wouldn't expect anything less than a bit of hard work in exchange for the rooms."

He cleared his throat and looked up the stairs. "Your friend. I'd like to help you find her."

"You want to get rid of me that badly?"

She expected him to frown, but he didn't. He simply looked at her. "Perhaps, in my own way, I wish to help those who find themselves in a basket as much as Mrs. Lancaster does. I just don't want to see anyone taken advantage of while they are helping."

Could she trust him? Should she trust him? Did she have a choice? She'd started off on this impossible search because she'd been desperate enough to cling to a rumor and hope, but she hadn't the slightest idea what to actually do now that she was here. "I'm afraid all I have is a letter mailed from here several months ago."

"Doesn't sound like that close of a friend," Mr. Banfield muttered.

"Doesn't sound like a very helpful sentiment," Margaretta returned.

"Mrs. Fortes—"

"Mr. Banfield, as Mrs. Lancaster so helpfully noted, I am weary from my travels. Perhaps your dissection and belittlement of my life could wait until tomorrow? You can stare at me suspiciously while I dust the shelves and assure yourself I've no intention of absconding with candlesticks."

His eyes widened, and then he coughed, possibly to cover a laugh, but she frankly didn't care anymore. Up these stairs was a chair that wasn't moving that she could sit in while she ate and a bed she could snuggle into afterward. At the moment, those two things sounded like bliss.

And if she imagined what it would have been like if the handsome Mr. Banfield had been as welcoming as the elderly grocer, well, that was no one's business but her own.

3

Nash sat in his office, trying to return to the work he'd been doing before Mrs. Fortescue had blown into town. He stared out the big window beside his desk, looking across High Street to the now quiet inn where the stage had unloaded hours earlier.

The ink on the tip of his quill had dried, so he gave up pretending and dropped the feather onto the desk surface.

A trio of children ran down the street chasing a dog and inspiring a small, sad pang in Nash's chest. Had his sister's baby lived, he would be about the age of those boys. But he hadn't lived and neither had Mary. And for a few years after, it had been a question of whether or not the husband she'd left behind would survive the loss. Nash had been prepared for his good friend to slip away like his father had after the death of Nash's mother, alive only in the most literal sense of the word.

It was a cruel twist that the baby his mother had died bringing into the world was felled by the same fate.

The boys shouted as the dog turned abruptly and began chasing them, yapping happily as they scattered down a side street.

Nash smiled at the antics even as he silently reaffirmed his commitment to remain free from the sort of entanglements that killed men while they were yet breathing. This town was his family. It gave him purpose and companionship. When the Lord called him home, there would be people who mourned. That was enough.

He was still watching the quiet street when Mrs. Lancaster shuffled past. He nodded to her when she caught his eye, and she smiled back. Eventually the walk back to the cottage she'd lived in with her husband would become too much for her and she'd have to move into the rooms above the shop, but for now she seemed content to travel back and forth up the hill each day, even though she had to come into town at an exceptionally early hour because Nash never saw her in the morning until she was sweeping the stones in front of her door.

Her walk home tonight, however, meant Mrs. Fortescue was now alone. Her unfettered access to whatever possessions Mrs. Lancaster had in the upstairs rooms was a nominal concern at best, but he still fought the urge to take a walk in that direction. Whether it was to make sure the downstairs doors were locked or that the woman on the run was safe by herself, he wasn't sure, and that question was enough to drive him away from the door and back to his desk.

The tin of peppermints in his jacket pocket rattled as he settled into his chair. He shifted to the side and fished them out, frowning at the tin before dropping it into a drawer. Metal clinked as it landed on top of the tin of peppermints he'd bought earlier in the week.

He was going to have to come up with a better reason to go by Mrs. Lancaster's shop tomorrow. If he bought any more peppermints, Mrs. Lancaster might hurt herself from laughing so hard. She'd barely contained her mirth this afternoon, and it had given him a modicum of pleasure to inspire the old woman to smile, even though that wasn't a very difficult task.

Mrs. Fortescue's near laugh flitted through his mind. How

much more heroic would it feel to be the one to make *her* smile and laugh?

Nash shook his head. Why did it feel comfortable to be a bright spot in Mrs. Lancaster's day but decided uncomfortable to consider being such for Mrs. Fortescue? His commitment to himself was certainly strong enough to withstand being the source of a full smile on a young, pretty woman.

Wasn't it?

◆

Noises from the street below were the first thing to break into Margaretta's sleep-soaked brain the next morning, but she kept her eyes pressed closed until she could work through the lingering fogginess. She was in a bed, that much she knew, but where the bed was located was still trapped in the black shrouds of drowsiness that were threatening to creep back over her consciousness.

The bedding was clean and smelled of fresh air and lavender, an unfamiliar but certainly not unpleasant combination.

She turned her attention to the vague noises that had woken her in the first place. Definitely not London. Raised voices, horses, and wagon wheels were all distinct from each other, instead of a large noisy blur. A small town then, or a less busy side street of a larger one.

A frown pulled her eyebrows together and sent cracks running through the last vestiges of sleep. Why wasn't she in London? She remembered traveling to Margate, but the sounds reaching her ears weren't those of the seaside resort town, either.

With great care she eased one eye open to look at the plain white walls and heavy, dark wood timbered ceiling. The visual inspection of her surroundings brought everything she'd done in the last three days swirling back. Complete consciousness caused something else to swirl as well, though, and she clamped her eyes shut again while taking deep, slow breaths and willing the seizing of her midsection to cease.

Once she had her body somewhat under control, she opened her eyes again to take in the room she'd done nothing but glance at the evening before. She hadn't known where the candles were and the energy to search for them had seeped from her very bones. After eating most of the bread and half of the fruit she'd purchased downstairs, she'd undressed and climbed into bed.

And apparently slept through the night and into the morning.

Not too far into the morning, though, based on the paleness of the light creeping through the uncovered window.

A low groan rumbled up from Margaretta's chest as she stretched and pushed herself to a sitting position on the side of the bed.

"Good morning."

Margaretta screamed and fell back onto the mattress, flinging the bedding up as if it would create a shield. After two heaving, terrified breaths, she eased the blanket off her face and looked toward the door. She had to peek over her feet as well as the blankets since her legs were now sticking over the edge of the bed at an odd angle.

Her heart pounded in her ears, drowning out whatever greeting Mrs. Lancaster was giving her as she brought in a small tray bearing a plate of toast and stewed apples, as well as a sturdy mug with steam curling over the rim.

With a hard swallow and a deep breath to calm her racing heart, Margaretta sent up a quick prayer that the steaming mug was a proper cup of tea. How she longed for a good cup of tea. The inns between mail stages had served something they called tea, but could more accurately be described as dirty water. Yet another thing she'd been taking for granted in her former life.

She pressed a hand to her middle. How quickly things could

change. Hopefully, one day she could return to such a life, though it would never be the same for her after this experience.

Margaretta pulled her legs in and pushed herself up to sit against the plain wooden headboard. "Good morning." She cleared her throat to ease the croak in her voice. "What are you doing here?"

Mrs. Lancaster chuckled while she arranged the tray and eased herself down to sit on the edge of the bed. "Why, I live here, dear. I've got a cottage up the hill, but my old bones don't like making that walk early in the morning, so I come back here to sleep every night. I was afraid I'd disturb you when I retired last night, but you didn't so much as shift a finger."

Margaretta lifted the mug and inhaled the steam, further quieting her senses. She cast her eyes about the room, taking in the carved wardrobe on the far wall and another small bed situated on the other side of the window from Margaretta's. Staying in rooms run by the older woman was one thing, but actually living with her? Did Margaretta want to do such a thing? How long would she be able to keep her secret if she was living in such close quarters with Mrs. Lancaster?

She only had another month or two with her secret anyway, but by then she hoped to have a better plan than wait and see if it was a girl. If only it didn't take so long to have a baby. The solution to her predicament would be much easier if she could simply hide away for a month or two and have the whole thing over with before anyone realized she wasn't in Margate after all.

Of course, having the baby was only the beginning of her problems. The question was what she was going to do with it afterward, particularly if it turned out to be a boy.

There was no way that Samuel would accept another person sliding in between him and his father's title.

As she nibbled on an apple, hoping her breakfast would stay

settled, she looked around the room once more. "I didn't take your bed, did I?"

Mrs. Lancaster waved a hand in dismissal. "One bed's as good as another. I never know which one I'll decide to crawl into until I come up here each night anyway. At least with you here, I'll have a bit of predictability in my day."

While Margaretta ate, Mrs. Lancaster talked, sharing funny stories from the many years she'd been living in the town, tossing in a mention or two of a specific townsperson's connection to more influential people, thankfully none whom Margaretta had ever met. There were tales from various markets, though if all of them were completely true, Margaretta would eat the plate her toast had been brought on.

Behind a screen in the corner, Margaretta washed the travel dirt off as best she could and dressed, taking care to shift her clothing so no one could see the slight swell in her midsection. After wearing the same dress for three days straight, it was bliss to feel clean clothes against her skin.

With Mrs. Lancaster unable to see her face, Margaretta tried to bring the conversation around to the women Mrs. Lancaster had supposedly helped over the years.

"There hasn't been that many, in truth. We take care of our own here in Marlborough, and it isn't often that women travel through by themselves."

A rustling cloth indicated that Mrs. Lancaster was setting the bedroom to rights. "Mrs. Wingraves' girl comes through and cleans up here every day, but she won't bother your things."

The only identifying or valuable thing Margaretta had was the valise, and she wasn't overly worried about a young country girl seeing it. The chances of her recognizing the stamped metal emblem or the custom craftsmanship were limited. She wanted to talk more about Mrs. Lancaster's girls, though. "Do you remember meeting Katherine?"

"I don't often exchange first names." Mrs. Lancaster chuckled. "Shall we place wagers on what Mr. Banfield plans to come in and buy today?"

Margaretta came out from behind the screen to find Mrs. Lancaster smiling at her. The old woman winked before retreating into the other room.

Obviously Katherine and the other girls were not open for discussion this morning. In a way, Margaretta was glad. She wouldn't want Mrs. Lancaster freely telling people about Margaretta's presence, either. The older woman apparently had no problem talking about the solicitor, though, and Margaretta needed to know if he was going to be a problem. "Does he stop by every day?"

"Hardly ever." A cackle shook the other woman's shoulders. "But he'll be in every day as long as you're living here."

Margaretta couldn't help but wonder what it would be like to have someone willing to go to that much trouble to watch over her. "He must care about you a lot."

"Probably more than he'll admit. Makes my heart break to see the man try and harden his heart. Bible's full of people with hard hearts, and I wouldn't want to be a single one of them."

Margaretta didn't know what to think of the way the old woman sprinkled God and the Bible into her conversation as casually as a Londoner might mention the traffic or haze. Even though she'd been attending church her entire life, Margaretta hadn't ever thought to make Jesus quite that versatile. She'd left Him in church where He seemed to belong, but Mrs. Lancaster appeared to think He belonged everywhere.

Margaretta listened to more stories as the women went down the stairs and into the back of the store.

"There's a broom and dusting things in this cabinet. The broom at the front is just for the porch. I sweep it off regularly. Helps cut down on the amount of sweeping we have to do in here and lets me know what everyone's doing in the town."

Mrs. Lancaster laughed to herself as she moved to the front of the store. Margaretta had never met someone who seemed to be so continually . . . happy. Despite everything going on in her life, all the uncertainty around her future, Margaretta couldn't help but smile. With her steps feeling a bit lighter, she opened the cabinet and tried to guess what was used to clean which things.

❖

The wavy glass that covered the front of Mrs. Lancaster's shop kept Nash from seeing any particular details, but it was clear that at least six women milled around near the front of the store, waiting for Mrs. Lancaster to help them. It was also clear that none of them were Mrs. Fortescue. Not that he'd had that much time to observe her, but none of them moved like her or even stood the way he remembered her standing.

Besides, she was supposed to be cleaning. Not shopping.

He slipped quietly through the door and eased it shut behind him so as not to draw notice of the chatting customers.

Was it possible Mrs. Fortescue had decided to leave already? Mrs. Lancaster's voice was as cheery and helpful as ever, so if the young woman had departed it must have been in an amiable sort of way. Otherwise, the old shopkeeper would have been spouting proverbs to everyone along with their purchase totals.

No, if she were still here, she'd likely camped herself in the back with the knick-knacks and other non-food goods. Someone on the run wouldn't want to be near the front when this many people were in the store. Nash nodded a greeting to one of the women and strolled around a set of shelves to head toward the back portion of the store.

Mrs. Fortescue was in the deepest corner, trying to juggle a brass barometer while running a cloth over the space it had occupied. Afraid that his sudden presence would cause her to

37

drop it, Nash crept up and lifted it from her arms. She was still startled, but at least the barometer didn't break as a result.

The rest of the shelving nearly did, though, when she squealed and spun around to press herself against the boards, her hand pressed to her chest and her breath coming in quick, short bursts. "Mr. Banfield," she gasped. "You gave me a fright."

"Obviously." Nash nodded at the now clean shelf behind her and held up the barometer. "May I?"

"Oh!" She scurried away from the shelf. "Of course."

"Why aren't you using the goose feathers?"

Mrs. Fortescue blinked at the cloth in her hand, coated with dust she'd just raked from the back corner of the shelf. As they both stared at her hand, a large fluffy grey clump drifted off the rag to the floor. She sighed. "Now I'll have to sweep again."

Nash's eyebrows rose. "You already swept? Before you dusted?"

Pink stained her cheeks. "No, of course not." She pushed her shoulders back and straightened her posture but then immediately slumped and folded forward again before turning back to the shelf. After shaking the loose dust from her cloth, she started on the next section. "What do you need, Mr. Banfield? I'm afraid I can't help you procure any goods. You'll have to wait in line with everyone else."

"And if what I came for was information?"

She snuck a glance at him. "I'm afraid I can't help you with that, either."

He settled his shoulder against the wall and fought a grin. This was almost fun. Where had the suspicion and worry from yesterday gone?

Was the considerable but misguided effort she was putting into cleaning the shelves enough to convince him she meant the shopkeeper no harm? It must have been, because all he felt when he looked at her was a swelling drive of curiosity. He really wanted to know who she was looking for, what she was running from, and why Marlborough had been the point between the two. It was enough to convince him that keeping her close was a very good idea.

"What if I didn't ask anything about why you were here?"

Mrs. Fortescue laughed, but it was brassy and bitter. She stopped pushing dust around to cross her arms over her chest. "What else could you possibly have to ask me?"

What did he have? His interest in learning about her felt vague and undefined. "Obviously cleaning is not something you're especially good at."

She looked like she wanted to smile but managed to restrain herself. "And I imagine you are perfection personified at everything you attempt?"

"Hardly." He smiled. He couldn't help it. She was so appealing when she smirked or smiled or anything really that chased away that desperate air she'd had about her when she got off the stage. Had it really been only yesterday? He leaned in as if he were imparting a secret. "I am absolutely terrible at shooting."

She went back to dusting, but her attention clearly wasn't in it. "That must make hunting parties nervous."

He shrugged and moved his way down the wall, staying close to her as she cleaned. The tasseled saddlebag on the shelf in front of him was crooked, so he reached out to straighten it. "I am, however, rather exceptional at riding, so they let me come along and chase the hounds. And now it's your turn to throw humility aside and confess what skills you're hiding."

What was he doing? Was he actually flirting with her? He hadn't even considered participating in a flirtation in years. And now he was doing so with a woman he barely knew, one he wanted to run out of town? It didn't make any sense, but he realized he was, possibly for the first time in a very long time, having fun.

"I cook."

Of all the things he'd have guessed she would say, cooking was the last one he expected. "You cook?"

She nodded.

"Well, perhaps I can get you to bring me nuncheon one day."

She blushed but said nothing. He didn't really expect her to. The idea had been planted in both their minds, spoken without any real thought behind the words, but now the idea of a pretty young woman stopping by the office to brighten his day and share a light meal with him was too enticing by far.

He needed to get out of here and think about what he was really doing.

"I'll be back tomorrow, Mrs. Fortescue. And here's fair warning that I intend to weasel out of you your favorite type of pie." He settled his hat on his head and tipped the brim. Then he turned and strode out of the store before she could say anything.

4

Margaretta ran the goose-feather duster around the jars of spices with a practiced swish. She wasn't an expert at cleaning by any means, but in the past week and a half she'd learned a thing or two about effectively dusting the shelves.

She'd also learned how stubborn charming old women could be. No matter what she asked, Mrs. Lancaster wasn't telling her a thing about whether or not she'd met Katherine. Margaretta wasn't getting very far on her own, either. The current post-master for the town had taken up his post only six months ago. Even if he had the memory of an elephant, he wasn't going to remember a girl posting a letter before he took the job. She also couldn't risk strolling through too many public areas because while Margaretta was looking for Katherine, someone else was looking for her.

More swishes of the duster accompanied her self-pitying sigh and sideways glance toward the front of the store.

He was late.

No matter how good she got at dusting, it was never going to be a chore she particularly loved. It seemed to pass much faster when Mr. Banfield stopped by to chat though, which he'd gotten into the habit of doing every day, just as the morning rush of customers subsided. It was why she'd altered her cleaning routine to save the back shelves for his arrival.

But today he hadn't come, and the sun had already passed its peak in the sky.

"Margaretta, dear," Mrs. Lancaster called from the front of the empty store. "I've something I need your help with."

Margaretta stored the duster back in the cabinet before going to the front of the store. Whatever the old woman needed, Margaretta was happy to do, or at least attempt to do. She'd been an utter blessing from the Lord.

A short laugh escaped through Margaretta's smiling lips as she shook her head. She was even beginning to sound like the old woman, thanking the Lord for things in the middle of the week. The truth was, though, that Margaretta didn't know what she'd do without the woman and everything she'd done for Margaretta. If that wasn't the definition of a blessing, she didn't know what was.

"Ah, there you are. I've got a delivery for you to make." Mrs. Lancaster set a small basket, filled to the top and covered with white muslin, on top of the counter.

Margaretta took the handle with a bit of trepidation but found that while it was heavy, it was manageable. "I'm afraid I don't know my way around town. I haven't ventured much past the store and the church yet."

The church had been another one of those places Margaretta had been hoping to catch a glimpse of Katherine. She'd spent more time inspecting the rows of people than listening to the rector the past two Sundays. No familiar blonde runaways had been in attendance.

Mrs. Lancaster waved a hand in the air. "It's not far. Just a bit down High Street."

"I'll need better directions than that." Margaretta smiled. She took a deep breath and plunged on, hoping she could catch

Mrs. Lancaster off guard and get a bit more information to help in her search. She was convinced the old lady knew something or she would have simply told Margaretta that she didn't know Katherine FitzGilbert. "Perhaps you need me to go by wherever Katherine stayed when she came through town?"

A pudgy, wrinkled hand waved through the air. "We've plenty of time to discuss this search of yours later. Right now we've got a quiet moment, so it's the best time to make a delivery. Just turn right and head down High Street. You can't miss Mr. Banfield's office. It's got a big window looking out over the street."

"Mr. Banfield?" Margaretta choked. What could possibly need delivering to him? He'd been in the store every day for the past ten days. Except of course for Sundays and then they'd seen him at church.

"That's correct. He was supposed to come in and get it this morning, but something must be keeping him. I don't mind going out of my way for one of my best customers."

Or sending Margaretta out of her way, as the case may be. "I know what you're doing."

Mrs. Lancaster's grin was infectious. "Good. Then you won't mess it up. Off with you now."

Margaretta laughed as she put on her pelisse and tucked the basket against her hip before setting off on her journey. Who needed subtlety when they had Mrs. Lancaster's charm?

His office was easy to find, and Margaretta enjoyed the short walk through town. She'd seen the market twice now from the window above Mrs. Lancaster's shop and both times had been an assault on all of her senses. The quietness of the rest of the week appealed to her more. It was an odd blend of feeling like the city and the country at the same time.

She took one last deep breath of fresh air before pushing her way into Mr. Banfield's office.

He was bent over his desk, the quill flying across the paper

A Search for Refuge

in tight, neat writing. She waited until he'd paused to clear her throat to catch his attention.

The bewildered expression on his face was darling. He looked from her to the window to the clock on his mantle. "Oh! I'm late." A blush rode his cheekbones. "Well, not late because I didn't have an appointment, but—"

"Mrs. Lancaster sent you this." Margaretta offered him the basket.

He took it apprehensively but broke into a wide smile after he pulled back the muslin. "Hungry?"

"What?" Margaretta's eyebrows pulled together until she looked into the basket to find a variety of fresh foodstuffs, including a loaf of the apple bread she'd made last night and a fruit tart left over from this morning. "I could eat."

That was almost a joke. She could always eat these days.

Still, it was nice to sit at the small table Nash led her to and dig into the basket with a handsome companion.

Not that she thought him handsome. Oh, very well, she thought him handsome. Who wouldn't with that shock of dark hair that didn't seem to want to lay right and blue eyes framing a strong, straight nose? Of course she found him handsome, but she didn't think it meant anything.

"And what has you working so diligently this morning, Mr. Banfield?"

He held up a section of apple bread. "Did you make this? It's amazing." He shoved another morsel into his mouth. "If you're going to be delivering me freshly made tarts and bread, you might as well call me Nash."

She looked around the office to keep from having to look directly at him. A blush was already threatening, and it would take over her complexion if her gaze remained locked with his. Bookshelves lined one entire wall while stacks of newspapers and magazines covered every other available surface. Obviously he kept abreast of news far beyond the borders of Marlborough. "I've never been in a solicitor's office."

"I would think not. It's not the normal domain of gently reared females."

He was fishing for information again, but she let it pass. She couldn't really blame him. The curiosity hadn't seemed rooted in any malice since her first day in town. That didn't mean she answered, though. Even if she found herself wanting to.

"It's an interesting look into your life."

Nash looked around with her. "What do you mean? It's mostly books and papers."

She turned back to him, wondering if her smile looked playful. Part of her felt like an imp, but the other part of her was really and truly curious to know what went on behind those serious blue eyes and shaggy dark hair. "You've a partner desk but no partner. That seems a rather poignant bit of symbolism."

He snorted a laugh and dabbed at his mouth with a napkin. "I assure you that it's not. It's simple practicality. The partner desk has more drawers."

The words were spoken lightly, but he still shifted in his seat, rolling his shoulders as if his jacket was suddenly uncomfortable. Had she hit the nail a little too close to the head? Was he alone in this world by something other than choice? A feeling of dread licked through her stomach before she could stop herself from wondering. Did he have a woman in his life who had left him heartbroken?

Not that Margaretta was in any sort of condition to mend it, if that was the case, but still. She hated to think of Nash hurting.

"You won't answer if I ask about your friend."

It was a statement, not a question but Margaretta nodded anyway. Katherine had disappeared in the midst of devastating rumor and scandal, the kind that ruined a girl's future. The letter Margaretta had gotten was essentially a good-bye. An assurance that Katherine had left of her own volition and was safe but wouldn't be returning.

Margaretta hoped that meant Katherine had figured out how to have her baby and protect both of them while she was at it. She'd also managed to stay hidden for eight months. Margaretta needed to know how she'd done both of these things.

Nash broke off another piece of apple loaf. "What about your husband?"

Margaretta's eyes opened wide. "What do you want to know?"

It was quiet for a few moments, Nash not meeting her eye. "Did you love him?"

They were getting too close. She was only in this town for a little while, and for the time she was here, she was essentially in hiding. Any sort of relationship with this man, even friendship, was unwise.

She murmured something about getting back to Mrs. Lancaster and rose from the table, leaving him to do whatever he wished with the remaining food.

Still, she stopped at the door and looked back at him.

He was watching her with softness around his eyes. Accepting what she was willing to give him without pushing for more. How had they come so far so quickly? Was a half hour of conversation here and there enough to make two people closer in such a short time?

It was. She knew it was because it had happened. Was happening. And since she wasn't willing to give him anything else, she gifted him the one thing she could. "Nash," she swallowed and licked her lips, "you can call me Margaretta. And no, I didn't love him."

And then she left.

Not knowing what else to do, Margaretta took the next two weeks to try to venture into the more public areas of Marlborough. She scurried along the edges of the market, looking at every vendor and shopper, heart pounding that she'd find someone she knew, but it wouldn't be the right someone. The trepidation she expected to feel at her continued lack of success never came. It was easy to forget, in her cozy rooms and quaint little village, that a real sense of urgency was needed.

The fact that Mr. Banfield didn't miss a single visit over those two weeks didn't hurt. Nash. Margaretta kept waiting for him to push more at the door she'd opened and ask about her husband, her family, but he never did. Instead their discussions had grown more playful and personal, the illusion of privacy the back shelves gave them lending itself to long stretches of uninterrupted conversation.

They swapped childhood stories, though Margaretta was careful to never mention the leather shop or horses. They talked about the Sunday service. They even got into a rather heated, good-natured debate on whether or not the new style of longer, looser trousers for men would become acceptable formal evening wear.

And he watched her. She knew he did because she couldn't stop herself from watching him, too. For a woman who had been comfortably settled with the idea of having her father arrange a marriage for her, the giddiness that ran through her when she heard Nash greeting Mrs. Lancaster was both foreign and exciting.

But as time crept on and her stay in Mrs. Lancaster's rooms extended into its second month, she felt uneasy. They'd been good weeks, if strange, and her days had fallen into a routine.

They would wake early and eat breakfast before going down to the shop. Mrs. Lancaster never seemed to mind that Margaretta came down after her, choosing to wait and dress after the older woman had left the rooms. The mornings no longer left her middle feeling queasy, but it was requiring more artful ar-ranging and fastening of her gowns to keep everything hidden.

Then she spent the day cleaning and avoiding the customers until Nash came to visit. Afterward, she would straighten the shelves and come upstairs to prepare dinner.

When Mrs. Lancaster closed the shop, she would come up and eat and then go for a long walk by herself. Margaretta of-fered to accompany her a few times, but Mrs. Lancaster always turned her down, saying a lone walk was good for digestion and reflection.

Margaretta spent the evenings reading or trying out a new bread or tart recipe. She'd taken to making baskets for Nash to pick up when he came into the store.

Then she would fall into the bed and not wake until the sun hit her eyes the next morning.

At least, that had been the pattern until three days ago.

Sleep had become an elusive friend, almost as difficult to find as Katherine was, and her body was feeling the loss.

Margaretta lay in the bed, listening to the deep breathing from the bed beside her. The fits and lulls of momentary un-consciousness she managed to find at night couldn't have ac-cumulated to more than a couple of hours if they'd been strung together. The level of exhaustion she'd been feeling every day should have meant she slept blissfully each night, but the still-ness of the night and the way the town actually quieted with the setting sun only gave her time to think about all of the things she pushed aside with the busyness of the day.

More than a month in Marlborough and she was no closer to finding Katherine than she'd been on day one. But she hadn't a clue what to do next. Mrs. Lancaster would talk about anything and everything under the sun except for Katherine. Whenever Margaretta raised the topic, it was brushed aside like the dust and dirt she'd gotten so good at cleaning.

Who else could she ask, though? Aside from Nash, she knew no one in town, and had deliberately avoided more than passing greetings with them all. Asking Nash would mean having to answer all of the questions they'd been dancing around. As close as they'd gotten, she couldn't ask for his help without expecting to give him some answers in return.

So where did that leave her? She was running out of time.

Margaretta pushed the covers down below her hips and pulled her nightgown tight across her middle. The false sense of security and comfort that hiding away with Mrs. Lancaster provided was shrinking, and Margaretta's middle was starting to swell. It wasn't much yet, certainly not anything a little slump and dress adjustment couldn't hide, but it was difficult if not impossible to ignore anymore. How much longer before she would have to find a way to procure new dresses? How many more days could she linger before she had to find a more permanent place to hide? If Samuel found her, there'd be no denying her condition soon.

Worries swirled in her head until she felt dizzy. She knew what Mrs. Lancaster would say, because she'd been listening to the woman prattle on for weeks. The shopkeeper would say that worries belonged to the Lord since He stayed up all night anyway.

The thought brought a smile to Margaretta's lips. A nice concept, letting someone else stay up and worry for you while you slept blissfully all night through.

She glanced over at the other bed, and the woman whose shape she could barely make out in the moonlit room. Mrs. Lancaster always left the drapes open, stating that the sun was ever so much nicer to wake up to than having Mrs. Berta Wheelhouse come round and tap on her window with that long stick of hers.

People like Mrs. Wheelhouse probably existed in London, going around and waking people at the appointed times in return for a small fee. Margaretta had never had to concern herself with that, sleeping as late as she wished for most of her life. If there was a need to rise at a certain hour, one of the servants saw to waking her. She'd never thought to wonder how they woke on time.

Right now, though, the room was dark, even with the open curtain, so the moon must have set, and the sun would soon start pinkening the sky. Then she would have to find a way to haul herself from this bed once more and go about cleaning the shop downstairs. Again. The chore was considerably more difficult than she'd expected it to be. Especially when she was fighting the desire to simply curl up in a ball in the corner and let the rest of the world carry on without her while she took a nap.

As exhausted sleep finally smothered the constantly swirling concerns, Margaretta had one last fleeting wish that she could return to those lazy mornings and let this sleep last for hours.

5

Bright sunshine made Margaretta wince the next time she tried to open her eyes. She sat up quickly in surprise, and instantly regretted it as the sudden movement sent her running for the chamber pot for the first time in more than a week. Once she could move comfortably again, she looked around the room.

A shard of sunlight cut across the wall and onto Margaretta's pillow from the bright beams edging around the dark green drape that had been pulled across the room's little window.

Rapid blinks were required to keep the sudden moisture in her eyes from turning into a bout of weeping. She'd been struggling with that a lot lately, had even had to claim to get dust in her eyes one or two times when the urge to cry had hit her while in the shop below. But this act of caring on Mrs. Lancaster's part when Margaretta was feeling so alone and bereft was simply too much, and a few drops of emotion leaked from Margaretta's eyes before she could contain herself.

A small smile tilted her lips, forming a track for the salty tears, and she wiped them away idly with her wrist while she pulled the curtain to the side and looked down at the town she was coming to know.

Mrs. Cotter was walking down the street with her mouth

set in the determined line she always got when she was planning on haggling Mr. Abbott about paying less for bread. She always visited the baker just after midday in the hopes that he'd be worried about selling everything that day. It never worked, but she kept trying.

Margaretta blinked. Could it possibly be noon already? Had she slept that long? If so, she'd missed her talk with Nash for the first time. What had he thought? What excuse had Mrs. Lancaster given him? The idea that Nash might think her the type of slothful person who would laze a day away just because she felt like it made Margaretta sad. He knew her better than that by now, didn't he?

A loud shout drew her attention to the right and the large three-peaked inn she took care to avoid. Its location in the middle of High Street meant that people from London were frequently coming and going from the center of town on their way to or from the popular city of Bath.

The stage pulling up in front of the inn now was nicer than the one Margaretta had traveled on, though still loaded down with as many people as it could carry. It wasn't a mail coach, so there was more room for people and luggage, and passengers scrambled down from every nook on the roof and sides. Finally, a footman stepped up to open the door to allow the interior passengers to disembark.

A man with thick, graying hair stepped out before settling his tall hat back upon his head. Even from this distance, she could see his hawklike nose and the sun glinting off the silver embroidery of his waistcoat.

Her gasp seemed to pull all the air from the room while squeezing all of the breath from her chest. She'd thought she had more time—that her story would hold for at least another few weeks—but there was no denying that her father was in Marlborough. She hadn't wanted to worry him, hadn't wanted him to blame himself for the fact that the man he'd married her to had a crazy brother who would do anything to move up from third to first in line for the title of Viscount of Stildon.

If Samuel Albany found out she was expecting his older brother's child, he'd either beat it out of her or find a way for it to meet an early demise once it was born. He'd all but told her as much when he paid his condolences after the death of his brother, John.

If there hadn't been so many witnesses to John's accident on the gangplank of the *HMS Malabar*, Margaretta would wonder whether Samuel had had a hand in it as well. But no, that had simply been an unfortunate incident, though the move from third heir to potential spare seemed only to whet Samuel's appetite for the title.

If her father was here, did that mean he knew she was no longer in Margate? Did Samuel know she was no longer in Margate? That she'd stayed there for a mere three days before the sight of Samuel's manservant sent her scurrying across the country on a circuitous route of mail coaches?

The *ifs* piled up until she began to feel sick again, but then the bottom fell out of her stomach entirely as another man emerged from the coach. A shorter man with a rounded hat already on his head. He stepped to the side and pulled spectacles off his face before taking a handkerchief from his pocket and cleaning the road dust from the lenses.

Margaretta tried to swallow, but her throat was dry.

Samuel was here. And her father was with him.

───◆───

Nash was working, trying his best not to worry about Margaretta, whom Mrs. Lancaster had said was feeling poorly this morning. Was she very sick? Did she need a doctor? Would she even be willing to see one? Until now, she'd been very particular about where she would go outside of Mrs. Lancaster's shop. If she wasn't trying to find her friend, Nash doubted she'd have gone anywhere other than church and that only because Mrs. Lancaster all but dragged her there.

The opening of his door was a welcome distraction, especially since he didn't know the two gentlemen who walked in. Strangers would consume his whole attention and force him to stop thinking about a particular dark-eyed, dark-haired fugitive.

Nash cleared his throat and set his quill aside on a stack of last week's newspapers before rising to his feet. "May I help you, gentlemen?"

The two men looked around Nash's admittedly messy office. Nearly half of his clients communicated with him via messengers, and most of the others were locals who were just as likely to have him over for tea as to meet in his office. Over time, he'd allowed the room to become a bit cluttered, though he still considered it quite professional. Would it look as such to two obviously well-to-do men from London?

Whether they decided it was professional or not, it must have passed muster because the younger man gave a stiff nod, and the two men came to stand by Nash's desk.

The older of the two men cleared his throat and glanced sideways at his companion. Tension ran underneath that gaze, and Nash couldn't help but remember the last tense, secretive person who'd walked into his life unexpectedly.

So much for the visitors distracting him from thoughts of Margaretta.

"As a man of the law, I assume you are man of discretion?"

Nash's eyebrows flew upward. How long had it been since someone questioned his character like that? When everyone knew everyone in a town, your reputation tended to precede you. "Of course," Nash stated. Was there really any other acceptable answer? "Have a seat, gentlemen."

They all made themselves comfortable in Nash's chairs, though the younger man's eyes never seemed to settle on anything for more than a moment.

The older man nodded and swallowed before clearing his throat again. "We need you to facilitate a meeting with the local providers of transportation. We need to inquire about moving about the country with a bit of, er, discretion."

A more vague and ridiculous request Nash had never heard. There was definitely something else going on here. He'd simply have to go along with their ridiculous wording until he learned what it was. "Of course. My name is Mr. Banfield."

The younger man sneered. "We assumed as much, Mr. Banfield. Your name is on the sign after all."

"Yes," Nash said slowly. "But as you did not come equipped with the same type of signage, I assumed we wanted to introduce ourselves like gentlemen."

"Yes, yes, of course," the older man said quickly. "This is Mr. Samuel Albany, third son—"

"Second son!" snarled the younger man.

The older man's eyes hardened and his shoulders stiffened. "Third son," he repeated with deliberate enunciation, "of the Viscount of Stildon. His elder brother, John, is recently deceased, however."

Mr. Albany's snarl deepened as he locked eyes with the older man. Their gazes didn't hold for long, though, and soon Mr. Albany was back to staring at the bookcases.

The old man gave a small nod and turned his attention back to Nash. "I am Mr. Curtis Fortescue of Fortescue Saddlery."

Thoughts pinged around Nash's brain like bullets shot into a metal bucket. He'd heard of Fortescue Saddlery, of course; everyone had. They were known for crafting beautiful, sturdy saddles as well as high-quality bridles and harnesses. Their leatherwork was exceptional . . . which brought to mind Margaretta's unique valise. He'd only gotten a glimpse of it that first day, but her last name and her overprotectiveness of the leather satchel merged with the presence of the men in his office. Nash had a feeling he was one step closer to finding what she was running from.

And how hard she was running.

The saddles were exclusively used by England's richest, noblest families. Anyone connected to that business wouldn't have the need to work in a shop. But how was she connected? Was this man her father-in-law? Or, Nash swallowed to ease the rising burn in his throat, was she possibly not widowed after all?

Mr. Albany swiveled his head in Nash's direction. "Fortescue Saddlery has partnered with my family to extend their line of saddles. We intend to take the racing world by storm and wish to travel anonymously until we choose to reveal the connection."

"Thus the discretionary transportation," Nash clarified. Now he knew for sure that these two were playing some sort of game. Marlborough was the last place anyone with a connection to horse racing would care to go. For that matter, Wiltshire as a county probably wasn't high on anyone's list. There was only one track of note in the whole county, and it was a good bit south of Marlborough.

If one was looking for a person, however, someone who would be looking to go somewhere with as many traveling options as possible, one couldn't do much better than Nash's little town.

"Yes." Mr. Fortescue turned toward Nash, but his gaze flickered almost constantly in Mr. Albany's direction. "We're exploring ways to travel around the southern half of England without anyone knowing we're there."

"And you wish to talk to the people who might help you do that?" Nash asked.

The two men looked at each other, both frowning, both seeming to be trying to glare the other into some sort of submission. Mr. Albany was the one to finally break the glare and answer. "Yes."

Nash couldn't tell which man actually held the power in the pairing, and that made his job considerably more difficult. Of course, it would be much easier if he knew what his job was supposed to be in this instance, because he was fast coming to believe that his role in this little tableau was to protect Margaretta. There was no doubt in his mind that she was who these men were really looking for, but Nash couldn't tell what they wanted to do when they found her.

Tension spiked up his neck until he was forced to roll his head along his shoulders to relieve it. He tried to cover the movement by reaching for a piece of paper and a quill, though he had no idea what he was going to write.

"I can certainly arrange for you to meet with a few people who might be amenable to arranging your travel needs." It wouldn't be difficult to keep them away from anyone who knew anything about Margaretta. Her dealings with the townspeople had been limited mostly to the women who came into Mrs. Lancaster's shop.

"All of them," Mr. Fortescue bit out. "We wish to speak to all of them."

Nash's eyes widened. "We've more than a dozen inns with stage stops in Marlborough alone. When you include the neighboring towns and villages, that number goes up considerably. Then there's the smiths and stables that rent out horses and carriages and—"

"This is ridiculous." Mr. Albany surged from his chair and paced to one of Nash's overflowing bookcases. "Your discretion is costing us precious time, Fortescue."

Mr. Fortescue's eyes narrowed. "And what alternative would you suggest?"

Nash waited, not daring to even breathe, but both men lapsed back into an angry silence, glaring at each other. Finally, Nash cleared his throat to break the tension. "If you'll give me your names and where you're staying, I should be able to make some arrangements within the next day or two." He looked from Mr. Albany back to Mr. Fortescue. He was an older man, but he carried himself well. He could be Margaretta's father or husband, possibly even her father-in-law, and Nash desperately needed to know which. "Are you traveling with wives, gentlemen? I would be happy to suggest a few entertainments for them while you are in the area."

"Women are a nuisance," Mr. Albany muttered while Mr. Fortescue looked at Nash with assessing brown eyes that went a long way toward convincing Nash he was looking at the father and not the husband. The shape and color were too familiar to Nash for this man to be anything other than a blood relation. Why give her name as Fortescue, then? The idea that she might not have married at all crossed Nash's mind, but he dismissed it. He had no reason to believe she'd lied to him at any other time than possibly that first day. And then it would have been understandable.

"The only woman in my life," Mr. Fortescue said slowly, "has been taking the waters for the past two months to see to her health."

Mr. Albany emitted a sound of disbelief. "Should have sent her to my estate in Shropshire. She'd have been safer there."

"Have you reason to believe her health is in danger where she currently is?" Mr. Fortescue asked pointedly.

The men were staring at each other again, struggling for power. What would happen when one of them actually came out on top? If Margaretta was caught in the middle of these two gentlemen, he could see why she would run away.

"I'm sure I wouldn't know," Mr. Albany finally said quietly. "But then again, neither do you."

Another tense moment passed before Mr. Albany straightened his coat and strode toward the door. "We're staying at The Castle Inn. My man arranged rooms for us there."

Mr. Fortescue's skin faded to a sickly gray that matched his hair. "Your man is in town?"

"Is that a problem?" Mr. Albany's eyebrows lifted, along with the corners of his lips. The smile was smug and even sent a shiver down Nash's back. "I've been sending him ahead of us to scope out the prospects. He seems to think this town very promising."

"Tonight." Mr. Fortescue snapped at Nash. "I want the first meetings arranged by tonight. We'll spend no longer in this town than we absolutely have to. You may join us for dinner with the details of the arrangements."

"Quite right," Nash said slowly, though he wasn't really sure what he was agreeing to. All he knew was a moment ago he'd been sure that these two men were the threat Margaretta was running from, but now he'd just learned there was a third man. One who might have been in town for a while.

It was a grim prospect indeed.

❖

It was nearing evening before Nash managed to enter Mrs. Lancaster's store. By then he was nearly trembling with worry. He'd wanted to go straight there after the men had left his office, assure himself that Margaretta was tucked away safely in the rooms upstairs, but knowing there was a third man, an unknown who Nash couldn't recognize, made him cautious. On the chance that he was being followed, Nash visited stables and talked to the innkeepers who dealt with the stages and mail coaches.

Every time he'd considered running for the store, he'd see a stranger or lock eyes with one of the townspeople he didn't know as well and cautiousness won out over panic and made him put every effort into looking as normal as possible. But now sufficient time had passed, and he couldn't stand the wait anymore. He had to see her.

She'd had a month—more than a month—to decide he was trustworthy and tell him her problems. Now that he'd been thrown into the middle of them without a single clue, she was going to give him answers.

Assuming, of course, that she was still safely tucked away above the shop.

Frustration and worry ate at him until his composure and patience crumbled, leaving him vulnerable and angry. He was nearly shaking with the emotions as he strode down High Street with the wind whipping his coat about. Rain was probably blowing in. It seemed to be that sort of day.

The store was blessedly empty when he walked into it. In fact, the only person he could see was Mrs. Lancaster.

"Where is she?" He knew the blatant question would give the meddling woman ideas, but he'd handle that later. She was already assuming whatever she wished. Right now, he needed answers, and he desperately needed to know that Margaretta was safe.

"Upstairs." Mrs. Lancaster shuffled toward the door and turned the sign to *Closed*.

"Are you certain? Have you actually seen her today?" Nash forced himself to breathe more slowly. What if they only thought she was upstairs and she'd actually been found by Mr. Albany's man or run away again so that they wouldn't catch her?

Nash couldn't wait for Mrs. Lancaster to work her way around whatever clever phrasing she felt like giving him today. He had to see Margaretta, had to know the worst thing that had happened was that she'd caught a head cold. He tore through the store and out the back door. He was two treads from the top of the stairs before he realized what he was doing. Was he really planning on storming up here, invading what was essentially her home? A gentleman didn't do such a thing.

The sick feeling he'd had when Mr. Fortescue's skin had paled welled up within Nash's gut once more until it squeezed his heart. Gentleman or not, he had to see Margaretta.

His pause had given Mrs. Lancaster time to catch up with him, though, breathing a little harder than Nash would have preferred. "Can't have you up here without a chaperone," she huffed before reaching past Nash and pushing the door open. "We've a guest, dear!"

A groan came from deep within the rooms, sending panic through Nash. Had Mr. Albany's man already been here? He nearly pushed Mrs. Lancaster into the front room, which acted as a sort of parlor and kitchen area. A worktable was positioned along the wall near the fireplace, and cooking hooks sat empty along one edge of the hearth. An iron rack cut across the middle of the fireplace opening. Three chairs sat around a dining table, while three more created a little seating area near the window. A door across from the fireplace stood open, and that was where Margaretta appeared, looking so pale that her thick dark brows and red lips stood out in shocking contrast.

"Nash, er, Mr. Banfield?" Her dark gaze swung from Nash to Mrs. Lancaster and back again. "What's going on?"

Relief took the strength from Nash's legs, and he braced an arm against the wall, forcing breath into his lungs. She was well. Everything was going to be fine. On the heels of relief came determination. Whatever was going on, he could keep her safe, as long as she finally gave him all the answers. But how to convince her to do such a thing? He'd asked more than once about her life, her past, and she'd proven to be quite silent on the subject, so trying to be delicate it about it was something he didn't have the time or inclination to do. So he decided to throw the largest rock he could into the pond and see what ripples it created. "I think it's time you told us about your husband."

6

Margaretta's insides clenched once more as a dozen possibilities tumbled over themselves in her mind.

Why was Nash pushing for information now? He'd been so patient. It couldn't be a coincidence that his urgency came on the same day Samuel and her father came to town. One or both of them must have encountered Nash.

But how? Why?

She couldn't believe her father would go alone with any scheme of Samuel's. He'd said he believed her when she told him she was afraid of Samuel. It was why they'd agreed to send her to Margate in the first place.

But now with both of them here together, she didn't know what to think.

"My husband is dead." She choked out the words around the knot of fear that had settled in her throat the moment she'd seen Samuel exit the carriage.

Nash drove his fingers through his hair before folding his arms over his chest, emphasizing the breadth and strength of his body. It was something Margaretta had quietly admired, his ability and willingness to do more for his clients than sit behind a desk and draw up paperwork. He walked all over town and involved himself in the more physical aspects of property management. But what did he intend to do with her?

"And your connection with Fortescue Saddlery?"

A chill wrapped around Margaretta's body despite the fact that she could hear Mrs. Lancaster poking at the fire, building it up until it crackled once more. What could she say? Nash had become a friend—she wouldn't let herself consider him anything more than that—and it wasn't as easy to lie to him as it had been when she first arrived in town. But keeping her father's business interests intact was the main reason she'd disappeared instead of asking him to help her. If he ended the business deal with the Albany family racing stables, it could ruin his reputation and his business.

Margaretta licked her lips. "I . . ."

He stared, face hard but devoid of any readable expression. Margaretta swallowed, wondering if, once he learned the truth, his sense of honor would compel him to tell her father she was here. What would her father do? He'd seemed confident that everything would work itself out when she'd last seen him, but now he was here with Samuel Albany of all people. What did that mean?

"Please don't lie to me," Nash whispered hoarsely, his blank expression giving way to a glimpse of the agony she heard in his words. "Because I'm fairly certain there's a bag in that room behind you that proves it."

She stared back at him, locking her gaze with his, trying to decide what she could say while desperately hoping he could hear all the things she couldn't bring herself to put into words.

The hiss and pop of boiling water followed by the rattle of crockery startled Margaretta, allowing her to finally look somewhere other than Nash's blue eyes, swirling with indeterminate emotion. She turned to see Mrs. Lancaster making yet another pot of tea. It was the only thing Margaretta had been able to keep down today, and Mrs. Lancaster had been running upstairs every hour and a half or so to make a fresh pot.

"Margaretta." Nash's quiet voice had lost the note of pleading, replaced by gentle strength.

She slumped against the doorframe, feeling tired and weak despite the amount of time she'd spent in bed today. An equal amount of time had been spent at the window—watching, waiting, hoping that her father and Samuel were simply passing through and would be taking the stage out of town.

They hadn't.

"Yes," she whispered, closing her eyes and letting her head fall against the wall. "I am connected to Fortescue Saddlery."

"And the Mr. Fortescue I met today? The one I'm supposed to be meeting for dinner in an hour?"

Margaretta swallowed, knowing her lies were about to catch her completely. "My father."

His eyes widened. "Why give us your unmarried name?"

Mrs. Lancaster bustled in and wrapped an arm around Margaretta's shoulders. "What does it matter right now, can't you see the poor girl's dead on her feet?"

Once Margaretta was in the vicinity of one of the chairs, she collapsed into it, unwilling to look at either of the room's occupants. Right now, these were her only two friends in the world, and she couldn't bear it if she saw distaste or distrust on their faces.

A cup of tea was pressed into her hands, and she sipped it gratefully, letting the hot liquid soothe her tight throat and settle her jumpy stomach. After half a cup, she almost felt normal again. Perhaps the tension of waiting to be discovered had been making her more ill than the baby or some other illness.

"It's no wonder she's unwell," Mrs. Lancaster crooned, smoothing a hand over Margaretta's hair. "She hasn't slept nigh a wink in at least three days."

"How would you know?" Nash asked.

That pulled Margaretta's attention from her teacup. Didn't he know she'd been living here with Mrs. Lancaster?

The old woman chuckled. "It's hard to miss when my bed's barely five feet from hers."

Nash's head jerked toward the door to the small bedroom. In two steps he was standing in the doorway, hands braced against the frame and leaning in to look over all the contents of the room. What did he see? Margaretta and Mrs. Lancaster were fairly neat—Margaretta more so because she didn't have enough possessions to make much of a mess, but the room was lived in.

His expression was incredulous as he looked over his shoulder, still braced in the doorway. "You're living here."

"Of course I am." Mrs. Lancaster set about cleaning up the tea, but kept her gaze averted from both Margaretta and Nash. The lack of eye contact was unusual and unnerving.

"But I see you walking toward your cottage every evening. You even wave at me through the window." Nash's tone was cold enough to pull Margaretta's attention once again. How in the world had this confrontation become about Mrs. Lancaster instead of her? "Why aren't you living in your cottage?"

It wasn't hard to guess why he was angry. Mrs. Lancaster's lonely evening walks had probably included a very deliberate path by Nash's office. As a man who liked to control everything, he certainly wouldn't like being fooled by an elderly shopkeeper. Despite the tension, Margaretta had to hide a small smile behind her teacup. Mrs. Lancaster was certainly sly.

The sly woman currently under Nash's scrutiny set down the kettle and turned to face him, her hands planted on her soft hips, making the flowers on her muslin print dress bunch together. "Because I leased it."

Silence fell, so stark that Margaretta didn't even risk taking a sip of tea. Even the fire refused to pop or crackle.

Nash's mouth pressed into a tight line. "You leased out the cottage?"

"Just said as much, didn't I?" Mrs. Lancaster bustled over to the worktable, her right foot dragging a bit with each step but looking as spry as someone half her age otherwise. She pulled a loaf of bread toward her and began slicing it. "I leased it to a lovely young widow and her companion." She gave a nod in Margaretta's direction. "Friends of yours, if I had to guess."

So Mrs. Lancaster had known something about Katherine! Hope surged through Margaretta only to fade as the full implications of Mrs. Lancaster's statement sank into Margaretta's weary brain. "I'm afraid you're mistaken. My friend isn't a widow."

"Nonsense." Mrs. Lancaster slid the slices of bread onto the rack over the low-burning fire. "There's more than one kind of widow, you know."

Margaretta glanced at Nash to see his eyebrows climbing up toward his hairline. "There is?"

"Of course. There's the woman who got married and then found herself without a husband." Mrs. Lancaster jerked her head in Margaretta's direction. "Then there's the one who simply doesn't want anyone to ask too many questions."

"So your tenant lies?" Nash frowned.

Margaretta bit her lip. Knowing how passionate Nash was about his clients' property agreements and contracts, the thought of Mrs. Lancaster, whom he felt so personally responsible for, making such an arrangement without him, and to someone potentially unscrupulous, had to be torture.

Mrs. Lancaster shrugged. "If you're narrow-minded in your definition of widow."

Margaretta blinked. How could the definition of widow be misconstrued?

Nash grunted in disdain, obviously agreeing with Margaretta's reaction. "She is a woman whose husband is dead. I'm fairly certain Johnson's *Dictionary of the English Language* will support me in that statement."

"And why does he get to decide?" The old woman's wrinkled hands settled onto her hips again and a frown pulled down the corners of her lips, making her round, normally cherubic face look distorted. "Besides, how do you know she's not a widow? There's no age limit on them. A woman can get widowed in a month if her husband ups and dies on her."

"Or less," Margaretta muttered. She didn't know if either of them could hear her, but the fact that she'd been married less than two weeks—a mere eleven days—had to be something of a unique achievement. And given that seven of those eleven days had been spent apart while he prepared to leave the country, she'd barely been married at all.

Nash glanced at her, and for a moment Margaretta thought he would latch onto her statement and demand more answers. Instead he sighed, rubbed a hand across his face, and looked back at Mrs. Lancaster. He must have decided her news was the most pressing. After all, Margaretta was someone he could dispense of with a simple visit to the inn where her father was staying.

She swallowed. Would he do that? Did he want to be rid of her? Would he even care to hear the rest of her side of the story? The intense desire to go back and change the last five weeks coursed through Margaretta. If she could, she would trust Nash sooner, break her silence and tell him everything. But she couldn't go back, and her time may have run out while she waited.

"Mrs. Lancaster, you just told me your tenant was lying."

Margaretta looked from Nash's frustrated expression to Mrs. Lancaster's determined one. This argument was going to be fruitless, but at least it was proving a good distraction for everyone in the room.

"Well, what do I know? I'm an old woman." Mrs. Lancaster scurried to the fireplace and picked up an iron rod from the hearth to poke at the dying flames.

Nash cleared his throat and ran a hand along the back of his neck. "Which is why we agreed to let me handle your legal documents. I never saw this lease."

"Of course you didn't." She used a long fork to flip the bread on the rack. "Because I didn't have one written up."

Margaretta laughed before she could stop it, and even though she quickly muffled it with both hands, it was enough to draw Nash's attention back to her once more.

An answering smile started to curve his lips, and the skin at the corner of his eyes crinkled before he shook his head and looked at the ground. A deep breath expanded his chest until she could see it pulling against the seams of his jacket. When he looked up again, his demeanor was serious once more but no longer appeared angry. "You can't do that, Mrs. Lancaster."

"Why not? It's my cottage."

Nash sighed. "Are they even paying you?"

Mrs. Lancaster shrugged. "We have an agreement. They uphold their end and I uphold mine." She glanced at Margaretta. "Well, usually I do. I just told Mrs. Fortescue here about her friend's presence, but she's been here long enough that I trust she means no ill will toward her friend."

"Of course not," Margaretta whispered. All this time Mrs. Lancaster had been helping her, she'd been trying to decide if Margaretta was worthy? If it was safe to take her to Katherine? Her hand drifted down to her midsection, an urge that grew daily that she tried her best to ignore. Did Mrs. Lancaster know Margaretta's secret?

Her eyes cut to Nash. Did he know? Mrs. Lancaster had just

revealed that Katherine hadn't wanted anyone to know she was here, yet Mrs. Lancaster had told not just one but two people. "What about Nash?"

"Oh, him?" Mrs. Lancaster sent him a wink and waved her hand as if disregarding his presence. "He can't help himself from protecting the innocent and disadvantaged. Keeping your friend a secret has almost been more about protecting him than her. Last thing he needs is another project." Her eyes cut to Margaretta. "Unless it's the right one."

Nash frowned. "I'm going to the cottage."

Before Margaretta could blink, Nash was striding toward the door, his boots hitting the floor with dull thuds.

"Wait!" Margaretta didn't know where the sudden burst of energy came from, but she surged out of the chair, laying a hand on Nash's shoulder. "What about your dinner with my father?"

Yes, the cottage and Katherine and everything she'd just learned was important, but Margaretta also needed to get her father and Samuel out of town. And the sooner Samuel did whatever he came here to do, the better.

Nash's eyes cut briefly to where Mrs. Lancaster was collecting the barely warmed bread from the rack and throwing a handful of dirt on the fire. It didn't take long for him to look back at Margaretta, though. "I'll tell him urgent business came up with another client. No one was available to talk to him and his partner until tomorrow morning anyway, so he'll simply have to accept the list then."

"Partner?" Margaretta choked out. Her father could not have accepted Samuel as a partner.

Nash's brows drew together and the worry that had covered his face when he'd first entered the rooms returned. "Companion? I don't know. There was something going on that I couldn't understand. And I don't know what any of this"—he gestured between himself and Mrs. Lancaster—"has to do with any of that"—his hand swung toward the window overlooking High Street. "But I know I can get at least a few answers at the cottage tonight."

Mrs. Lancaster pressed the two pieces of bread into Margaretta's hands on her way to the door. "Well, you're not going anywhere without me. It's my cottage after all."

"And you are my responsibility," Nash answered. "I promised your husband."

She flipped one hand through the air. "The dear man's dead. What he doesn't know can't hurt him."

Nash opened his mouth to answer but closed it with a sigh.

Margaretta bit off a piece of the toast, the first thing she'd actually felt like eating all day. As her two friends headed out the open door, a tingling crept up from Margaretta's feet. Could the woman in the cottage actually be Katherine? Could Margaretta risk waiting to find out? Her father and Samuel would be ensconced in their inn by now, preparing for dinner. Was there really much risk in her leaving the shop?

Clasping the unfinished bread in one hand and grabbing her cloak off the wall hook with the other, Margaretta ran out the open door just before Nash could close it behind them. She took a deep breath and looked from a frowning Nash to a smiling Mrs. Lancaster.

"I'm going as well."

Nash and Mrs. Lancaster looked at her, their expressions as different as could be. The concern in Nash's face warmed Margaretta's heart, settling her stomach even more. "I don't know." He sighed. "Mr. Albany said his manservant was in town. I didn't—I don't like this situation and I'd rather you stay here until I know more about it."

Mrs. Lancaster pushed past Nash on the little landing. "Of course you're coming, dear." She draped the large yellow cloak over Margaretta's shoulders and flipped the hood up to cover the dark curls. "It's your friend we're looking for after all."

And if Katherine could disappear once, she could disappear again. Eight months ago, she'd left society so completely that Lord FitzGilbert didn't even acknowledge her existence anymore. What was stopping her from running again if she learned Margaretta was in town?

"No," Nash said. "It isn't safe." He reached for the older woman's shoulders, the care in his gesture easing the lines of frustration and anger on his face. "First, we're going to see what business you've mucked up with your cottage."

"I've mucked up nothing." Mrs. Lancaster sniffed. "Everything is exactly as I wish it to be."

Nash closed his eyes and sighed again.

Mrs. Lancaster took the opportunity to head down the stairs. Margaretta followed before Nash could lead her back into the safety of the little rooms she'd been clinging to all day. It would be better if she stayed behind, there would certainly be less risk, but seeing Mrs. Lancaster standing up to Nash, revealing all she'd managed to do without anyone knowing, had given Margaretta a bit of courage.

Yes, life had thrown her a problem, but it was time she took steps toward solving it. Even if the person in Mrs. Lancaster's cottage wasn't Katherine, Margaretta was done waiting for someone else to tell her what to do. She'd been hiding behind Mrs. Lancaster's care and even Nash's protectiveness, hoping to find an old friend who would give her an easy solution. It was time she found one of her own.

By the time they reached the alley at the bottom of the stairs, Mrs. Lancaster was nearly skipping like a child on a treasured outing while Nash practically stomped his way down the uneven stone pavement.

Margaretta considered the future as she trotted along behind the others, occasionally stuffing a bite of bread into her mouth. Part of her was still exhausted from the emotional and physical toil of the day, but hope was a powerful animal and she would ride it as long as it allowed her to run after her companions.

It wouldn't be so bad, being a country matriarch. True, she'd never lived anywhere in her life besides London, but it wouldn't be such a bad life if she could establish herself in a little village, grow old, and then force everyone to her will the way Mrs. Lancaster seemed to be doing. It was the last thing Samuel would expect her to do. There had to be some way she could establish herself somewhere, perhaps a village less passed through by aristocrats and London's wealthy elite.

The idea of leaving Marlborough, leaving Nash, made her heart pound in her chest again. Or perhaps that was the fact that they were getting farther away from the safety of the store. Yes, that had to be it, because with the baby, she couldn't afford to form any attachments that might influence her thinking.

They strolled down narrow alleys and back lanes, Mrs. Lancaster waving a greeting to everyone she saw. Several people seemed to be on their way home for the night, probably planning their dinners and when to put the children to bed.

Lack of physical energy forced Margaretta to slow her steps a bit, and she fell back. Every few steps, Nash would glance back and adjust his pace so she wasn't too far behind him, but Mrs. Lancaster simply shuffled on, her skirts doing an odd swish with every drag of her right foot.

As they moved out of town, the businesses and shopfronts gave way to rows of homes. The buildings became simpler and the road a bit rougher, especially on the hill away from the market area. Tile still graced the walls that weren't made of brick, but the mouldings became plain and the structures more square. Some even seemed to tilt from the weight of age.

Could Katherine really be living in such a place? While Margaretta had flitted on the edge of society, Katherine had been exceedingly popular before her fall from grace. Could she have left behind the jewels and dozens of servants to live in such reduced circumstances?

Immediately Margaretta knew the answer was a resounding yes. If the rumors were true, if there was even the slightest accuracy in what they said, then there was every possibility that Katherine had turned her back on all she knew. Given the chance, Margaretta certainly would. If it meant the difference between death and survival for the innocent life she carried, she'd sweep and dust until she couldn't hold a broom. The simple life hadn't been as bad as she'd feared.

And if anyone had enough resilience to make it work, Katherine did. It was why Margaretta was here. She had to know how Katherine had managed to make it all work.

Had to know if there was a way to redeem such an impossible situation.

The road they were climbing suddenly opened up, spilling them into a large open green area lit brightly by the sun perched on the horizon. Homes surrounded the green, and a few children chased each other with long, flat paddles, their game of cricket abandoned in the name of pursuit.

"William," Mrs. Lancaster called, "does your father know you've run off with his cricket bat again?"

One little boy stumbled to a halt, dirty blond hair flopping into his eyes. He bit his lip, revealing a gap where one of his front teeth had fallen out. "No, Mrs. Lancaster."

"Well, then." The old woman braced her hands on her knees. "You rush home and do an extra good job brushing your father's horse tonight and we'll say nothing about it."

The little boy grinned, revealing a second hole in the lower half of his smile, and rushed across the green to hug Mrs. Lancaster.

Margaretta felt a pang in her chest at the sight of the happy little boy. Whatever had pushed her to find the strength to walk up that hill drained away. She hadn't thought past the fact that she was going to have a baby, hadn't let herself imagine what came next because she simply didn't know how to protect such a dependent, helpless being.

She hadn't let herself consider the fact that the baby she was carrying would one day, God willing, grow up. Be a child. Run around and play cricket.

Unless Samuel Albany found him first.

7

Nash took a deep breath. He knew the children running around on the green, getting hugs from Mrs. Lancaster before running off to their homes. Of course he knew them. They even shouted their greetings in his direction as they ran off.

He always found it a bit difficult, though, dealing with the children. Awkward. The younger they were, the more he wondered whether or not their mothers had suffered in bringing them into the world. It was always a vague uncomfortableness, a hazy impression of guilt that inspired him to keep a modicum of distance between himself and the younger generation.

Tonight, however, his unease didn't feel so very abstract. It felt specific. Personal. And he wasn't sure why.

His sister's boy would have been older than the ones currently running away from the green, but that didn't stop him from wondering what his life would have been like if she had lived, if he'd watched her son run around the green with a cricket bat. If she and Lewis had grown their family. What would that have meant for Nash?

He'd likely have married. But watching Lewis nearly let go of life had convinced Nash that perhaps the danger was a bit too great. Perhaps it was a risk not worth taking. Without a child to hold, a future to cling to, Lewis had given himself over to the melancholy for almost three years.

His business had faltered and he became nearly destitute. Friends and family had been worried, trying to deal with their own mourning while at the same time encouraging Lewis to keep living.

Eventually, he had started living again. Turned his business around, remarried, even had two young children.

Despite his recovery, one thing Lewis said during those three years had stayed with Nash beyond any of the other painful ramblings. Lewis hated himself because he'd been the one to do that to Mary. His loving Mary had eventually killed her.

Nash didn't think he could live with such a sentiment.

Especially now that the vague emotion was starting to sharpen into a familiar face. Was that what had him thinking so much about Mary and Lewis tonight? Margaretta's presence at his side? The one woman who had cracked his resolve ever so slightly?

As the children ran off, laughing and happy, Nash thought through the families they represented. Many of them had brothers and sisters who hadn't lived through infancy. Two had lost their mothers—one to childbirth and another to illness.

Despite this, the families seemed, for the most part, happy and healthy. But sometimes pain could fester unseen, allowing you to fool the world at large.

The last boy disappeared over the rise, leaving Nash alone with his obscure remnants of pain.

Margaretta squeezed his arm and offered him a small smile, a soft look in her eyes that seemed to reassure Nash that he wasn't alone. She didn't even know why he hurt, what he'd vowed, but she could sense his inner torment. The fact that he wanted to wallow in that sympathy, to lean into her and seek the comfort of her presence, shocked him out of his stupor.

Mrs. Lancaster. The cottage. The mysterious tenants who didn't seem to actually be paying their way for anything. These were the things he needed to be focusing on.

The cottage wasn't very far from the green, just two turns down a rutted side street, and they were standing before it. The walls tilted slightly, showing the age of the house. When it had been built originally, it had probably stood alone, overseeing a sheep pasture outside the village, but Marlborough had grown to eventually swallow the pasture and the house.

Margaretta's breathing increased even though their pace remained slow. The harsh rattle of her shallow breaths concerned him, as did the fact that she'd grown so pale that her face was nearly translucent.

He fell back a step to stand near her but resisted the urge to take her hand or wrap an arm about her for support. Despite the depth of their conversations over the last weeks, he'd never touched her. Never sought to bridge the distance between them. If he did that, if he changed the tenuous definition of their association, he was afraid he'd forget the vow he made to himself and his sister, the quiet promise he'd made to the town that became his family.

Mrs. Lancaster lifted one fisted hand and rapped her gnarled knuckles against the thin wooden door.

The panel swung open to reveal a pretty girl about Margaretta's age, with blond hair pulled into a simple bun and a pale green muslin dress that had once been fine but was now showing wear from multiple washings.

Nash fell back half a step as Mrs. Lancaster pushed into the doorway, cooing over the baby in the woman's arms. The woman said nothing, simply stared at Margaretta, eyes wide and expression blank.

The baby gurgled as Mrs. Lancaster continued her attentions. A hard lump settled in Nash's throat. Babies made him even more nervous than young children did. Babies meant that very recently a woman had potentially been at death's door and only God's mercy had kept her from it, though how God decided which mothers got to live was beyond Nash's understanding.

Margaretta reached over and clasped her fingers around his hand. The feel of her skin against his, even if it was only their hands, nearly broke the wall he'd constructed around his heart. Her nails dug into his palm, but the sharp pain didn't disguise the warmth of her touch or the softness of her hands. She'd run out tonight without her gloves, and every detail of her skin implanted itself on his brain without waiting for his permission. His thumb traced over a spot that was beginning to roughen and callus because of her daily use of a broom.

Margaretta had every ounce of his attention, but he didn't have hers. She was staring at the woman in the doorway, her mouth moving but no sound coming out. Finally she managed to swallow and clear her throat. "Katherine."

"Margaretta." The blonde, apparently the missing Katherine, licked her lips before pressing them into a firm line. Her voice was flat, and when she finally pulled her gaze from her Margaretta, she spared Nash only a glance before glaring at Mrs. Lancaster.

The angry stare didn't bother the old shopkeeper, who was too busy with the baby to pay much attention to the woman holding him. "As lovely as the weather is, dear," Mrs. Lancaster said, finally straightening away from the baby, "perhaps you could invite us in? The chill of night is coming, and we don't want darling Benedict to catch cold."

Katherine's gaze cut to Nash once more before she looked over her shoulder into the depths of the cottage. Tension pulled her face tighter, making the lines of her neck stand out. But then she nodded and stepped back into the house, leaving the door open in silent invitation.

Nash considered leaving. If he hurried, he'd only be a few minutes late to his dinner meeting. But before him, if he were willing to brave a room containing a baby, were the answers to all Margaretta's secrets. This was who she'd been looking for. Her quest was complete. She could soon be leaving Marlborough, and Nash didn't want to be asking himself *what if* for the rest of his life.

With a sharp inhale that did nothing to steady his heartbeat, he followed Margaretta over the threshold.

———◈———

Margaretta didn't realize she'd grabbed Nash's hand until she had to let go in order to follow Mrs. Lancaster into the cottage. She had to make a conscious effort to let go of him, but she wasn't going to miss her chance to talk to Katherine, and Nash didn't seem in any hurry to follow their hostess into her home.

The interior was considerably darker than the street outside, and Margaretta blinked to accustom her eyes to the dimness and to the unexpected surroundings. She remembered visiting Katherine in London, remembered the silk-hung drawing room, the plush Aubusson carpet in her bedchamber. The contrast between those memories and the stark simplicity in front of her now was startling.

The wide-planked wood floor was swept clean, and two plain but comfortable-looking wooden chairs flanked a fireplace, where a fire burned low. On the other side of the room, a smooth wooden table, a bench, and three more chairs sat in front of a basic kitchen work area. Two doors led from the room, presumably to the bedchambers.

Even assuming that the chambers in the back of the house combined to the size of the room in the front, the entire living space was smaller than the double drawing room in Katherine's father's house where Margaretta had attended more than one social gathering.

Mrs. Lancaster moved comfortably about the room, taking the baby in her arms and making her way to a rocking chair in the far corner. It was obvious she had done more than give these women a home. She'd been visiting them with some frequency, probably when she'd taken those long evening walks.

Margaretta stared at Katherine. Her old friend stared back. From the corner of her eye, Margaretta saw Nash shifting his head back and forth as he looked from one woman to the other. How strange it must seem to him that she'd been so desperate to find this woman and now that she had, she was saying nothing.

What could she say, though? How did one broach such a subject?

"I see the rumors are true." Margaretta winced. That had probably not been the best way to open the subject.

Katherine's eyebrows lifted, and she looked over her shoulder to where Mrs. Lancaster was rocking and cooing at Benedict. One side of Katherine's mouth tipped up into a sad smile. "Not as true as you think."

The baby let out a gurgle that slid into a bit of a whimper, as if to call Katherine's statement a lie. Margaretta said nothing, allowing the circumstances to ask her questions for her.

"Mrs. Lancaster didn't tell me you were here." There was an undeniable note of censure in Katherine's voice, even if the look she sent Mrs. Lancaster's way was edged with indulgence.

"Of course I didn't, dear." Mrs. Lancaster never looked up from the baby. "You'd have taken this precious boy and made a run for it. When I said I'd protect you, I never said that didn't include protecting you from yourself."

A sigh that could almost past for the beginning of a laugh deflated Katherine's chest as she looked at the floor and shook her head. When she finally looked up, her expression was a little softer. "Won't you sit? You may select a chair from the table if you wish to join us, Mr. Banfield."

The man choked. "I beg your pardon; have we been introduced?"

The impish smile that flitted across Katherine's face was familiar enough to send a pang of sadness through Margaretta. Would her own smiles soon become a mere memory? Something that only hinted at the carefree girl she used to be?

Hadn't they already become so? Her smile had returned easily after her husband's death. Perhaps a bit too easily. But then they'd hardly known each other, had both considered the marriage a prudent match that would secure a future between Fortescue Saddlery and Albany's racing stable. John's death, though tragic, had seemed more of an inconvenience than a devastation, but then it became apparent that Margaretta's future hadn't simply been delayed. It had been threatened.

She hadn't smiled much since.

Katherine sat in the other chair flanking the fireplace, looking as serene and graceful as she had during her Season in Town. "I make it a point to know all the important people in my area, Mr. Banfield," she said smoothly. "Besides, Mrs. Lancaster speaks highly of you." She then turned toward Margaretta. "How have you been?"

"Well." Margaretta said hesitantly. "I've been married."

Katherine looked like she didn't quite know what to do with that information. "Congratulations."

"And widowed," Margaretta continued.

"Oh." Katherine's eyes widened, and her hands gripped each other in her lap. "I'm so sorry."

As the baby let out another loud cry, the door behind Katherine opened, and another young woman stepped out. Margaretta's jaw went slack. She recognized the woman with the round face and the nondescript brown hair as the friend who had followed Katherine around almost like a companion. "Miss Blakemoor?"

The woman blinked in Margaretta's direction. She coughed. "Miss Fortescue?"

Nash, who had stood upon the other woman's entrance, shot an accusing look Margaretta's way. A reminder that he hadn't forgotten the news that had been dropped on him earlier this evening.

Margaretta cleared her throat. "It's Mrs. actually."

Miss Blakemoor coughed and darted a look in Mr. Banfield's direction. "Oh, er, I'm actually a Mrs. as well."

The dizzying weakness from earlier crept into the edges of Margaretta's brain as she tried to make sense of everything she was seeing and learning. What was real? What was pretense? Perhaps if she gave a little information the woman, or apparently women, she'd come to see would provide some answers as well. "Mine was a very short marriage," Margaretta said with a smile that attempted to break the tension in the room. "It is sometimes difficult to remember I received a new name."

Nash crossed his arms over his chest and narrowed his eyes at her. "What else are you forgetting?"

"Nothing that need concern you."

"Too late. I find my concern growing by the moment."

Margaretta stared at her hands. He sounded almost hurt, as if he, too, had found himself in a strange place these last few weeks, wondering about their burgeoning friendship. Had he grown feelings for her the way she was deathly afraid she'd grown feelings for him? Margaretta wasn't willing to name the thing that made her heart pound whenever she heard him greet Mrs. Lancaster during his daily visit. To do so would mean one more thing she had to leave behind when the time came.

The baby cried once more, this time refusing to be hushed

and calmed by Mrs. Lancaster. "I do believe he's hungry, my dears, and I'm long past the age of being able to help him with that."

Margaretta clamped her teeth together to hold in her shocked laughter, while Katherine and Miss Blakemoor felt no such compulsion to restrain theirs. Nash emitted a low groan.

Miss Blakemoor crossed to the rocking chair and lifted the bundle in her arms. "I'll see to him, Mrs. Lancaster."

And then she disappeared back into the room she'd come from.

Katherine looked at Margaretta pointedly. "Rumors rarely get everything correct."

Nash pulled his chair over to the grouping and settled into it. "Are you from London as well, Miss FitzGilbert?"

Katherine's pointed look narrowed into a glare as she shifted her gaze to Nash. "How do you know my name? Yours is blazoned across the sign outside your office. Mine, however, is certainly not."

"Margare—er, Mrs. Fortescue, I mean—" he cut himself off with a sigh and pinched the top of his nose as he took a deep breath. "Margaretta came to town looking for a Miss Katherine FitzGilbert. As she appears to have been looking for you, I'm assuming that you are the Miss FitzGilbert in question. Or have you suddenly remembered a name change as well?"

Katherine pressed her lips together. "No name change, but I would thank you to forget you ever heard mine."

He lifted one eyebrow. "I never forget anything."

The look he shot Margaretta's way made her sweat.

Mrs. Lancaster popped up from the rocking chair. Nash rose slowly as well, his eyes staying on Margaretta the entire time. She'd come to learn his different expressions in the past month, but this one was unreadable. What was he thinking?

"As long as we're all making confessions here this evening,"

Mrs. Lancaster said, stepping closer to the chairs where Katherine and Margaretta sat, "we might as well get one more out of the way. Then we can all start to move on from this secrecy."

Margaretta didn't know how she felt about the word *confessions*. Uncovering of secrets was probably more accurate, since none of the parties involved had given their information voluntarily, but if Mrs. Lancaster had something she felt she needed to say, Margaretta certainly wasn't going to stop her. The woman had been a blessing, and she deserved peace if some secret was tormenting her.

"Of course," Margaretta said. "You can tell us anything. I believe everyone here can say they owe you loyalty."

Nash and Katherine both nodded, their faces mirroring the concern and confusion Margaretta felt.

"That's nice of you, dear, but it's not my confession." She smiled as if whatever she said next would be the best news in the world. "It's yours."

Margaretta's mouth dropped open as she looked in Mrs. Lancaster's kind, smiling eyes. The woman looked almost excited about putting Margaretta on the spot. Or was it the news she expected to hear that made her so happy? Margaretta's attempt to swallow almost choked her. The shopkeeper knew. How long had she known? How long had she suspected?

"I . . . I . . ." Margaretta looked over at Nash but quickly dropped her gaze to the floor. "I'm sure I don't know what you mean."

"It's why you're here, isn't it?" Margaretta could hear the frown in Mrs. Lancaster's voice, and it made her wince. But then one wrinkled hand landed on her shoulder and gave an encouraging squeeze.

Why couldn't she say the words? Margaretta swallowed. It wasn't as if she'd done anything wrong. She had been married. But somehow she knew the news would change everything.

Yes, she'd never claimed to be anything other than a widow, but other than that one conversation, she and Nash had never acknowledged her past. Once he knew the truth, there'd be no ignoring it. "I . . . I can't."

Another squeeze encouraged Margaretta to look up into the face of the woman who had filled the role of friend and mother for the past five weeks. "It's time," Mrs. Lancaster said. "You might as well tell everyone about the baby."

8

"Baby?" Nash shot to his feet. He looked to the door where the woman whose identity he hadn't known had disappeared with the baby. Surely they weren't trying to say that the baby was Margaretta's, were they?

When he finally pulled his gaze back to Margaretta and saw her hand pressed to her middle in a gesture he remembered his sister doing countless times, the bottom fell out of his world.

Images and memories he'd kept locked away flooded to the surface. The joy and laughter that abounded when Mary and Lewis had shared their news. More laughter, as well as the occasional good-natured complaining, as she'd grown too large for public outings and never seemed to be able to find a position that stayed comfortable for more than five minutes.

The devastation when Lewis came to Nash's house and simply sat, unable to bring himself to say the words and actually tell Nash what had happened.

Miss FitzGilbert finally coughed, breaking the silence before speaking into it with a quiet voice. "You were actually married, weren't you?"

Margaretta didn't stop looking at Nash. He wished she would. Then maybe he could stop looking at her as well.

"Yes." Her voice was just as low and quiet as her friend's. "I married Mr. John Albany, and we spent three days at his father's country house in Surrey. Then we returned to London so he could prepare to leave with his regiment. They were to set sail from London one week after we came home."

She swallowed visibly. "He slipped on the gangplank and hit his head. By the time they could fish him out of the Thames, he was dead."

No one said anything. As the shock of Margaretta's announcement wore off, questions filled his mind, warring with a mixture of other emotions.

"A tragedy to be sure," Katherine said quietly, but without the sort of emotion one would normally expect behind such words. "But why are you here? You've nothing to hide."

Margaretta closed her eyes. Tears welled along the compressed lashes before streaming in twin tracks down her cheeks. "John's younger brother wants nothing more than his father's title." Her eyes opened, deep brown pools of utter despair. "If he finds out I'm with child, he'll stop at nothing to make sure the baby never has a chance to inherit."

Nash grabbed on to the back of the chair, gripping it until his knuckles whitened and the wood threatened to break the skin. The uneasy feeling he'd gotten in his office that morning grew to a spine-tingling premonition. The man who had come to his office, traveling with her father, inquiring of discreet modes of transportation. If that was him, if that was the brother . . .

The implications slammed into Nash faster than he could process them. If what Margaretta said was true, what in the world was she going to do?

❖

Margaretta pressed her hand against her middle, where the softness she'd known her whole life had given way to a firmness that wouldn't let her forget the impossible situation she was in. It was the crowning example of the fact that life was not fair. She'd done everything right, all that was asked of her, and still this had happened.

Somehow, once she started telling the story, finally admitting it all, it felt less daunting. The last vestiges of the hope that had carried her to Katherine helped stem the tears that were dripping onto her skirt. She also couldn't stop the story now that she'd started, even if she wanted to keep as much as possible to herself and only answer the questions they asked. In a fit of nerves and energy that propelled her from the chair and sent her pacing across the floor, the words poured out of her.

"Of course, his family was anxious to know if it was possible a baby had come from the brief union. John's older brother left for India years ago and married there. He and his wife have been to England to visit a time or two, but there's been no children. John knew he was likely to inherit, but he joined the navy anyway. Our marriage was more of a business union than anything: Fortescue Saddlery and the Albany racing stables. It made sense."

She took a deep breath and pressed on, staring at her toes as they tried to dig their way into the wide-planked floor. "Samuel was the most insistent. After a couple of weeks, he became agitated, and I panicked. Told them that there was no baby. I thought it was the truth, thought it had to be the truth. My parents were married for years before I came along."

"That's not how it works for everyone, though," Katherine said softly.

"No." Margaretta sighed.

"And Samuel Albany knew that, too," Nash murmured.

His soft words forced Margaretta to look at him, even though she'd been avoiding it. More of that unreadable expression met her gaze, so she let her eyes fall back to her clasped hands.

"Yes. He works a lot with the racing stables, and he kept visiting, saying he had business with Father, but making a point to see me every time. I think he was bribing my maid because he seemed to know almost as soon as I did. He got angry, made veiled remarks about ways he'd heard women got rid of unwanted children. My father and I didn't know what he would do, so Father sent me on a sea-bathing trip with Mrs. Hollybroke and her daughters. Father said he'd join me there in a few weeks."

Margaretta took a deep breath, knowing the next thing she'd done had been foolish. "But Samuel's man followed sooner. I'd been in Margate but three days when I saw him outside the house where we were staying. I got scared. So I ran."

The tears returned. A slow steady trickle down her cheeks that blurred her vision and added to the misery coursing through her.

Strong arms suddenly wrapped around her as Nash pulled her to his chest, making her feel truly safe for the first time in months. She curled into the steady warmth, her body beginning to shake from the overwhelming emotions. For just a moment, part of her believed everything was going to come out right in the end.

Mrs. Lancaster sniffled in the corner, not even bothering to hide the fact that she was crying.

"But why did you come here?" Katherine was standing now, but still looked wary, staying several feet from Margaretta and Nash.

Margaretta straightened within the circle of Nash's arms so she could see her old friend better. "When you left London, there were whispers. They said you were with child, and I couldn't imagine another reason you would have left like that. I had hoped you would know what I could do, where I could go. A way to hide my condition and never let the world know it happened.

All I had was the letter you sent me from Marlborough, so I came here. I didn't know what else to do."

The slow stream of tears became a flood as Margaretta finally allowed herself to feel everything. She sobbed into Nash's chest. Tears of freedom from finally sharing her burden with someone else. Tears of hopelessness because it didn't appear that Katherine had found a real solution either. All the tears she'd done her best to hold back for months came pouring out. She cried for John, perhaps the first time since he'd died, and she cried for his family, who mourned ever so much more than she had. Mostly though, she selfishly wept for herself, for the unfairness of life, for the strength she didn't know if she had.

Another set of arms wrapped around Margaretta's shoulders and pulled her away from Nash, toward one of the doors off the main room.

She didn't want to leave his warmth, didn't want to leave him. Desperate for one last look at his face, she tilted her head up as his arms fell away from her. More tears spilled, blurring the lines of his face and preventing her from reading the expression in his deep blue eyes.

She tore her tear-filled gaze from his, unwilling to drag out the breaking of her heart any more than she had to. Would she ever see him again?

Would he tell her father? Did it matter?

Would Katherine be able to give her any answers? She was living alone with Miss Blakemoor and her baby. How were they surviving? Whatever resources they had, Margaretta didn't have access to similar ones.

The room Katherine took her to was warm. Margaretta couldn't see through the tears, and her eyelids were starting to puff and swell from the force of her crying. But she could feel the blessed softness of a mattress and soon the welcoming darkness of oblivion silenced her pain.

A hearty wail broke into Margaretta's slumber. As she blinked awake, she tried to remember where she was, a problem she'd never had until a few weeks ago, having spent most of the first twenty years of her life waking up in her father's London townhouse. She eased her eyes open. The room was dim, too dark to be the rooms above Mrs. Lancaster's store. Plastered walls painted a light yellow surrounded her as she snuggled under the pieced scrap quilt. Low murmurs came through the wall, and the baby who had woken her soon silenced.

Katherine's home. Or Mrs. Lancaster's cottage. Whichever way she wanted to think of it.

The chirping of birds greeted her as she got up and found her clothing draped over a chair in the corner. How heavily had she slept that she hadn't even noticed when Katherine removed her dress and shoes?

The room was small, but comfortable, with a bed, chair, and small washstand. The lone window looked out over a small vegetable garden and let in the morning sun.

Tears threatened again, but her head was already pounding from everything that had happened the day before, and she was so very tired of crying. She took a deep breath and pressed her palms to her eyes until the urge subsided.

A sense of urgency swelled in her throat as she dressed, but she delayed leaving the room. Katherine had been Margaretta's last hope, but what help could she really offer? Even if Katherine knew a way for Margaretta to hide and to then provide for the baby, there was still her father and John's parents to consider. She couldn't disappear like Katherine and Miss Blakemoor had.

She also couldn't just go back to London and hope Samuel would come to his senses. She couldn't even afford to leave this cottage until he was gone from Marlborough.

But one thing was certain: She wasn't going to find any answers in this little room.

Miss Blakemoor was sitting in the rocking chair near the fireplace, feeding the baby, as Margaretta stepped out into the main room. "Good morning."

"Good morning, Miss Blakemoor."

She laughed. "Call me Daphne. There's little reason to stand on ceremony here."

Her gaze dropped to Margaretta's middle before looking down at the baby she held. Her smile never faltered.

Margaretta eased forward and sat in one of the chairs. "Everyone thought it was Katherine who was in a delicate condition. They swore it was her who had been caught with Mr. Maxwell Oswald." With a wince, Margaretta realized she'd never even wondered where Daphne had disappeared to. Neither had anyone else. "I'm afraid no one even considered it was you."

"I know." Daphne's smile turned sad. "They probably didn't even know I was gone. Katherine was ruined in their minds, and I was ruined in real life, so we convinced our fathers to give us our dowry money and we would disappear. Mine wasn't very large, of course, but Katherine's . . . we figured it would be enough to get us somewhere, to get established until we could find a way to provide for ourselves."

She rose to walk, the baby on her shoulder as she patted his back. "We'd intended to go east and then up the coast, find a little bungalow in a seaside town. But the carriage ride made me ill, and then we met Mrs. Lancaster. We'd intended to only stay until I was feeling up to traveling, but that was nine months ago and we're still here."

They fell silent, and Margaretta tried to find the courage to voice the questions she didn't dare ask. Did the father know? Did they intend to live here forever and raise Benedict themselves? They'd had nine months to think about the future, and

Margaretta was deathly afraid that it hadn't been enough time to find a solution because the problem was an impossible one.

"Were you truly married?" Daphne asked quietly, apparently not as petrified as Margaretta was about propriety.

"Yes, I really was. John and I met a few times at parties in the two years I was out in society. Then Father brought him home, proposing the benefits of a connection between our families. I barely knew John, but he seemed nice enough so I agreed."

Silence fell again. Whether or not both women were thinking the same thing, Margaretta couldn't say, but it felt to her like the unspoken question on both of their tongues was *What are you going to do?* Margaretta imagined they both wanted to ask each other the question but each felt she couldn't since she didn't know how to answer it for herself.

A grumble from Margaretta's empty belly broke the silence, prompting her to inquire about food. Each bite she took of her simple breakfast sounded loud in the silent room. Perhaps taking her chances in Mrs. Lancaster's tiny rooms would be better than this, even though being in the center of town greatly increased the chances of Samuel or his man finding her.

The front door opened, and Katherine bustled in with a basket full of fabric. She dropped the basket next to the door and looked from Daphne to Margaretta and back again. "Have you been like this all morning?"

"Kit . . ." Daphne's voice was low.

Katherine rolled her eyes at her friend. "Do you really think proper parlor manners are called for here?" She took off her pelisse and hung it on a hook by the door before moving to sit across from Margaretta. "What are you planning to do?"

Apparently Katherine had no problem voicing the question. She always had been a bit more blunt than most.

Margaretta sighed and put down her tea. "I don't know. I

spent days in my room pondering that question, praying in ways I never had before. Then I remembered your letter—"

"You sent letters?" Daphne paused in the act of putting her son down in his cradle. "We agreed to disappear."

Katherine didn't even look ashamed. "I wanted to say good-bye to a few people, let them know I was leaving and not dead in a ditch somewhere. Besides, I didn't think we were going to be staying in Marlborough for more than a day. It seemed like a safe enough place to mail them from."

Daphne dropped into the third chair at the table. "How many?"

Another sigh and another eye roll. Perhaps that was how Katherine expressed herself when she felt backed into a corner. "Only three."

"If it's any consolation, I don't think anyone else will be looking for you." Margaretta hesitated, but perhaps they all needed a bit of Katherine's blunt honesty. "I probably wouldn't have remembered it except that I found myself desperate to know what you'd done if the rumors were true."

"But you're a proper widow." Daphne picked at her fingernails.

"A fact that actually has me in more danger at the moment than the alternative would have."

"But if the child is a girl, you could simply go home." Katherine fixed her own cup of tea from the pot Margaretta had made earlier.

"Yes." That was the best outcome she could hope for. But even then she'd be taking a child home to what? Care and comfort, yes, but Margaretta was now a widow with limited prospects. Could she take the child and live with John's family, knowing the kind of man Samuel was? Would she stay home and wait for her father to marry her off again? What sort of man wanted to marry a woman who came with a daughter?

The idea of marrying again threatened to send Margaretta

right back to bed, where she could cry herself into oblivion. Where she had once welcomed the security of an emotionless marriage, it had lost a great deal of its appeal in the past month. She'd learned that relationships could be different, and it was difficult to go back to thinking otherwise.

"Will you take a boy to the foundling house then?" Katherine's question was quiet. So quiet Margaretta wasn't sure she simply hadn't thought it.

Because she'd thought it before. Thought it often.

"I can't." Margaretta's throat seemed to swell. The words she knew she needed to get out felt thick and syrupy as they slid through the thin passage, fighting for space with Margaretta's shallow breaths. "I thought maybe I could, but I can't. I didn't love John, but this child is from a marriage that, however short, happened. I can't leave him on the doorstep, to be scorned and treated like an unwanted blight on the world."

"No child should be left to think that of themselves," Daphne added with a look toward the cradle in the corner. A look that said she loved her son more than anything, more than the tough road she'd been forced to walk to get here, more than the mountains they would still have to climb.

Margaretta looked back and forth between the two women at the table. "How are you going to do it? Mrs. Lancaster isn't going to live forever."

Katherine nodded to the basket she'd dropped by the door. "We take in some sewing. A bit of mending, some work for the church, making clothes for the people in the workhouse. It's all arranged through a local seamstress, a friend of Mrs. Lancaster's. All those years of embroidery mean I can sew a pretty straight stitch. We've enough to purchase a house when it comes time. As long as we make money for food, we should be able to survive, possibly even thrive eventually."

Daphne splayed her fingers across the table and then curled

them into fists. "Mrs. Lancaster said that once the baby is weaned, she'd find a way to make sure he was taken care of." Her gaze shifted again to the quiet baby in the corner. "But I can't do it. I can't spend these first months with Ben and then give him up."

Katherine reached a hand over and wrapped her fingers around Daphne's fist in a show of silent support.

There was no way Margaretta could mimic their plan. She hadn't the funds or the help. But another idea crept into her mind.

"I could send money."

She winced. That wasn't how she'd meant to broach the idea.

Both women looked at her with raised eyebrows.

Margaretta cleared her throat and forged ahead. What was the worst that could happen? They would say no and kick her out of their house? She'd be no worse off than she was right now, except that she wasn't sure how to get back to Mrs. Lancaster's store. "I'll get pin money. I could send some. To help."

"Help who?" Katherine asked.

"Help you. If the baby is a boy . . . If I left him with you, could you keep him? . . . Could you give him a good home?"

9

Nash hadn't slept. Ideas and inclinations had run through his head, distracting him to the point he'd nearly cut himself while shaving. He was drowning in the very thing he'd spent nearly a decade determined to avoid: emotion so crippling that he couldn't live his daily life.

Behind him, his desk was strewn with work, but he hadn't done any of it. Despite the fact that he was considerably behind, he stared out the window.

Not that he saw much beyond the glass. He was too busy remembering the look on Margaretta's face as she'd let her hand trail over his arm while Katherine led her away. She'd been pleading for something, using those bottomless dark eyes to try to rip his soul from his body with the claws of her dripping tears. But Nash had left. Even before Katherine had closed the door to the bedroom, he'd fled the cottage. Nothing would ever be the same for him. Or for her.

Recognition of two of the men walking through the morning hustle and bustle of High Street broke through Nash's ponderings. Mr. Fortescue and Mr. Albany were walking down the street, presumably in the direction of Nash's office. The older man's face was set in determined lines while the younger man curled his lip in distaste. Whether his disdain was for the early hour or the town itself, Nash couldn't tell. Nor did he care. After everything he'd learned over the past twenty-four hours, Nash wasn't inclined to like the man.

In fact, his inclinations veered much closer to running Samuel Albany out of town than ensuring his welcome to the local stables and coaching inns.

There was nothing he could do, however. Nash's opinion of the situation didn't matter. In the eyes of the law, the man had done nothing wrong. If possessing ambition and desiring to inherit a title were criminal offenses, quite a bit of England's aristocracy would be rotting in Newgate.

Margaretta's husband had died nearly four months ago, based on all the information Nash had put together over the past few weeks. That was more than enough time to know if she'd gotten with child during her short marriage, and the fact that she was running, hiding, would only serve as evidence to Samuel Albany if he was, indeed, as crazed and obsessed as Margaretta believed.

As the two men crossed the street, Nash could see that they were arguing, with Mr. Fortescue looking nearly ready to explode into a tirade. Whether that would manifest itself as a physical or verbal assault on the younger man remained to be seen, but it settled some of Nash's fear that Margaretta's father was somehow betraying the safety of his daughter.

The two men stopped outside the door to Nash's office, but his position at the window allowed him to hear their hushed, angry voices.

"One has to wonder how well you can control a business if you can't control your daughter, Mr. Fortescue," Mr. Albany snarled.

The threat didn't seem to do anything to fluster Mr. Fortescue's composure. It was easy to see where Margaretta had gathered the strength to set out on her own.

The older man flung open the door to Nash's office and strolled in. "A business is ever so much more predictable than a woman." He sent an inquisitive look in Nash's direction. "Wouldn't you agree, Mr. Banfield?"

Given that Nash's ability to guess what a woman was about was essentially nil, he had to agree. He nodded. "Of course, sir."

The younger man grunted and narrowed his eyes in Nash's direction. "You didn't come to dinner."

Nash turned, maintaining his position by the window. "Urgent business arose with another client. As only a few of the men you requested to speak with were interested and none available until today, I decided to wait until this morning."

"We wish to speak to them all, Mr. Banfield." Mr. Albany's lip curled. "If you can't make that happen, I'll find a solicitor who can."

There were only two other solicitors in Marlborough, one of whom was nearly seventy and wrote simple contracts at a small desk in the corner of his drawing room, so Nash wasn't incredibly worried about the threat. What did concern him was getting Samuel Albany out of reach of Margaretta as quickly as possible. Yes, he felt betrayed that she'd kept such a secret from him, and the discovery left his chest feeling like it had been hollowed out with a cricket bat, but he still wanted to make her happy, keep her safe.

"Perhaps, gentlemen," Nash settled himself into the chair behind his desk and steepled his fingers underneath his chin, "I could be of better service if I knew more about what you were actually looking for."

Mr. Fortescue's eyes narrowed, but Mr. Albany's gaze became hazy and unfocused as he paced across the room to the window. "I intend to make my name known across the country, Mr. Banfield. My grandfather may have started our racing stable, but I intend to bring it into the nineteenth century. We will be the stable that everyone talks about, the one that the Arabian princes come to visit. And I intend to be the one who makes it so."

A fiery passion rode his features as he turned back to Nash and braced his hands against the desk to lean forward. "One day, the Albany racing stables will be mine, and then—" His words broke off, and he hung his head, taking a deep breath as if collecting his thoughts. "The Albany racing stables are an important part of my family legacy, Mr. Banfield, and I *will* be a part of it."

Nash glanced at Mr. Fortescue, noting the paleness of the man's skin behind the determined set of his jaw. Thoughts tumbled over each other in Nash's head, the foremost of which was that Samuel Albany didn't seem to be in complete control of his faculties. He was a man obsessed with power and prestige, none of which he could expect to gain as a third son unless he took it for himself. And that made him dangerous to Margaretta.

A niggling thought tickled Nash's mind, a vague memory prodding an idea. Was there any chance Samuel's passion could be redirected? Was it possible Nash could point him in a direction that would let him make a name now instead of waiting to inherit control of the family stable?

"Passion for a family legacy is admirable." Nash cleared his throat and rose, walking slowly to a stack of magazines on a low table. The article he was remembering was a couple of months old, but if he could find it . . . A copy of *Sporting Magazine* lay at the bottom of the pile, its edges curling around themselves. "Perhaps that could be better found in making a mark on the sport as a whole."

Nash's heart threatened to pound out of his chest as he took the magazine back to his desk and settled into his chair once more. He had to tread very carefully through this conversation. He couldn't give away that he knew anything about Mr. Fortescue's daughter or Mr. Albany's family situation. One word, one slip could be a disaster. The safest thing would have been to remain quiet, but he'd just introduced a suggestion that required he drive the conversation.

Oh well. In for a penny . . . "There's a new style of racing in Ireland."

He plopped the magazine on his desk, open to an article entitled, "A Curious Horse-Race." Mr. Albany scooped up the paper and settled into a nearby chair to read, but Mr. Fortescue remained focused on Nash, his eyes assessing and thoughtful.

Nash swallowed. "I'm not much of a sportsman, gentlemen, but it seems to me that the right leadership could take the idea of this idle wager and turn it into a horse racing empire." That was possibly laying it on too thick, but Nash couldn't back off now.

Mr. Albany looked up. "They had jumps in the race?"

"Yes." Nash looked at Mr. Fortescue out of the corner of his eye. "And if someone were to make a special saddle for just such a race, it would no doubt be to the racer's advantage."

"No doubt," Mr. Fortescue murmured. "It would be quite a coup to be the first to introduce such a novel thing to England's shores. Surely not something an Irishman would be capable of."

Mr. Albany slapped the magazine down onto his leg. "Fortescue Saddles will not take the credit for this. Any saddle you make for this will be for Albany use only."

"Of course." Mr. Fortescue cleared his throat. "But I'd need to study how this racing is done."

Nash shuffled some blank papers on the surface of his desk. "We could draw up an agreement now, if you wish, that any development in saddles made for this new style of jump racing will be for the exclusive use of the Albany stables."

Mr. Albany seemed to preen under the idea of exclusive rights to anything. "Yes. We could even name the saddle after us. It would need to be a priority development."

"Of course." Mr. Fortescue seemed to sink into his chair with a sigh of relief. Perhaps this was the first time he'd relaxed in weeks. How long had he been following this madman around the country?

"We need to take control of this soon," Mr. Albany declared, then paused. "But we cannot neglect our . . . current project."

Mr. Fortescue tightened back up in his seat. "Nothing will change in the time it takes us to travel to Ireland and study this. We can address the issue when we return."

Nash knew the man was hoping that by the time they returned the issue would have settled itself, and Margaretta would have either had a girl or found a safe place to hide the baby if it were a boy. The alternative, that Margaretta or the baby didn't survive the duration of their absence, was probably eating through Nash's thoughts alone. No father would want to consider such an end for his daughter.

"I suppose." Mr. Albany looked back at the article in his lap before nodding at Nash. "Draw up the papers."

❖

Margaretta was placing small, neat stitches in the ripped shoulder seam of a rough white shirt when Mrs. Lancaster came through the door around midday. The women were still seated at the table, discussing the possibilities open to Margaretta, though Katherine had declared that they at least needed to do something worthwhile as they talked.

Where Margaretta's cleaning skills were decidedly lacking, her sewing was almost as accomplished as her cooking. She'd already set a pot over the fire to heat a stew for their supper.

Conversations stumbled to a halt as Mrs. Lancaster let herself into the tiny cottage. She beamed at the three of them. "Look at you ladies. Making the most of life when the devil would rather strike you down. I'm proud of you."

Daphne blushed but didn't look away as the old woman came forward to look at the bundle in her arms.

"Ah, such a sweet little one." The shopkeeper looked up and smiled. "And our other sweet little one? Have we settled things there?"

Katherine and Daphne looked at each other for a long moment. While many potential details had been discussed, an actual agreement had yet to be reached. Finally Katherine gave a little nod. "We're keeping Margaretta's baby."

Mrs. Lancaster's smile fell as she looked straight at Margaretta. "You'd leave your baby behind?"

Until that moment, Margaretta hadn't really let herself think of it that way. She'd thought of it more as taking care of someone in need. Like a charity that could be done impersonally with a bit of separation. But at that moment, with the sadness and possibly even disappointment on Mrs. Lancaster's face, her baby became just that. *Hers.*

It didn't change the facts, though. "I haven't a dowry to bring or anything to start my life with. If I go home, marry, seek the life I was born for, I'll have money that I can send back to help. If it's a girl, I might be able to keep her. Otherwise—" she lay her hand over her middle—"it's simply not a risk I can afford to take."

Katherine sighed. "For what it's worth, I think you should tell John's family. I think they would protect you."

"Samuel is the only son they have left living on English soil. I can't take the chance that they'd believe him over me." Margaretta paused so she didn't stab herself with the needle. "And they'll insist I come live with them, under their roof. Hiding from Samuel wouldn't be an option anymore."

It was a great risk she was taking, not telling John's family about the baby. If it turned out to be a boy, if he was in line to inherit, would they believe her when she claimed it was John's? Or was she dooming her child to a life without his birthright?

Mrs. Lancaster came around the table to hug Margaretta tight. "Don't you worry none. God's not surprised by one bit of this. Mark my words, my dear, He's got a plan big enough for everyone. And sometimes"—she pressed a kiss into Margaretta's hair—"those plans are hard to understand."

Margaretta didn't know what to do with the open affection of Mrs. Lancaster, but it felt like a balm on her aching heart. Daphne and Katherine reached their hands across the table and twined fingers with Margaretta. The moment was solemn, like a vow between the women to do the best they could with these lives that they'd been entrusted with for whatever reason. Emotion overwhelmed her, led by fear that they were doing the wrong thing.

These babies needed so much guidance, so much education, so much of everything if they were going to make their ways in this world. Could four ladies who didn't know what they were doing manage it?

It was enough to make her want to slink to her bed and not come out for a week.

Then Benedict peeked around his blanket, blinked at her, and burped.

As the most basic of noises broke the solemn silence, the four women gave into laughter instead of tears, and Margaretta knew that Mrs. Lancaster was right. No matter how lost she felt, none of this was a surprise to God.

❖

Working out the contract took the better part of the day, but by the time evening rolled around, both men were smiling. Well, Mr. Fortescue was smiling. Mr. Albany looked like a smug cat who'd stolen the cream.

Nash promised the men he would make clean copies of the agreement and have it messengered to London, as well as to Newcastle, Ireland, where the men were intending to travel.

Hands were shaken all around, and Mr. Albany made noises about whether or not it was too late to catch the stage. He eventually decided they would wait until morning. Neither Nash nor Mr. Fortescue offered a thought while Mr. Albany discussed this decision with himself. They simply nodded in agreement.

Mr. Fortescue never stopped eyeing Nash with a bit of skepticism before saying quietly, "I'd still like to discuss those travel arrangements some time."

Nash debated how to answer. He knew that traveling to Ireland and abandoning his daughter had to be a difficult prospect for the older man, but he would do it to keep her safe. Mr. Albany currently didn't seem to care about anything, having been convinced that his name would become synonymous with this new style of horse racing within a year. Nash wasn't willing to test that new fascination, though, by speaking in anything other than vague terms with her father.

"I'm sure I can be of service in that area when the time comes."

Mr. Fortescue's eyes narrowed, probably trying to read Nash's hidden meaning. Then his eyes widened as he took in something beyond Nash's shoulder.

Before Nash could turn and see what had garnered the other man's attention, the door opened, allowing a slight breeze into the office along with Mrs. Lancaster. "Good evening, gentlemen."

Nash swallowed, trying to keep himself from panicking as Mrs. Lancaster waltzed right by Mr. Albany with Margaretta's bag held in front of her. She nodded to the men and came around the desk to set the valise on the ground, out of sight. "I don't mean to interrupt. Mr. Banfield simply agreed to help me with my deliveries today. These old bones can't do quite what they used to."

She cackled, seeming completely at ease and ignorant of the tension her presence had created. Thankfully, Mr. Albany seemed equally ignorant.

Mr. Fortescue, on the other hand, was staring at Nash's desk as if he could see the bag sitting on the floor behind it. His gaze turned hard as it finally flicked up to meet Nash's. "This . . . agreement. I trust you've seen to my interests in it? All of my interests?"

Nash considered playing dumb, just in case Mr. Albany was more astute than he thought, but he couldn't do that to the man. Any father who was willing to set aside his normal business and travel all the way to Ireland simply to protect his daughter deserved to know that she was safe. "Of course, sir." Nash swallowed, but there was no moisture left in his mouth. "I'll make sure that everything of yours is protected."

Mr. Albany huffed. "Yes, yes, isn't that what we just spent that past several hours discussing? Now, let's be off. I need to send my man ahead to inquire about passage to Ireland."

Tension Nash hadn't known he was holding seeped from his muscles at the news that Mr. Albany's man would be traveling with them. With one last glance, Mr. Fortescue rose and followed Mr. Albany to the door. He paused at the portal. "Any updates you feel this . . . agreement needs. You'll send me word?"

Nash nodded. "I'll send it express, sir."

Mr. Fortescue looked sad, but he nodded and followed Mr. Albany out into the street.

Nash collapsed into his chair, exhausted.

Mrs. Lancaster smiled. "Well, that seems to have gone well."

A groan escaped Nash's chest as he laid his head back on his chair. "What are you doing here, Mrs. Lancaster?"

"You need to deliver this to Margaretta tonight. I don't think my legs can take the walk up that hill again."

Nash couldn't help the smile that rose to his lips. Mrs. Lancaster could probably walk halfway to Avebury before feeling a twinge, despite her strange shuffling gait. Still, he could never call her a liar. That didn't mean he wanted to deliver the bag, though. He wasn't ready to see Margaretta. Wasn't sure he would ever be.

She was with child. He knew what that meant in such vivid, horrid detail, knew the ultimate risk, the possible devastating outcome. And he didn't want to think about it.

"She needs her things." Mrs. Lancaster frowned, an expression so foreign that her face seemed to crack in order to make the muscles move into the necessary position. "And you're going to take them to her."

10

Nash took Margaretta her bag because, well, because he couldn't figure out a way not to. That didn't mean he had to see her, though. He'd left the bag on the stoop and then knocked before running away like a pranking child, fleeing from the cottage as if it contained the plague instead of a baby and an expecting woman.

He'd included a note, though, stating that her father and Samuel Albany were leaving town, their search for her suspended for the time being. The note was light on details and probably raised more questions than it answered. Was part of him hoping she'd seek him out and demand more information?

If so, he was doomed to disappointment. Two weeks passed without a word.

She didn't return to Mrs. Lancaster's shop, either, choosing instead to stay with the other women at the cottage. Cooking, gardening, and sewing were now taking up her days. He knew because his near daily visits to Mrs. Lancaster's shop had continued. Even though he told himself he was better off without Margaretta in his life, he couldn't help wondering how she was, what she was doing.

At first, Mrs. Lancaster had been happy to tell him things,

even saying that the women had a plan for Margaretta's baby. As the days passed, though, Mrs. Lancaster's updates turned into frowns and glares.

Yet still, Nash returned day after day because it was the only way he would learn anything. If something important happened, surely Mrs. Lancaster would break her self-imposed silence.

Though he knew he shouldn't care.

Nash stared at the papers in front of him. The same ones that had been spread across his desk for two days now. While it was true that life in the country moved at a slower pace than that of the city, his clients still expected him to actually do the work they paid him for.

He grabbed a quill and set it to paper, intent on writing out the new dowry agreement for Mr. Jacobson's daughter. It was a straightforward sort of thing, a sum of money determined by her parents' marriage contract. It shouldn't have taken Nash more than an hour to complete it.

Yet here he was, taking the better part of the morning to even set quill to paper.

He was two lines in before he realized he'd never dipped the nib into the inkwell.

Throwing the quill down on the scratched but blank sheet of paper, Nash shoved away from his desk and stalked across the room. Looking back at his desk, he was haunted by the knee hole and drawers facing him.

You've a partner desk but no partner.

While it didn't make sense for him to have a partner here in his little Wiltshire solicitor's office, the statement seemed to echo around the empty halls of the rest of his life as well. He didn't have a partner. Didn't have anyone, really. Even the townspeople who he claimed to feel so beholden to, so protective of, he kept at arm's length.

But still he cared, knowing that one day death would knock

on the door of those he'd become accustomed to seeing. Mrs. Lancaster would follow Mr. Lancaster to heaven eventually. Henry Milbank would be replaced by a younger, stronger person when he could no longer handle delivering coal to the businesses in town. Already the man was slowing down and talking of taking on an apprentice.

Because he had no son to train. Life had left Mr. Milbank scarred, and he'd never tried again.

But at least he'd tried. Like Lewis and Mary. Nash couldn't claim such a feat.

Nash had walked away from life, thinking he could limit his involvement and therefore limit his hurt. Just as he'd walked away from Margaretta. He couldn't let her in, couldn't give her his heart, only to have to bury it alongside her should she suffer the same fate as his sister.

The idea that Margaretta might not survive the birth of her child rocked through Nash, sending him to his knees. He groped his way to a chair and pulled himself into it before dropping his head into his hands and taking great, gulping gasps of air into his lungs. The air rushed in and out of his heaving chest until his lips begin to tingle.

It was too late.

If Margaretta died, he would be crushed. Even the idea that she would suffer pain caused tears to spring to his eyes. And what if she lived? Would she change her mind and keep the child? Would she stay here? She had no money, no job, no place to live unless she stayed with her friends who, from all appearances, were already on limited funds.

Nash knew, from all the contracts and documents he'd written over the years that her choices were more than limited. They were nonexistent. She would have to marry.

And she would marry someone who wasn't Nash.

Because he had walked away from her. Did she ask Mrs.

Lancaster about him? Did she feel betrayed by his absence? She had to feel like he'd rejected her. After all, he hadn't been to see her once since her secret had been revealed. It was likely that she had—quite accurately—guessed that he was unable to handle her situation.

But could he? If he could take back the past two weeks, if he could go back and assure her that the feelings that had grown unacknowledged between them were true and real, would he? Was there a way back from his quiet rejection?

More than that, could he take the risk? He hadn't fathered the child, but he could be the one to suffer if there were consequences. Did it matter?

The door to his office clicked open, and he made himself stand to greet whoever came in. There was still a business to be run, after all, and it was distinctly possible that this business would soon be all he had.

❧

Margaretta rubbed the side of her growing middle. It seemed in the past week she'd gone from slightly rounded to obviously enlarged. It was enough to keep her inside no matter how badly she wanted more space to breathe fresh air. Marlborough was currently filled with England's elite on their way to their summer abodes. She couldn't risk word of her location or condition getting back to Samuel, even in Ireland.

For now she'd have to content herself with circling the small room in Mrs. Lancaster's cottage.

A sudden lurch against her hand brought her stumbling to a halt. Was that . . . could it be?

With one hand braced against the wall to steady her suddenly weak knees, Margaretta took her other hand and pressed it hard against the place that had just fluttered.

There it was again.

The briefest shift, barely anything and not much different that the other minor aches and pains she'd been experiencing, except that she knew it was different. She knew it was her baby.

There was a baby inside her, a living thing, and no longer was it something she knew, like she knew her sums and who the King of England was. This was real. She was growing a brand-new human being. A child who would one day run and laugh like the neighborhood children.

A son who would have to learn to grow up and be a man with someone else leading the way.

Or a daughter who would have to be equally as strong as she grew up without a clear sense of belonging or purpose, bearing a dead man's name, assuming John's parents would even acknowledge her after Margaretta had claimed to be without child. They had no real motivation to claim her. For most, a daughter was simply a bargaining tool to be married off for social or economic gain.

Margaretta slid to the floor and wrapped her arms around her middle, praying it was a son. She knew she'd have to leave him behind if it was, but Mrs. Lancaster had assured her that he would be taken care of in this small town. It'd be a simple life, not worthy of his father's lineage, but he'd be safe, perhaps even loved.

Leaving him would be in the name of survival, but Margaretta wasn't sure she would survive it. It would difficult, but at least she'd know. She wouldn't have to wonder every day for the rest of her life if he was well. Which would be worse? To watch her daughter struggle to find her place in life, trapped between her mother's rich merchant upbringing and her father's younger child aristocracy, or miss out on the smiles and hugs with her son?

She'd seen Daphne cooing and laughing with her own son, had cheered along with Katherine when Benedict picked his head up all by himself and waved his little fist in the air.

Margaretta's trembling hand ran over her belly once more. There was every chance she wouldn't be a part of cheering for this little one.

Salty tears pooled against Margaretta's lips as she leaned her head back against the wall. Mindlessly, she swiped at her face, almost surprised that her hand came away wet. Was she crying for the child or for herself? Did it matter? With that single flutter, everything had changed. Margaretta would never be able to completely separate herself from this baby ever again. Not in her heart, anyway.

Just as she knew that even if she married again, it would be as practical as her first marriage.

Fresh tears streamed down her cheeks. It hadn't mattered that she'd told herself not to fall in love with the solicitor, that a life with him was as likely as a life in which she got to keep her child.

It wasn't fair. She wanted to scream at God and yell at the ceiling. She'd done everything right. She'd been the perfect model of what a young English girl should be, seeking to advance her father's position by aligning with a family higher on the social ladder, even if he was a second son with very few prospects.

She'd done everything right. So why was her life falling apart now?

Nash stopped at the end of the alley, looking at the boys playing on the green, remembering an evening not too many weeks ago when he'd watched a similar scene, unaware of the fact that everything he thought he knew about life and himself was about to change.

Three boys ended up in a pile on top of each other, laughing and squealing while the other four boys circled around them and cheered.

Would Margaretta's son play on this field one day? Would there be a child with pale skin and dark hair lining up with the other neighborhood children on market day, hoping that the sweets vendor decided to give them the broken candies for free?

This was assuming, of course, that mother and child even survived the birthing process.

Richard, the fourth son of an innkeeper, broke away from the pack, spinning some sort of cloth over his head. Jeremiah, the eldest son of the town banker, ran after him. The chances of the boys remaining friends when they were too old to run around on the green were slim, but the future wasn't stopping them from enjoying life right now. Neither was the past.

There was something to be learned from that. Perhaps that was what Jesus meant when he said, "Take therefore no thought for the morrow: for the morrow shall take thought for the things of itself." Perhaps that was what living for today was, because there was certainly enough right here and right now for him to concern himself with. And if he were living for today, why was he doing things to make his day so miserable?

He nearly ran the rest of the way across the green and down the street to the little cottage. Was he really going to do this? Go through that door and do everything he'd vowed to never do?

Yes, he was. Because he already loved her.

The only question was whether or not he'd spend whatever was left of their lives together showing her how much. A smile graced his face for the first time in weeks, free because he'd finally decided to let go of that fear and hold on to the joy they seemed to bring each other.

His knock went unanswered, so he pushed open the door, worry nibbling away at the fragile hope he'd just found. With three women doing their best to be forgotten by the world, shouldn't at least one of them be home?

The door creaked on its hinges as he pushed it open.

He winced, hoping Benedict wasn't sleeping in the main room.

The baby was the last thing on his mind, though, when he saw Margaretta huddled in a ball against the wall.

"Margaretta?" He half ran, half slid his way across the room until he was on his knees at her side. "My love, what's wrong?"

"Don't—" she took a deep shuddering breath—"Don't call me that. I don't want to remember you calling me that."

He cupped her face and slid a thumb along her cheek to catch a tear. "I want you to hear it. I want you to know it. Because it's true. You are my love, and I'm so very sorry that you've had to live these past weeks without knowing that."

Her answer was a shaky, trembling wail that shot to his heart, breaking down the last part of the wall he'd built to try to protect himself. He settled onto the floor next to her and scooped her into his lap. She felt so right in his arms, making him feel whole when he hadn't even known he was missing anything. As she cried into his shoulder, he held her, rubbing a soothing hand across her back or over the curls that that had escaped her bun.

A shot of guilt niggled at the back of his mind. He didn't have the right to hold her like this, not until he knew she was in agreement with the direction his mind was rapidly taking. It was as if the moment he'd given himself permission to feel again, to join life again, he'd surged toward the one thing he wanted more than anything else.

Margaretta.

Already part of his mind was filled with thoughts of marriage, debating which church to read the banns in since she didn't really live in the town. Perhaps he should take the stage into London and see about getting a special license so they could avoid the complications altogether and just marry quietly.

He leaned his head back against the wall and tried not to laugh at himself. When he changed his mind, he did it wholeheartedly, didn't he?

A final sob escaped Margaretta, and she sat up in his lap, wiping furiously at her tearstained face. It was splotchy and a bit swollen, but he didn't care. To him, it was beautiful, because it meant she was letting him in, letting him see her vulnerabilities and inner fears. It meant something when a woman let a man see her cry.

"You don't mean that," she whispered.

"Yes." Nash swallowed. "I do."

She placed a hand on the middle of her belly and looked down. Curled up as she was, it was impossible to see the slight bump he knew was there, the curve that her loose skirts could almost hide until the wind pressed them against her body. Was she thinking his love didn't extend to that part of her? To the baby she created with another man, a man he knew she hadn't loved?

Nash covered her hand with his. "I love your child, too. Our child. Or at least he can be." The breath Nash pulled into his lungs made him shudder. "If you marry me, I can have you both—love you both. Show you that every day is made for living, just as God has showed me."

Watery brown eyes rose to meet his.

"I haven't been living," Nash whispered. "I've been hiding from life, thinking that staying safe was the way not to hurt, but it was only a way to die before death actually came calling. I don't want to be like that anymore. I want to live, with every breath God has left to give me. I want to live, and I want as many of those breaths as possible to be shared with you."

Something he thought was hope rippled through her eyes, only to be dimmed once more. She caught her lip between her teeth. "Samuel—"

"Has nothing to do with us. I'll claim this baby as mine, and the world won't be able to say differently unless we admit it."

If it was a boy, there might be complications, guilt that they were possibly keeping him from a greater purpose in life. But were titles more important than love and safety? Was there anything being the potential heir presumptive could bring this child that Nash couldn't provide, aside from a position at the edge of the aristocracy?

He took a deep breath, knowing that he'd let Margaretta decide. If she wanted, they would go to her late husband's family and tell them everything; but if she didn't, he would gladly raise this child as his own.

Nash began to talk. He drew a picture in her mind of what their life could be. Of the way he'd imagined this child—their child—playing with the other children in the town, looking forward to market day and growing up to become a solicitor or a soldier or anything else he wanted to become. He talked about sneaking the child peppermints from Mrs. Lancaster's store while Margaretta pretended to glare at him for spoiling the children.

With every sentence he felt her relax, settle deeper into his embrace. Occasionally she chuckled. Eventually her arms unwrapped from around her middle and eased their way around him, bringing her fully into his embrace.

Where she belonged.

Nash took a deep breath. "Marry me, Margaretta. Stay here. Love me. Let's build this life together."

In answer, she leaned forward and pressed her lips to his. He could taste the salt of her tears, feel the trembling of her body.

A soft click sounded through the room, but it took him more than a moment to realize what it meant.

"Well, I hope this means you're getting married." Katherine

leaned back against the door and crossed her arms over her chest, a frown on her face.

Beside her, Miss Blakemoor was grinning from ear to ear while she snuggled a wrapped baby to her chest. "Of course they are. They love each other."

One side of Katherine's mouth lifted. "I guess they do, don't they."

EPILOGUE

Two months later, Nash was sitting down at the dining table in the house he'd leased for himself and Margaretta, just a little ways down the road from Mrs. Lancaster's cottage. He'd received a letter from Margaretta's father that morning, letting them know that he and Samuel Albany were engrossed in designing and testing a new saddle, one that would be perfect for the new style of racing. The idea wasn't quite taking off yet, but Samuel had found a new obsession and was determined to bring the style into the sport.

Nash wished him every bit of luck as long as it kept his focus off Margaretta.

A smile touched Nash's lips as his wife maneuvered around her extended belly to serve dinner to their friends. Katherine and Daphne had taken to bringing little Benedict by and spending the evening with Margaretta at least three times a week. Sometimes Mrs. Lancaster joined in.

Usually the evening was loud and joyful, but tonight Daphne seemed subdued. Her spoon scraped against her plate as she pushed the food around instead of eating it.

Margaretta set aside her own spoon and frowned. "What's wrong, Daphne?"

Daphne looked up, her sweet round face pinched and serious. "I was just wishing that everyone had a Nash. You're so fortunate, Margaretta, so blessed."

Heat crawled up Nash's cheeks as everyone took turns glancing from him to the cradle Benedict was currently sleeping in. It wasn't hard to tell where Daphne's sadness had come from. While the two girls had been incredibly happy for Margaretta, there was no running from the fact that no one had come to Daphne's rescue.

Katherine reached a hand across the table and wrapped her fingers around Daphne's. "We'll do it. We'll be someone's Nash."

Margaretta's wide eyes met Nash's. "What do you mean?"

"Well, we were willing to raise your child for you, but now we don't have to." Katherine swallowed and squared her shoulders as if the idea she was proposing scared her even as she was determined to do it. "So we'll do it for someone else. We all know there are more girls out there facing this impossible position."

"But we can't help them all," Daphne said quietly.

"No," Katherine answered. "But we can help one. And maybe . . . maybe that's enough."

The group around the table fell silent.

An idea formed in the back of Nash's mind. It was possibly unscrupulous, and definitely not what his client had in mind, but Nash couldn't deny that the solution seemed like a perfect one. One that might have been created by God himself. Still, he couldn't bring himself to do more than whisper, "What if you could help more than one?"

Three sets of eyes swung his way.

"We can barely support ourselves, Nash," Daphne said just

as quietly. "Taking in even one more is going to be difficult enough."

Nash swallowed. "What if we could fix that?"

The sun was starting to crawl down the sky by the time Nash had borrowed his neighbor's horse and wagon and convinced Mrs. Lancaster to watch Benedict. There should still be enough time to show the women what he meant, which was good because he didn't think he could find the words to explain it. Partly because he still couldn't believe what he was suggesting.

As he drove the wagon down a rutted road leading out of Marlborough, Nash wasn't sure which was pounding more, his brain or his heart. What he was about to propose went against every cautious bone in his body. If he did this, if they did this, what would it mean for their lives? He glanced at Margaretta, snuggled up against him.

But what would it mean for so many other lives? For the women like Margaretta who had no way of supporting themselves, much less a child? Women who were forced to consider extreme measures to ensure survival?

Visions of what Margaretta would have done if he hadn't followed her into Mrs. Lancaster's shop that first day tried to crowd his mind. Nausea rolled through his stomach as he thought about what might have been. What would have happened if she'd been forced to return home and face Samuel. What would have happened if she'd chosen not to return home at all.

He shook his head and guided the horses onto an overgrown lane, branches and vines dragging against his head.

None of the things he was picturing had happened. None of them would happen. Margaretta was safe at his side, and just that morning he'd felt his child kicking away.

The women giggled and pushed through the trees that fell toward the wagon. This property hadn't been in Nash's care long, and clearing the drive hadn't been his top priority, especially since the solicitor who contacted him about finding a caretaker hadn't bothered making arrangements for the property, even though his client had owned it for years.

Nash saw no reason why the caretaker couldn't be a couple of women and a handful of children. There were a few men in the town who would support such an endeavor, see to the more laborious tasks. And with the neglect and overgrowth of the surrounding lands, no one even had to know they were here.

They broke through the overgrown brush and pulled up in front of an estate house that hadn't seen residents in well over a decade.

The giggles subsided.

Katherine leapt from the wagon bed as it rocked to a stop. "Nash, this place is enormous."

It was. Giant two-story columns rose from the front porch, flanked by two large sets of stairs climbing to the house's double doors. Two wings stretched out from the central section and a third stretched backward, though the women couldn't see that yet.

"It needs a caretaker. I've been charged with setting up a long-term solution."

Katherine looked from the house to Nash and back again. Then her gaze swung to Daphne. "What do you think?"

Daphne pressed a hand to her mouth and looked at Margaretta, then back to Katherine. "I think I'd have been in even more dire straits than Margaretta if you hadn't saved me. I'd like to pass that on."

Margaretta wrapped her arms around Nash's arm. "And you won't be alone." She looked at Nash. "None of us will be."

Katherine blew out a breath. "There's things we'll have to consider. The caretaker's funds won't support a passel of children. We'll have to decide what we can actually handle and how to know who to help." She looked around the property again. "But if you want to do it, then I'm in agreement."

Nash couldn't look away from Margaretta as a feeling of purpose swelled in his chest alongside the love that threatened to explode out of him now. "We'll figure it all out. Together."

"Together," Margaretta whispered back.

Nash smiled before he leaned in to give her a quick kiss. Living again felt wonderful.

SUMMER *of* DREAMS

A
FROM THIS MOMENT
NOVELLA

ELIZABETH CAMDEN

1

"You want me to do what to a birdcage?"

Clyde Brixton stood in the superintendent's office at the United States Military Academy at West Point, not quite certain he understood the bizarre order correctly. Superintendent Draper sat behind the imposing mahogany desk flanked by two American flags.

"General White's daughter wants a fountain added to her birdcage, and you are going to build it for her. Or would you prefer to have your disciplinary hearing now, instead of at the beginning of the next semester?"

Clyde swallowed hard. If the hearing was held before he had a chance to work off his demerits, Clyde would be expelled from West Point. No cadet was allowed more than two hundred demerits, and as of this morning, Clyde had just hit that dangerous number. He hadn't expected the penalty for his jaunt to Washington to cost a staggering forty demerits, and his academic career was hanging by a thread. Working off demerits was possible, but difficult. In Clyde's case, it was going to involve pandering to the general's spoiled daughter.

"You are going to build the general's daughter a fountain in her birdcage, or we will proceed to an expulsion hearing immediately. Is that understood?"

After three years at West Point, Clyde knew there was only one correct response. "Yes, sir."

"You have yet to demonstrate the ability to follow orders," the superintendent barked. "You started collecting demerits your first week on campus by dismantling the Olsen canon and putting it on the dormitory roof, just to see if it could be done. Then came insulting the library's collection of chemistry texts. Then carousing on the Fourth of July. You knew you had an appalling number of demerits, but you still went traipsing off to Washington on a lark. It was reckless and irresponsible."

Not if Clyde wanted to get his patent filed before a rival team of inventors in Baltimore beat him to the patent office. Clyde's design for a safety switch on an electrical fuse was a meaningful contribution to the field, but he had plenty of competition. Inventors bombarded the patent office daily. He couldn't afford to wait the three weeks until a formal leave of absence was granted. He was only a year away from graduation, but he was willing to risk it all in exchange for getting that patent filed ahead of the Baltimore team working on a similar idea.

"Yes, sir. It was irresponsible," Clyde said, but the triumph he'd felt when that patent-pending documentation had been handed to him still brought a surge of pride. It was hard to suppress the twitch of his mouth, the nascent beginnings of a smile.

Superintendent Draper noticed. "You think this is funny, Brixton? Maybe I've been too generous offering you the opportunity to work off the demerits. I can assemble the disciplinary council and proceed to a hearing immediately."

"No, sir. I'm happy to work them off, sir." Panic clouded the edges of Clyde's vision, and he fought to hold his breathing steady. "Please, sir. West Point is all I've got."

He had no money, no connections, and his widowed mother

was barely scraping by until Clyde could graduate and begin getting money to her. His only advantage in the world was a sharp mind capable of grasping the rapidly evolving concepts in engineering. It made him a valuable asset to the army and had earned him a coveted appointment to the U.S. Military Academy. He had already won the right to work alongside military engineers as they designed plans to lay telegraph wires beneath riverbeds, a task far more challenging than any of his peers had been awarded. What twenty-one-year-old student in the country had such an opportunity?

Although the other cadets sometimes grumbled about the stodgy military rules, bland food, and rigorous academics, Clyde loved it here. West Point had dormitories with roofs that did not leak and a mess hall with bottomless pots of nourishing food. They provided brand-new uniforms and shoes with no holes in them. He wouldn't leave before earning that degree, even if it meant building the general's spoiled daughter the Taj Mahal of birdcages.

"I will complete my final year without a single demerit, sir. And I will gladly build the general's daughter a fountain for her birdcage, dollhouse, or any other toy she desires."

For the first time this morning, there was a slight softening of the superintendent's ruddy features. "Your engineering abilities are the sole reason we've tolerated you," he said. "If it were up to me, you would have been kicked out after that stunt with the canon, but General White needs men like you in the Corps of Engineers. I'm warning you in advance: the general has no tolerance for impulsive or reckless engineers. So build his pretty little daughter a fountain for her birdcage, and if you impress him, perhaps you'll have a shot at an appointment to the Corps of Engineers. Otherwise, the army simply has no use for men like you."

Clyde breathed a sigh of relief as he accepted a card with

the general's address. Building a child's birdcage had no place within his ambitious daydreams, but he'd happily jump through whatever hoops were necessary to salvage his position at West Point.

~ ❧ ~

Evelyn felt the muscles in her face tighten as she stared at the note from West Point, informing her of the imminent arrival of Cadet Clyde Brixton, who would assist her with the installation of a hydraulic pump for her fountain. Her jaw clenched, and she was tempted to rip the note to shreds, but to the outside world, she knew she looked as serene as a statue of the Madonna.

Evelyn was accustomed to suppressing any visible show of emotion, even though today had delivered a series of crushing blows, beginning with the letter from her father this morning. He had bluntly refused to pay her college tuition to Yale, even though the college was willing to admit her to next year's class of freshmen students. All her life, Evelyn had hungered for the realms of pure elation that came from immersing herself in the world of learning, but if her father had his way, she would suffocate in the miasma of afternoon teas and the social obligations expected of a hostess. He insisted the study of science and engineering was unladylike and refused to send his only daughter into a man's field for which she was biologically unsuited.

Biologically unsuited. Those were the exact words he'd used in his letter. How would her father know about her suitability for anything? Over the past ten years, he had been in West Point less than an accumulated total of six months. Her childhood had been spent migrating like a seasonal bird among the houses of various relatives while he traveled the nation to oversee the design and installation of the country's most impressive engineering projects. Now she was eighteen years old and craved the chance to go to college, but it looked as though that would never happen—unless she could somehow convince her father she had a genuine aptitude for engineering.

Perhaps it had been a mistake to write to him for advice, but she'd thought engaging him in a correspondence on the design of a hydraulic pump, complete with a pressurized piston, relief valve, and a cistern, would demonstrate her technical abilities. Her pump had worked fairly well, but it had failed after only a few hours of operation, and prompting her to ask for his advice.

Instead of answering her question, her father apparently made arrangements to send an engineering cadet from West Point to install a proper pump for her. She glared at the note. Clyde Brixton would arrive this afternoon to inspect her work, make the necessary adjustments, and pat her on the head.

She wasn't going to let him in. It was important to show her father she had no need for a West Point cadet to come riding to her rescue. Not that a successful hydraulic pump would win her father's approval for college, but it *would* force him to admit she had a capable mind. With cool poise, she folded the note and inserted it back into the envelope. She opened the desk drawer with whisper-soft grace and deposited the note inside, closing the drawer soundlessly. No show of childish tantrum, no volatile emotions. She had a mission to accomplish, and pointless outbursts of emotion would not help remedy her failing pump.

She withdrew a fat volume on hydraulic engineering written by an English inventor who had designed the fountains at Buckingham Palace, then set to work revising her design. Even now, she could hear the trickle of water from the backyard, where her rudimentary pump labored to propel water up and over a series of rock formations she and her cousin had carefully designed.

The doorbell rang precisely at two o'clock, but Evelyn did not lift her head from the pages spread out on the desk before her. The young cadet was punctual, but she had no need of his help. The scratching of her pencil did not even falter at the interruption.

The doorbell sounded again. It was Sunday and the maid's day off, so there was no one to answer the door and send him away. She held her breath, hoping he would leave. She didn't like being rude, but if she accepted his help, it would confirm her father's belief that she was incapable of solving a rudimentary engineering problem on her own.

When the doorbell rang a third time, she sighed and closed the book on English fountain design. If the English could survive invasions from the Celts, the Vikings, and the Spanish Armada, she could handle a lone cadet from West Point. Besides, sitting here like a sulky child was needlessly rude to a young man who did not deserve her ire.

She set down her pencil and left the library, walking through the perfectly symmetrical hallway to the front door. Like all houses built in the Federal design, there was a rigid formality to the floor plan, with identically proportioned rooms on each side of the straight hallway. The redbrick home was shaped like a perfect box, an homage to the principles of rational design. Evelyn thought it an homage to lack of imagination, but her father's position required a certain amount of respectability.

The doorbell had just rung for a fourth time when Evelyn opened the door to a young man in the gray uniform of a West Point cadet. He was quite handsome, with finely molded features, clear blue eyes, and dark blond hair cut short in military precision. His tanned face spoke of good health, and he looked like someone who enjoyed being alive. Were he not a West Point cadet, Evelyn would have found him attractive.

"Can I help you?" she said politely, even though she knew very well what he was here for, and she had no intention of cooperating.

"I'm here about a birdcage," the young man said.

She wrinkled her brow in confusion. "A birdcage? Why would we want a birdcage?"

"I gather General White's daughter has a birdcage. She wants a fountain installed in it. I am here to help."

A reluctant laugh broke from her. To call her exotic experiment in the backyard a *birdcage* was the understatement of the century, but not entirely inaccurate. "Is my father really calling it a birdcage?"

He blinked in confusion. "Are you General White's daughter?"

"I am."

A flush stained his cheeks, and he stood a bit straighter. "M-my apologies, ma'am," he stammered. "I assumed General White's daughter was a child."

So did General White. "I'm sorry for the misunderstanding, and even sorrier that your Sunday has been pointlessly interrupted. I am quite capable of designing the necessary hydraulic pump and won't keep you from enjoying the rest of your day."

"Can I see it? I've never seen a hydraulic pump small enough to fit inside a birdcage, and I'm curious."

There was no condescension in the young man's face, only genuine interest, and Evelyn always felt an immediate connection with someone who shared her love of a clever design. It wasn't the cadet's fault her father was such a troglodyte about women's education, so she opened the door wide. "Come on back and I'll show you."

Perhaps it was vain to be so proud of the architectural and technical marvel she and her cousin had been building in her backyard, but this project meant a lot to her. The *birdhouse* was actually a spectacular greenhouse that sheltered a variety of exotic plants, butterflies, and now hummingbirds. She and Romulus had been working on it for years.

"Here is my birdhouse," she said as she opened the door to reveal the enormous greenhouse. It was a paradise under glass, with soaring Gothic arches painted white and looking like the closest thing to heaven Evelyn could imagine. The glass panes glinted in the sunlight, and the inside of the greenhouse was filled with palms and lime trees imported from Florida, orchids from South America, and newly hatched swallowtail butter-flies. The greenhouse's latest residents were four hummingbirds Romulus had impulsively caught for her.

Hummingbirds were the most elusive of birds, seeming to appear from nowhere in a whir of buzzing sound, hovering in the air while sampling a bit of nectar, then zooming out of view just as quickly. When Evelyn had mentioned that she fancied a chance to study them more closely, Romulus had taken up the challenge, capturing four hummingbirds merely to prove he could do it.

Evelyn walked into the greenhouse, enjoying the look of wonder on the cadet's face as he stepped inside and felt the warm air. He looked as though he had just stepped into an Arcadian paradise, which was rather how she herself felt each time she visited the greenhouse.

She passed by a cluster of hydrangeas in the far corner of the greenhouse. "Here is where I've installed the hydraulic pump, but the pressure to the fountain usually fails after only a few hours."

"That's not a fountain, that's a waterfall!"

She grinned. "Isn't it amazing? My cousin helped find the boulders from an abandoned quarry near Rochester. They are the same kind of quartzite used in the Sistine Chapel. Romulus never does anything halfway."

Clyde picked his way across the smaller rocks at the base of the waterfall to examine the pump concealed behind a cluster of peonies that had just begun to bloom and fill the space with their heady fragrance. He scanned the network of pipes she had installed to shoot trickles of water through the rocks at three artfully selected spots. When working, the waterfall looked en-tirely natural, but she could see by the anemic dribble of water that it was already losing pressure and would fail again soon.

"Your pump is too small for a fountain of this height," he said. "If you lower the pipes a few feet, it will work better. What are they now, ten feet?"

The fact that he could assess the fountain's height so accurately made him even more interesting to her. "Yes, but I'm afraid a small fountain won't do. I want a real waterfall. Ten feet tall, at the very least."

It might sound a little spoiled to issue such an audacious request, and she was about to explain their need for proper humidity control when his smile made her lose her train of thought.

"Then you shall have one," he said confidently. "I can get a higher-powered pump working for you within the week."

"I don't need any help," she countered. "I'd much rather accomplish this on my own."

"Not with that undersized pump, you won't. You need something at least twice that size for a waterfall this high. No wonder it's been failing."

She lifted her chin a notch. Pump capacity was probably something students learned in their first year of engineering studies, but she'd never been to college and probably never would if her father had his way. She glanced at the pump. The last thing she wanted to do was accept help sent by her father, but she was hungry for information. And she needed to make this pump work, for more than her pride rested on the results.

"What size pump do I need?" she asked reluctantly.

"It depends. How many hours do you want it to operate each day?"

"Twenty-four hours. All day, every day. Until August."

He looked at her in confusion. "Pumps ought to rest for a few hours each day. They can overheat otherwise."

She shook her head. "I need it to operate continuously." She hoped she didn't sound too petulant and demanding. She couldn't pinpoint why his good opinion was so important to her, but perhaps it was because she recognized a tiny sliver of a kindred spirit in him.

"Come over here, and I'll show you why," she said, skirting a cluster of calla lilies and heading toward the ficus trees grouped near the other side of the greenhouse. She padded softly up the slate terracing that raised the beds several feet in the air and gently pulled aside a frond of the tree to reveal a small bird's nest. The cadet looked hesitant to approach, but she gestured him closer to peer down into the nest, where three tiny eggs lay clustered in the bottom. Each egg was no larger than a marble.

"They are hummingbird eggs," she said. "My cousin fancies himself a naturalist, and he captured the hummingbirds a few weeks ago so we could study them. We had no idea they would . . . that they would so quickly . . . well, we didn't expect *this*."

At first she had been charmed at the prospect of watching baby hummingbirds emerge from the nest, but Romulus had been appalled. "Do you know how fragile hummingbirds are?" he had said. "The conditions have to be perfect . . . temperature, humidity, nutrition."

"Can't we let them go?" she had asked. "Set the nest outside?"

But Romulus warned that birds often rejected nests that had been tampered with and said he thought it would be better to make the greenhouse a suitable environment for humming-bird hatchlings. Hence the waterfall and its ability to provide a proper amount of humidity.

As she explained this to the young cadet, his eyes narrowed in concentration, and she was relieved that he seemed to be taking her seriously.

"You will need a more sophisticated setup for that kind of pump," he said as he scanned the interior of the greenhouse. "What you've got here is all wrong. You need electricity to make your pump function the way you want."

"I don't know anything about electricity," she said. It was one thing to tinker with hydraulics, quite another to risk electrocution merely to prove a point to her father. "I'll add another pump. Or buy a larger piston unit."

"I doubt you'll be happy with the results," the cadet warned. "The pump you have isn't going to work. It's completely inadequate for the task. Totally wrong."

Each time he criticized her design, it was another dart to her pride. This man was the recipient of one of the world's finest engineering programs all because he had been born male, while she had to learn by plundering her father's library and sitting at the back of lecture halls on the rare occasions members of the public were allowed onto the hallowed campus of West Point. It was unfair and annoying.

It also wasn't his fault she was in a snit over her father's stubbornness, but her battered pride needed to complete this task on her own. If her father believed the cadet he sent to her rescue was responsible for making the fountain work, it would reinforce his antiquated belief that women were incapable of participating in the renaissance of modern technology.

"Thank you, but I'm confident I can correct the matter on my own. I won't keep you from your responsibilities on campus any longer."

The young man acted as though he hadn't heard, squatting down to tilt the back of the pump, disconnecting the relief valve from the cistern to get a better view.

"Your house isn't wired for electricity, is it?"

"No, it's not."

"That won't be a problem," he said. "I can install a small generator out here and get your pump working in short order. It will power your fountain with enough energy to shoot an arc of water that can hit the ceiling of the greenhouse if you want."

The prospect of an ugly, noisy generator in her idyllic greenhouse was appalling. "I *don't* want an electrical generator. And I don't want any help fixing my pump, so please, don't let me stop you from the rest of your day."

The way he flinched at her brusque dismissal was a little upsetting. She didn't like being so curt, but he had ignored her more subtle suggestions. He placed the pump back in its original position, stood, and brushed the grit from his hands, his gaze darting around the interior of the greenhouse.

"It's no bother, ma'am. I'd truly enjoy helping you get this waterfall working properly."

It would be embarrassing to reveal her father's disdain for her intelligence, but it seemed that was the only way to get him to leave. "I'd like the opportunity to show my father that I am capable of installing a simple hydraulic pump. Accepting help from you would undermine that objective, so please . . . let me solve this on my own, all right?"

His shoulders sagged a little. "Oh," he said. Oddly, he seemed a little queasy as he fidgeted before her. "Here's the thing, ma'am. I need to work off some demerits, and it was suggested that helping you with this problem was my best shot for making that happen." He swallowed, his Adam's apple bobbing above the collar of his uniform. "It's pretty much my only hope."

Understanding dawned. Having been born and raised within the shadow of West Point, Evelyn was well aware of the awesome set of rules and responsibilities heaped on the cadets. They were destined to become army officers. Judging a cadet's academic abilities was easy, but it was much harder to assess their potential for leadership. The demerit system was a time-tested method of winnowing out students who lacked the self-discipline to be a good officer. A single demerit was used for minor offenses, such as poorly polished shoes, but more serious offenses, such as missing classes or insubordination, could be assigned ten, twenty, or even more demerits. There were no exceptions to the rules. Originally, popular or well-connected cadets could pull strings to remove demerits from their record. All that was a thing of the past. There was no favoritism, no exceptions. The only way to remove a demerit was to work it off, and it was much harder to erase demerits than it was to have them assigned.

The young man who had entered her house with laughing eyes and a confident air was gone, replaced by an ill-at-ease cadet whose clenched fists revealed his anxiety. She wished the academy had not seen fit to snatch her project away and give it to a cadet to work off demerits. She had so few opportunities for intellectual challenges . . . but the deed was done, and it would be horrid of her to refuse this man a chance to redeem himself.

She glanced at her pump. Her inadequate, underpowered, failing pump. Soon she was going to have a set of baby hummingbirds on her hands, and the pump needed to be operating reliably before then. She glared at the pump, then back at the sweating cadet.

"Oh, all right," she grumbled. "You can help with the electricity, but I want to do all the hydraulic work myself. I need to show my father that I am competent."

The relief on his face was humbling. "Thank you, ma'am!"

"You'd better call me Evelyn if we are going to work together."

His smile grew even wider as he agreed and asked her to call him Clyde in return.

"I dread the prospect of an ugly, noisy generator in here," she said.

"Then I'll install it outside and tunnel the cable beneath the greenhouse frame."

"We'll still be able to hear it, won't we? Generators make quite a racket."

"I'll figure out sound-proofing," Clyde said quickly. The spark of excitement in his eyes was familiar. It was exactly how she felt at the beginning of a daunting technical challenge. "I can insulate the casing with cotton batting. And maybe transplant some shrubbery to screen the unit. You'd be amazed at how much landscaping can disrupt sound waves."

She nodded in agreement. "I read an article in last month's *Journal of Science* about acoustics and sound disruption in natural settings like farms and orchards."

"I read the same article! It was what gave me the idea. I've never tried it, but I'll bet between the two of us, we can get it done."

Her heart skipped a beat. The way he automatically included her in his plans was heartening. All her life, her cousin Romulus had been the only person to ever take her ambitions seriously, and her sphere of people who respected her abilities had just doubled.

They were grinning stupidly at each other when a loud buzz sounded behind Clyde's left ear, making him startle and almost trip. A blur of green and scarlet zoomed past him and headed toward the vine of honeysuckle behind him. He stared in drop-jawed wonder at the hummingbird hovering near his shoulder as it drained the blossom of its nectar. Just as quickly, the bird rocketed out of sight.

"That was a ruby-throated hummingbird," she said. "A male. The females don't have that patch of red. They are quite lovely, aren't they?"

"I couldn't tell," he said. "He came and went so quickly, I'm still not sure what I saw."

She followed his gaze to the cluster of palms the bird had disappeared into, a faint whirring noise coming from where she suspected he was happily feeding away. "Are you sure you're willing to do all this?" she asked. "It seems rather extravagant to add electricity all so three baby birds can be hatched. These hummingbirds are in no way rare or valuable."

Clyde only smiled. "I don't want to do it because it's a life-or-death issue . . . I want to do it just to see if we can."

Another chink in her armor dropped away. The unabashed pursuit of an engineering challenge was what gave meaning and purpose to her life. Suddenly, she felt as if these next few weeks of discovery were going to open an entire new world for her.

2

Evelyn had hoped to spend the evening telling Romulus about her plans for solving their problem with the greenhouse. Romulus was her official chaperone for the rest of summer, having returned from Harvard three weeks earlier. His willingness to move into her father's house meant Evelyn was finally able to leave her aunt's home, where she had been sleeping in the guest bedroom for a year. She truly loathed being a visitor in other people's homes, but as the general's unmarried daughter, it was unthinkable that she should live alone while her father was stationed out West. Most of her life had been spent bouncing between the guest rooms and trundle beds of various family members, but Romulus was now twenty-two and old enough to serve as her chaperone, so they were spending the summer at her father's home.

So far, they had stocked the greenhouse with orchids imported from Peru, shepherded a dozen swallowtail caterpillars to the butterfly stage, and were in the process of perfecting the waterfall. It was Romulus who had alerted her to the extraordinary needs of the hummingbirds, and their inability to get the hydraulic pump working had been weighing on both their minds. She was looking forward to telling him of Clyde's visit and the plan to install an electric pump, but that was before Romulus stumbled through the front door with a tremendous bruise swelling his right eye shut.

"What on earth happened?" she gasped out. "It looks as if you ran smack into a speeding train!"

Romulus flashed a pained smile. "I ran into a second lieutenant's right hook during a boxing match." He gingerly lowered himself onto the bench in the front hall, wincing as though every muscle in his body had taken a pounding . . . which it probably had.

"Stay right there while I fetch the ice." There was an icehouse out back, and her hands shook as she wielded the ice pick to knock a chunk free.

It wouldn't be the first time she'd tended Romulus after a bout in the boxing ring. Why a man of his intelligence and effusive charm enjoyed leaping into a boxing ring was beyond her, but Romulus was now captain of Harvard's boxing team and loved challenging the West Point officers to impromptu matches whenever he was home.

After wrapping a chunk of ice in a towel, she sat beside Romulus on the bench, wincing along with him as she pressed the ice to the side of his face. Although one side of his face was bruised and swollen, the other side looked as though it had been sculpted by a Renaissance artist seeking to create the perfection of a fallen angel. With chiseled cheekbones, a strong jaw, and flashing black eyes that matched his ebony hair, Romulus was appallingly handsome—and he knew it, too.

"You've spent three years stuffing your head with arcane knowledge, then you come home and let some stranger at West Point pummel it all out of you."

He grinned. "There is always more where it came from. Lugging all this brilliance around is my burden in life."

But he wasn't brilliant enough to get that hydraulic pump

working. In short order, she told him of Clyde's visit this afternoon and the prospect of a new and better waterfall. She feared he might fuss over the noise of a generator and had been marshalling her arguments in support of it all afternoon. To her surprise, Romulus not only endorsed the idea of the generator, his flamboyant mind already had additional plans for it.

"Moon lighting," he said. "I saw it at a public garden in Boston. We can string light bulbs in the trees. When turned on at night, they emulate the moonlight streaming through the leaves. It will be as if Monet himself has designed the garden."

Honestly, sometimes Evelyn suspected she had been put on this earth to reel in Romulus from his excessive ambitions. "Let's not get carried away again," Evelyn said. "All we need is to create a suitable environment until the baby hummingbirds are hatched and weaned. Then we can dismantle it."

Romulus looked appalled. "Did King Arthur destroy the Round Table after he assembled his knights? Will Paris dismantle the Eiffel Tower after the World's Fair? If we are to install electricity, I want a waterfall and moon lighting and landscaping to rival the gardens of Versailles. And for once, I want you to snap out of that hidebound practicality that sucks all the joy out of life. Were you an Indian, your spirit name would be Dream Killer."

She lifted a brow, giving her best General White impersonation. "Because I don't believe a greenhouse needs simulated moonlight, it makes me a dream killer?"

Although now that he had planted the idea in her head, it did seem rather appealing. Already she could imagine the sound of water trickling over rocks while the lighting created dappled patches of moonlight on the ground. It would be both a technological and artistic challenge, but a fun one.

In a perfect world, she would be allowed to go to college and have the chance to participate in the burgeoning technological revolution. That dream was already fading and disappearing into the horizon, but that wouldn't stop her from experimenting in her own backyard. Her greenhouse would never earn her fame or fortune, but that was okay. She didn't hunger for that sort of acclaim, she did it for the sheer joy of discovery.

Dreams had always been hard for her. In the still of night, she'd harbored spectacular dreams, only to watch them wither in the practical realities of daylight. But this summer she would savor working alongside Clyde Brixton and learn all she could from him. He had the dreams and ambitions to go after exactly what he wanted, and for a few weeks, it would be a wonderful adventure to work right beside such a man.

<hr />

"Tell me everything you can about Evelyn White," Clyde said as he tightened the top hinge on the newly installed screen door to Smitty's modest three-room house. Smitty sat on the front stoop, still wearing his janitor's uniform and handing Clyde tools as needed.

"Why do you want to know about Evelyn White?"

Because she's a stunner. Because she's smart and funny and I've never met a girl whose good opinion I've craved as much as hers. "I'll be doing a bit of work at General White's house over the summer," he hedged, reluctant to reveal how deeply he had already fallen for the general's daughter. When she'd opened the door to him this afternoon, the sight of her had driven the oxygen from his lungs. She had glossy dark hair and high cheekbones that set off her intelligent eyes. Despite her calm demeanor, she seemed the most alive, intense girl he'd ever met. And when she'd spoken about the properties of hydraulic pumps and atmospheric pressure, he'd fallen for her swiftly, plunging inescapably down like an anchor flung overboard . . . but he had no desire to save himself. Rather, he wanted to fulfill her every request. If she wanted electricity in her greenhouse, he'd bring it to her like Prometheus carrying fire down from the mountaintop.

He didn't have much to offer a girl like Evelyn, so he needed to know everything about her, from her family background to the kind of tea she liked to drink. Knowledge was power, and there was no better source for information than Smitty Jones.

As the janitor for three decades at West Point, Smitty had his ear to the ground and knew more about the happenings on campus than any officer or cadet. Nothing escaped Smitty's attention, and he was the first person to notice when a cadet with nowhere to go over the long Christmas holiday had taken to hiding in the library overnight. It had been Clyde's plebe year. When the dormitories had closed in mid-December and all the other students headed home, Clyde hadn't known what to do. He would eat nails before confessing he had nowhere to go and no money for lodgings, so he holed up the library, hoping no one would notice the lone student who lingered in the book aisles after closing.

Smitty noticed, and he invited Clyde into his home until the dormitories reopened in mid-January. Clyde didn't have a dime to compensate Smitty for his hospitality, so he offered to install gutters on the janitor's modest clapboard house. While on the roof, Clyde had spotted some rotting shingles and replaced those, too.

The arrangement worked well for them both. Smitty was a childless old widower who welcomed a younger man's company over holidays and summer break, but no matter how kind he was, Clyde refused to accept Smitty's hospitality for free. The summer of his plebe year he'd painted the house and repaired the crumbling front porch. The following summer, he'd installed running water to the kitchen and washroom, making Smitty's house one of the finest in the neighborhood. Today he was working on adding a new screen door while Smitty handed him tools and filled him in on Evelyn's background.

"Her mother died when she was only a toddler, and General White wasn't in a position to care for a child. The girl was farmed out to other family members around the state. She seems bright. I see her at all the public lectures on campus, and she must have fifty books checked out from the library."

"Is there anyone special in her life? A man?"

"She won't look twice at a cadet," Smitty warned him. "Plenty have tried, but rumor has it she is chillier than an arctic wind. Any man who approaches her risks frostbite, hypothermia, and certain failure."

"She didn't seem chilly to me."

Smitty gave an ironic smile. "I'll bet you weren't flirting with her in hopes of cozying up to her father. That girl has no interest in any man in a uniform."

Being as she was the daughter of a powerful general, Clyde suspected plenty of cadets and army officers were eager to court Evelyn. She was right to be cautious, and given Clyde's ambition to rise within the Corps of Engineers, she'd be doubly suspicious of him.

And why was he even thinking of her like this, anyway? His sole ambition in life was landing a solid job as an engineer so he could start earning a decent income. Anytime he lost sight of that goal, the memory of his mother's hands, cracked and bleeding from the harsh lye soap she used at the laundry, snapped him back on track. He couldn't afford to aspire to someone like Evelyn White. Someday he would wear an officer's uniform. He would have money and prestige and the ability to get his mother out of the rooming house where she'd lived ever since his father had died and left them with nothing but debt.

"How many demerits are they going to scrub from your record for working at the general's house?" Smitty asked.

"It will be enough." But he was sweating as he said it. He'd been stupid to rack up so many demerits during his early years, mostly over trivial pranks. He'd never imagined his jaunt to Washington would result in such a steep penalty, and it imperiled everything for which he'd worked so hard. With luck, the patent he'd filed for last week would someday earn good money. At the very least, it ought to earn enough so he'd never have to pawn his old textbooks for money to buy soap, the only item West Point did not provide for free. It was embarrassing to be poor as dirt, and even more so to be on the verge of expulsion over those stupid demerits. There was no need for Evelyn or Smitty or anyone else to know of his precarious position at the academy.

Clyde squatted down on his haunches to drill the next holes for another door hinge. The scent of fresh sawdust prickled his nose as he wound the hand crank, grinding forward into the wood and wishing he could talk about anything other than how close he was to being kicked out of school.

Smitty must have read the tension in his voice. "Try to walk a straight line this year. I've seen plenty of lightweights get booted out of West Point over demerits, but you've got what it takes to be one of the great ones. Don't let your impulses get the better of you."

Clyde swallowed hard as he finished drilling the final hole. "I'll do whatever it takes to graduate," he said firmly.

Because if he lost his appointment at West Point, he'd have nothing in the world.

3

Evelyn was sitting at the breakfast table opposite Romulus when a wagon of bricks was delivered to the house, along with a note from Clyde Brixton. The bricks were leftovers from a new dormitory, and he'd been granted permission to use them at the general's house. Supplies for building the generator were also being provided by the academy, for West Point looked after the family members of officers posted on long-term assignments.

Evelyn raced outside to accept the delivery, excited at the prospect of beginning work on the generator. Romulus joined her outside as she scanned the note once again.

"Clyde's note suggests we lay the bricks on the flat surface just south of the greenhouse," she said. She was proud of the perfect calm in her voice, especially given the way her heart picked up pace at the prospect of seeing Clyde again. Not that it meant anything. She was simply excited to get started fixing her waterfall.

She summarized the rest of the note's instructions for preparing a proper surface. She might have been reading lists from the West Point student directory for how bland she sounded.

Romulus's eyes gleamed as he leaned a hip against the side of the cart. "Did you know your cheeks just flushed a shade of crimson to rival a damask rose?" he asked. "I suspect that a West Point cadet might be responsible for your alarming surge in blood pressure."

She lifted her chin a notch. "I have no interest in any West Point cadet and never will."

"Are you sure? You sounded pretty impressed with him the other day."

"Then let me clarify," she said calmly. "The earth will stop rotating, the moon will drop from the sky, and the sun will burn to ash before a man in uniform will ever appeal to me."

And it was true. From the time she was old enough to crawl from her crib and take notice of the world, she had witnessed army wives being abandoned by their husbands, and children raised with no fathers. As a child, there were years Evelyn couldn't even remember her father's face; the best she could do was recall the scent of starch from his scratchy uniform.

"No need to supply all the details of the apocalypse," Romulus said. "Let's get these bricks carted to the backyard."

The rest of the morning was spent perched on a bench, giving Romulus instructions for digging a shallow trench and laying out the bricks according to the plan sent by Clyde. Being female had few compensations, but she was prepared to take full advantage of the excusal from manual labor. Romulus shed his shirt and donned a pair of work gloves as he began cutting into the sod.

As much as she adored Romulus, he was family and could never fill the hollow part of her heart that longed for a man in her life. The only men she met at West Point were in the army and destined to lead the same kind of itinerant life as her father. She wanted to meet other young men who were interested in the same things she was—men she would be free to court or someday marry.

"Could I come visit you sometime at Harvard?" she asked impulsively. "You know I love going to the lectures, and I wouldn't mind meeting some of your friends."

Romulus straightened, then sank the tip of the shovel firmly into the ground. He swiped the sweat off his face and peered at her through his still-swollen black eye. "Which of my friends do you want to meet? The young and handsome ones?"

Romulus could always read her like a book, and it was embarrassing. "Good looks don't matter," she said. "I'd like to meet someone who is intellectually curious. Someone who likes to tinker with things and likes a good challenge. Someone who'd be willing to install a generator or a waterfall to see if we can create an environment for hummingbirds."

Romulus grinned as he started shoveling again. "Someone like Clyde Brixton?"

"Someone like Clyde Brixton without the looming army career. He'd be perfect but for that."

"Did someone say my name?"

Evelyn gasped, for there was Clyde, standing beside the greenhouse with a bag of sand precariously balanced on one shoulder. If the earth could have split open and swallowed her whole, she would have been happy, for if the widening of Clyde's smile was any indication, he'd heard everything she'd said about him.

Romulus saved her, tossing down the shovel and brushing the grit from his hands. "If you're selling something, we're not interested. If you're the engineering cadet from West Point who is going to install an electric generator for our greenhouse, let me scatter rose petals in your path."

Clyde grinned, leaning over to let the heavy bag of sand roll from his shoulder and thump on the ground. "I'm the guy who sent you all those bricks. And the brick pad will last longer if we add a layer of sand before you set the bricks, so I brought a bag. I knocked, but the maid said you were out here." He looked at Evelyn with curiosity. "What were you saying about me just now?"

The heat in her cheeks grew. She cleared her throat and nodded to his note. "I was saying how I appreciated your instructions for making the brick pallet. They were very clear."

He beamed at her with an impossibly blue gaze. She hoped he wouldn't challenge her, for what could she say? That she had been thinking of him almost nonstop for the past three days? That she had never met another young man she'd felt so instantly attuned to?

"Good!" he said. "Can I stay and help?"

Clyde couldn't believe his good fortune. He'd only intended to deliver the sand and then return to Smitty's house, but he was almost certain he'd interrupted Evelyn talking about him, and the snippets he'd heard made him dizzy with anticipation. He'd spent a few sleepless nights worrying she might somehow learn about his mortifying collection of demerits or about the desperation move he'd made to get admitted to West Point. He wanted her to see him as a hero, yet there were so many ways she could have heard about his checkered history.

But miraculously, it seemed he was already on his way to making a favorable impression. He rolled up his sleeves alongside her cousin and set to work digging the shallow trench, exquisitely conscious of Evelyn's presence just a few yards away, watching his every move.

"So you attend Harvard?" he asked the man laboring beside him. "What are you studying?"

"Natural science," Romulus replied. "After graduating, I'm thinking of going to Yale for another degree in animal science."

"And what will you do with that? Become a college professor?"

Romulus shrugged. "Who knows? It's mostly just an excuse

to avoid gainful employment for a few more years. What will you do after you graduate?"

Get a job with Evelyn's father. The best possible appointment for someone like him was to become an officer in the Corps of Engineers, but there was no need to state it so bluntly. "I'll go wherever the army sends me," he said. "Maybe drilling tunnels through the Rocky Mountains or working on the canals in the Great Lakes. Or a bridge somewhere. I've never worked on a bridge before."

Romulus shuddered. "It sounds like the inner rings of Dante's inferno."

That attitude confounded him. All his life, he'd only wanted to earn a degree, start working, and make money. Anything that interfered with that was a problem.

He split the top of the sandbag with the tip of his shovel and dumped a generous amount of sand into the trench to serve as a drainage bed for the bricks. "All I've ever wanted to do was build things," he said.

Romulus grabbed a rake and began spreading the sand, then abruptly stopped. "Brixton," he said in a pondering voice as he straightened and looked directly at Clyde. "Any relation to Fleetwood Brixton and the refrigeration project?"

Clyde felt his stomach drop. There were plenty of painful details about his personal life he didn't particularly want to share, but the final, humiliating years of his father's technological debacle were at the top of the list.

Both Evelyn and Romulus awaited his answer, studying him with curious eyes. He looked away and raked the sand flat. "Fleetwood Brixton was my father," he admitted, still not looking them in the face.

"Who is Fleetwood Brixton?" Evelyn asked, and Clyde winced. If all had gone according to plan, his father's name would have been as famous as Thomas Edison's. The compact, insulated refrigeration boxes would have been a standard feature in every American kitchen. Instead, Clyde had to sell his father's watch just to afford his casket.

Romulus supplied the answer. "Fleetwood Brixton developed a clever means of keeping a box refrigerated for weeks or months at a time. We had a prototype at our laboratory at Harvard to keep biology specimens fresh. I think it would have worked quite well had the drainage problem been solved."

The drainage problem surfaced in the refrigeration boxes after about a year of operation. The slow, gradual drip in the evaporator coils was unnoticeable at first, but over time it soaked the insulation, corroded the wires, and made the refrigeration box inoperable. His father had invested his life savings into the invention, as well as one hundred thousand dollars from a slew of investors, in order to rush his invention to market and begin earning a return. After the invention failed, his father faced lawsuits from both customers and his investors, and was forced to default on a bank loan. He'd died after a bout with pneumonia three years ago, depressed, bankrupt, and with an inventory of two thousand useless refrigerator boxes filling a rented storage space.

Clyde hadn't known what to do. He was eighteen years old and knew little of the world other than what he'd learned in his father's workshop. His mother paid as many of the debts as she could, but it hadn't been enough. They were left with nothing. His mother moved into the top floor of a boarding-house in Baltimore, where she did the laundry in exchange for room and board.

And Clyde ran away. West Point was the only school that would pay the full freight for a student to receive a fine engineering degree. He didn't want to become like his father, whose self-taught knowledge of technology was full of gaps and had led him into disaster.

Getting into West Point required connections, and Clyde had none. He needed to be nominated by a congressman, senator, member of the president's cabinet, or higher. He had excellent grades, an aptitude for technology, and a total lack of fear. It was his willingness to boldly fight for what he wanted that prompted him to beg rides from Baltimore to Washington. It took two days of riding in the back of hay wagons, sleeping beneath the trees, and walking over twenty miles by foot, but when he arrived in Washington, he paid for a bath in a rooming house and got his hair trimmed. Then he steeled his resolve, walked up to the home of the vice-president of the United States, knocked on the door, and asked for a nomination to West Point. It had been a long shot, but Thomas A. Hendricks had an appreciation for unvarnished audacity, and after a brief interview, he'd agreed to nominate Clyde.

Evelyn looked at him with curiosity, but he couldn't meet her eyes. Evelyn White's father was in command of the U.S. Corps of Engineers, charged with overseeing the transportation and telecommunication systems that would lead the country into the next century. His own father's legacy was a storage shed filled with useless refrigeration boxes.

A niggling sense of embarrassment drove him to boast. "I filed for a patent on my own invention just last week," he said. "For an electrical switch that can automatically shut off when it gets damp." And that wasn't the only patent to his name, although it was the only one that might someday earn money. His other three patents were mere technical curiosities with little practical application, such as the automated dispenser for feeding house cats. Even thinking about those useless patents made him feel small and frivolous beside this girl whose father was helping build bridges that spanned miles.

"Sometimes I wish that I were a man," Evelyn said.

Romulus choked on a mouthful of water, and all Clyde could

think of was the terrific waste if this glorious woman were to be transformed into a crude, run-of-the-mill man.

"If I were a man, I could do interesting things like you," she said. "I could study engineering and file patents and build useful inventions. I wouldn't have to run to the superintendent at West Point for help with a hydraulic pump any plebe could install."

"No plebe could have built that pump," he said truthfully. Considering Evelyn was entirely self-taught, her accomplishments were extraordinary, but he hesitated to praise her too openly. He sensed a wariness in her, a natural self-restraint she hid behind like a shield, and he needed to tread cautiously. Caution was difficult for him, but he would master it in order to gain Evelyn's trust. "I think the sand ought to be adequate for the drainage needs," he said. "Evelyn said this generator only needs to operate until the hummingbirds have been hatched and are ready to be released back into the wild."

Evelyn glanced at her cousin, a wealth of unspoken communication flying between them. She looked a little embarrassed as she turned back to him. "We've changed our minds about that," she said. "We want to build something that will last. We never planned for this to happen, but now that it has . . . well, it is a grand experiment, isn't it? Like Lewis and Clark setting off for the great unknown."

"Jason and the Argonauts searching for the Golden Fleece," Romulus added.

"Gutenberg inventing the printing press," Evelyn said.

"Are the two of you always this prone to exaggeration? We're discussing a pump, not the—"

"Stop!" Romulus said. "This greenhouse is mankind's war against mediocrity and acquiescence."

"We can and we *must* build something better," Evelyn said with the dignity of a queen, but her eyes were laughing.

As the afternoon unfolded and they completed laying the

generator pallet, Clyde felt a surge of happiness unlike anything he'd ever known. Sometimes in life a person was lucky enough to stumble across someone for whom an immediate sense of camaraderie bloomed, and this was just such a moment. Times two. Evelyn and her cousin could not be more different in temperament and comportment, but he liked them both enormously. The three of them clicked in perfect harmony, and he was sorry when the pallet was complete.

"I'll be back tomorrow with the pieces to assemble the generator," he said, thrilled to see the anticipation in Evelyn's sparkling eyes.

There had never been a challenge he'd set for himself that he'd failed to meet. The academic demands at college were easy. Avoiding demerits was harder, but all that would take was a little more self-discipline. And maybe, just maybe, he could aspire to win Evelyn White, as well.

***

Evelyn snapped awake before the sun was in the sky the following morning. Even the thought of tampering with electricity was mildly terrifying, but she'd read the chart Clyde had showed her, and it was already preserved like a photograph in her memory. Perhaps she didn't have the makings of a natural engineer like Clyde Brixton, but she had a memory that worked better than any camera, and that was a valuable asset when working with technology. If everything went according to plan, it would take only a few days to assemble the generator, and then they would have all the power they needed to run the waterfall for as long as she wanted.

She threw on her work clothes, a simple cotton frock with an apron she always wore in the greenhouse.

Then she discarded the apron. She didn't mind looking frumpy before Romulus, but it was different with Clyde here. The indigo dress might have been washed countless times, but it showed her figure to its best advantage, and she didn't want an apron messing it up. She took a few extra minutes before the mirror to coil her hair into a becoming twist at the back of her head.

The sun still hadn't risen by the time she dashed down the staircase, but to her surprise, a wagon was already parked before her house, with Clyde folding down the back and unloading a box of equipment. She opened the door. "Have you had breakfast?" she asked.

He shook his head. "Too excited to get started. What about you?"

"You can't do manual labor on an empty stomach. I'll get Romulus out of bed and make us all some eggs. Then the real work begins."

It took three days to install the generator, and Evelyn enjoyed every moment. True to his word, Clyde limited his work to the electrical components and let her take complete charge of adapting the hydraulic pump. While Clyde assembled the generator, she climbed to the top of the waterfall to fit the pipes in the spaces behind the rocks. Romulus dug a trench to accommodate the buried cable line that would feed electricity to the water pump. Clyde used coiled copper wire and clunky magnets to hook up a Beckwith motor, all of which would be set inside a metal casing to shelter it from the elements.

It was amazing how quickly Clyde fit in. She and Romulus had known each other since childhood and had their own unwritten language that could be communicated with nothing more than a glance, but Clyde seemed immediately capable of reading it and joining in. He teased Romulus for wearing a satin vest while performing manual labor, and Evelyn warned him he was treading on sensitive ground. The only thing Romulus loved more than his extensive wardrobe was a professor's daughter named Laura, and anyone who insulted either was in peril.

"So who is Laura?" Clyde asked Romulus one day as they buried the underground cables.

Romulus threw down his shovel. "Laura is the beginning and end of every romantic sonnet ever written. Her laughter is music. She has a lethal sense of humor but the wisdom to know when to use it."

"But who *is* she?" Clyde pressed.

"She's the woman who has agreed to marry me as soon as I graduate. She's studying languages at Radcliffe College, but sometimes she comes to classes at Harvard. We met in a class on botanical nomenclature. Her Latin is excellent. I never knew how attractive it was to listen to a beautiful woman reading botanical treatises in the original Latin until I met Laura Hartley. I was smitten within the hour."

Near the end of the third day, the generator had been assembled and was ready to test. Evelyn hoped that someday they could use the electricity to power a strand of light bulbs suspended from the taller plants, but the first step was to get the waterfall working. After the cable was routed beneath the soil and up into the greenhouse, Evelyn held her breath as Clyde made the final connections to the pump.

"Be careful," Evelyn cautioned. "I'd feel terrible if you got electrocuted."

"At least have the decency to delay the electrocution until the waterfall is working," Romulus added.

"If I die from this, I want a monument dedicated to me in your fancy greenhouse," Clyde said, grinning as he twisted the wires to connect them to the generator, utterly fearless. His easy confidence made him even more attractive to Evelyn, and she felt lightheaded as she awaited the final few moments before the test.

After the last connection was made, Clyde went outside to fire up the generator. He warned her not to be alarmed by the racket, for soundproofing would be added later. Even with the warning, the bangs from the generator were startling. All four hummingbirds zoomed about the enclosure at the rackety noise, but after a few moments, the generator calmed to a rhythmic mechanical thumping, exactly as Clyde had said it would.

And a second later, the hiss and gurgling from the pipes indicated water was being drawn upward in the tubing behind the rocks. Evelyn held her breath, thrilled as water finally reached the top of the artfully arranged rocks and began cascading down the front in white, frothy streams. It was dazzling, with more than twice as much water flowing over the rocks than with her earlier effort. The patter of falling water even helped mask the noise of the generator.

Clyde raced around the enclosure to witness the waterfall in action.

"Well done!" Romulus said.

Two of the hummingbirds were still careening around the greenhouse in annoyance, but the others had disappeared into the shrubbery. Clyde moved beside her to gawk at the cascading water, and the three of them stood shoulder-to-shoulder in speechless delight. It was hard to believe that only a few days earlier the waterfall had barely enough power to dribble a little water for a few hours. Now it was a splendid sight . . . thrilling and beautiful . . . and yet she was sorry they'd accomplished it so quickly. The past three days had been the most fun in her memory.

She wished her father were here to see it.

That thought was a damper on her mood. Clyde was the person deserving of the credit for this, not she. Her hydraulic pump would never have been so impressive without Clyde's electricity. If she bragged to her father about her brilliant accomplishment, it would endanger the credit due to Clyde, for she mustn't forget that Clyde had been sent here specifically to help clean up his record at the academy.

"This ought to earn you goodwill at the academy. How many demerits will it erase?" She intended her question to be light-hearted, but Clyde's reaction was the opposite. Every muscle in his face tightened, and the corners of his mouth turned down.

"I'm sure it will be adequate," he mumbled.

Romulus pounced. "Exactly how many demerits do you have? They must be bad for you to need to work them off. Come on, how many have you got?"

Evelyn thought the question terribly rude, like asking some-one about his grades or how much money was in his bank ac-count, but perhaps this sort of teasing was normal among men.

Clyde shrugged. "I've got a few. Most cadets do."

"A hundred?" Romulus asked. "A hundred and fifty? Come on, don't be ashamed to own up to it." The flush on Clyde's face darkened, and he looked away. "Two hundred?" Romulus pressed.

"That's ridiculous," she defended. "If he had two hundred demerits, he would have already been kicked out."

Clyde didn't look like he was enjoying this. "I don't have two hundred demerits," he snapped. "I am in no danger of being expelled, I simply wanted to help with this project. Could we drop this?"

The magical feeling of just moments ago evaporated, and Evelyn wanted to shake Romulus. Mercifully, Romulus showed unusual sensitivity by quickly diverting the conversation.

"What do you think about adding a koi pond? I think the hummingbirds will fancy a little company, and Evelyn's pump ought to provide adequate power to oxygenate a pond, don't you think?"

To her relief, Clyde's tension eased, and a hint of a smile lurked at his mouth. "I think it is an excellent idea."

Another flare of attraction surged through Evelyn. She loved the way Clyde seemed ready to tackle anything. Seize any idea.

Other people laughed at the way she and Romulus tinkered with their greenhouse, but Clyde wanted to roll up his sleeves and play along.

Even better, adding a koi pond meant Clyde wouldn't be leaving anytime soon. There would be more afternoons like this, more long summer days laughing and working together toward a common goal. More time with a man she found irresistibly attractive.

She winced at the thought. Clyde would return to West Point in August and graduate in May. He was destined for a military career. She could never, under any circumstances, align herself with a military man. She'd already lived through a childhood of abandonment and would not allow herself to become an abandoned wife, as well.

That vow had never been difficult before now. Somehow, deep in her soul, Evelyn knew she would never be able to fully erase Clyde Brixton from her heart.

4

The imposing Gothic buildings of the West Point campus looked softer in summer, surrounded by lush trees and spacious lawns of neatly trimmed grass. Evelyn always loved this walk, especially since she was headed toward the library, her favorite building in the entire area.

She was here to meet Clyde and perform research. Romulus fancied trying to make the greenhouse look like the famed Hanging Gardens of Babylon, one of the seven wonders of the ancient world. None of them had the slightest idea of what the gardens looked like, but Romulus liked the sound of it and Evelyn was game to try. Clyde had suggested she meet him in the library to research the details of the gardens. Romulus was in Boston buying supplies for a koi pond, but she secretly thought it all an excuse to sneak a visit to his beloved Laura. New York City was much closer if all he wanted were supplies for the artificial pond.

It didn't really matter why Romulus was gone, all that mattered was that she was going to be entirely alone with Clyde. The fact that they would be surrounded by dozens of people in the library hardly mattered. She would have the chance to work alongside a recklessly attractive man, their heads bent over a book, figuring out how to translate their far-flung dreams into reality.

And she would be a perfect lady the entire time. Just because she liked fantasizing about a dalliance with Clyde didn't mean she intended to act on it. Clyde was forbidden fruit, and she would be as proper as the Queen of England in her dealings with him.

It was hard to remember her good intentions when she rounded the parade field and saw Clyde sitting on the wide front steps of the library. He sprang to his feet with military precision, although there was nothing military about the grin he beamed at her or the way his eyes lit with anticipation.

"Brotherly," she muttered to herself. "Clyde Brixton is to be just like a brother."

"Hi Evelyn," he said as she approached. She even liked the way he said her name, a little breathlessly, as though he'd been looking forward to this afternoon as much as she. "Are you ready to rediscover the Hanging Gardens of Babylon?"

"Okay." Couldn't she think of anything more original to say? The wonderful ease she felt when Romulus was with them had evaporated. Now they were just a young man and the girl who couldn't stop staring at him. Her brain contained all the intelligence of a newly sprouted lima bean.

But it didn't seem to matter once they stepped inside and began hunting through the aisles. They were two explorers in search of knowledge, prowling through history texts, old art books, and archaeological treatises. Ensconced on the second floor beside the art history section, they undertook a thrilling quest for insights into the ancient world. It didn't take them long to discover that nobody knew what the fabled gardens looked like, but that didn't stop artists and historians from speculating. They found dozens of illustrations that bore little resemblance to one another.

Clyde wasn't satisfied with the speculation. "We'll disappoint Romulus if we come back with anything less than a fully realized master plan, possibly complete with one of those getups for his wardrobe," he said, gesturing to the page of Bronze Age jewelry that had been excavated from a Mesopotamian tomb.

She froze. It was impossible to deny that Romulus had outlandish taste in clothes and jewelry, but she couldn't tell if Clyde was mocking him.

"Don't tease," she warned. "Romulus is my best friend in the world." Her only friend, really, aside from Clyde himself.

He looked taken aback. "I wasn't teasing. I've just never met a man who puts so much thought into his clothes."

She sighed. "I'm sorry if I'm too protective. It's just that Romulus is the only person I had when I was growing up."

An avalanche of painful memories stirred to life. As a child, she'd been shunted among a series of relatives who had agreed to look after her. Not wanting to impose too much on any one relative, her father never left her in a household for longer than six months. Her earliest memory was when she was five years old and being dropped off at yet another strange home an hour from West Point and being introduced to a stern-faced lady named Maude, a distant cousin of her father's. She'd been afraid of Maude and had started crying when she understood she was to be left there. She clung to her Aunt Bess and begged not to be abandoned at this new and strange house. Maude had a teenage daughter named Caroline who was ordered to let Evelyn share her bed. Caroline didn't seem any happier about the arrangement than Evelyn. That first night Evelyn had lain stiffly on the mattress, listening to the voices of the adults from below.

"She's not usually so whiney," Aunt Bess had said. "And she'll only be here for a few months until the general can make other arrangements."

Evelyn wanted to start crying again, but it would wake up the older girl beside her, and Caroline didn't seem very nice.

On that night she'd resolved never to cry or complain again in Maude's house, no matter how scared she felt. No one seemed to want her, so she'd tried not to be any trouble. At meals she sat at the dining table quietly, listening and trying not to make any noise. She ate whatever was set before her, even though her tummy hurt whenever she had something with tomatoes in it, and Maude served tomatoes a lot.

She knew her sixth birthday was coming up soon, because Maude kept a calendar from the *Farmer's Almanac* hanging on the wall of the kitchen. If Maude asked what she wanted for her birthday, Evelyn planned to ask for new shoes. Her shoes had been too small even when Aunt Bess had brought her here, but now they'd gotten so small her toes had to crinkle up just to fit inside. Her feet hurt and grew blisters, but it was important not to complain since Maude was doing her father a big favor by letting her stay here.

Maude never did ask what she wanted for her birthday. It seemed no one even knew it was her birthday until two weeks later when a package arrived from the Dakota territories, where her father was helping build a railroad. It was a box for her birthday, containing toffee candy, picture books, and a brand new doll with three different sets of clothing.

But no shoes.

No one noticed she didn't have proper shoes until a picnic on the Fourth of July. They went into town and she saw her cousin Romulus, who was nine years old and preferred kicking around a ball with the other boys, but he always made a point of welcoming her whenever she joined a family gathering. When he saw she didn't have anyone to play with, he offered to teach her how to skip stones on the pond. It was so nice to have someone to play with again, and she babbled nonstop as they skipped the stones. Romulus was a lot better at skipping stones than she, and she wanted to impress him somehow. The only thing she could think to do was recite all the states and their capitals in alphabetical order. Memorizing things had always been easy for her, and Romulus pretended to be impressed.

"Listen to you, Smarty," Romulus said, but he was smiling as he said it, and she liked the way it made her feel. "I'll bet you're going to make good grades in school, probably way better than mine."

That was when he'd noticed her shoelaces were untied and the flaps pulled as wide as they would go.

"You'll trip if you don't tie your shoes," he cautioned.

She shrugged. "It's okay."

But his eyes narrowed, and he told her to sit down and take off her shoes. He gasped when he saw the blisters running across the tops of her toes. "How come you don't have shoes that fit?"

She didn't know how to respond, but a few days later Maude took her to a shop and purchased new shoes for her. She didn't know what Romulus did to make it happen, but from that day forward he had been her hero.

No matter where she lived over the coming years, Romulus would come visit. "Hello, Smarty," he would say as he breezed in the door, and she secretly loved that he called her Smarty. It was a special name between the two of them, and it made her feel good whenever he said it.

Over the years, she was sometimes sent to live with Aunt Josephine, who was Romulus's mother. Those had been the best times, for it meant she and Romulus were like a real brother and sister. They walked to school together, ate meals at the same table, and had chores together. It wasn't quite as good as living in her own house, but at least she wasn't scared at Aunt Josephine's house.

She didn't want to share any of this with Clyde. There were

plenty of genuine orphans who'd been left with nothing, and she never bemoaned her migrant childhood. What good would dwelling on it do? But that didn't mean she would let anyone belittle Romulus.

She lowered her voice so the people reading at the next table couldn't hear. "Romulus may dress like a dandy and pretend he doesn't have a care in the world, but he is one of the kindest men you'll ever meet," she said. "Even when we were children, he was always looking out for me. I'd do anything in the world for him."

Clyde gazed at her, a troubled look on his face. "I didn't mean to insult him," he said. "And I've never seen a bond like the two of you have. I'm in awe of it. That kind of friendship is rare in the world, and I'm glad the two of you have made room for me, even if it's just for a few weeks."

The muscles in her body eased, for his apology was genuine. Clyde's straightforward way of expressing himself made him even more appealing to her. All her life, she'd been cautious and reserved, and she wished she could be as open and trusting as he was. And the way he gazed at her was mesmerizing. His eyes were so blue . . . although to call them *blue* was something of an understatement. They were cerulean, or maybe azure, or something close to the shade of cobalt she had seen at the mineral shop.

She tore her gaze away. *Brotherly*. She must maintain a brotherly relationship with Clyde, nothing more. Scooting her chair a few inches away, she turned her attention back to the books spread before her. She scrambled for something to say. "If we can't find any reliable images of the Hanging Gardens, perhaps if we know why they were built we would have a better idea of what to include."

Clyde reached across the table for a text from the ancient historian Diodorus Siculus. She loved watching the intensity on his face as he flipped through the pages until he landed on a passage. He scooted closer to her as he read in a quiet voice. "'The Syrian king built the gardens to please his wife, Queen Amytis, for she, being a Persian by race and longing for the meadows of her homeland, asked the king to emulate her native land through the artifice of a planted garden.'"

Evelyn looked at a hand-colored engraving of how an artist imagined the gardens might have looked. It had alabaster columns and terraced beds brimming with flowering blooms and trees laden with fruit. There were staircases spiraling up to ever higher levels, each draped with fruiting vines and lush plantings. The effect was like a mountainside, each level more spectacular than the one before.

She traced a finger along an edge of a terrace. "It's hopeless," she sighed. "We can never emulate this kind of terracing. Last summer, Romulus and I worked for an entire month to install a single terrace, and it's only three feet from the ground."

Clyde drew closer, his leg almost touching hers as he peered at the engraving. His eyes softened as he scanned the lavish gift from a long-dead king to his beloved wife. Then he turned to her, his voice so low she could barely hear it. "If it were in my power, I'd build you a monument like that."

She drew a quick breath. There was no mistaking the implication of that sentence, and there was nothing brotherly about it. A nervous glance at the cadets studying at nearby tables showed that no one was paying them any mind, even though her heart thumped so loudly it could probably startle the crows in the belfry.

"I can't . . ." How could she put this into words? She'd spoken softly, and Clyde leaned even closer, expectation in his eyes that hurt to see. "I can't become close to any cadet," she whispered.

His brows lowered. "Is it because of your father?"

Her father would sing from the mountaintops if she married

into the army and became a respectable officer's wife. It had been hard enough being the abandoned child of the army, the last thing she wanted was to become the wife of such a man.

"I know what is expected of officers' wives," she said. "Most of the aunts and relatives I've lived with over the years were like widows when their men left them for years at a time. Their children had no real father in their life. There were times I couldn't even recall my father's face. That's not the kind of life I want. All I've ever wanted was a stable home where I could set down roots. Preferably with a husband who lives with me."

And that meant someone free of military obligations. The hopeful light in Clyde's face faded, and his head dipped a bit, but his eyes were still gentle. "It doesn't have to be that way," he said. "Some wives travel with their husbands. It can happen."

She shook her head. "I know, but I want children who aren't uprooted with each new season. *I* don't want to be uprooted with each season. You can understand that, can't you?"

He stared at her a long time before nodding. "I understand. Pretend I never said anything."

His tone was light and his smile was easy, but it didn't quite reach his eyes. A moment later, even the smile dropped from his mouth, and he turned away, pulling a book before him. He looked demoralized. Deflated. As though the sun had just slid behind the clouds with no hint of relief on the horizon.

He scrubbed his hand across his jaw, and that was when she noticed his hand was trembling. She clenched the seat of her chair, wishing this conversation had never happened. She struggled for something to say.

"We'd better finish our planning so it can be ready when Romulus gets back, right?"

She feared he might push away from the table and leave. Or perhaps he'd ignore her completely, as Maude had done whenever Evelyn had displeased her.

But he did none of those things. He gave a resigned nod and a gentle smile. "Yes, we will do precisely that."

Clyde watched Evelyn depart from the library, her notes from the afternoon's explorations tucked under her arm. He put the books on the re-shelving cart and tried to pretend that he was tough and confident and didn't feel like his heart had just been stomped flat beneath Evelyn's pointy little boot heels.

Which was hard. Evelyn White seemed perfect for him on every level. She shared his love of tinkering with things. She was smart and curious and funny—oh, and she was a stunner. He'd known she would be hard to win, but he'd thought it would involve overcoming her mistrust of men angling to get closer to her father. Turned out, that would have been an easier challenge.

Because what she'd said about the wandering life of an engineer was correct. If all went according to plan, he would win an appointment to the Corps of Engineers and would spend most of his career traveling, whether it was to build bridges and harbors in distant lands in times of war, or to help lay the nation's infrastructure of railroads, tunnels, and telecommunications in times of peace. He couldn't offer Evelyn the kind of stability she craved.

But he could build her a better terrace in her greenhouse. Even if he couldn't court Evelyn, he still wanted her as a friend.

As the next few weeks passed, it was exactly as he'd hoped. May turned into June, and as the summer turned warmer, his friendship with Evelyn and Romulus deepened. He had never made such fast friends before. Evelyn and Romulus welcomed him into their lives, and as they transformed the greenhouse, they formed a bond as tight and glorious as The Three Musketeers. They soundproofed the generator. Then they dug, lined, and installed the koi pond. Clyde showed Evelyn a more efficient way to add another terrace atop the existing one, and within a week they had a third level in the greenhouse. Romulus made a journey back to Boston to purchase another batch of exotic orchids for the new terrace, as well as a dozen fish for the pond. He brought the fish back to West Point by train, holding the glass jars filled with live koi fish on his lap the entire journey. They released the large, placid goldfish into the pond, and the three of them stood over it, gazing like proud parents as the fat, slow-moving fish explored their new home.

Clyde spent most of each day in the greenhouse, for it was a magical place, and he was wise enough to know such periods of happiness were rare. He helped Evelyn plant lemon verbena and Irish moss so that they lined the new terrace like a carpet. Romulus bartered his Japanese cloisonné cuff links for a mature holly shrub, and its height made the new terrace look as if it had been there for years. All the while, swallowtail butterflies fluttered in the greenhouse, scattering only when one of the hummingbirds came zooming into view.

And the hummingbird eggs were going to hatch soon. Last week, Clyde had propped a mirror high over the nest so they'd have a perfect view without disturbing the birds, and Romulus had noticed a slight change in the eggs' color. He was convinced they would hatch sometime on Thursday. Clyde arrived early that day, but even though he stayed through dinner, there was still no sign of the eggs hatching.

But he couldn't leave. It seemed even the hummingbirds anticipated that the hatching was imminent, for they hovered near the nest most of the day. It was odd behavior for hummingbirds, which rarely loitered anywhere for long, so Romulus was probably right.

Clyde had worked hard to make this environment perfect for those birds, but that wasn't the real reason he wanted to stay. It was because Evelyn and Romulus were both bursting with excitement, and he wanted to be here when those tiny birds, probably no larger than his thumbnail, finally emerged from their miniscule eggs.

They had plans to install the moon lighting later in the summer, but the wires had not been laid yet, so Evelyn brought a pair of lanterns from the house to cast soft illumination in the corner of the greenhouse. They ate apples and cheese and jam tarts, trying to keep their voices low in deference to the hummingbirds, but it was hard when laughter was always just beneath the surface.

Romulus said he'd changed his mind about graduate school and was contemplating a three-year expedition to Brazil to study wildlife. Laura said she would like to go along, and the two of them would spend the first years of their married life on a grand adventure.

"I'll bet the army would hire you," Evelyn said. "Father says they are hiring naturalists these days."

Romulus shuddered. "I could never spend my life in a uniform. Drab beige might be good enough for Brixton here, but he's got no sense of style. Beside, I'd have to work too hard in the army."

Clyde grinned. "You'll have to get a job eventually, won't you? You can't sail through life based on your ability to match your socks to your ties."

"Noticed that, did you?" Romulus asked with pride.

Who else wore green socks to match a green tie? Clyde figured Romulus had them custom-made, but he still wanted the answer to his question. "I'm serious. What is your plan?"

Romulus sobered. "I don't know what I want," he admitted. "In a perfect world, Laura and I would run away together. Maybe live on an island off Capri or carve out a haven in the wild Scandinavian fjords. We'd live off the fruit of the land, dance in the rain. That's the thing about Laura. Her dreams are as wild as mine, and we'll figure things out as we go." He slanted a narrow glance at Clyde. "People like you who know exactly what they want drive me crazy."

Clyde only smiled, because it was true. He'd always known what he wanted, but it wasn't until he met Romulus that he realized what a gift that sense of purpose was.

"Romulus . . ." Evelyn whispered. Her eyes were fixed on the mirror propped above the hummingbird nest. Clyde followed her gaze and saw that the female hummingbird had settled into the nest, something she hadn't done all day. She bobbed her head low into the nest, as though engrossed.

They had been anticipating this from the beginning. Clyde held his breath as the three of them moved to stand beneath the mirror, entranced by the activity inside the nest.

The mother's body blocked some of the view, but alongside her was the unmistakable sight of a wriggling, red, featherless little creature. It was alive! Clyde smiled so wide his face hurt.

"Look at them," Evelyn whispered in awe.

He didn't know how long they stood there staring like besotted fools, but this moment was perfect, and nothing in the world could tempt him away.

It wasn't until the last rays of sunlight disappeared and the lanterns burned out that it became impossible to keep observing the hummingbirds. Clyde knew it was past time for him to leave, but he didn't want to go yet. He wanted to carve every moment of this perfect day on his soul, for it was quite possibly the purest moment of happiness he'd ever known. This had been the best summer of his life.

"I hope we will have more days like this," he said, surprised at the sudden swell of emotion.

"I do, too," Evelyn said instantly, which made the lump in his throat grow even larger. What a sap he was, but at least he wasn't alone in this feeling. He felt as though he'd found two friends for a lifetime.

And if Evelyn never welcomed him as a suitor? At least she would be his friend, and perhaps that would be good enough.

Then again, he'd never been the sort to settle for *good enough*. The hope and energy racing through his veins made him believe anything was possible, and that kind of feeling made a man bold. He wouldn't give up on Evelyn without a fight.

5

The pungent scent of corn grain and fertilizer made Clyde's nose wrinkle as he stepped inside the Farm and Feed Supply store. The August heat made the scent especially strong, and his gaze wandered over the barrels of grain and other supplies stacked to the rafters of the modest store. He'd come with Romulus to buy some kind of fertilizer Romulus thought would help revive the struggling peonies in the greenhouse. They headed to the back counter of the store, where Romulus greeted the proprietor like he was an old friend.

"Hello, Jason," Romulus said with an easy smile. "I need a good nitrogen fertilizer, and a little chicken manure, please."

Clyde struggled not to laugh, for surely Romulus was the only man alive who would wear an emerald tie clip while ordering chicken manure. Clyde shrank back a few inches as the store owner opened the lid of a barrel behind the counter and scooped a sandy gray substance into a sack, but Romulus did not flinch. The store owner asked Romulus's suggestions for handling root fungus on his mulberry trees, and it was impressive how easily Romulus rattled off a stream of instructions. Clyde knew next to nothing about plants or chemistry, but Romulus loved discussing both.

And wouldn't stop. Clyde shifted from foot to foot. He'd accompanied Romulus here today to pick the man's brain about how to soften up Evelyn. No one on the planet knew Evelyn better than Romulus, and if Clyde had a prayer of winning her, he needed Romulus's help. The summer was almost over, and he didn't have much more time.

To make things worse, Clyde had never once in his life had a girlfriend, and he was completely ignorant of how to go about things. Evelyn had told him that Romulus had had dozens of girlfriends, beginning when he was thirteen and a cluster of neighborhood girls had drawn straws to see who would get to bake him a cake on his birthday. Romulus never bragged, but he'd kept company with a slew of girls from Radcliffe College while he was at Harvard. All that had stopped two years ago when Romulus had become obsessed with Laura Hartley, on whom he lavished an endless stream of gifts, poetry, and outrageously priced chocolates. Clyde suspected that most of Romulus's jaunts back to Boston this summer had been as much about visiting Laura as they had been to buy koi fish or fancy orchids.

During his entire three years at West Point, Clyde had avoided the cotillion parties because he tended to be tongue-tied and clumsy around girls. That wasn't the case with Evelyn, but he still didn't know how to overcome her instinctive reaction against men who served in the army. There was no point in mincing words, and as soon as their fertilizer was loaded into the back of the wagon, Clyde cut straight to the point. "What is the best way to help Evelyn get over her aversion to a man in uniform?" he asked bluntly.

If Romulus was surprised, it didn't show as he casually flicked the reins to prod the horse along faster. The cart bumped and jolted over the craters in the unpaved road, and Clyde clenched his fists, awaiting the answer.

"Hopeless case there," Romulus said without looking at him. "She'd rather court her backyard lemon tree than a man in the army. Sorry, Clyde."

Clyde had expected a little resistance and was prepared to keep digging. "What about if I helped persuade her father to let her go to college? Would any of that gratitude rub off on me?"

"Nope. Try again."

"Money. What if my patent goes through and I make a ton of money from it? Will she look at me then?" Evelyn didn't strike him as a girl overly impressed by money, but that was probably because she'd always had it. She'd surely want to marry a man with money, as well.

"Will you still be in the army?" Romulus asked.

"Probably."

"Then probably not." With a gentle tug on the reins, Romulus guided the cart toward the side of the road and stopped the horse. "Look," he said, not unkindly, "Evelyn had a tough time growing up. Even now, she still has to go from house to house because her father won't let her live alone. As soon as I go back to school, she'll be moving into our Aunt Bess's house. Do you know what it's like to always be a guest in someone else's home? Never have a place of your own?"

He did, actually. The last few years while his father had been alive had been spent moving in and out of increasingly seedy boardinghouses. It wasn't until he'd landed at a dormitory in West Point that he'd slept in a place where he could breathe easy.

"I'm not interested in all the reasons I can't court Evelyn. I only want to know how I *can*."

Romulus glanced at him. "You might start by not wearing that awful uniform all the time. It's a constant reminder of the sad fate that awaits you after graduation."

"You mean work? Actual work for which I will be duly compensated?"

Romulus flicked the reins and eased the cart back onto the street. "Work." He sighed. "Such an unfortunate concept. Yes, I mean work in the army, which will ship you off to Timbuktu or wherever they need engineers. Given General White's position, Evelyn has had a front-row seat for what awaits an army engineer. So that uniform is a constant reminder."

Clyde looked away. He wore his uniform all the time because he didn't have any other clothes. His roommate his plebe year had been so appalled at the grubby clothes Clyde had arrived in that they'd held a bonfire to send the threadbare clothes to their eternal rest. He loved wearing all the various pieces of his uniform because they were well-made and tailored in a way that made him look like a man of consequence.

"Evelyn also likes gifts," Romulus said. "She was overlooked as a child. People never remembered her birthday and at Christmas she only got a token gift. It doesn't have to be much. Any simple gesture means a lot to her."

They rode along in silence. Clyde had a little spare money from working odd jobs over the summers, but most of that was funneled to Smitty to help cover expenses, but he'd think of some way to get a gift or two—or ten—for Evelyn.

"Next week we'll be closing up the house before I go back to Harvard. I'm supposed to drive Evelyn and her belongings to our Aunt Bess's farmhouse, where Evelyn will stay until Christmas. I suppose I could default on my promise if you'd like to drive her instead."

"Oh, twist my arm," Clyde said with relish. He'd had plenty of time with Evelyn over the summer, but Romulus had usually been just a few yards away.

As much as he mourned the end of this magical summer, it was time to start courting Evelyn in earnest.

❖

Clyde borrowed a set of civilian clothes from Smitty. If the sight of a cadet's uniform kept Evelyn at arm's length, he wouldn't wear one. Smitty's clothes were humble, but at least they didn't have patches on the knees.

Smitty had immediately suspected the reason Clyde wanted to borrow the clothes. "Be sure to go into that fancy washroom you installed for me and give yourself a nice clean shave before you go call on that girl . . . the general's daughter."

"I'm not calling on her. I'm just helping her move to her aunt's house." Was his infatuation for Evelyn so obvious? But he was grateful for the advice, because it hadn't occurred to him to shave again.

He was also grateful Romulus had carried through on his promise to become unavailable to drive Evelyn. Today would mark the end of the best summer of his life, but perhaps it would be a turning point into something better between him and Evelyn. He'd also taken Romulus's advice about a gift. It was a modest present, but still one he couldn't afford and had bartered with a day of labor at the curio shop in exchange for the gift. He'd carefully wrapped it in tissue paper and set it in a wooden box at the back of the cart so it wouldn't get crushed.

The borrowed clothes were ill-fitting and felt strange as he mounted the steps of General White's home. Evelyn answered the door promptly after he rang the bell.

"Clyde! I almost didn't recognize you in your civvies."

He felt heat gathering in his cheeks. "I didn't want to mess up my uniform in case there is heavy lifting."

"But it's only a few satchels of clothes, nothing like the mucking about we did in the greenhouse all summer."

Mercifully, she didn't press the point. She merely held the door wide and beckoned him inside. "I can't tell you how grateful I am that you're helping me out. It's strange for Romulus to abandon me like this, but I gather a rare meadowlark has been spotted east of town, and he is keen to go see if he can find it." She slanted him a humorous gaze and lowered her voice. "Personally, I think he's merely lazy and using it as an excuse to slough off work."

"Romulus isn't lazy, but let's go." In short order, he had her bags loaded into the back of the cart. On the entire drive across town, he was too tongue-tied to broach the subject that had been burning inside him all summer. All too soon he was pulling the cart up before a white farmhouse on the outskirts of town, a covered porch stretching across the front of the first story.

"Well, here we are," Clyde said, pulling on the brake and preparing to spring off the seat, but Evelyn hadn't moved. She was staring into the distance, where a line of sycamore trees abutted a field of barley, the golden fronds swaying gently in the breeze.

"The barley is almost ready to be harvested," she said. He had never heard such despondency in her voice. "I guess summer really is over."

"I wish it weren't." In the past, Clyde had always been anxious to get back to school and the joy of delving into the world of knowledge, but this year was different. If he could, he would live in this summer forever.

But there was no help for it. He lugged her bags up the wooden steps and onto the porch, setting them down with a hollow thud. Evelyn knocked, but no one answered the door. They stood awkwardly on the porch, and he could sense her misery, waiting to be admitted to a house where she would once again be a seasonal, mildly unwelcome burden.

A middle-aged woman with the tightest bun Clyde had ever seen finally answered after Evelyn's third knock. "Oh, Evelyn," she said in a sleepy voice. "I didn't realize you'd be here so early.

I was sleeping. Well, come in. You know where Josie's old room is. I should go check on the pickles. It's canning day."

And that was the extent of the welcome Evelyn received. Clyde carried the bags down the first-floor hallway to the room where Evelyn would be staying. Their footsteps echoed on the hardwood floors in the eerily quiet house.

"Is she the only person who lives here?" he whispered, wondering if his voice carried.

"For now. Her daughters are both married, and her husband is in Texas. There is an army post there."

It seemed such a desolate place to leave someone as vibrant and curious as Evelyn. There were a few other houses several acres away, but here there was only a disinterested woman and a field of barley to keep Evelyn company. And even the barley would be gone soon.

"Come on," he urged, "let's go for a walk. I've brought you a present."

Given the way her face lit up, Romulus had been right about her love of gifts. It seemed Aunt Bess wouldn't be much of a chaperone, for she barely glanced up from her vat of pickles when Evelyn asked permission.

Evelyn clasped her hands as Clyde lifted something wrapped in tissue paper from the box in the back of the wagon. It was no larger than a baseball and barely weighed anything. She loved presents. It was embarrassing and silly to be so thrilled with this unexpected gift, but she wanted to savor this moment.

"Be careful," he said as he placed the tissue-wrapped gift in her hands. "It's breakable."

"What is it?" she asked.

"Open it and find out."

She wanted to draw this out as long as possible. Leaning

against the side of the cart, she cradled the present gently and then, with exquisite care, peeled back the first layer of tissue paper, trying to guess what could possibly be so light. She sniffed it. No smell, so it couldn't be food. Only after peeling back several layers of plain white tissue paper did she see a flash of purple inside. She caught her breath. In her palm was a hand-blown piece of purple glass, shaped into a tiny hummingbird.

"It's just a little something to help you remember this summer," Clyde mumbled. "You can hang it on a Christmas tree. Or set it on a window ledge."

"Oh, it's perfect," she said softly, a little tremble in her voice. "Thank you! I won't need any help remembering this past summer, but I will love this forever." When she held it up and let it dangle from the wire hanger, sunlight sparkled and flashed off the glass.

"Evelyn," he said in a hesitant voice, "do you think you'll ever change your mind about men who serve in the army?"

She lowered her hand, the hummingbird still cradled within. It hurt to look at the anticipation on his face, for Clyde was such a good friend, and disappointing him felt awful. She turned away, still leaning against the side of the cart but gazing out over the softly swaying barley. It would be so easy to imagine herself alongside Clyde. The idea of living with him, laughing with him, curling up with him every night—it was the most tantalizing daydream she'd ever toyed with. But it was only a fantasy. If she aligned herself with Clyde, she would end up rattling around an empty house like Aunt Bess.

She lowered her head, still cradling the hummingbird. "No, Clyde. I'm not sure what my life has in store for me, but I want more than what Aunt Bess has."

"Then reach out and grab it!" His voice startled a pair of blackbirds from a nearby tree, but it brimmed with hope and excitement. He grasped her arms and turned her to face him.

"I'm going to be an engineer someday. We live at a time when everything is changing so fast, and it's going to be the most thrilling ride in history. Ten years ago, no one had ever even heard of a lightbulb, and now we are stringing them up inside greenhouses for fun. Engineers are in a race to see how we can use electricity to revolutionize the world, and I'm going to be a part of that race. I can take you with me. We can run this race together."

How desperately she wanted to let herself be carried away by the enthusiasm coiled in his voice. "How—how would it work?" she stammered. "Where would we go?"

"Wherever the army sends me."

The tempting vision he was spinning for her collapsed. "Out West to build telegraph wires to nowhere? Why can't you be an engineer for someone else, like Mr. Edison or Mr. Westinghouse? Why must it be the army?"

"Because if I quit the army after taking an education from West Point, they'll throw me in jail." He dragged a hand through his short-cropped hair in frustration. "You want to design a perfect world and fill it with handpicked people in a controlled environment like in the greenhouse. Life doesn't work that way. Sometimes you have to grab whatever opportunities are in your path and seize them, nurture them, make them grow and thrive. I can't promise to deliver everything you want, but Evelyn! Give us a chance. We can do something amazing, don't you know that?"

It felt like her chest was splitting open. "All I know is that, aside from Romulus, you are the only real friend I've ever had, and I don't want to lose that. Can't we just go on like we have been?"

"No, we can't," he burst out in frustration. "I've never learned how to give up, and I'm not going to start now. I care for you too much to keep going on as we are. I want to court you properly. If you don't want that, tell me to go away, and I'll try to accept it."

His eyes simmered with a combination of excitement and frustration. Could she risk joining her life with his? The world he painted seemed daring and adventurous, when all she wanted was a home with her own garden, her own bedroom, and children she could raise in a safe and permanent place.

"Well?" he challenged. "If you let me court you, I'd be the happiest man on earth. Otherwise, tell me to go away, because I won't waste time fighting a losing battle."

Her jaw dropped, completely unprepared by the gauntlet he'd just tossed down. Why did he have to be so insistent? Why did he have to keep pushing like this?

Because that was who Clyde Brixton was. She'd known it since the day he'd arrived on her doorstep convinced he could solve anything. Maybe, just maybe, Clyde would be bold enough to figure out a way to make this work for both of them. She glanced at the isolated farmhouse, sad and lonely in the middle of a barley patch. "It will be hard to court a girl so far from campus."

He didn't move a muscle, but his eyes lit with anticipation. "I don't mind hard," Clyde said. "I kind of specialize in it."

And he did. Already in his life he'd overcome insurmountable hurdles simply because he refused to give up.

She took a step closer to him, leaned in, and kissed him on the mouth. Halfway into the kiss, he started grinning too much to kiss her back properly.

"Is that your answer?" he said, still smiling.

"That's my answer. I hope we both don't regret this." Letting Clyde into her heart might be a huge and painful mistake, but cutting him out would hurt even worse. He was worth the risk.

6

Autumn rolled forth in its traditional glory as the mountains around West Point were blanketed in shades of scarlet, orange, and yellow. October faded into November, and the leaves dried, curled, and dropped off to scatter across the damp earth.

Evelyn had been right in predicting Clyde would figure out a way to court her. The greenhouse needed considerable preparation for winter, and it was the perfect spot for her to meet Clyde for a few stolen hours every Saturday. Plants that couldn't survive a freeze were potted and brought indoors, while they mounded thick beds of mulch around the hardier shrubs. Evelyn drained the waterfall pipes, and Clyde dismantled the generator, moving it inside.

The koi were going to be a problem. Like many of Romulus's ideas, they began with the grandest of intentions but collapsed under impracticality. Even Clyde wasn't daring enough to try to build an electric heater for the water.

"Could we let them go, like we did the hummingbirds?"

"I suppose we'll have to," Evelyn said, and one Saturday afternoon they carted them to a park near the edge of town, setting them free in a deep lake where she hoped they would survive the winter. After releasing the fish, they sat on the park bench, and Clyde's hand sneaked out to hold her gloved hand in his palm. They kept their eyes fastened straight ahead at the lake. It was considered unseemly for a cadet to show signs of affection in public, but their clasped hands were disguised in the heavy folds of her skirts.

The contact was entirely chaste, but still thrilling. Clyde Brixton was the smartest, handsomest man she'd ever met, and the fact that he used his precious little free time to be with her was a compliment she didn't take lightly.

They spent every Saturday together. When she mentioned she'd like to learn how to distill elderberries for making her own perfume, he borrowed the equipment from the academy's chemistry lab. They made the elderberry oil together. After they distilled the oil, they didn't have the foggiest idea how to proceed with the perfume, but neither of them really cared.

"Give some to me," Clyde said. "I'll wear it like it is."

For the next two weeks, he had the wonderfully woodsy scent of elderberries on him when she met him on the steps of the West Point library.

She felt bad about Clyde spending Thanksgiving alone, but he assured her he always visited his friend Smitty Jones for the holidays.

"He's a lonely old man," Clyde said. "He's got no family, and I'm on my own up here, too. It works out well."

To her surprise, Clyde then invited her to Thanksgiving dinner at the janitor's house. If she accepted, it would mean leaving Aunt Bess alone, and that didn't seem right either. In the end, Clyde said both Evelyn and Bess were welcome at Smitty's house for the holiday meal.

Evelyn brought a big shank of ham, slowly cooked and glazed with maple syrup and honey. She brought enough so that Smitty ought to be able to eat for a week after they left. The ham was heavy as she carried it to the kitchen table, landing so hard it made the silverware rattle.

The compact kitchen was barely large enough for the four of them to squeeze around the table, but Evelyn could not help being impressed with the fully operational sink and washroom.

"I've got the fanciest house in the neighborhood." Smitty preened, nodding his head to Clyde in warm approval, almost as if Clyde was his own son. Any man would be proud of Clyde's accomplishments. Even her father would be impressed, and it took a lot to impress General Thaddeus White.

Who was returning to town soon. Although she welcomed the chance to return to her own home while her father visited, he had far more rigid standards than Aunt Bess, and the opportunity to sneak Saturday afternoon jaunts with Clyde would have to come to an end.

"My father is arriving back in West Point on Wednesday," she announced. "He will stay until the first week of January."

In Evelyn's eighteen years on the planet, she had spent a grand total of three Christmases with her father, so the month-long release was highly unusual. She looked forward to the visit with a mix of anticipation and dread. She rarely saw her father anymore, and he could be such a daunting man.

Clyde met her eyes across the small table. "So General White is coming home?" The eagerness in his voice was as though he was asking after Santa Claus.

She finished swallowing a bite of ham. "Yes, for a month."

Smitty leaned across the table to cuff Clyde on the shoulder. "That will be a good opportunity for you, won't it, laddie?"

Clyde locked eyes with her. "It would, Evelyn. It really would."

She set down her fork. The last thing she wanted was for her father to meet Clyde. She'd become very protective of Clyde, and her father could be so blunt and cutting. "My father is a terribly intimidating man. When I was seven years old, I wrote him a letter to his post in Texas. He sent it back with my spelling errors marked and asked me to resubmit."

"My spelling is perfect," Clyde said with a grin, and she had to laugh at his buoyant confidence.

"Even so, I don't think there is much point in it," she said. "My father doesn't have anything to do with the initial assignments of graduating cadets. I think that's handled entirely by the superintendent."

"It would still be good to make the connection," Clyde said. "There are thirty of us graduating with engineering degrees and only a fraction get assigned to the Corps. I'd give anything for one of those slots. That is my goal. It's *always* been my goal."

Clyde watched her with fierce anticipation on his face. In the past, she'd always been suspicious of West Point cadets who paid special attention to her in hopes of getting close to her father, but after the past months it was impossible to believe that of Clyde. Every Saturday they clicked along in perfect mutual harmony, so why should she block access to her father? She wanted Clyde's career to soar and did not doubt his motives.

"All right, you can come to dinner," she conceded. Clyde leapt into the air and reached out to give Smitty a tremendous hug. The two of them looked like they'd just struck gold.

"Thanks, Evelyn." Clyde grinned when he finally took his seat again.

Evelyn could only clasp her hands and pray this wasn't the biggest mistake in Clyde's professional career.

❖

Evelyn peered out the front window into the darkening gloom, twisting her hands and wondering when Clyde would get here for dinner with her father.

Thank goodness Romulus had agreed to come, as well.

Romulus had returned for the Christmas holidays, and she'd begged him to come tonight because he could be counted on to keep the conversation moving. She dreaded having her father and Clyde come face-to-face, but Romulus promised to bring a bottle of cherry brandy, which was her father's favorite drink in the world.

She spent the afternoon baking her father a warm vanilla soufflé, something he complained he could never get army cooks to master. But for all her planning, this evening's dinner was already turning into a disaster, and Clyde hadn't even arrived yet.

Her father had been surly ever since this afternoon, when he'd read about the election of the nation's first female mayor in Kansas. Mrs. Susanna Salter had won the election on a temperance ballot, further enraging her father.

The newspaper trembled in his hands. "Are we to be ruled by a petticoat dictatorship?" he growled. "Who is this woman to suggest a man can't have a drink of wine with his meal?"

Evelyn knew a rhetorical question when she heard one and went about setting the table without commenting, which was good, because her father was on a roll. The deeper he read into the newspaper account, the angrier he became.

"She's pregnant!" he roared. "The woman has the gall to assume a man's duties while about to give birth. And what kind of husband would permit it? Has this nation lost all sense of decorum? Of decency? This is ten kinds of disgraceful, irreverent, reckless, and irresponsible!"

"Is someone speaking about me?" Romulus asked, still standing in the front doorway, wrapped in a greatcoat and carrying the bottle of cherry brandy in his hands.

Her father crumpled the newspaper into a ball and flung it aside as he stood to greet Romulus with a condemning stare. "Close the door before we all catch galloping pneumonia. What kind of man wears a plaid scarf? And those shoes! Don't they sell boot blacking at Harvard?"

The grousing continued even after Romulus poured her father a snifter of brandy. Cherry brandy was impossible to get here, and Romulus had carried it all the way from Boston, but her father didn't even notice as he took a swig.

"I probably shouldn't be drinking," he grumbled. "Gout, you know. This cold weather is murder on the joints, and alcohol makes it worse."

Oh dear. If her father was in pain, this evening was going to be excruciating. "Why don't I make you some willow bark tea?" she suggested. "Or perhaps I can warm some towels and wrap your feet?" Anything to soothe the raging beast. Clyde was about to walk into a lion's den, and it was all her fault for inviting him when she knew how volatile her father's temper could be.

Before her father could respond, the doorbell rang. Romulus sent her a look of sympathy, then went to answer the door. He and Clyde hadn't seen each other in months, and there was a good deal of backslapping and laughter as they greeted each other.

Clyde had arrived in full dress uniform and looked outrageously handsome in the form-filling swallowtail coat with its triple rows of gilt buttons. It also appeared he'd just had a haircut, and his boots were polished to a high shine. Even her father would be unable to fault Clyde's appearance.

"Father, this is Clyde Brixton, class of 1887 at West Point."

With surprising alacrity, her father strode across the parlor, hand outstretched. "Welcome, young man! Good of you to brave the weather on such a freezing night."

"The honor is all mine, sir."

Evelyn held her breath, waiting for the inevitable negative comment from her father, but all he did was gesture Clyde into the parlor, offer him a drink, and ask about the rumor that West Point had plans to field a football team.

"I think it is still in the planning stages, sir."

"Just so long as they can beat the Naval Academy, I'll be happy."

At first, Clyde looked a little dazed at the general's warm welcome. Frankly, she was stunned, too, but she dared not intervene because it seemed the two of them were getting along well. By the time they moved to the dining room for dinner, her father and Clyde seemed like old friends. General White took his seat of honor at the head of the table, laughing as he cut into the roast beef. Platters of herbed potatoes and buttered peas circulated, and the tension in Evelyn's spine relaxed a tiny bit. Only a fraction, though, for her father's irritability could emerge quickly.

When everyone had been served, Clyde asked her father's opinion on the Washington Monument, which was scheduled to open to visitors next year. The Corps of Engineers had helped design and install the steam-driven elevator inside the monument, and Clyde and her father carried on a fascinating discussion about the challenges of housing steam-powered turbines in a tower of that size. The technical issues flew entirely over her head, but she tried not to interrupt.

"What are the possibilities of converting the elevator to run on electric power?" Clyde asked. "It seems a more elegant solution to the problem than steam."

Her father set down his fork, and Evelyn cringed. Here it came. For Clyde to question her father's judgment on such a prominent building was poking a hornet's nest. Her father finished chewing, took a long, slow drink of water, then set down the glass while Evelyn held her breath.

"Excellent question," he said. "The problem is that electrical design is evolving so fast, we dare not convert too quickly. Within the next decade, I expect electric motors to be slim enough that we won't need to redesign the shaft. But you're thinking along the right lines. The future belongs to electricity, not steam."

Evelyn was so dazed she felt light-headed, and the evening only got better. She prompted Clyde to talk about the generator he'd installed behind the greenhouse this summer, and how smoothly it powered the waterfall. They'd even had enough power remaining to string up Romulus's light bulbs.

"We need men like you in the Corps," her father said once they all retreated to the parlor to enjoy plates of warm vanilla soufflé. Clyde and her father sat in the two chairs flanking the fireplace, while she sat beside Romulus on the settee, thrilled her father had been so receptive of Clyde.

"In the next decade, the government plans on a wholesale rebuilding of Washington, D.C.," her father said. "They've got plans for a new Library of Congress, a separate building for the Department of Justice, and an annex added to the Capitol for congressmen's private offices. There are decades of work ahead, and we'll need good men on the job. Men who understand electricity."

"Yes, sir!" Clyde said, flush with excitement. "It makes sense to wire for electricity from the outset, rather than trying to add it later."

"That Beckwith motor you used in the greenhouse generator will be outdated soon, but it was probably the best choice for so small a task," her father said, continuing to outline generator and turbine development—but something about what he'd just said didn't make sense.

"Father, how did you know Clyde used a Beckwith motor in the greenhouse?"

"He just told us at dinner how he built that generator," her father said.

Evelyn closed her eyes and recalled the conversation in her

mind. She had an exceptional memory and was quite certain the word *Beckwith* had never been mentioned. "No," she said pointedly, "all he said was that he used a pre-built motor in the generator. So how did you know it was a Beckwith?"

Her father looked annoyed at her comment, but she wasn't going to let this drop. Something was going on here, and she intended to get to the bottom of it. She glared at Clyde, then back at her father.

The details were starting to click into place. Her father wanted her to quit dreaming about college, forget about her improper interest in technology, and get married to a respectable army officer. He was well aware of how much she despised the prospect of being married to an itinerant soldier, which was probably why he'd spent so much time at dinner blabbering about the possibility for Clyde to be stationed in Washington, D.C., for the great renovation of the city.

"Have the two of you been conspiring behind my back?" she demanded. "Does this account for Father's bizarre good mood?"

Clyde looked startled. "I don't know what you're talking about . . ."

"Don't look so innocent," she snapped. "How would my father know about that Beckwith motor unless you told him?"

This was simply awful. She had trusted Clyde and considered him one of her dearest friends, but how foolish she'd been to forget Clyde was the most ambitious, driven, money-hungry man she'd ever met. Had their entire friendship been launched as a means of getting close to her father? While she had been savoring the memory of last summer, while they built the waterfall and waited for the hummingbirds to hatch, had Clyde been there for an entirely different reason?

Clyde stood. "Evelyn, I've never met your father before tonight. I swear—"

"Did you exchange letters? Speak on the telephone?"

Her father used his booming general's voice. "Your manner is most unbecoming for a respectable young lady."

"It's my fault, Evelyn," Romulus said. "Clyde didn't have anything to do with this."

She stared at Romulus, aghast. "You did what?"

"I knew Clyde needed to meet your father. I've never known a man so suited to the world of engineering as Clyde, and I wanted to smooth his way. I've been keeping your father informed about Clyde all along. I think you've been a bit stubborn about holding Clyde at arm's length, and your father agreed."

She turned to look at her father, who matched her glare for glare. It appeared Clyde had been handpicked to be not only appointed to her father's Corps of Engineers, but to have his daughter's hand, as well.

Clyde beckoned to her. "Evelyn, could we go for a little walk? I think I could use some fresh air."

It was snowing outside, and the air was freezing . . . but he was right. They didn't need to have this conversation before prying eyes.

⬧

Clyde's heart pounded in a combination of panic and exhilaration. He'd never asked Romulus to intercede on his behalf with the general, but he was grateful that it had happened. He only prayed Evelyn believed it.

Everyone studying engineering at West Point knew of General White's cantankerous temper, confirming all of Evelyn's warnings. He'd been as surprised as she by the jovial man who greeted him at the front door. He couldn't blame Evelyn for being irked at the interference, but as they stepped outside, he scrambled for a way to sooth her ruffled feathers. The sleet had subsided and had been replaced by fat, puffy snowflakes gently falling in the moonlight.

"Let's go down the front walk," Evelyn said. "Otherwise, I'll suspect my father of eavesdropping."

The walkway was slippery, and she accepted his hand to guide her down the steps and the path. That was a good sign, wasn't it? They both wore gloves, hats, and scarves, but holding her hand still felt marvelously intimate.

"It's true what your father said about Washington."

"About all the construction?"

He nodded. "By the turn of the century, it will look like an entirely new city. The old brick buildings will be torn down, replaced by buildings and monuments to rival the glories of Ancient Greece. It's going to take decades to build."

And Clyde wanted to be a part of it. He didn't care where he lived, just so long as he could use his God-given talents to be a part of the technological revolution that was sweeping the nation. If General White was willing to appoint him to one of the long-term projects in Washington, what was to stop Evelyn from considering his suit? They could settle into a nice home together, and he could provide Evelyn with the stability she'd always craved.

"I see," she said pensively.

"Do you? Do you understand what this could mean for you? For us?"

She stopped walking and turned to face him. Her skin looked pale in the moonlight, so lovely she could be an alabaster cameo.

"You are putting a lot of faith in my father. He could assign you to a project in Washington, then move you to Montana the following year. Or a war could break out, and then he'd have no choice but to send you wherever the Corps is needed."

How was he going to break through the natural layer of caution she hid behind like a turtle retreating into its shell?

"Evelyn, just for a moment, can we forget that I'm destined for the army and admit that what we have between us is something extraordinary? This kind of attraction and unity is rare in the world, and we can't be careless with it. I love you. No matter how much you push me away or wish I was something other than what I am . . . I love you."

Evelyn's eyes widened at his declaration, and she turned her head away, but she didn't look displeased. "I don't know what to say," she said. "I'm a very cautious person, and I don't rush into things—"

"We've known each other for seven months, and I've been in love with you for six." He hadn't meant to reveal so much, but this evening had gone so perfectly he felt invincible. For the first time, he could truly envision a life that would suit both him and Evelyn down to the ground. There were colleges in Washington that accepted women, and if he was an officer, he could afford to send her to one of them. He could work on the construction of monumental buildings that would survive into the next millennium.

Evelyn never wanted to risk things unless she could see the plan before her in exquisite detail, so he would paint that picture for her.

"There is a neighborhood in Washington that's lined with poplar trees that shade the walkways in front of the shops and cafés. We could have an apartment there, one that overlooks the park and is a quick walk from the cafés below. I would work on the new government buildings, while you could go to college."

Evelyn looked dazzled, her eyes wide and mouth open, but she struggled to keep a thread of practicality in her tone. "My goodness, you are quite the dreamer," she said, even as she clasped his hands tighter.

"Dreams are all I've got, but they're a powerful force. They forge nations and spur revolution. If I weren't a dreamer, I'd still be off-loading crates in the Baltimore harbor." Hope gathered inside, growing stronger and more powerful.

He pulled her into his arms, and she didn't resist. Her hair was soft along the side of his face, smelling of lavender and endless years of happiness. "In the mornings we will go downstairs to the café to have coffee and sweetcakes while I read the newspaper and you prepare for class. What would you like to take your first semester? Chemistry? Philosophy?"

"Something fun and frivolous," she whispered. "Maybe the history of engineering."

He smiled and drew her tighter against him, the snow settling softly around them. Evelyn White might possibly be the only woman in the nation who thought a class on the historic principles of engineering would be fun and frivolous, but that was one of the reasons he adored her.

"Trust me," he said, barely able to speak through the grin on his face. "We can be brilliant together despite this uniform."

<hr />

Her father left in the middle of January, and Evelyn returned to Aunt Bess's home on the outskirts of town. The distance from campus made it hard for Clyde to visit, so she met him each Saturday in the library. For the most part, they simply studied side by side at one of the worktables. While Clyde studied for a demanding round of engineering tests, she sat beside him and read quietly on her own. It seemed such a charming, domestic activity, and she loved every moment of it.

Everything in her life was falling into place. Against all odds, she'd found a man whose love of technology matched her own. Even better, Clyde was willing to support her ambition to go to college. While he prepared for his final exams, she studied for entrance into college.

By April, it was time to begin preparing the greenhouse for the next season. She'd written to Romulus for advice on the best fertilizer for spring but had yet to hear back from him, which was odd. Normally he wrote to her weekly, but perhaps his final semester of classes was as demanding as Clyde's, for she had not heard anything from Romulus in almost a month.

She and Clyde always sat at the same table, on the second-story balcony overlooking the reading room below. One of Aunt Bess's requirements for allowing her such freedom was that she be in plain view the entire time she was with Clyde. Not that Clyde would dare take liberties with General White's daughter, but it was best for both their reputations to obey her aunt's instructions.

The fact that they remained in the same spot each Saturday was how the senior cadet on duty at the library was able to find her so easily. She was studying the nutrients to add before spring planting, and Clyde was looking at a page of mathematical equations that looked like ancient hieroglyphics, when the young officer approached and leaned over to whisper quietly to her.

"Miss White? You are needed downstairs. A woman is here to see you."

What an odd comment. "A woman? My Aunt Bess?"

The young officer cleared his throat. "She doesn't look like anyone's aunt, ma'am. It would be best if you came downstairs to handle the situation immediately."

She and Clyde exchanged confused glances, but both pushed away from the table and followed the officer down the winding staircase.

Oh my . . . she could understand the officer's embarrassment. The woman loitering in the lobby wore face paint and a bodice cut so low she was in danger of exposing herself.

"Can I help you?" Evelyn asked the woman, whose shocking red hair was a shade that surely could not be found anywhere in nature.

"Yes," the woman said. "I'm Nellie Sweetwater. I work in a dance hall in Boston, and Romulus and I used to be . . . well, special friends, I suppose you could call it. That is, we were until that Laura woman got her hands on him. Now she's all he can think about."

Evelyn's mouth went dry. Whatever this woman's association with her cousin, this didn't seem good. "And?"

"Romulus is in trouble," Nellie said. "Something really bad has happened, but he won't tell me what. No one can get him to come out of his room, and the other men in the dormitory say he is crying all the time."

Evelyn was so aghast she couldn't even draw a breath, but Clyde took over.

"Crying?" he pressed. "That doesn't sound like Romulus. He's always in good spirits."

"Not anymore," Nellie said. "He stays in his room and drinks until he's sloppy drunk, then he starts blubbering like a baby. I don't know what to do for him, so that's why I thought I'd come to you. Someone needs to do something before he drinks himself to death."

Evelyn's fear ratcheted higher with every word Nellie spoke. It sounded so uncharacteristic of Romulus, but the fact that she hadn't received any letters from him in weeks gave credence to Nellie's story. Something was deeply wrong.

"What about Laura?" Clyde pressed. "Does she understand what's going on?"

Nellie's painted mouth pursed as though sucking a lemon. She leaned in to whisper. "I think maybe she's thrown him over. No one has seen her for weeks, and Romulus is in a bad way. He's quit going to classes, and one of the men in the dorm said he lit a fire in his trash can. A bunch of fellows had to burst inside to put it out before it spread."

"I've got to get to Boston," Evelyn said.

"I'll come with you," Clyde responded.

"Can you?" She held her breath. She had no idea what she

would be confronted with in Boston, and the prospect of deal-ing with this on her own was terrifying, but Clyde wasn't a free man. "Are you sure you'll be able to—"

"I'm coming," he insisted. "So long as I'm back by Monday morning, it will be fine."

The resolve on his face reassured her. Somehow, she knew she could conquer anything so long as she had Clyde Brixton by her side.

7

Clyde held Evelyn's hand the entire four-hour train ride to Boston. She was so tightly wound her spine never touched the back of the seat. He ached to comfort her, but until they understood what was wrong with Romulus, there was nothing meaningful he could say.

The dance hall girl sat on the bench opposite them but had little additional insight to share. All Nellie could tell them was that Romulus had been his normal, easygoing self until about a month ago, when he quit attending class and seemed determined to live the life of a drunkard.

They reached the Harvard campus late on Saturday afternoon, and Nellie guided them to Romulus's dormitory. She had a performance that evening and could not stay, so Clyde and Evelyn approached the front of the dormitory on their own. A handful of students lounged on the steps of Stoughton Hall, swigging from a bottle passed around the group. When Clyde inquired about Romulus, their mood sobered. The students confirmed everything Nellie had said. Romulus was drunk and despondent, and no one had been able to help him.

"We are friends of his from home," Clyde told them. "We'd like to go up and see him."

It was an all-male dormitory, and when one of the young men suggested Evelyn would need to wait outside, she lifted her chin a bit but kept her voice calm. "I can see you are men of good character," she said. "Men who would never make low assumptions when a woman comes to her cousin's aid. I'm so grateful we share the same values."

There was no more talk of barring Evelyn after that. One of the young men sprang to his feet and walked them up to Romulus's room on the third floor. Their footsteps echoed down the dimly lit hallway, and Clyde braced himself for what he might find on the opposite side of the plain wooden door.

He knocked, but there was no response. He wiggled the knob, but it was locked. He tried knocking again, this time hard enough to make his knuckles ache. "Romulus? It's Clyde and Evelyn. We know you're in there."

This time they heard some shuffling from behind the door, but it took several more knocks before a muffled voice replied. "Go away. I'm fine."

The only thing Clyde knew for certain was that Romulus was *not* fine. He glanced at Evelyn, whose face was pale with fear. "Let me borrow a hair pin," he whispered.

He ended up destroying three of Evelyn's hair pins, unfolding and twisting them to pick the rudimentary lock on Romulus's door. "We're coming in," he warned one final time before opening the door.

Romulus was sitting on the floor, legs stretched before him, leaning against an unmade bed, glowering at them from bleary eyes. He held a half-empty bottle of something in one hand, and he raised it toward them. "Can I offer you a drink?" he asked.

Clyde said nothing as he guided Evelyn inside the room and closed the door. It was a tight fit for the three of them, feeling even smaller since the desk chair was overturned and the wardrobe doors hanging open. Evelyn crossed the small space to close the wardrobe and set the chair upright. The only other pieces of furniture in the room were the bed and a desk beneath a window overlooking a leafy green.

"Who told you?" Romulus said.

"A girl called Nellie," Evelyn answered as she lowered herself onto the mattress next to where Romulus leaned against the bed. "She came all the way to West Point to tell us you were in trouble, but she didn't know anything else. Romulus, what's going on?"

Romulus made no attempt to reply, merely took a swig from the bottle.

"Nellie said you're not going to classes," she continued. "Is that true?"

"True."

"Why?"

Romulus let out a tremendous sigh, then rose on unsteady feet. Clyde darted to the door, leaning against it and barring any attempt Romulus might make to bolt from the room. It didn't matter. All Romulus did was heft himself up onto the mattress, landing with an ungainly bounce. With the saddest eyes in the world, he stared across the room to the maple tree outside the window.

"It doesn't really matter," he said. "Look . . . I appreciate that you came all this way, but there was no need. There's nothing you can do to help, and I'll figure this out on my own."

Clyde kept a close eye on Evelyn, who looked torn between weeping and lashing out in anger. The bond between Evelyn and Romulus went back to childhood. As much as it hurt for him to see Romulus like this, it must be devastating for Evelyn. He wanted to lunge across the room and shake some sense into a man who appeared to be throwing his life away.

He forced his voice to remain calm. "You're not alone," he said. "Tell us what we can do to help, and we'll do it. You know we will. Whatever it takes."

Romulus dragged both hands through his hair, drawing a shaky breath. "Thanks, but there is nothing you can do. It's about Laura. She told me it's over, and . . ." His voice trailed off so that it could barely be heard. "And I've managed to pretty much destroy everything."

Romulus had always been prone to exaggeration and over-blown language, but Clyde couldn't doubt the hollow despair in each of Romulus's words.

"Rom, there'll be other girls . . ."

"Maybe, but not for me. Laura was pretty clear about my many failings, and the worst of it is, everything she said about me is right."

Evelyn bristled. "What bad things did she say about you?"

"That I'm scatterbrained and disorganized. That I've changed my course of study five times and can't commit to anything. That I know a little of everything but not a lot of anything—"

"Doesn't she get it? That's what makes you so interesting!" Evelyn said.

Romulus snorted. "That's what makes me unemployable and a total failure, and she's right. She says I'll never be able to hold down a job. That I couldn't be depended on to support a wife and children, and I wouldn't be a good husband."

"Nonsense!" Evelyn said. "Any girl would be lucky to have you. You're smart and funny, and I shouldn't say this because your head is already too big, but you are probably the handsom-est man in all of Boston. Can't she see that you're brilliant?"

Romulus usually preened in the face of Evelyn's adoration, but he just hung his head and stared at nothing. "Evelyn, I'm really not," he said softly. "I can put on a good show, but there's not a lot underneath it all. I guess she finally figured that out. And I love Laura so much. It wasn't just that she is smart and pretty, it's that she knows how to dream. We had such plans to see the world, to build a house with our own two hands, to write a symphony together. But as graduation got closer, she started changing. She's gotten very practical all of a sudden, and she thinks I won't be able to make it in the real world." His voice became tense and ragged, as though the words were torn from his throat in a sudden rush. "She's in my blood and bones and every dream about the future I've ever had. No woman will ever be able to surpass what I've felt for her. So I guess she's pretty much ruined me for any other woman."

A fat tear rolled down his face. With a flick of his palms, Romulus scrubbed his eyes and drew a heavy breath. "I quit going to class," he admitted. "At first it was because I didn't care, but now it's too late to repair the damage. I'm going to fail trigonometry, so I won't even be able to graduate."

Over the next few minutes, Romulus outlined his situation. Harvard's attendance policy was lax, but three weeks of missing classes could not be overlooked. A disciplinary hearing had been called, which he did not bother to attend. He gestured to a stack of papers heaped on his desk.

"Those are the disciplinary reports," Romulus said. "A copy of everything was sent to the people organizing the expedition to Brazil, and they've cut ties with me, too. They said I lack the character necessary for an expedition of that caliber. Everything I've ever worked for is over. Ruined. It's all my own fault, which makes it doubly humiliating."

Clyde frowned. He didn't know much about the culture at Harvard, but West Point cadets were trained never to accept defeat. He skimmed the disciplinary report and Romulus's academic scores to date, including a zero on a trigonometry test he'd missed. He closed his eyes and ran the mental calculations. It would be hard to overcome a zero on a test, but it was still mathematically possible for Romulus to pass if he could sober up, hit the books, and fight for something better than seeing the bottom of a whiskey bottle. It was going to be a close call, but there was valor in fighting all the way to the end.

"Look, you did something really stupid," Clyde said. "You've dug yourself into a hole, but now it's time to start climbing out, and guzzling whiskey won't help. The only way to find your dignity again is to stand up, admit your mistakes, and fight for what you've always wanted. For what you *still* want."

"The life I wanted is closed to me," Romulus said.

"Then make a new one," Evelyn replied. "Don't you think I know about having doors slammed in my face? I won't let you give up your future over one mistake."

Clyde set down the papers, flipped the desk chair around, and sat directly in front of Romulus, who was still slumped on the mattress, staring at the ground.

"I'm willing to tutor you," he said. "You can't give up yet. I've been trained to go down fighting. We've got four days until your final exam in trigonometry—and a fighting chance at getting there. We may not make it across the finish line. You might spend the next four days working and striving, and it still won't be good enough . . . but we can't give up until it's over. If we die on this field, we die as fighters, not quitters."

For the first time since they'd entered this room almost an hour ago, a spark of hope lit Romulus's reddened eyes.

Perspiration beaded up on Clyde's palms. He had planned to take the train back to West Point tomorrow afternoon. If he missed class on Monday, he'd be slammed with a whole new set of demerits. He'd worked hard all year to remove some of his demerits, and he was in good shape, having cleared away almost sixty demerits. But graduation was less than a month away, and it was impossible to know how many demerits this would cost him.

He swallowed hard as the full understanding of everything he risked by staying to tutor Romulus washed over him. A degree from the nation's finest engineering program and the automatic commission as an army officer hung in the balance. All his life, he'd focused, with steely-eyed determination, on his plan to achieve, strive, and conquer. He'd earned his first patent when he was only seventeen. He had the audacity to get into West Point by knocking on the vice-president's front door and asking for a recommendation. He'd never looked back, never let another person divert him from the goal of a West Point diploma.

But that was before he'd learned the meaning of friendship. Was there any price he would not pay for the gift of a genuine friendship? There was no greater love than to lay down one's life for one's friends. He'd never fully understood the meaning of that passage until this very moment.

Romulus was his friend, and Clyde would do what was necessary to lift him back onto the right path.

❖

As Clyde started tutoring Romulus, there was little for Evelyn to do other than tidy the room, but soon enough it became a genuine team effort. She ran to the grocer's shop a block from campus for some sandwiches and a jug of tea, as it appeared Romulus had not had a decent meal in weeks. While Clyde went over the principles of how to calculate distance equations, she wrote out study questions from a trigonometry book. It seemed as soon as she had them copied, Clyde was sliding them before Romulus, who attacked them with growing confidence.

It was a little embarrassing when she ventured outside the dormitory room. It was impossible to blend in when she was the sole woman in a building of two hundred men, but after some initial awkwardness, everyone was quite decent to her. Romulus was a popular man on campus, and his fellow students did their best to help however possible. They brought hot coffee and extra blankets and pillows. One of them even dragged in a pallet, for Evelyn, Clyde, and Romulus would be sharing this tiny space for the next few days.

They worked well into the night. The moon rose, and they lit a lantern, and eventually there was nothing else for Evelyn to do but curl up on the corner of the rumpled bed and listen to Clyde's patient voice coaxing Romulus through the problems. The window was open, and she could hear shouts of male laughter and carousing from the courtyard below.

A sense of well-being flooded her as she realized that this was her first night of college. She wasn't enrolled, and her time here would amount to no more than a few days, but for this snippet of time, she shared in the comradery and pursuit of knowledge here on campus.

Romulus insisted she take his bed, while he and Clyde stretched out on the pallet, but she was still stiff and cramped by morning, and she knew she needed to get another telegram to Aunt Bess. She'd sent a message to her aunt yesterday, alerting her of an urgent need to see Romulus but assuring her aunt she would return soon. That wouldn't be the case now, and she composed a carefully worded telegram to explain that circumstances would prohibit her return until Wednesday evening.

Romulus was still asleep, and she tried to be silent as she straightened her blouse and smoothed it back into her skirt. Clyde was awake, swigging from a carafe of cold coffee. She couldn't help but smile at the way he didn't even wince as he swallowed what surely must be a truly awful mouthful of coffee. He'd probably endured far worse during his training at West Point, but she loved the way he never complained. He simply rolled up his sleeves and tackled the chore at hand with good humor.

She'd bring him back a nice, steaming pot of coffee after she sent Aunt Bess the telegram. She was about to leave the room when a terrible thought struck. Romulus was heading into his final weeks of college, but so was Clyde. She leaned in, whispering so as not to awaken Romulus.

"Don't you have class on Monday?"

Clyde glanced away as he set down the flask of cold coffee. "Don't worry about it."

"Won't you get penalized? Another round of demerits?"

"Maybe, but I can work them off, you know I can."

She also knew it was hard to work off demerits once they'd been accumulated, but Clyde was an intelligent man and wouldn't be careless with his entire academic career. "Do you want me to send a telegram on your behalf to campus? Alert them ahead of time?"

Clyde flashed her a quick smile. "It will be easier to apologize afterward, rather than let them know of an infraction in progress. I'll be fine."

"If you're sure, then . . ."

She let the sentence dangle, but all he did was smile. Romulus was starting to groan and awaken, and the sooner she could be out of the room, the faster they could get some coffee into him and get back to work.

She sent the telegram to Aunt Bess from the local pharmacy. On her way back to Stoughton Hall, she stopped for coffee and a copy of the *Harvard Crimson*, the student-run newspaper that was produced every day. There wasn't much for her to do while Clyde tutored Romulus, but over the coming days, she eagerly read each issue of the *Crimson*. She almost felt as if she was part of the college as she read gossip about various professors, the results of intramural athletic teams, and even complaints about food served in the meal hall.

A few times, Romulus lost hope. "I'll never get there," he muttered on Tuesday morning after Clyde had graded a sampling of trigonometry equations. He'd scored an eighty-one percent on the test and was going to need at least a ninety-seven percent to pass the class.

"Nonsense," Clyde said. "You just need a little more exposure to my brilliant tutoring."

And as she watched Clyde patiently tutor her cousin, Evelyn understood the meaning of real love. Love wasn't the dizzying rush she felt when she saw Clyde standing proud and handsome in his dress uniform. It wasn't the thrill she felt when he kissed her, or the way he could make her explode in laughter at his jokes.

Real love was far more humble. It was hours spent together, drinking lukewarm coffee, tutoring a friend, and laughing over the silly comics in the daily newspaper. It was sharing aspirations for the future while working the mundane, workaday tasks required to make those dreams come true.

And she was grateful she'd had the wisdom to realize it before Clyde graduated and was lost to her forever. She had been selfish and narrow-minded when she'd insisted she would only settle for a man who could provide her with the comforts of a settled home. Perhaps it would be years before Clyde could do that for her, but she was no delicate flower powerless to adapt and bend. Clyde was a man whose honor and ambition was going to serve them both well, and if he asked her to marry him, she was going to do so, joyously.

<hr />

Clyde had known there would be consequences for what he'd done. He just hadn't expected them to arrive the moment he stepped off the train in West Point.

He and Evelyn had caught the last train back to West Point on Wednesday evening. Clyde was so tired and bleary-eyed from four straight days of staring at trigonometry equations that he'd let Evelyn read the train schedule to get them both home. Romulus would take the final exam on Thursday at noon. Maybe he would pass, maybe not, but either way, Romulus had a fighting chance of graduating on time.

On the ride home, Clyde held Evelyn's hand as she said a prayer for Romulus to face the next day's test with honor and courage. Her voice was soft but confident as she spoke the prayer, and he was once again awed by her combination of gifts. Evelyn was the embodiment of faith and gentle compassion, but it hid a core of steel. She never raised her voice or lost her poise, she simply accomplished the task, whether it was building a habitat suitable for hummingbirds or helping prop up Romulus to face a difficult class.

He squeezed her hand harder and added a silent prayer for himself. Missing three days of classes was going to result in a steep penalty, but he had earned a lot of goodwill on campus over the past academic year. He hadn't earned a single demerit and had worked off scores more. It was almost a month before graduation, and he would do whatever was necessary to repair the damage this trip would cost him.

He and Evelyn both jostled forward as the brakes began slowing the train as they approached the station. Faces of people awaiting the train's arrival slid past the window as they drew near. Both he and Evelyn were jerked back into their seats at the final jarring stop. Steam hissed as gears clanged and the pressure valves released.

He stood, muscles stiff after the long train ride. "Shall we?" he asked. As difficult as these past few days had been, they were a memory he'd never forget. It was the hardest things in life he was most proud of having accomplished, and he was proud of how he'd stood by Romulus.

"There's my Aunt Bess," Evelyn said as she peered out the window.

His mouth went dry as he saw the stern-faced men standing beside her. One was the commandant of cadets, the officer responsible for student conduct at West Point. And Clyde had just absconded with General White's daughter for a four-day jaunt to Boston.

The railway car was crowded as passengers stood to dis-embark, and Clyde was momentarily tempted to stay on the train and simply keep traveling to the next town.

But there was no escape, and he knew it. He stood, making way for Evelyn to step into the aisle ahead of him.

"This doesn't look good," Evelyn said as they inched their way toward the exit door, but he was too nervous to respond. His heart thumped and he could barely breathe, but he tugged his uniform straight and held his head high. This was going to be bad, but he'd face it with dignity.

The stench of coal steam hung in the air as he stepped onto the platform. The commandant stepped forward. Two members of the military police were with him.

"Cadet Brixton, you are charged with being absent without leave and conduct unbecoming a cadet. It will be categorically impossible to expunge this conduct prior to graduation. You will be escorted to campus, where you will be restricted to your room and be held pending the disciplinary hearing."

It felt like he'd just been kicked in the gut, but he couldn't let it show. Evelyn was watching. He schooled his face into a calm mask and sent her a quick, reassuring gaze, the best he could muster. Her face was pale, hands twisting as she watched the two military police step into position on either side of him. At least he was spared the humiliation of handcuffs.

"It's going to be all right, Evelyn."

But it wasn't. The commandant of cadets had just told him he was going to be expelled. The only thing left to be deter-mined was what additional penalties, or even imprisonment, he would face.

As much as he loved Evelyn, that dream was probably over, and all he could see on the ride back to campus was the image of his mother's hands, cracked and careworn from years of laundry. There would be no quick end to his mother's problem, or for Evelyn either. He needed to find a way to salvage this, but he didn't have the first idea of how to do it.

⟨◈⟩

Evelyn watched in disbelief as Clyde marched between the two officers to an awaiting carriage, torn between fear and outrage. How could Clyde have misled her so? She'd known he had a few demerits for the pranks he'd racked up in his early years, but she'd never imagined he was this close to expulsion.

She whirled on her aunt. "Did you do this?" she demanded.

"*He* did this," Bess replied. "I don't know what insane notion prompted you to go traipsing off to Romulus, but Clyde Brixton has responsibilities here and had no business accompanying you."

Evelyn closed her eyes. How foolish she had been to accept his careless assurances that all would be well. Clyde had always been reckless. She should have known he might minimize the potential for trouble.

Her aunt's hand encircled her elbow and propelled her toward the waiting wagon, but there was a telegraph window there in the train station, and Evelyn intended to contact her father immediately.

"I need to post a telegram," she told Bess, pulling her arm away.

"I think you've had quite enough fun and excitement for now. You are going nowhere but home."

She knew Aunt Bess referred to the white clapboard farmhouse on the outskirts of town, but Evelyn was not going to cooperate.

"I have no home," she said quietly, but in a voice vibrating with conviction. "I have lived in houses and on trundle beds and in guest bedrooms, but the closest I've ever come to a real home is wherever Romulus White is. And after this past year, I consider Clyde Brixton in the same category. I won't abandon either of them in their hour of need, and right now I intend to contact my father for help. I hope you will wait for me to post that telegram, but if not, I am nineteen years old and of age to declare my own independence. Please don't require me to do so."

Aunt Bess backed down.

Evelyn was still shaking with anxiety as she waited in line to post the telegram to her father. She wasn't quite sure what to say—the situation was far too complex to boil down to a few lines in a telegram—so she would simply have to plead for him to return home as soon as possible. He was currently posted in New York City, only a few hours away by train. Clyde was in over his head, and if she had to beg and plead with her father to intervene, she would not let pride stand in her way.

❖

To her amazement, her father arrived at Aunt Bess's house early the next morning. Although he usually arrived in town with the acclamation reserved for conquering generals returning to Rome, he pulled up to the farmhouse in a rented carriage and wearing civilian clothes. Instead of his typically fierce expression, his eyes were clouded with concern.

"What's going on?" he asked the moment she opened the door. "Are you all right?"

The concern on his face caught her by surprise. She was usually so intimidated by her father that his concern undercut every one of her defenses, and her eyes flooded with tears. She lifted her chin to prevent them from spilling down her cheeks.

"Clyde is in trouble," she whispered.

Her father tugged her outside and onto the wooden porch, closing the door on Aunt Bess's inquiring face.

"Tell me," he said once they were both seated on the bench.

She told him everything, including what Romulus had done to ruin his academic career. There was no way for her father to understand why Clyde had been so desperate to help Romulus without that insight.

"Is there anything you can do?" she asked. "You know Clyde will be a brilliant engineer. Surely the army won't throw him away over this."

Her father let her ramble without interrupting, but when he did speak, there was rare sympathy in his eyes. "I'm sorry, but the rules about demerits are inflexible. They are designed so no one gets special privileges or escapes responsibility for his actions."

"But what about loyalty? Can't the army understand basic loyalty?"

"Yes. We have loyalty to the country, to our fellow soldiers, and to the rules that maintain order in the army. How can we depend on an officer who breaks those rules on an impulse? And not just once—Clyde has flouted army discipline time and again."

"But he did it for a good reason. Please, Father . . . can't you intervene? Can't you do something?"

"The army's rules may seem overly rigid in times of peace, but we train our officers so their adherence to discipline comes automatically, not merely when convenient. Once a war breaks out, it is too late to start instilling that discipline. It's why we begin training our officers in those rules on the first day they arrive at West Point. Can I intervene for a man who, with all knowledge and foresight, impulsively breaks rules despite repeated warnings?"

"I don't know!"

Her father's smile was patient. "But I do. Clyde Brixton has the makings of a brilliant engineer. He is a true and loyal friend, but he does not have the makings of an army officer. I stand by his expulsion."

Her dream of living in Washington as Clyde participated

in the grand transformation of the city, her dream of going to college . . . all of it was slipping away. Clyde's dreams were ruined, too.

"What will happen to him?"

"He will have a choice. Two years in jail or two years as an enlisted soldier in the army. The country has invested a great deal into this young man's education and deserves to be repaid."

"And if he enlists . . . what happens to him?"

"It would be a waste to send a man like that to dig ditches, but make no mistake, he will be an enlisted private in the army and will perform whatever task he is assigned. Go wherever posted. His freedom to control his destiny is gone."

She knew what that felt like. She had been helpless her entire life, drifting from one household to the next, always rootless, always alone. Only when she was with Romulus or Clyde did she have a sense of belonging.

And that sense of belonging with Clyde had happened even though they had no home together. They had only each other and their wild, ambitious dreams.

What if she could be as bold and daring as Clyde? What if she stepped out from the shelter of her father's protection and created a new life for herself, instead of passively sitting here waiting for it to happen?

The trembling began in her hands but soon consumed her entire body, for the thoughts whirling in her mind were daring and frightening. She'd been passive her entire life. Clyde had shown that it was possible to step out into the world and act.

Her gaze trailed across the fields. Did she have the courage to implement such a plan? And if she did, would Clyde even allow it? She smiled a little. Even if he didn't, she was sick to death of wandering from house to house, doing nothing meaningful with her days and waiting for something to happen. It was time. She was going to *make* something happen.

"Father, I'd like to ask a favor," she began.

She suspected he would pitch a fit, and he did. For once, Evelyn was grateful for the isolation of Aunt Bess's house in the middle of a barley field, for otherwise the neighbors would have overheard hours of blustering about inappropriate females, reckless actions, and the likelihood of Evelyn falling flat on her face.

Everything her father said was true. The possibility of failure was high. If she botched this, within a few months she might well be crawling back to West Point to fall on his mercy, but at least she would have tried.

At the end of the evening, he had agreed to her plan, and for the first time in her life, she saw genuine respect in her father's eyes.

8

Clyde had never realized how forced inactivity could weigh on a man. For the past five days, he'd been confined to his room with no visitors or responsibilities, nothing to do but lie on his bed, stare at the ceiling, and fear for his future. It was draining and demoralizing. The formal disciplinary hearing would be held this afternoon in the commandant's chambers, but he already knew what to expect. He was going to be expelled from college, demoted to the rank of private, and agree to serve two years as an enlisted soldier wherever the army chose to send him.

And he'd probably never see Evelyn White again. He'd managed to smuggle a message to her aunt's house the day after arriving back on campus, but that was four days ago and still no response. Could he blame her? All spring, he'd been spinning daydreams about what their life in Washington, D.C., would be like. She could go to college while he worked on the grand renovation of the city. She would be an officer's wife. They would dine in the city's famous cafés, take long walks in the parks, and curl up before the fireplace in a home of their very own. Those dreams were all in ashes now.

Perhaps a clean break was best, but it was hard.

Two years as an enlisted soldier wasn't so bad. He'd do his best to keep abreast of the developments in electricity, and the instant he was released from service, he'd race to Menlo Park and beg a job from Thomas Edison. If he could become successful, a man whose skills were sought after by the world's best engineers, maybe Evelyn would look at him again. He couldn't give up on her. Not yet.

The worst thing about being confined to quarters was that he still heard the normal activities of campus. The trumpet blast of reveille each morning, the shuffling footsteps of cadets scrambling to inspection, the bugle calls for meals, the laughter of his classmates at the end of the day.

Clyde was isolated from all of it. He couldn't even open the door to exchange a quick greeting. The only person he saw was Smitty, who brought him three meals a day and emptied the trash can. Despite all the trouble he'd gotten into over the years, he had loved being a West Point cadet. The comradery and the rigor, the chance to work alongside hundreds of other smart, driven men. It was going to hurt to be severed from it.

A tap broke the silence, and Clyde rolled from the bed, prepared to help Smitty in with his lunch tray. Smitty had been like a father to him since his first year on campus, and these few minutes of accepting food ought to have been a comfort, but it was difficult to see the disappointment in the old janitor's eyes each day.

To his surprise, Smitty had a stack of clothing over his arm. "You're to put on your full uniform for the hearing today," he said as he hung the formal wool uniform from the hook on the door. "After the hearing, you'll be changing into these," Smitty said, his voice radiating sympathy as he set a stack of light brown clothing on the bed. It was the uniform of a private. "I'm sorry, laddie."

Clyde tried to smile. "It's okay. I don't regret anything. I'd do it again."

He mostly believed it. Romulus had been a great friend, and even if they never crossed paths again, last summer in the greenhouse had been an experience he'd treasure for the rest of his life. He'd never known anyone like Romulus, a brilliant man who hid a staggering array of interests beneath a glittering, flamboyant exterior. And Evelyn . . . so cautious and contained. She and Romulus were complete opposites, yet they brought out the best in each other. And for a few glorious months, he'd been allowed into that friendship. It had been a privilege he would never forget.

He changed into his dress uniform. The swallowtail dress coat, tailored to military precision and heavy in his hands, was the finest article of clothing he'd worn in his life. He tried not to think that this was the last time he'd ever wear it. Standing before the small mirror on the back of the door, he adjusted the stiff collar so it was in perfect alignment beneath his chin. The silk braids and rows of brass buttons across the front of the coat gave him a look of bearing and distinction. Tugging on his white gloves, he stared at the mirror, trying to memorize this sight, for in a few hours he'd never see it again.

Even in hindsight, he would go to Romulus's aid again. He wished the price wasn't so steep, but he couldn't regret that show of loyalty and friendship. For the next two years, while he was toiling at some army outpost, he would have the knowledge that he was a loyal friend until the end.

✦

Evelyn had never been inside a third-class railway car before today, but she was pleased as she wriggled into an open spot on the bench between a postman and a woman with a caged chicken on her lap. It would take five hours to get back to West Point, but her mission in Boston had been successful.

Now she just had to get back in time to intercept Clyde before he was sent off to his posting. It was going to be a close call. Her errands in Boston had taken considerably longer than she'd anticipated, and Clyde was at his disciplinary hearing at this very moment. Would he still be in town by the time she arrived? Or would she have to hop back on a train and chase him to Fort Slocum?

It was hard to guess what Clyde would think of her actions. He might be proud of her, but he was just as likely to be embarrassed and humiliated. Even if he shuddered and wanted nothing to do with her plan, it was done, and there was no going back. She would carry it through—hopefully with Clyde, but she was prepared to go forward on her own if necessary.

She had a job! It had taken her two days to find someone willing to hire a girl with no work experience and soft, smooth hands unaccustomed to manual labor, but she was going to start work at McKendry's Dry Goods Store in the north end of Boston near the marketplace. It wouldn't require much skill, merely weighing out sacks of flour and oats and making proper change for customers. Apparently Mr. McKendry had difficulty with clerks who struggled to calculate the right cost for customers, but Evelyn was able to demonstrate her mathematical abilities with ease.

Her wages wouldn't quite cover the cost of an apartment, but Evelyn had anticipated the problem and brought a few pieces of her mother's jewelry to help fund her first few months alone in Boston. She had no memories of her mother but liked to imagine she would be proud to see her ivory brooch and gold bracelet being used to help make her daughter's dreams come true.

The money from pawning the jewelry was used to lease a one-room apartment over a delicatessen near the Boston harbor. She had some left to buy a little bit of furniture and the train tickets to get back and forth to West Point. Her father had steadfastly refused to help fund even a dime of her "harebrained scheme," but he'd given her something far more valuable.

He'd told her where Clyde's first military assignment was to be. She also suspected he may have used some of his influence to ensure Clyde would be sent somewhere close and where his engineering skills would be put to good use.

The army was upgrading their telegraph and telephone communications, using underground conduits to ensure more reliable transmission. Boston was the testing ground, and the army needed skilled men to dig, lay, and install those systems. Clyde would not be designing the systems, but her father had gruffly assured her it would be good to have a man of his talent in the field.

That meant he would live in Boston.

And so would she. The shabby, one-room apartment had only a single window with a view of the neighboring building's brick wall. It was a far cry from the idealized house of her dreams. There was no spacious lawn of soft grass for her children to play on, no huge oak tree from which to hang a swing, no plot of land for a rose garden.

But there was room enough for a kitchen table and a bed big enough for two. She just hoped she could get to Clyde in time to make it all happen.

<hr />

It was as he'd suspected. After standing at attention while the list of his accumulated demerits was read out before the board, Clyde was informed that he was expelled from the academy and ordered to serve two years as an enlisted soldier.

He'd expected it, but it still hurt to stand at attention and hear the words said while maintaining an expressionless stare. He wanted to run away, break something, rip the list of his demerits from the commandant's hands and tear it to shreds. Instead he stood and accepted that his life had just taken a huge downturn.

To make it worse, Evelyn's father had been there for all of it. General White's face was stony as he watched the proceedings with a detached air. The only flicker of acknowledgment came at the very end, as Clyde left the superintendent's office.

"Enjoy digging ditches," General White whispered in his ear.

There was only one appropriate answer. "Thank you, sir. I will."

His first assignment was for two months at Fort Slocum, which was on an island off the coast of New York. He'd be trained in the basics of military procedures. It seemed pointless, as Clyde had close to four years of military training, but then again, he'd been trained as an officer, not an enlisted soldier.

Back in his dorm room, he avoided the mirror as he peeled off the formal dress uniform for the final time. No matter where his life took him, it was hard to imagine he'd ever wear a coat of which he was so proud. He hung it carefully in the wardrobe before pulling on the light brown fatigue uniform. It was going to be humiliating to walk out the door in this uniform, but maybe it wouldn't be such a bad thing. All his friends would see what happened to a man who squandered a gift, and if it helped them toe the line, that would be all to the good.

There was a knock on the door, and one of his former roommates tipped his head in. "There's a lady downstairs to see you," Jake said.

"A lady?"

"General White's daughter. She wants to see you."

Clyde closed his eyes. He couldn't bear to see Evelyn right now. This was probably the most difficult day of his life, but he'd been plowing through it with his head held high, spirits more or less steady. Even the taunt from General White had glanced off his hide, but Evelyn?

No, he didn't have the strength to see her now and maintain an even keel. Not while wearing these clothes.

"Tell her I'll write," he said.

Jake nodded and left to carry the message downstairs.

Clyde felt horrible, but writing was the most he could promise. The image of Evelyn's desperate face as he was led away at the train station would haunt him for years. Once he got to Fort Slocum he'd have the time to draft a letter that put the best possible spin on things. Of all the people he'd disappointed, Evelyn was at the top of the list.

Maybe someday he'd be able to dig himself out of the hole he'd gotten himself into. He'd earn riches from his patents, acclaim from engineers and architects. Perhaps she would look at him again with that same sort of awed pride as when he'd hooked up the generator in her greenhouse. Or when she'd kissed him on the snowy winter evening the night he'd met her father. Those were the memories he wanted of Evelyn, not her look of pity and disillusionment as he set off to Fort Slocum.

Jake burst back into the room. "She won't leave. She says she needs to see you before you get on that train, and she's planted herself at the front door."

He exhaled and plopped down on the mattress. He should have suspected Evelyn would be difficult, for it simply wasn't in her nature to give up.

Nor was it for him. He glanced out the window, an ironic grin twisting his mouth. At this point, it didn't really matter if he racked up more demerits, did it?

Evelyn might not budge from the front door, but there were other ways out of this dormitory than walking out the main entrance. His career at West Point had begun with a string of infractions, and it seemed appropriate that he'd leave the same way. He flashed a grin at Jake as he yanked the window sash up. "If you don't want to be party to an infraction of the rules, look away now."

"You are *not* leaving out that window," Jake said, but his voice was full of admiration.

"Watch me." He scooped up his canvas rucksack, already packed with his meager earthly possessions, and swung a leg over the windowsill. In his pocket he had orders and a train ticket to get to Fort Slocum, and he'd obey them, but he'd do so on his terms.

A gutter pipe was in easy reach, and the brackets anchoring it to the brick wall served as toeholds as he scaled from the third floor, past the fourth floor, and onto the roof. Some of the cadets in the field below noticed and called out encouragement.

"Brixton, you maniac!" someone hollered up from the field. Others applauded in vigor.

He tossed them a hearty wave of acknowledgment. He couldn't help himself. He loved it here, and he loved the men with whom he served. He didn't want to be hustled off campus like a criminal. His feet were nimble as he scrambled over the roof and to the adjoining building, one that had an escape ladder welded to the outside.

He gave one final, wholehearted wave to the cadets below. It was a wave of friendship, of farewell, of regret. As he picked up his sack, the shouts of encouragement from the men in the field filled him with the fierce joy of having once been a part of something great.

He got to the ground quickly, then made a dash to the cover of the oak trees bordering campus. No one was in a hurry to turn him in, and he sprinted toward the main gate and soon was on Thayer Road, walking toward the train station.

Onward toward the next great adventure.

———❖———

Clyde managed to hitch a ride on the back of a farmer's wagon and arrived at the train station with almost an hour to spare. It was his last hour of freedom, and he didn't intend to waste it. A couple of boys waiting on the platform tried to play jacks, but their technique was all wrong. Clyde dumped his rucksack, sat on the floor beside them, and showed them the proper technique. He loved playing with kids and hoped to have some of his own before too long.

He pushed the thought away. There was no point in wallowing in his mistakes—he would simply enjoy the adoration in the boys' eyes as he taught them how to twist their wrist faster and improve their take.

At last it was time to board his train. It would be a two-hour ride to New Rochelle, then a short ferry ride to David's Island, where Fort Slocum was located. This wasn't the career he'd hoped for, but he'd try to do a good job. And as soon as he had a chance, he'd figure out what to write to Evelyn to explain his cowardice in not being able to face her this afternoon.

He stepped into the third-class car as soon as the doors opened. There weren't many people onboard today, so he had his pick of seats. And third class wasn't so bad. He'd walked and hitchhiked too many times not to appreciate a good, forward-facing bench all to himself. The train was bound to get more crowded as they got closer to Manhattan, but for now the air was clean, and he had room to breathe.

The stationmaster announced one more minute until the doors would close. One more minute before this chapter of his life was over forever.

A woman with her skirts hiked up around her knees came running toward the stationmaster. Clyde nearly choked. Evelyn?

There was no mistaking her. Even scurrying across the platform with her skirts wadded in one hand and a traveling case in the other, she had the willowy grace that was unmistakably Evelyn. His eyes widened as she boarded the car.

She spotted him immediately, and her smile lit her entire face. She marched down the aisle and plopped into the empty space beside him.

"This seat isn't taken, I hope?"

She was breathless and beautiful as she looked at him. He couldn't even speak. Evelyn seemed remarkably even-keeled for a woman whose sweetheart had just scrambled over rooftops and hitched a ride to town to avoid her.

"Be my guest," he said.

"I've been hiding behind the screen of mulberry bushes and spying on you playing jacks with those children. I feared that if you saw me, you'd make a dash for freedom again." She grinned. "Honestly, Clyde! Am I that terrifying?"

He risked a glance at her. Yes, she was indeed terrifying. She was beautiful and brilliant and he'd been reaching way too high when he'd aspired to win her. At least as an officer he'd had a chance. Now he was Private Clyde Brixton, future ditch-digger.

"I'm sorry about this afternoon," he admitted. "I've let a lot of people down, and I just wasn't up for seeing you. Your father can be a trying person."

She smiled. "You're just now realizing that?"

"He wished me luck in my future digging ditches."

The stationmaster walked along the platform, calling, "All aboard!"

"Look, you'd better get off now," he said. "I'll write, I promise." He stood and grabbed her satchel.

"I'm going with you to New Rochelle," she said. "Then I'm heading to Boston. I'm moving."

He looked at her blankly. "You're moving to Boston? Why?"

She bit the corner of her lip and seemed to shrink a little. For the first time since boarding the train, she looked nervous.

He sat and grabbed her hand. "Evelyn," he whispered urgently, "what's going on? Tell me. Tell me what I can do to help." Because somehow he suspected he was the cause of this and, if so, he needed to repair it. He could take anything but disappointing Evelyn.

"I got a job," she said, her voice a mixture of pride and trepidation. "It's not much, just weighing and selling things in a dry goods store, but it will help pay my expenses in Boston. I've rented an apartment just a few blocks down from the store."

If she'd told him she'd sold all her earthly belongings and was moving to the North Pole, he couldn't have been more stunned. But he was proud of her. She was withering on the vine in West Point, and anything that got her out of there was good. The fact that she was doing it on her own? Truly amazing.

His smile was genuine. "I'm glad for you, but did you have a falling out with your father? I don't understand . . ."

"My father has been wonderful. He was the one who told me about your future as a ditch-digger."

Clyde sighed. He'd be two months at Fort Slocum for training, but his life after that was still a mystery. Apparently General White knew where he'd be sent, as did Evelyn.

"And did he say where I'd be digging ditches?" He braced himself, dreading the answer.

"Boston."

He blinked. "Boston? That doesn't make sense."

"It does if you realize the army is upgrading their telephone and telegraph capabilities. They are experimenting with setting the cables into underground conduits, and guess where that work is beginning?"

The thud of his heartbeat had just doubled. "Boston?"

"Boston!" she exclaimed, her voice triumphant. "Rumor has it that one of the enlisted soldiers assigned to work on laying the cables is a smart-yet-reckless young man. He's no good at following orders, but he has a way with electricity."

He reached out for her hand, squeezing it hard. He wasn't able to speak yet—the lump in his throat was getting in the way. What a relief to be assigned to meaningful work that would take advantage of his skills. He'd still be a private in the army, but he craved the chance to use his God-given abilities to their fullest potential.

His breath froze as another realization blazed to life. "And why are you moving to Boston?" he asked, barely able to get the words spoken without shaking.

"Because that is where you will be. And for me, that's home."

His breath left him in a rush. It was impossible to believe this beautiful, talented woman would actually want him after all he'd done to destroy his own career. He had *nothing* to offer her. The extent of his worldly possessions fit into the rucksack at his feet.

"I don't know if I can give you what you need. I'm a private in the army; I'll be paid a pittance, and half of that will go to my mother."

"That's why I got a job, Clyde. We'll do this together. I want to do this together."

Her words were meant to be reassuring, but all he felt was a growing terror. His father had disappointed his mother time and again, and he didn't want to be the kind of man whose wife feared how the next month's rent would be paid. Evelyn could have anyone. She was beautiful, intelligent, and well-connected—she didn't need to settle for a job in a dry goods store. Once she left home, her father might not even take her back if things went badly.

This discussion was too important to couch in vague terms. He needed to lay it out bluntly. "I'm afraid you will give up everything for me, and then I'll let you down. I'm a *private*, Evelyn."

"I didn't fall in love with a rank or a uniform. I fell in love with *you*. A man who could build a generator to hatch hummingbird eggs. Who dropped everything to rescue a friend. And Romulus passed his test, did you know? He earned a perfect score and will graduate on time, all because you were there when he needed someone to help him through a rough patch. No man with that kind of heart will ever let me down."

Evelyn's smile was growing wider by the second. It was hard to believe this was happening. Was she really moving to Boston because of him? It was wonderful and terrifying and quite possibly the answer to all his prayers.

He grabbed her other hand. Okay, he'd better not muck this up. "It would be pretty scandalous if we ran off to live in sin, wouldn't it?"

The glare she pinned him with assured him he was well on his way to mucking things up. He cleared his throat and started again. "What I meant to say is that I'd be honored if you would consent to be my wife."

"Of course I'll marry you—"

He cut her off with a kiss. What had begun as the worst day of his life was ending as his best. "I can't believe this is really happening," he said.

Laughter mingled with her smile. "It seems we have a history of doing everything the hard way."

He bent his head. Everything about the next two years was going to be hard, and it was entirely his fault. All the early demerits, rescuing Romulus, his impulsive show of bravado leaving campus rather than facing Evelyn directly . . . all of it had taken him a little farther from the safe, respectable life Evelyn deserved.

"I can do better," he vowed. And he would. He loved Evelyn too much to fail. What had started as a summer of dreams was going to become so much more.

He held her close, thankful he'd been given the chance to build a fountain for her birdcage, and that she'd been able to see past his uniform to the man beneath. It would be a challenge to be worthy of her, but with God's grace, he had been given a chance to prove himself. Marriage was a serious commitment, and from this day forward he would strive and pray to be worthy of Evelyn's trust. He would hold fast to her, love and cherish her, through all the joys and sorrows that lay ahead.

UP *from* the SEA

❧

A
WHOSE WAVES THESE ARE
NOVELLA

AMANDA DYKES

For April. My sister, my friend.
Because . . .
History.
Courage.
Hearts beating with the song of redemption.
Sandwiches in the forest.
Things I like about you.

They shut the road through the woods
Seventy years ago.
Weather and rain have undone it again,
And now you would never know
There was once a road through the woods. . . .

Yet, if you enter the woods
Of a summer evening late . . .
You will hear the beat of a horse's feet,
And the swish of a skirt in the dew,
Steadily cantering through
The misty solitudes,
As though they perfectly knew
The old lost road through the woods . . .
But there is no road through the woods.

—from *The Way Through the Woods*
by Rudyard Kipling

PROLOGUE

The forest floor came alive that night. Footsteps pounding upon it, roots forging slow paths on dark soil. Two worlds about to collide. The young woman flew through the trees, the frantic swishing of her skirt masked by the sound of wind through the bending pines above.

Something snagged—a bramble against her white lace shawl. With a rip that matched the rending of her heart, she freed herself and continued on, one arm holding fast to the boxy bundle wrapped within her shawl.

There, on the back side of a mountain, she broke into a clearing. Her destination. The place where a massive stump of freshly cut white pine looked like an altar in the moonlight. And well it might, for the sacrifice it had made. Spiced soil was soft beneath bracken as she fell to her knees and began to dig with cold fingers.

Setting her bundle within the fresh hole, she made quick work of mounding soil over and around it. A wooden box, its wood and paper contents nestled inside—and atop it, the roots of a sapling tree. All her regrets, and all her hopes.

She'd thought herself alone. Just her, the moon, and the secrets she'd buried. But a stone's throw away and off in the shadows, a solitary figure on horseback looked on. If she had known, perhaps she would not have spilled her tears into the earth, watering that tree with her very soul.

Perhaps she would not have pulled out the dull knife from the pocket of her mud-splattered skirt. And perhaps she would not have etched in that young trunk, three deep scars that would mark the living wood for centuries to come.

But she did. And as the man watched on, two words that would have gone unheard, instead became a legend.

"Forgive me," she said. She slipped back into the darkness, the sound of her feet vanishing against the haunting echo of her words.

1

ONE HUNDRED FIFTY-ONE YEARS LATER
OCTOBER 1925

Ragtime music spun around Savannah Mae Thorpe. Even as jaunty measures of the string quartet pulled couples onto the glow of the resort's wooden dance floor, it slipped right through her with a whisper: *Come away. You don't belong here.*

The temptation was strong. From an open window beckoned a pine-laden breeze, laced with the sound of the sea. A step to the left—and then another, careful to keep her borrowed gown as still as possible so as not to let its blue-on-white sequins catch attention—and she was nearly to the door. No one would ever notice her absence.

Her eyes fell upon her cousin Mary across the avenue of cologne and fringed garments. Mary was Savannah's opposite in every way. Flaxen-haired, fair-skinned, and blue-eyed was she, where Savannah's eyes matched her dark hair, which escaped from a simple braid most days. Her face sported freckles from so many days running in the sun and sand as a girl. Freckles she'd never given a thought to, until arriving here.

Bedecked in a black beaded dress and a cloak of buoyant laughter, Mary caught Savannah's gaze and lifted a single brow.

As if she knew precisely what Savannah was up to. Her admonition from earlier that evening echoed in Savannah's mind: "*No slinking off like one of your Georgia swamp possums tonight, Savannah. You're one of us now.*"

"It's O-possum," Savannah said under her breath, pasting on a smile and nodding a greeting to her cousin. The ragtime band struck up again in the corner. They did so every night as the well-to-do descended from their rooms at the Gables, having changed from their rowing and lawn tennis outfits into their evening wear, to fill the ballroom with merriment.

Couples around the room began to move again in spins and flails of the Charleston—Mary along with them, and Aunt Fern watching on approvingly from a red velvet-backed chair. Her mother's sister, though the two were as opposite as the north and south they'd each occupied all of their adult lives.

Soon, Cousin Wilbur was on the dance floor, too, spinning around a pretty girl whose cheeks flushed with the heat of the room. A fresh breeze blew in from the window. This was Savannah's chance. Ushered by bright notes, she slipped out, hurried down those curving stairs with a branch-woven railing, and disappeared into the tree line.

Pressing her back against a towering pine, her pulse slowed to the easier cadence of the forest. *Freedom.*

The treetops swayed, and it was as if they'd been waiting for her. There was something breathtaking about it—that trees standing for a century or more before she was even born would play a symphony of wind and leaves for her now. It was silly, perhaps. A vestige of her mother's vivid imagination, inviting her into a fairy tale right here at the edge of the forest.

Or maybe it was something more concrete that made these trees feel like a home to her. The knowledge that they were hers by rights—or rather, the wilderness up the mountain was. Her inheritance, though she could not touch that inheritance until she turned twenty-one. Another two years. Two years of slipping out of dances and frippery.

Closing her eyes and inhaling, she savored this moment. She could get by for two more years this way if she had to. Limping along from stolen moment to stolen moment. Couldn't she? Still, something within her yearned for more than mere survival. Here in this land where her absentee uncle, always off in New York minding bank business, left her to the whims of her cousins.

The brass clasp of her tapestry purse unlatched easily at her touch. The metal was as worn as the threads were bare, and she'd never seen her mother leave the house without it a day in her life. Try as she might, Mary could not convince Savannah to lay it aside for something "with a little more shine to it." When Savannah ran her fingers over its stitches, the ache in her heart for her departed parents took on a gentler pang.

Slipping her hand inside, she pulled out the old piece of paper. The only thing of her mother's she'd brought back with her to this harbor, her mother's childhood home. A map of her young adventures—pine trees everywhere, a castle in the woods. A mind alive with possibility and imaginings—so fitting for the way she lived this life. Savannah's gaze landed on an arrow to a clearing in the heart of the woods with Mother's scribbled words: *Atonement Tree.*

What an atonement tree was, Savannah had no idea. But she intended to find out, despite her relatives' appalled reaction whenever she mentioned venturing farther into the mountains. It was the only link here to her past—and somehow, at least she hoped—her future.

A twig snapped in the distance, wrenching her wonderings from that map and the thousand explanations she'd imagined for it. Following the noise with her eyes, she spotted the swing of a lantern, broken up by intermittent tree silhouettes. Metal creaked, the sound of time-worn wheels.

She'd been out here every night for a week and never seen another soul. Never spotted a path, either. Not into the woods, anyway. All roads led to the sea here, where everyone preferred to paddle their days away among the islands in the pocket harbor of Ansel-by-the-Sea.

Her pulse stuttering, she pushed off from the trees and made to slip away from the sound—but before she could, the swing of the lantern stilled just yards in front of her.

2

W ho are you?" a voice said. Deep and steady, but wary.
"Who are *you*?" She swallowed, lifting her chin with
courage she did not feel. She couldn't see the man's face at the
angle he was holding the lantern.

After a pause, he lowered the lantern. Her eyes adjusting,
the spill of moonlight showed a man not more than twenty-five
or thirty stepping nearer. Behind him sat an old wooden cart
laden with logs.

Savannah took a step backward, folding the map and tuck-
ing it into her purse.

He paused, perhaps sensing her unease. "I'm Alastair," he
said.

"Alastair," she repeated the name, narrowing her eyes to see
him better in the dark. Strong features, eyes that held a gaze
fast. Seeing, not hiding behind a mask of pretension. So unlike
the others gathered inside.

He nodded. "Alastair Campbell MacGregor Bliss."

Savannah smiled. A name as storied as his presence.

"Who are you?" he asked again. With a glance at her attire,
he pulled a newsboy cap from his head and pressed it against
his chest, between suspenders looped over his flannel shirt. Her

beaded white skirt sparkled in the moonlight and she felt as out of place in it as he apparently did in her presence, the way his thumb tapped against his chest atop that cap, as if keeping time with his thoughts. Or maybe marking moments until he could be done with this wandering forest waif. She opened her mouth to answer, but the sound of the veranda door's hinges silenced her.

"Savannah!" Mary's voice cascaded down to where they stood in the dark. "Where has she gone to? I swear, that girl is intent on nesting with the loons, the way she's always disappearing out here." Two of Mary's friends giggled in response, traipsing behind their leader.

"Don't be so hard on her," Wilbur's voice replied, bringing up the rear of the gathering. Mary's brother, Will, extended a kindness to Savannah that the others did not. Though he spent money like it came in with the tide and fancied himself a jollier version of Jay Gatsby from that new novel, he meant well.

Alastair ventured a step closer. "That's you? Savannah." He said her name like it was a journey, not a black mark across the place of her birth, as Mary did.

She nodded. "Savannah Mae Thorpe." She felt the roundness of her Southern words keenly against the edge of his Northern speech.

"Savannah Thorpe!" Mary said again, and she was nearly upon them. "There you are." Mary's quick eyes pinned her. "Come, cousin," she gave a cursory glance at Alastair and reached out for Savannah's hand. "Join us inside for a dance or two."

The invitation sounded kind, but there was something about the way Mary's eyes flicked to the others, as if ensuring they would all be witness to Savannah's next bout of blundering.

"Thank you . . ." She scanned the place, desperate for an excuse. The nightly events held at the Gables were nothing like the country square dances back in Georgia. Lace instead of calicos, flapper dresses instead of aprons. In the distance, smoke curled from the chimney, chasing away the autumn chill. "I'll come inside," she said, "but if it's all the same, I'll skip the dancing. I'll just see to the fire." It wasn't her job, as a guest for the evening, but she felt leagues more at home stoking coals than shuffling her feet to a dance.

A cry of delight escaped Mary. "See?" She clapped, turning in triumph to face her friends. "*Far*. Instead of fie-er. Isn't it quaint?"

Heat crept up Savannah's cheeks. Hadn't her cousin tired yet of showcasing her like a pet pony? And butchering the beauty of the way people spoke back home, too. Missing every nuanced curve of it.

Savannah shot a glance at Alastair who, though shadowed and hard to read, stood stalwart and solid in the dark. She could sense her own anger bouncing off him—or amplified by him.

Mary's laughter fell down a musical scale. "Oh, cousin, how glad I am that we inherited you."

The words scrubbed embers of grief into her. "Glad?" Savannah pushed past her fury and pasted on a fake smile to match Mary's. "How convenient that my parents' demise brings you amusement."

The smile disappeared from Mary's scarlet-stained lips as she looked around at her friends.

"Don't worry, Mary. I'll be sure not to embarrass you any further tonight."

The words were fire on her tongue. She regretted their tone even as they poured forth, and Mary's face went from ashen to scarlet. This woman had once been her faithful correspondent, back when they were nine and Mary's Maine world sounded full of enchantment. She'd done it again, letting her temper get the better of her, hasty words like weapons. They'd been friends, once. And she prayed they could be again. It was just that Savannah was floundering, the sophisticated creature of society before her a far cry from the girl who used to send her pressed leaves every fall. But perhaps Mary felt the same, this gap between their grown selves and their young selves stretching wide between them.

What would Mama have done? The epitome of spunk tempered with grace even in their simple home, she certainly wouldn't have erupted like Savannah was doing now. She bit down on her bottom lip to shackle the deluge of scathing words that threatened. Judging by the fire in Mary's eyes, she'd done enough damage for one evening.

Savannah dipped her chin, hoping the show of remorse might be a peace offering. "Forgive me," she said. "I am grateful for the home you and your family have so kindly offered."

That much was true. Drenched in pomp it may be, and perhaps she was a fish out of water way up here in Maine, but it was a roof over her head. And they were family, after all.

Sensing she'd blundered enough for one night, and with everything from her way of speaking to her untamed anger on display, Savannah picked up her hem and made for the Gables. The lodge—half stone, half timber, angled around an open green. She crossed the fading lawn and climbed the steps, returning to the ballroom.

3

Savannah was well inside by the time Mary caught up, grabbing Savannah's arm with a gloved hand.

"Don't be cross. I think your way of speaking is charming, truly I do." Mary's own words gleamed, finished off by a school for young ladies in Boston. "Don't bother with the fire. See?" She pointed at a door to the side of the lodge's stone fireplace, where Alastair entered with an armful of logs. "That's his job."

The young man looked their way, his blue eyes piercing and his face solemn. In the low light of the chandeliers, Savannah could see him better. He looked like he'd been carved by the Maine wind itself. Rugged and strong, with a wild air about him, barely tamed by the square set of his jaw.

"He's our lumberjack, you know."

Mary meant well, Savannah was certain. She'd never known any different, and perhaps didn't hear the condescending superiority in her voice when she said "lumberjack," as if the man were her lackey.

Mindful not to let anger slip back into her own voice, Savannah schooled her tone into gentleness. "I hadn't realized lumberjacks were owned by anyone," she said. With the proud set of his jaw and his determined stride, she had a feeling he didn't care a pinch for what Mary and her people thought.

His dark hair fell over his forehead at an angle as he set to stacking the logs against the wall.

"You know what I mean. He works here. He's one of those winter people who live here all the year through. Rough sorts, you know. He'll stay after we've all cleared out next month, back to civilization."

The band pulled the music into the final measures of the tune, and as applause sounded, couples drifted to the outskirts of the room. Intermission, time enough for the band to eat their own dinner and come back for round two of lively dancing. The Gables played host as the social highlight of the summer for locals and "summer people" alike. This corner of Maine was remote, nearly north enough to be claimed by Canada, and the same families had been returning to the resort every summer for decades. Escaping the heat of the cities, but bringing their cities' glitter with them into the wilds.

"What a dull bunch you all are," a male voice piped up. Wilbur circled the room and scooped an arm through the air to rally the party. "Let's have us a scrum, shall we?"

His trio of friends raised their glasses in the air with hollers of affirmation.

Mary wrinkled her nose. "A *scrum*? I swear, Will, these ideas of food that you bring home from your travels like so many stray dogs—"

Wilbur landed an arm around his sister's shoulder. She beheld it as if it were a fly, and brushed it off in like manner.

"A *scrum*, dear sister, is from rugby. Jolly old England. Good fun. The fellows mob together like a pack of wolves with the ball at the center and paw at it with their feet while pushing at each other with their heads and a few tons of flesh, and—"

"As I said," Mary interjected. "Stray dogs." Mary turned

a gloved wrist as if cuing the jingle of laughter from her own friends.

"Don't be daft." Will rolled his eyes. "We don't do an *actual* scrum. The fellas and I invented our own sort on the boat back stateside last week. Didn't we, blokes?" His attempt at a British accent on the last word brought more laughter. He lowered his voice and leaned in as if to impart a great secret, the group gathering around in response. "See, we all sit around the fire"—he tipped his head toward the great hearth—"and take turns entertaining the rest. Then the next person tries to top the last performance, and so on. A story, a charade, a joke—a song, even, until everyone's had a chance to use their head"—he tapped his forehead twice—"to win the game. You see? Scrum!" He gestured with both arms, as if he'd just revealed the secret to life.

"Brilliant." Mary's smile spread unnaturally wide, a glint of mischief in her eyes. "No one in history has ever before thought of such a thing. Or called it, I don't know, *an evening's entertainment*."

Will leaned in farther. "That wasn't very entertaining. You lose, sister. Next up?"

"Oh, hush. Do step back and let me have an honest go at it," Mary said. This was the cousin Savannah remembered. Spunky, with an uncanny way of uniting a group with her charisma. The small cluster of young people parted to make way, then drew into a semicircle around the fire. "Come," she said. "Gather the chairs." She glanced to the door, where Mrs. Flint, proprietress of the inn, bustled in with the customary intermission tray of silver-pitchered hot chocolate and popping corn. Her son, Abner, toddled in behind her.

Savannah's heart soared. It was a rustic tradition, but one the Flints held to nightly, making the glamour of the lodge feel inviting. The corn was harvested from their own garden last fall, dried for months in anticipation of nights like this. Served up alongside a crock of fresh melted butter for the ladling, with cinnamon and maple sugar to top.

Tonight, though, she kept to the back of the crowd. Arranging chairs bedecked in silk around their log frames, as the others rustled over with their refreshments and the kernels popping over the flames began.

A *thump* sounded, a log rolling from its place where the wood was stacked against the wall. Wilbur craned his neck to spot the lumberjack at work. "There. Al! Tell us that story you know."

A murmuring swept the group as they followed Will's lead in singling out the man behind them.

Savannah flushed at Wilbur's treatment of him. *That story you know*? As if the man was only good for one thing. "Alastair," she spoke before she could think. "That's his name." His name felt far away on her lips, holding the promise of something unseen. She felt a pull to bring him in. To smooth over her cousins' jabs at the man.

The drill of the group's eyes on her jolted her into realizing she'd spoken his name and nothing more, like a numbskull. "We—" she cleared her throat—"we'd surely like to hear a story of this home of yours." She spread a gloved hand toward the open windows, where a wind rustled pine boughs outside. "If you might lend us one, that is." She lowered herself into one of the chairs in the fireside circle, part of her wishing she could disappear.

"That's right!" Wilbur piped up. "That's exactly it. The story of your land and that lady. Tell us, old boy."

Alastair capped the pile of logs with a splintered one and rested his hand there. "Sorry. I've got work to do."

"Oh, never mind. I know the one. I'll tell it." Mary moved toward the hearth, her beaded dress of black sparkling.

Savannah's cousin drew in a dramatic breath, raising her slim shoulders and circling them back. She was relishing this, born for the spotlight. "You've heard, of course, about the woman in the woods."

A hush fell like a curtain over the room. *The woman in the woods.* Her mother's very words, whenever Father would stir their beach campfire for story time, Savannah burrowing her feet into soft Georgia sand and leaning forward to soak in the magic of this tale.

"It was two hundred years ago that she walked those paths. All in white, every night."

Savannah's heart pulsed with the rhyme. It was the very same story. A fairy tale from her mother's vivid imagination, she'd always thought. But here—it was fact?

Mary continued, her voice hushed to draw the crowd in.

"She was a broken soul, who never slept a wink. Wandering beneath the moon, wailing as she went."

No . . . this was wrong.

"Until one night," Mary said, her eyes growing wide, "a man upon horseback came upon her. He was utterly spellbound by her beauty, and watched her there for three nights more, until he summoned the courage to speak. 'My lady,' he said. 'Ask anything of me. If you will but lend me your smile, your love, your hand in marriage—'"

What on earth? This was nothing more than an overdone, simplified caricature of a fairy tale. Nothing of the haunting hope and beauty that was supposed to live in this story.

"No." The word escaped from Savannah before she could stop it. And by the look on Alastair's face off in the corner, she wasn't the only one revolting against this gothic version of the tale. Something that belonged in the pages of *Red Book* magazine. All the grit of it was gone, and with it, the magic.

"Oh?" Mary's hand lingered in the air, as if she held the

final punctuation mark of the story in the palm of her hand. "You know the story? Do, let's hear your version, Savannah."

Savannah gulped. She stole a glance at Alastair and felt his ire at Mary's telling simmering from where he stood in the corner. She did not understand his reaction, but it echoed a similar fury in the embers of her own soul. The woman in the woods had lived as a beacon in her young mind. On dark nights, when the cries of the red foxes had kept her awake and her mind had sparked with shadowed imaginings, she pressed her eyes shut and imagined that woman with her lantern in the woods. Savannah had held up her own lantern in the dark. *Lord, you created the dark just as you created the light. Help me find life there, and not fear.* Her prayer, tucked up around herself just like a blanket each and every night.

Yet here and now, it wasn't the foxes hovering just outside the circle of light, but Savannah's sense of aloneness. An outsider, who had no right to roll over the traditions of these people.

Still, the story would not slumber. "The woman in the woods was not a lovelorn damsel," she said. She smiled, hoping to invite them into the spellbinding version of the tale. "She—at least in the account I've heard—was the very soul of bravery."

"You're not proposing she's real." Mary's narrowed eyes held their old condescending mischief, and her friends stifled laughs.

"No," Savannah replied, her voice holding a steadiness she did not feel. The crowd, which had begun to fidget and whisper amongst themselves, fell silent. "I mean yes. Perhaps, once. But in the story, she did not wander the woods wailing night after night."

Savannah tucked her hands behind her, clasping them to keep from fidgeting out of nerves. She did not like this—being the center of attention. She was no storyteller.

But her mother had been. She had woven magic around it

with her words. Closing her eyes, Savannah reached back into those fear-laden nights, when her mother had knelt at her simple cot and taken her hand.

"Darkness comes, Savannah my girl. But don't you let it steal your light. Remember that woman, how she slipped out into the night when her whole world shook . . ."

Savannah pulled the stream of words from their deeply buried place in the past, and spoke them. "The woman lived in a castle," she said. "Right up here in the woods of Maine. She lived with her uncle, and when she was a girl, she traipsed through the forest with him day after day, gathering berries and helping him fell trees. She thought he was a brave man, the way he traversed those woods like they were a part of him. Never getting lost in their sprawling magnitude, always letting her get lost in their wonder."

She paused, taking in the smirks of her peers.

Wilbur took a swig from his glass and raised it to her. "Go on, cousin," he said. His jolliness, at least, seemed sincere. "Tell us more about little red riding hood."

"Well, she—she loved her uncle, very much. She loved her king, across the ocean from her place in these colonial woods. And she loved this new brave land where they'd come to settle, after her uncle left the king's troops to ply the lumber trade. He'd take her high up on the cliffs to look out over the waves far beyond. 'See that?' He'd point at the ships in the harbor. 'There they go, floating on water with trees that grew right beneath our feet. And now they're carrying men across oceans, to the far corners of the world.'" Her mother had made ships seem like magic things, in the words of the story.

"They were happy. Building a home in the woods for the two of them, log by log. Felling trees and watching them be transformed into ships to carry men far away, across a great blue expanse that should be uncrossable.

"Sometimes, they would come across the special trees. *Treasure trees*, her uncle called them. With a marking carved into them—two angled slashes and a straight line between them, the shape of an arrow. Three blows of an axe, transforming an ordinary tree into something majestic—the Broad Arrow, the mark was called. 'It points up, because these trees are meant for great things,' he said. 'Great things.' He'd get a faraway look in his eyes when he repeated those words. These trees he would leave, and whenever they came back across them later, there would be a stump. She loved to wonder where they'd gone and when. What 'great things' they were doing. Plowing through waves as a ship, carrying princesses, perhaps. Or carved with care into a throne, royal wood that it was.

"So they lived for many years. They completed their cabin. Their lumber business grew. And so did the girl. Life was simple and happy up from the sea, away out there in the woods. Fewer and fewer were the times they spotted trees marked with the Broad Arrow. She came to learn that they belonged to King George across the ocean; that he had need of those trees, as they were the tallest of the white pines, and they would be the proud, strong masts of ships of his royal fleet, his own country's tall timber having long since been sacrificed to that cause.

"People around here didn't take too kindly to that, believing the trees were theirs by rights. That a king so far away had no business marking and claiming the best of their lumber, when they were the ones to toil and work the land. But it mattered not, since there were fewer and fewer of the king's trees left. Rare jewels now, when they were found. The girl knew of only one still growing, high up on a peak."

Mary stifled a yawn. "Do tell us that is not the end of the story."

"Oh, no." Savannah could not keep a laugh from surfacing. Her favorite part was coming. "One day, from her old overlook, the young woman spied a royal ship just outside the harbor. It was there again the next day, and the next—just bobbing there, too close to the cliffs for comfort. She learned in the nearest town that their mast had broken, and the British soldiers aboard were trying to track down a new mast pole or a tree large enough to be made into one.

"She ventured to the village to buy her weekly parcel of brown sugar. And as she slid her humble coins over to pay at the general store, she heard low voices in the storeroom beyond—speaking of the plight of those sailors with no mast tree to be found. Yet their tone was not mournful. No trace of compassion. They spoke of 'dispensing justice upon them,' tones lower and more severe with every mention of tyranny and taxation. These voices—the men they belonged to had been watching the sailors and making plans.

A heavy urgency burrowed into her stomach and the young woman ran home to tell her uncle. Desperate for him to help her cut down the one tree she knew of, solitary up on that peak—to help these souls, stranded and plotted against, pawns in a battle between powers and ideologies.

"Together, they went in search of that tree. The walk was long and hard, a great effort for an older man and a young woman. Whenever they caught glimpses of the sea, they used his old telescope to spot the boat and the stranded sailors.

"On the third night of their sojourn, they made camp in a clearing and she prayed with all her might that God might send a way for these sailors to be spared. Beneath the light of the moon, she laid her head down on that ground to sleep. As she looked up at the stars, she watched the pine boughs wave, and then—for a split second—" Savannah paused, just as her mother used to. The others were rapt, and even Mary's bored face flickered interest. "She saw it. The king's Broad Arrow. Emblazoned on the tree, pointing up to that star-studded sky."

"So the sailors were safe?" Wilbur narrowed his eyes. "Awfully convenient. You sure it's not a fairy tale?"

Savannah shook her head. "That is where the tale's mystery begins. No one knows what became of the sailors . . . or the tree. The next day, she flew down the mountain to tell of their discovery and gather men enough to transport the tree. But when she returned—the tree was gone."

"Well, then. They clearly took it," Mary said, "to the ship. Made a mast and sailed away. I don't see what's so remarkable about that."

"Perhaps. But one man could not have pulled that tree down the mountain. There were no tracks where it had been dragged, no sign of her uncle. Only a tall stump, and a ship full of sailors left to perish."

"Nonsense!" Wilbur piped up. "They would have abandoned their ship if things were really all that rotten."

"They can't always do that," Alastair said, speaking for the first time. A man of few words, but his eyes were alight in their blue depths.

Savannah's heart sank. "Or . . ."

He fixed those unflinching eyes on her, listening.

"Maybe somehow, they did get the tree down. We don't know the end of the story. Only the part about her weeping. The account says a woodsman happened upon her, witnessed this moment."

"So she *did* moon about like a banshee." Wilbur looked satisfied.

"No," Savannah said, voice hushed. "The story says that whatever the end of the account, it brought her to her knees in that place on the mountain. To bury a small wooden chest deep in the earth, and atop it, a young tree. With a knife, she marked it deeply with the king's arrow. And the only words she could summon were . . ."

Savannah pulled in a breath. Words she wanted to cry out every day of her own life, but could not.

"*Forgive me.*" This, from Alastair.

Savannah's eyes stung, pricking from her own heart's cry. Her prayer every night. She blinked back hot tears, and nodded. "Yes," she said, her voice hoarse. "Forgive me."

The words hung like spun glass turning over the held breath of everyone listening.

"Well!" Wilbur's buoyant declaration shattered the effect. "A far cry from the wailing waif, eh? I say this leaves only one option."

"Indeed," Mary said. "Lay these fairy stories to rest and get back to the real fun." She dipped her head toward the band members, who were trickling back in and toward their instruments.

"No, not that!" Wilbur grinned, his voice rising above the resuming ragtime notes. "The woman in the woods. Let's find her!"

"Don't be ridiculous, Will," Mary said. "She's long gone, whoever she was. *If* she ever really was."

"I don't mean find *her*, herself. Let's find the clearing! Whatever she buried. Let's unearth her secrets. Or whatever that woodsman knew, whoever he was. They've got to be somewhere out in those woods."

Savannah swallowed back a bitter taste. Whatever the woman buried—whatever troubled her heart so—she somehow couldn't bear the thought of a bunch of strangers digging it up from its resting place.

"You're game, right, cousin? Let's get up a plan. We'll take to the woods tomorrow!" Wilbur sidled up to Savannah.

She couldn't help but smile at his friendly enthusiasm. And a pang pricked her heart, for he was always "getting up a plan," especially on the tails of his father leaving for yet another trip to New York. Lining Will's palm with money instead of giving in to his son's request to come along. Wilbur was eager to make something of himself, to prove his hand in his father's banking business. But his father, apparently, did not think him up to the task.

So she felt bad for what she was about to say, but could not muster the desire to go digging in chapters of history best left shut. "I think I'll stay behind," she said. "But thank you for including me."

And with that, as couples returned to their dizzying orbit on the dance floor, she saw her chance to slip outside once more.

Just as she reached the door, though, she paused. The sensation of being watched, heavy upon her. With a glance over her shoulder, her eyes landed on Alastair Campbell MacGregor Bliss. Who stacked logs, and met her gaze with words unspoken.

4

Say what one might about Wilbur Hapley, he knew how to hatch a scheme and carry it out. Savannah watched from the kitchen window of the family's Victorian home on Everlea Island—just across the harbor reach from the Gables—as Wilbur plopped a metal canteen down onto the growing mound of "necessities" for the grand expedition up the mountain. Beside the stack of suitcases, Mary sat perched upon a crate, fingering the blue feathers sprouting from her cloche hat.

Savannah tugged at her calico apron, a far cry from Mary's smart pants and blouse. Mary even dressed up for the bears and moose, it seemed. But Savannah's faded yellow chintz print felt more like home than all of Mary's fashion, however magnanimously it was loaned.

"What is that heavenly smell?" Wilbur burst into the kitchen rubbing his palms together. "Please tell me it's that hazelnut pie again."

"Wouldn't you like to know?" Savannah winked, handing him a paper-wrapped slice of her mama's best recipe—true Southern pecan pie. But with no pecans, she'd found the beaked hazelnut shrub on the island to be a boon, foraging nuts and whipping up a makeshift pie to stem a tide of homesickness last week.

With a drizzle of fresh maple syrup, it had given true pecan pie a run for its money. Will had been clamoring for more ever since.

"I wrapped up the rest in slices for you to take up the mountain," she said.

"You sure you won't come?" Will spoke between bites, crumpling the paper and tossing it into the wicker wastebasket in the corner.

She was about to explain herself for the third time to him, when he waved her off. "I know, I know. Leave the past alone. That's all well and good if you're not bored out of your mind, I guess. Anyway, thanks for the pie."

"Off already?" She had to admit, part of her did long to go with them. To break free of this house and head out into the wild.

"Ayuh." Will nodded, giving emphasis to the Mainer word for *yes*. If Uncle Albert heard him speak so, he'd lower his newspaper just barely, enough to remind him why he never took Wilbur into New York to the bank. "I've got to dig out the lanterns from the boathouse—could you be a sport and pop upstairs to Dad's office for the map? It's in the top right drawer." He gave her a grin and ducked out the door before she could protest.

It wasn't that she minded helping. It was just—she'd never set foot in the office. Uncle Albert seemed to prefer solitude, and after a very cold, formal reception upon her arrival that left her feeling more like a piece of acquired furniture than a close relative, she was happy to leave him be.

But what would a man like that, with his three-piece suits and pocket watches, be doing with a map of the backwoods of Birchdown Mountain?

The stairs creaked along with her apprehension as she climbed. Placing a hand on the cold metal of the office door, she opened it. It was silly to be nervous—Uncle Albert was off in New York for the rest of the week, and Aunt Fern was taking tea at the Gables. No one to disapprove of her presence here.

Crossing to the imposing desk of rich wood, Savannah pulled the shiny brass handles of the top drawer. It slid out smooth as velvet, exposing a stack of neat papers. They looked official—an embossed seal upon paper bordered in intricate loops, script certifying Mr. Albert M. Hapley as owner of stock in companies of ironworks, railroads, and automobiles.

But no map. Top right drawer, wasn't that what Wilbur had said? Or maybe he'd said left. But that only revealed neatly ordered trays of pens and ink, and monogrammed stationery. Her uncle's rigid handwriting punctuated one of the pages with a few jotted notes: *Trustee-Fiduciary duty—manage trust to benefit of beneficiary. Definition by law.*

These words should have been comforting, seeing as how Uncle Albert was the trustee of her estate for a few more years yet. But something about their appearance here turned her stomach. "Quit that, Savannah," she scolded herself. "You're here for a map, simple as that."

Another rifle through the right-hand drawer proved her uncle's affinity for the stock market again—until her hand came up against something hard just behind the certificates. A piece of wood, lighter in color than the rest of the drawer. Strange . . . the other drawer hadn't been so short.

As her hand ran against it, the panel fell forward. After a quick feel around, she pulled out a crisply folded map.

Downstairs the door opened and shut.

"Wilbur?" Good. He could take this, and she could step away from this room that made her feel like an intruder. But no answer came. A quick glance out the corner window showed Mary's former place on her crate was empty now. "Mary?"

Footsteps came, and Savannah unfolded the quadrants of the map to make sure she'd found what Wilbur needed. There—Birchdown Mountain, rising up just beyond the town of Ansel-by-the-Sea, which curved around the harbor like a gentle smile.

And beyond it, mountains and land that she'd never once set foot in . . . but which she owned.

It was a strange sensation. Holding this map and beholding the land that was hers. She did not like it. It should be her mother's, still. When her grandfather, a Victorian lumber baron, had divided these lands between the two daughters as their inheritances, he surely never imagined it would split his family. That Fern would marry old money from Newport and enter "proper society," far from the wilds where she was raised up here. And that Mother, feeling abandoned by her sister, would vanish away as far as she could get. Away down South to where the family's Georgia pulp holdings were centered. Where she would fall in love with a farmer and raise her daughter to run wild and free on the sands of the South.

But here she was, right back where it all started—in a home that would one day be hers, staring at the land that would one day be hers.

Something about the map in her hands felt oddly familiar, though she was certain she'd never beheld a depiction of the place before. And something was strange about it, too. Pencil lines were drawn upon it, sectioning off parcels, with dollar figures centered upon each one. As if they were items poised for auction.

"I'm not intruding, I hope."

Startled by the voice, Savannah dropped the map. Fumbling to pick it up, she closed the drawer and slipped from behind the desk to face her uncle.

A thin man, he was tall, and he let his pacing with words fill a room where his physical stature did not. Every word was measured, each one landing in a way that seemed to push her farther out of his world.

"I'm sorry," she said. "I was just looking for a map. The others are headed out on an excursion, and I—"

"Sit," he said, gesturing to the wooden seat on her rightful side of the desk. He slid his rich leather briefcase onto the smooth surface, its quality spoken in the whisper of noise it made. Easing into the wingback chair, he steepled his hands.

"You came looking for a map," he said.

"Yes, sir." She gulped. "Wilbur and Mary and some friends of theirs are going into the mountains and needed a map to guide them. Wilbur asked if I might—"

"And what did you think of your land?"

Her mind paddled to keep up. He slipped around the conversation at odd angles, keeping her off-kilter.

"My land . . ." Her eyes grew wide at the wonder of uttering this phrase for the first time. She knew that though it was hers by rights, it was technically under his control. She was a formality, really. An afterthought.

"It's good land," he said. "I trust you saw the itinerary?"

"Itinerary?" Good gravy, she sounded like a parrot. If she didn't gather her wits, she'd wilt here like the Southern weed he apparently thought she was. *Stop it*, she thought. He had taken her in, after all. Provided her a house to live in, if not a home to belong to. It was more than she could ask for. "I . . . did see markings on the map." Plans. Calculations.

"Yes," he said. "I've had that drawn up with experts in matters such as these. An itinerary, if you will."

She shook her head. "I don't think that land is packing its bags anytime soon." She laughed, hoping beyond reason to lighten the atmosphere.

Opening his top right drawer, he pulled out the tidy stack of stocks, and fanned through them with smug approval. "My wife is a brilliant businesswoman," he said.

She reeled, trying to keep up with another sharp turn in topic. "Aunt Fern," she said. "Yes, she seems . . ."

"Intrepid, really. She had much land in these woods, as you may know."

Had. Past tense.

"Yet unlike your poor mother, she sold them. Liquidating those assets." He looked up from the stocks, meeting Savannah's eyes for the first time. "That means she turned them from immovable, into something she could use in a profitable way."

She bit her tongue, wanting to retort that she knew what "liquidating assets" meant. His remark felt like a kick toward her mother's memory. *Help me bridle this beast of a tongue. . . .* Her prayer climbed through the heat she felt gathering inside.

She cleared her throat and prayed there would be restraint and respect in her own voice. "As did my mother. Who chose—also as a brilliant businesswoman—to keep that land." *For something that matters, someday.* That's what Mother always said.

His eyes barely registered interest. "That may well be. And perhaps she was right. We may be able to fetch a higher price for this land than we did even for ours." The shift in his language was seamless. Not *your land*, but *this land*. Not *Fern's*, but *ours*.

"As you'll see, Savannah Mae Thorpe, you might fetch a tidy sum for your parcels as well. Freeing you up to purchase fifty . . . sixty . . . maybe seventy thousand dollars in stock."

The number was enough to make Savannah swallow her own tongue. "That's impossible," she said. Not to mention irrelevant. If Mother wouldn't sell her land for profit alone, Savannah would stand her ground, too. "These figures"—she tapped the map—"they're nowhere near that. Even if I did sell, we'd fetch, what?" She did a quick calculation. "Eight hundred dollars, at best."

"Nine hundred fifty-four." Her uncle slid the stocks back into his drawer. "And seventeen cents. But that's the beauty of buying on margin. The stock exchange is a thing of magnificence. We live in an enlightened and opulent age, you know." He gestured widely, ending at the window toward the mainland. "This whole place, just a few hundred years ago, was nothing more than a fisherman's shack on the shore, and a few fledgling lumber operations scraping by in the mountains. A hundred pounds back then—*pounds*," he laughed. "Not even dollars, we knew so little of independence—why, it was equal to what thousands of dollars are today. At least. We'd be fools not to make the most of a time like this. For you to—*benefit*."

The way he emphasized that final word brought to mind his notes scratched upon that stationery in the drawer. As her trustee, he had a—how had he written it? *A duty to benefit . . .*

A shiver shot up her spine. He meant to sell her land.

"Progress, progress," he said as he fisted one hand into his palm. "We must not live in the past. Margin lets us move beyond anything our forefathers ever dared to dream."

She'd heard him speak of margin before. Of brokers loaning huge amounts, and people becoming wealthy beyond belief as a result of their investments.

She blinked and saw her mother's hands scooping up sand, letting it slip through her fingers, sparkling in the moonlight. *"We have all the riches in the world, Savannah Mae."*

She stood. "I don't wish to sell." And for emphasis, she crisply folded the map and slid it across his gleaming desk to him. The sound of Will and Mary's banter drifted up, muted through the mottled window glass.

With his fingertips, he slid it back to her. "Take it," he said. "Go with the children." He spoke of his grown offspring as if they were playthings. "See your woods. I'd wager you'll have your fill of moss and mosquitoes and come back ready to part ways with it. Use the money for something . . . worthwhile."

She lifted her chin, inhaling to calm the sharpness threatening to come out. "And if I'm not?" She knew what was on the line here. Uncle Albert and Aunt Fern were legally in control of her possessions until she was twenty-one. "Will you agree not to sell the land?"

He leaned back in his chair, stroking his chin. "I fear you'd be doing a dreadful disservice to your legacy. I could place your funds very shrewdly in the market. Bring me one solid reason not to sell this land—one solid *monetary* reason—and we'll talk."

She thought of that sand trickling through her mother's fingers. The way she used to brush her knuckles across Savannah's freckled cheeks. With her mother's silvery laugh strong in her memory, Savannah dared to challenge more from this stalwart man. She stuck her hand out across the desk, proposing a handshake. "If I bring one solid reason not to sell, we will lay this conversation to rest once and for all," she said.

Something sparked in him then at her firmness. Something in between respect and disdain.

He shook her hand, a condescending presence easing over him. "Very well. Go on up from the harbor. Get into the woods. And tell me what you find."

Retreating from the room, the world grew muffled as her pulse pounded. What had she just done? Wagered her inheritance on a fairy tale?

She closed her eyes and prayed that somewhere out there, the fabled castle in the woods might hold hope for the land of her mother's heart.

5

Thwack. The axe fell against a stump, and Alastair added one more reason to the long, long list of why life out here in obscurity fit him so much better than the tailored business coat he'd once bumbled about civilization in. This was his ritual now. For every fall of the axe, another reason listed. A rhythm, the only thing that made sense.

Reason number twenty-seven today: the flight of a blue heron made infinitely more sense to him than the dances at the Gables. One was all grace, the other all frenzy.

Thwack. Reason number twenty-eight: the ragtime band had its competition cut out with the call of the loon over on Cathance Lake.

Thwack. Life was simple and happy up from the sea, away out here in the woods. Wasn't that how the girl had said it last night? Where she'd come from, he did not know—blowing right into his woods in the dark like the sea breeze blew her in from away. Far away, by the sound of her words. And far from the pretenses of that crowd she was with. There'd been some kind of force in her, like an unbridled zephyr off the mountains, and the rest of them didn't quite know what to do with her.

Neither did he. Except for one thing: let that wild wind keep blowing her right on through, away from his thoughts. Last time someone had planted themselves in the soil of his mind, only disaster had resulted.

He needed to focus on the task at hand—chopping the rest of these stumps in Mrs. Bascomb's yard, so he could disappear for a few more weeks into the woods. Focus, and not think of the girl's words, nor the spark of her brown eyes that flashed with unhindered frankness. He gathered the logs in his arms, turned to take them over to the white clapboard home on the far side, to keep them away from the sea spray as much as could be. But when he turned, pushing the girl from his thoughts—there she was.

"Mr. Bliss," she said. Eyes wide, and looking as startled as he, she had her hand raised as though having meant to tap him on the shoulder. In pulling her hand back, she accidentally knocked loose a log from the stack in his arms.

"Would you look at me," she said. "Jumpier than a long-tailed cat in a room full of rocking chairs. Here . . ." She stooped to retrieve the piece of wood and stacked it right back on top of the others. Then, pushing her mouth to the side as if in deep consideration, she shook her head. "Nope, never mind. I'll take that back."

She went to snatch the wood away and he shifted to the side. "You can't," he said. "These are Mrs. Bascomb's."

"Of course they're Mrs. Bascomb's. Whomever that may be. I'm not trying to rob her of her firewood—I only meant to help you carry these sticks wherever they're going." She dropped her gaze to the earth between them. "Seeing as how I'm fixing to ask you for a favor."

She held on to one end of the stick, he the other. He cleared his throat, easing it from her grip. "A favor?"

She looked at him, puzzlement crossing her face. "You sure aren't one for many words, are you, Mr. Bliss?"

"Only when they matter," he said.

A breeze picked up and blew her dark hair off her shoulders, away from where sprigged flowers scattered in print across her dress's fabric. This girl was a mystery. A sea of spunk capped with waves of a gentle kindness. Worn-out clothes, living right there in Everlea Estate with all its ruffled trimmings.

She planted her hands on her hips and blew out her cheeks. "Well, then. I'd better cut right to the point, hadn't I?" She took a deep breath, shoulders lifting. "Mr. Bliss? I'd like to hire you." She lifted her chin in a way that said she'd worked herself up to this, that maybe she'd never hired a soul in her life.

He wasn't looking for more work. He was looking to get out and away from town as quick as he could, actually. Back to the honest work of hauling wood for the coming season. The sap of the pine had a way of cleansing his hands from the grime of his past.

But the way she shifted her weight and her near-worn-through shoes tilted on their sides, betraying her nerves, made him stifle a smile. And maybe want to keep her wriggling just a minute or two longer.

He tipped his head for her to follow as he crossed the fading-green lawn to stack the wood. She scurried to keep up with his long strides, but once at his side, did an admirable job matching his speed. Her cheeks flushed pink beneath a scattering of light freckles, setting off dark and wide eyes that held no pretense.

"What did you have in mind, Miss Thorpe?"

"Savannah," she said. "I don't think I'm quite old enough to call for all this 'Miss Thorpe' business." Her smile eased the discomfort in her words. She rallied, standing straighter. "But one thing I know is, my cousin Wilbur is heading out today to conquer those mountains. Taking Mary with him, and a few others." She cast a worried look at the mountain rising behind them.

Alastair ceased stacking wood and looked to the mountain with her. Mary and Wilbur Hapley versus Birchdown Mountain? The thought sent chills down his spine. He'd seen more on that mountain than the two of them could imagine.

"It's a romantic notion, this wilderness expedition . . ." Her voice trailed off, and it was admirable, the way she struggled to put it kindly.

"But?"

She ducked her head. "But . . . I fear they may be about to be eaten alive by it, to tell you the truth."

"That, we can agree on." He strode across the yard to return to work, and she followed, not missing a beat. Making sure she was at a safe distance, he picked up his axe and steadied a new stump to chop, raising the tool to swing.

"I'm going with them."

The axe froze in midair. He lowered it slowly to his side, turning to face her.

"You just told me you feared for them."

She nodded. "Yes."

"And now you're joining them?"

She rose to her full height—still petite, but the presence she summoned in that slim stature was a force to be reckoned with. Maybe the wilderness should be the one to fear her, not the other way around. "I grew up running the rivers with my papa every summer in Georgia. And if I can survive the alligators, and mosquitoes straight out of the Exodus plagues, I think I can contend with a few moose."

"And black bears."

She flinched. Swallowed hard. And drew her shoulders back, as if to defy fear. But her eyes flicked to the side, belying that summoned courage.

"What I *can't* do," she said, "is find a needle in a haystack I've never climbed."

"I don't follow." Alastair picked up his axe and resumed swinging. *Reason number twenty-nine—trees don't ask for favors.*

She stepped closer and took a map from her apron pocket, unfolding it and smoothing it out across the stump.

He planted the axe blade-first into another stump and folded his arms, zeroing in on one piece of land in the upper-left-hand corner of the map near her thumb. His one and only claim in that broad expanse of trees.

"You need to find something in there?"

"I think so. See, look." She unfolded a much older, smaller piece of paper. This one oddly resembling the larger in its lines and topography, but askew somehow. As if viewing it through a warped magnifying glass. The labels scratched upon it looked firm but faulty—that of a child bent on adventure.

"Here." Savannah pointed to an ink-blotted rectangle on the child's map. *Castle in the Woods*, it said. "This is what I need to find. And I'd surely appreciate your help, since you know these lands so well. I'll pay you the going rate of a guide. . . ." Her voice trailed off as she seemed to notice anew the run-down state of her own faded red shoes. "Somehow."

She fell silent, eyes falling on the map and brows pushing together as if she beheld an unsolvable puzzle. But her reverie did not last. She abruptly drew herself up with a quick intake of breath and folded the paper into its familiar creases.

"What did you mean last night?"

Savannah Thorpe reminded him of a rock skipping over water, shifting topics as fast as a pebble skims ripples.

"Last night?" He narrowed his eyes. "When, in the woods? I meant what I said. 'Who are you?' You looked . . ."

Now she was the one narrowing her eyes. "I looked what, Mr. Bliss?"

Like home, he thought. And she had. Freckled and spunky

and lovely and like she was born for moonlight. But what he said was, ". . . far from home." Which she had.

And she felt it, too, judging by the stricken look on her face. Like he'd said too true a thing.

"Well, that may be," she said. "But what I meant was, what did you mean about the ship?"

"The ship."

"Yes, the British sailors? You said that they couldn't always abandon a ship when it was stranded. What did you mean?"

He went back to chopping wood, giving thought before he said, "You ever hear about the *Gaspee*?"

"The what-ee?" She planted a hand on her hip, tilting her head to the side.

He pulled in a smile. She was completely without guile. "The *Gaspee* was a ship stationed down the coast in Rhode Island right around the time of your story. Full of British soldiers, and the locals were none too happy about the way they policed the comings and goings of the merchants there. True, it was their duty, but there was a whole lot of resentment about that, and not a whole lot the colonists could do about it. Until—" He stooped to pick up the newly split wood and flinched when something pierced his palm.

Pulling his hand in to examine the offender, he froze when she caught his hand in hers. She drew her face close as if she'd done this a thousand times.

"I can manage," he said, beginning to tug his hand loose. But she shot him a look that told him he'd best let her alone.

"You grow up around a lumber mill, you learn a thing or two about putting splinters in their place," she said.

"You mean taking them out of their place."

"Same thing." She bent her head to examine it, and the warmth of her breath stroked his hand, her nimble fingers gently coaxing the sliver. "Carry on, Mr. Bliss. The sailors?"

He cleared his throat. Tried to concentrate on a ship from seventeen-seventy-something when a very vibrant girl in the here and now was so close he could smell lavender in her hair.

He cast his gaze to the sky, where a few wayward clouds scudded. "Well, the ship ran aground while giving chase to a merchant ship," he said. "They were stuck. Also like your tale." He paused. She turned her face to his, sensing there was something he wasn't saying.

"Well, go on, Mr. Bliss. I'm not a Southern rose ready to wither at bad news, contrary to what you might think."

"The fact is, some people think the legend of the woman in the woods is just a different version of the *Gaspee* story. The ships stranded in small colonial harbors, the British in danger from the locals . . . there are a lot of similarities."

"Danger from the locals," she said, undeterred. "Now we're getting somewhere. Tell me about that."

"It was a revolution, after all," he said, and she released his hand. Not a trace of the splinter left as he pressed his thumb over the wound. "There were those who would see the British thwarted. And there were some who would even see them . . ."

"Go on," she said, eyes wide.

"Well—the captain of the *Gaspee* was shot, presumed dead at first. The ship itself was burned and sank to the bottom of the harbor. These were not accidents. After that, a stranded ship of Redcoats was a sitting target around here. So in your story, if they didn't get a mast and get out of there, it could have been only a matter of time before some of those with dark intents gathered from up and down the coast and made their attack."

"Do you think that's what happened?"

He shook his head. "There's no way to tell. Barring diving to the bottom of the ocean to see if there's any hint of a ship there."

She laughed. "Not likely, unless you're in an H. G. Wells

story." A thoughtful look crossed her face, and she pulled her map back out. "But what if we could find an answer by going the other way?"

He waited.

"Up." She gestured at the mountain rising in the distance beyond the harbor. "The story, the markings on this map—I can't help but think they're related. That the mountain holds answers."

He examined the map again, trying to make sense of it. He'd traveled up that way a hundred times at least, and never noticed a thing there other than ferns and fallen moss-draped logs in the understory. And, this time of year, leaves drifting to the ground in all their autumn color. Then again, it was another world up there—and in it, he knew, were worlds hidden within worlds, the woods were so thick at times. "You're that eager to find out if the story is true?"

Her cheeks flushed. "Not exactly. Will wants to find some proof of the woman in the woods. But I'm on the hunt for something else."

"And what might that be?"

She traced the rectangle with her finger.

"A miracle."

6

"Let me get this straight," Alastair said. How he'd let himself get roped into this wild-goose chase, he did not know. Or did not want to acknowledge that it might have something to do with the freckled firebrand whose long braid swung down her back on the mountain climb in front of him. Yet here they were, half a day's journey in, with afternoon stretching into evening.

Wilbur and Mary squabbled somewhere behind them, a scattering of their friends trailing even farther back. They'd long since passed the new lumber camp, where Savannah had stopped to talk with the men breaking up logjams along the creek bank. Some were spearing the logs with their long poles, others were finishing off the last of what they called their "second lunch"—boiled ham, boiled eggs, and doughnuts.

She'd leaned in to hear over the rush of the current, asking them about life up here, about how they were treated, about what they were doing to safeguard young growth. It quickly became clear that she knew her way around a lumber operation.

Alastair, looking on, couldn't help but scratch his head when she pointed at the logs in the water, then at a particularly tall fellow's boots. He couldn't hear what she said, but the man lifted up his foot to show the sole, where metal spikes protruded like teeth all over the surface. She folded her arms and nodded with approval.

"What was that all about?" he asked when she'd rejoined him.

She shrugged a shoulder. "This was my aunt's land, before Uncle Albert sold it. I just wanted to see what sort of hands it fell into and how they're taking care of it. And of the people working for them." She glanced back at the men, who gawked like they didn't know what sort of human—part honey, part tempest—had just blown through their camp. "If I should have to sell . . . I'd just want to know," she said.

"But you won't have to, you said."

"Not if I can find something of value," she replied.

"On your own land."

"That's right." Savannah tossed the words into the air as if this all were the most natural thing in creation.

"And if he sells it . . . then what?"

She shook her head. "He wants to invest the profits."

"On your behalf?" Something wasn't adding up about this.

"So he says. But I'd venture a guess that the company he has in mind would benefit him, were he to own more shares."

She was a sharp one. "You don't seem one to venture," he said, and was rewarded with her melodic laugh.

"You're right about that. But Uncle Albert is, and that's what scares me."

"And you think your best bet at finding something of worth is by following this map of your mother's"—he bent to toss a rock out of the path up Birchdown Mountain—"which she created when she was, what? Nine?"

"Mmm-hmm." There was melody in her voice.

"You don't think it might have been—" he searched for a way to put this kindly—"the workings of a very creative mind?"

"You mean made-up." She cast him a glance over her shoulder. For someone who wanted a guide, she sure did like to take the lead on the trail.

"Well, if you want to put it that way . . ."

"With my mother, it's hard to say where imagination and reality divided." She turned, catching her breath and facing him. "That was Mama's beauty. Everything was magic to her. Moonlight on waves down in Georgia was the sea coming alive and bringing us silver on shore. The heavy air before a storm was the sky making a promise, and the rainfall was an invitation to dance in that promise." She unscrewed her canteen and took a sip, furrowing her brow. "It's hard to say *if* imagination and reality could divide for her. They were one and the same, everything a miracle."

"Sounds like the soul of a poet," Alastair said.

Savannah laughed. "Yes. Maybe it skips a generation, because I certainly did not get that gift."

"That makes two of us," he said, and couldn't keep a half-smile from breaking.

The others drew closer, their off-tune rendition of "It Had to Be You" fracturing the forest.

Savannah pursed her lips and met his gaze in unspilled laughter. "I'd say you've got things right, Mr. Bliss." His name sounded melodic in the honeyed hues of her accent. "Sometimes it's better to be a man of few words than—"

"Say!" Wilbur burst upon them through quaking aspens. Their leaves quivered as if they'd never been so rudely treated. "We there yet?" The fellow was so affable, it was hard not to like him despite his volcano-like tendencies.

"Where's that, Will?" Savannah asked.

He shrugged. "Camp. Dinner. Waif-woman's hollow. Wherever. Are we any of those places yet?"

"Afraid not, old boy." Alastair used Will's favorite phrase, clapping him on the shoulder good-naturedly.

Wilbur scrunched up his face as his stomach growled ambitiously. "Afraid so, old boy. It's time." Wilbur returned the shoulder slap and looked around. Spotting a clearing with a pile of imposing boulders, he brightened. "There! The promised land."

By now Mary had caught up, as well as the others. All clad in khaki and white, the crisp lines of their ironed adventure outfits smudged and wrinkled despite their best attempts to hike pristinely. And as if the clearing were the Ritz-Carlton Hotel, they hoisted down wicker packs from the packhorse one of them led, and began pulling out pieces of a silver tea service, hampers packed with paper-wrapped sandwiches from the kitchen of the Gables, and jars of colorful confections. Linen tablecloths were spread upon the ground and a scattering of stumps, making for a fine dining experience right in the middle of the wilderness.

"It would appear we're outnumbered," Savannah said.

Alastair heard regret in her voice, knowing she wanted to press on as much as possible before sundown.

"We could go on ahead," he said. "Search the area, see if there are any signs of castles . . ."

"You don't have to make it sound so farfetched." She feigned offense, but he saw the spark of humor in her eyes.

"We really could, though. Explore some, and then rejoin the others before sundown."

The others were making appreciative work of their meal, with declarations of the savory goodness. And while he wanted to soldier on and get this job done, too—his appetite had other ideas. A low rumble sounded from his stomach. His face grew hot, and Savannah pursed her lips as if stifling a laugh.

"Come on, you two!" Will hollered and scooped the air to gesture them over.

"Come on!" Savannah echoed Will's invitation. "Adventurers need to eat too, after all."

Soon they were settled with a bare stump between them, devouring cucumber sandwiches, buttermilk fried chicken, and the fattest, sweetest blackberries he'd had all summer, mixed with fresh mint. To finish the feast, there was a Thermos of tea and slabs of a pie, the likes of which he'd never tasted before. Thick-crusted on the bottom, and that crust soaked with rich maple tones holding a filling of hazelnuts together.

He took one bite and froze, the flavors drawing him in.

Savannah laughed. "Something wrong with that pie?"

He finished his bite, turning the rest of the piece in his hand. "Wrong? If this pie could be served to everyone in the world, a whole lot of problems would be solved." He tried to wait for her reply, but with the rest of the confection calling him, couldn't. Chomping down, he savored the sweetness of the dessert and the way it wrapped right around the chime of her laugh.

"An old family recipe," she said. "Well, sort of. All but the hazelnuts."

"You made this?"

She nodded, smiling.

Finishing off the last crumbs, he folded the paper it had been wrapped in and tucked it into his back pocket. "That," he said, "was a pie to remember."

The sun dipped low over the trees, and Alastair saw Savannah's countenance fall with it. Looking at the others, and then back in the direction they should be headed, she was clearly torn.

Maybe it was the way her tale had drawn him in the night before. Maybe it was the way she took to this mountain unafraid, slashing underbrush with the best of them right there in her yellow sprigged dress. Or maybe it was that when her eyes settled on him, he felt . . . found out. As if she'd seen him there in the shadows he so favored, and she was inviting him to step into the light. Whatever it was, something in Alastair rose up in defense of her, wanting to go to battle on her behalf. But he knew asking this crew to venture farther today was a use-less task; they were settling in around a campfire for a game of charades, and if he knew anything, this was just the beginning of a long string of diversions. They were here for amusement, after all. Savannah, on the other hand, was on a mission.

Mary sauntered over to them and lowered herself with af-fected grace to her cousin's side. "Daddy says he had a—how did he put it?" She directed her large eyes to the side, blinking as if it took great and impressive prowess to recall what was said. "He said he had an 'enlightening heart-to-heart' with you about the future."

Savannah's countenance fell, and suddenly it was Alastair who wished he could bring the light into her world for her.

"I suppose you could say that," she said. "But the only things he was interested in discussing were stocks and land. If you ask me, the future is a bit more than that."

"Oh? And what are stocks, then? Surely you've seen what investments are doing for our country. Why, people who had hardly two cents to rub together just a year ago are building their own mansions in Newport now. If that's not the future, then what would you call it?"

Alastair blocked the rush of words that wanted out. *Fraud. Pride. Riches. Poverty.* All rolled into one, as he'd learned the hard way. But not everyone involved in the stock market fell hard to its lure as he had. Some were wise. Careful. Prudent. Everything he should have been. He'd do well to remember that.

Savannah studied her cousin. "I'd call it . . . maneuvering."

"Well . . ." Mary examined her fingernails. "*Maneuvering* is imminent, then."

Savannah sat up straight. "What do you mean?"

"Daddy says he'll be headed back to Wall Street at week's end to conduct this business on your behalf."

Savannah clambered to her feet. "That's not possible."

"That's the beauty of the world we live in, dear cousin. Anything is possible." And with that, Mary lifted a hand. It took a moment for Alastair to register that the motion was, apparently, his cue. Standing, he offered the expected hand and helped the girl to her feet. She meandered back to her gaggle of friends, apparently satisfied at the wreckage she was leaving behind.

Beside him, Savannah's breath came quicker, her cheeks flushed as she fumed.

"The nerve," Savannah said. "I bet he was just trying to get me out of the way, sending me up here on a wild-goose chase." She fisted her hand, her string of mutterings growing lower and faster until Alastair couldn't decipher them. But there was something more than anger in her, the way her gaze followed Mary like she'd lost something dear.

"What is it?" he asked.

Savannah shook her head. "She wasn't always like that."

"Mary?"

"Yes. She used to be . . . I don't know. You've seen the way she can hold a crowd. That . . . charisma. That's always been there. It used to be her beauty, back when we wrote letters to each other. The few Christmases we spent together. Sometimes it almost felt like she was the sister I always wished for. She could take an ordinary gathering and make it come alive."

"And . . . now?"

Savannah shook her head, tossing a pebble. Looking at her cousin as if beholding a puzzle. "Now, I doubt she'd be caught at an ordinary gathering. And yet"—she smoothed her worn dress, tugged at her braid—"the ordinary has up and come to her."

Alastair was beginning to think that nothing could be further from ordinary than the creature before him.

"Listen," he said. "They're going to be up far into the night. And when they do that, they sleep half of the next day away." He didn't blame them. It was just the way of the life they led, and truth be told, he'd slept many a morning away after staying up late himself. His reason just happened to point skyward, to the shows the heavens put on each night.

Savannah laughed. "At this rate, we'll climb this mountain in—oh, I don't know. Three months? What do you think?"

She tilted her head as if calculating in earnest, softening her words into humor.

"I wonder how they do it sometimes," she confided. "I've tried, truly. Mary was so eager when I first arrived to 'acclimate me to the life I deserved.'" Savannah smoothed her words into an uncanny impression of her cousin. "She means well, I know. And I'm thankful; she didn't have to acknowledge me, let alone try and bring me into her world. I'm just . . ." Savannah shrugged. "No good at it. My brain shuts down with the sun, and my limbs are ready to rise with it. A lifetime of being a farmer's daughter doesn't quickly leave a body," she said, her smile carrying a tinge of sadness.

A struggle he well knew, from his own foray into another life. The memory of it—of feeling all his sharp edges scrape against a rounder sort of world—made him want to grasp her hand and dig her a tunnel out. "We can be up with the sun," Alastair said. "Let them get their sleep, and we'll go on the hunt."

Turning, she studied him, her face earnest and fresh.

"Why, Mr. Bliss. That is an inspired idea." But the delight on her face fell quickly.

"What is it?"

"I'm worried," she said. "About how to pay you. I do want to do right by you. And if we find what we're looking for, maybe there will be something—"

"How about this," he said. "If we don't find what you're looking for, no need to pay me."

She looked ready to protest, and he rushed in with the most important part of the bargain. "And if we do—" he pulled the paper back out of his pocket, creasing the edges that had once held her pie—"you can pay me in something golden, and round, and rich."

As though sensing what he was about, a slow smile formed. Her eyes were bright. Merry. And focused on his in a way that told him she'd be more than happy to oblige.

"Doubloons?" Her smile told him she knew full well he wasn't referring to the currency of pirates. She fingered the long grass, letting her gaze follow. "If it's a pie you're after, I fear you'll be poorly paid," she said with a hint of color in her cheeks. As though realizing what he wasn't quite saying—that for very little, he would brave this land. This walk that had them steadily side by side for the whole day through and with the promise of more to come.

7

Savannah's worn old boots carried her through a tangle of pale morning light. This place—the Hinterwood, they called it—she'd expected a daunting wilderness, rugged and cold. The farthest reach of forest on Birchdown Mountain. And while it was indeed rugged—every muscle in her body ached from the ascent—the only thing she felt even in the chill of morning . . . was warmth. A homecoming she could not explain.

This was a storied place. Sowed with time and history. A glance at her mother's map, and a second at Uncle Albert's, which Alastair now held, told her that if they were to find this fabled place . . . it should be right here.

And yet every square inch around them was covered in evergreen. Spruce and balsam, hemlock and pine. Some towered above them, others sat like pupils at their grandparents' feet, covering the area in a sea of soft young growth to be waded through.

Savannah ran her hands along them, letting their waxy soft touch usher her deeper in. And yet—no sign of any sort of structure.

Alastair scratched his head, looking from the map to the trees to the sky, where a crow cried at them from above.

"Castle in the woods," he said. "You're sure it was an actual building?"

Savannah turned slowly, narrowing her eyes to take in every detail of this place. "I'm not sure of anything."

The crow cawed again, and beneath his cries, Savannah heard the faintest whisper of another sound. She froze, listening. Alastair did the same.

"Is that . . ."

Her mouth twitched into a smile. "Water." The hushed flow of it, coming from just to their left. "If you were to build any kind of structure way up here, what would you want it to be next to?"

"Ideally? Nothing and nobody. That's why most people come out here, to get away."

Savannah noted something personal in his voice. As if what he said was far more than speculation. "Yes, but even hermits need . . ."

The trickle of flowing current encircled Alastair's answer. "Water." Without a word more, they walked toward the sound. As they rounded into a new view, two giant hemlocks stood guard, their branches interlacing like a fence of evergreen. Pausing at the living wall, they exchanged a glance before pushing through the gateway. More thick shrubbery lined the avenue, vestiges of a true path, long gone. But now, the lines of trees served as arms reaching out to stop them.

At last, they broke through the spiced halls of green and into a clearing. Savannah's arms tingled, her fingers curling in anticipation of what they might find. Could there truly be a castle? She'd heard tales before of wealthy generals building their own fortresses to retire in, or millionaires staking a claim for European-style castles up in these New England mountains. Perhaps her wondering might not be so crazy.

Alastair reached for her arm, stopping her in her tracks with a strong but gentle grip. "Look," he said, pointing with his free hand. "There."

Savannah gulped. His words were simple but the way her heart raced, he may well have been a herald with brass trumpet in hand, declaring, *Behold! Your palace!*

She inched toward the direction he pointed, scanning. Ferns grew in a perimeter, and moss covered something with a thick carpet of green. A . . . a wall?

Together they moved toward it, his hand sliding down her arm and, rather than releasing her entirely, encircling her hand instead. He surely felt her pulse pounding, clumsy girl that she was. But how often did one discover a long-lost—

They skirted a stand of aspens, and the wall came into clear view. The "palace," if this was indeed what was depicted on her mother's map . . . was not a reaching edifice of stone. It was a rustic building of stacked logs, wide chinking, and lopsided roof. No bigger than the boathouse back at Everlea Estate.

There was something about its sleepy windows and squat stature that seemed friendly yet forlorn. As if it were Rip Van Winkle himself, waking to find an entire revolution had passed while he slept.

Savannah pulled out the hand-drawn map, tracing the sketch. "Castle in the Woods," she murmured. "So much for that." She laughed, imagining how this place must have looked to Mama's girlish eye. It had probably seemed a castle to her back then—though a body would have to pay someone to take ownership of it now.

Here was her inheritance, then. How Mama would have delighted in the irony of it all—and how she wished she could laugh with her now.

Alastair slid a hand to hold the paper steady as a breeze toyed with its corner. Looking from the paper to the cabin, a low laugh rolled from within him. "Yes," he said. "I could see this old place seeming castle-like to a ten-year-old. Can't you?"

Savannah scanned the chinked wood lengths, could almost hear them groaning with time. "Especially if that ten-year-old is my mother." She smiled.

"She had a good imagination, then?"

She laughed. "She was imagination itself." It felt good to speak of her with laughter, to feel the jagged edges of grief gentled with fond memory. "There—that door may as well have been a drawbridge over a gator-infested moat to her."

"Drawbridges were meant to be crossed." Alastair slung his pack over his shoulder and strode toward the door. He paused there, letting her be the one to unlatch its moss-covered latch.

Inside, she resisted the urge to call out *hello?*—for the walls seemed alive in their tired strength. Above them, something fluttered from its roost and swooped over their heads, through the door. The sudden movement sent Savannah's pulse racing, hand to her heart. She gulped.

"Just a barn swallow," she said, coaching her voice into an easy tone belied by her fast breathing. "Do you think it's safe in here?"

Alastair pointed at the roof, its sagging form around a hole showing a snatch of blue sky above. "That's the work of a long winter," he said. "Anything that was going to fall, fell with snow heavier than you and I combined."

"Still," she said. "Be careful."

She began to work her way around the snug cabin clockwise, and Alastair moved the opposite way.

There was an eeriness here, a sense that the place had stood still in time for longer than Savannah could fathom. Cobwebs and shadows, striped chinking in between stalwart logs. An earthen floor. And then all around the perimeter upon these rough-hewn logs, an odd touch of domesticity. Framed needlework pieces—most askew, many of the glass plates cracked. Thread stitched delicately and framed with rustic wood. Each one held a single line of a verse in the old way of writing: the letter *s* appeared as an oddly slanted, uncrossed *f*. Each rectangle was stitched with meticulous care until a forest of green vines and leaves grew amongst the words in thread.

The frames hung at odd intervals and height differences that made no sense. Some just a log or two up from the ground, others at eye level, and still more near the roof line. Dipping and bobbing in a way that made Savannah's insides do the same. But the order of the poem was linear, stringing together a hope that plucked a chord of longing in Savannah's soul:

> Though my sins are of a crimson stain
> My Savior's blood can wash me white again.
> Though numerous as the twinkling stars they be,
> Or sands along the margin of the sea,
> Or as smooth pebbles on some beachy shore,
> The mercies of the Almighty still are more.

The words undid something inside her. Making her feel seasick with their odd placement, yet carried along by their light.

On the timbered mantel, a collection of dirt and leaves, acorns and pine needles had gathered over the years, enrobing a solitary portrait. A man sketched in black ink, standing beside a girl seated upon a chair. She wore simple clothing, a dress unadorned by lace or ruffles. And he was sketched in a suit of black.

It was striking, the effect. Perhaps not the art itself, for in some ways it was rudimentary, compared to other family portraits rich with color and hue and detail from that era. But the way the two beheld each other—the girl with a smile that skimmed the surface of hope and the man with such kindness in his face—the artist had roped it into her quill and poured it out upon the paper in simple lines. In the bottom right corner, precise but girlish letters read *Lissette and Uncle John*. And then Lissette had signed it with just her first name, dated 1768.

Savannah ran her hand gently over the old frame, taking care around the single crack that ran the length of the glass. It was tiny, all told—no bigger than the palm of her hand. And yet somehow, it shook Savannah's entire world. What would it be like, to be the ward of an uncle who cared like that? To not be seen as a commodity, an inconvenient means to wealth?

A shiver traversed her spine as she set the image carefully back into its nest. "What *is* this place?" she murmured.

"I don't know," Alastair said, "but whoever lived here thought a thing or two about King George and jolly old England."

Savannah turned to see him holding several books and papers. He set them down on the old table, a pile of dust releasing into the air. Vague light seeped in through a window whose wavy glass dripped with time.

Joining him at the table, she pulled one of the papers toward her. *The Massachusetts Spy*, the newspaper's masthead said in intricately scrolled letters. Beneath it, a length of a great snake, segmented and labeled with initials of what she thought were the colonies, or at least several of them, and facing a dragon crouched in imminent attack. "'Join or die,'" she said, reading the words above the snake aloud. She'd seen this before—in her school days, studying the works of the engraver Paul Revere.

"'Do thou Great Liberty, inspire our Souls—And make our Lives in thy Possession happy—or, our Deaths glorious in thy just Defence.'" It was dated 1774.

"Look at this." Alastair pulled two small pieces of fabric from the pile. Each was the shape of a small flag and roughly embroidered. The first, nine uneven red and white stripes, painting the cloth top to bottom. And the other, a red flag with a white square in the corner, emblazoned by red lines into quadrants with a pine tree nestled in the uppermost corner. "Sons of Liberty," Alastair said, tapping the first flag. And then the second, "The flag of the Pine Tree Rebellion."

A solitary feather lay nestled in the papers, tucked inside a yellowed pamphlet reading *Common Sense*. And an old leather journal, marked with scribblings so old it would be a miracle to decipher their splotched form. Something about *forgive*—and there, a few lines down, *allowed to live*.

"What is all this?" Savannah asked. The words were familiar, but she felt as if she'd stepped from her ordinary world into one lined in shadows and hushed with secrets.

Alastair shook his head. "Pieces of a puzzle," he said. "Best I can tell, we've set foot in the cabin of a Patriot." His brow furrowed as he ran his fingers down the spine of the old journal.

"A revolutionary?" The stories of colonists rising up against their motherland of England punched into her memory from dusty history books in her old Georgia schoolhouse. Well over a century ago now this had all taken place—so distant, yet touching these things made it feel as if the stirrings of such a time had only just laid themselves to rest, here in the cabin.

Alastair nodded, fingering the small embroidered flags. "Someone bent on separation from England and its Redcoat soldiers. These are relics of a time leading up to what became a free America," he said. "The Pine Tree Rebellion. It stretched way up into these woods, when the king claimed the best lumber for his own ships. He needed them for tall masts, while the ones who dwelled and worked and lived off these woods suffered for it. And the Sons of Liberty—"

"Ah, the fellows that cooked up the Boston Tea Party," Savannah said. "Right?"

Alastair nodded. "Among other things, yes."

"How do you know all this?"

He patted his back pocket, pulling out a small volume of his own. "Lunch breaks," he said. "It's the best reason to be a lumberjack. Sit and eat and read with only the trees to look on."

Savannah smiled. "What, to behold their future as paper? Perhaps discover the fate of their long-lost cousins?" She shook her head. "Trees to pulp to paper. I used to watch them churn pulp at Mama's mill when I was a girl. It's always amazed me to see what a minuscule amount of pulp a giant of a tree can make."

"And what a giant of a thing can be written upon such a small amount of pulp." He held up Thomas Paine's *Common Sense* pamphlet.

"Touché," Savannah said. A handful of words could change the world, this was true. She began to move around the cabin again, hunting for more that these walls might tell them. "So you spend your meals with books in your pocket," she said. "What do you have there now?"

He tapped the volume in his hand. "*Rob Roy*." A roguish grin spread over his face. "Forefather of my ancestors' clan. Father of heroes."

Savannah took the pages and smiled. "Wasn't he a thief?"

"That depends. Would you call Robin Hood a thief?"

"Yes."

She'd stumped him.

"Well, then—yes, I suppose Rob Roy was a thief, too. They called him the Robin Hood of Scotland. But more than that, he was a MacGregor!" Alastair clenched a fist of pride in front of him. "Clan of warriors, back in Scotland. And if I'm ever blessed with sons, I hope I'll be able to give to them what Rob Roy has given me."

"A book in their pocket?"

"A legacy of courage." He stuffed the book back in his pocket and gestured at the table. "Which appears to be what the man in this cabin hoped for, too."

Savannah ran her hand over the wall beside her, its texture rough to her touch. "Strange," she said.

"That's not so strange. I'd think most people would want to leave a legacy."

"No, I mean—yes, of course." She wanted that, too. To pass on a legacy of courage. Though she perhaps did not deserve such fortune. "I was just thinking—these logs are so rough on the inside. Is that usual for a cabin in these parts?"

Alastair palmed a log, running its course with his hand. "No," he said. "They'd be smoothed or at least hewn. These still have the bark intact in some places."

"But not all places." Savannah scanned the room, the way dust mites spun enchantment into sunbeams from the missing portion of the roof. "Look," she said. "Everywhere one of the framed embroideries is hung, the bark is intact behind it." Other places, too, but—the only constant was the frames.

Heartbeat quickening, she made her way to the nearest one, just above her head. Gingerly, she lifted it up and away from its rusted nail mounting on the wall. And there, shrouded and kept out of sight by a stitched line of poetic lines about mercy, lay a carving in the wood.

A broad arrow.

8

〰❀〰

"That's not possible." Alastair strode to Savannah's side, running his thumb over the etching and feeling the depths of its grooves. These blows were solid and fierce. Placed by a hatchet at least, if not something more. Its three lines lay dark against the lighter tone of the old bark.

"King George's mark?" Savannah's dark eyes were wide. "The Patriot used the king's trees. But wasn't that considered—"

"Treason." He finished the sentence when she paused. "Yes. And punishable by a hundred pounds back then."

Savannah thought of her uncle's speech. How lucky they were to live in a time when a hundred pounds from that long ago was equal to over a thousand dollars today—at least. How proud he was of his own thousands, his savvy investment of them.

"But that means . . ." Looking around the room, she counted up the other frames. Five more. She moved to the next one, stooping to remove it from its post near the ground. There, just as she'd thought, burrowed another of the king's arrows.

She rose and reached to reveal the next—and the next, and the next. Picking up speed between each one, clutching the framed samplers to her dust-laden frock.

She stood in the center of the room, felt it spinning in revelation around her. This run-down shanty in the woods, standing—barely—where her mother had drawn this castle on the map . . .

Savanah let out a slow whistle. "This place had more money in its markings than I'll ever see at once in my life."

"May as well be a palace," said Alastair.

"Castle in the Woods," Savannah breathed. "But who would do this?" Savannah crossed the room to a dark corner she had yet to visit. "Why use royal wood to build—this? Way out here?"

"I'd venture a guess it goes back to all that." Alastair tipped his head back toward the table, the revolutionary papers. "Whoever this was, he was a man with a mission. It seems he was out to thwart the king however he could."

"But this goes beyond independence." She laid her hand on a door handle and tried it with a tug. It was stuck. Probably a closet, by the look and size of things. She tried again, pulling with all her weight into it. "This is personal. Calculated. More like—"

The door swung open, sending her stumbling backward as something musty spilled out onto the floor before her. The heap of dust-covered crimson fabric was a tangle of jackets, brass buttons, boots, and black tricorne hats with their three corners squashed at grotesque angles. The uniforms—or rather, what was left of them—of three British soldiers . . . in the closet of an American patriot. Three hats. One jacket, dark stains stubborn upon it where someone had tried to scrub it clean. One pair of boots—and another boot, all lopsided in its loneliness.

And suddenly this castle felt more like a crypt. What skeletons lurked here?

"More like vengeance," Savannah said.

That night, Alastair's dreams were fits of closeted uniforms and rhyming verses. Arrows carved into the marrow of a home and covered up with letters spelling out *mercy*. It all twisted together, not making sense.

The next day felt like a fog of the same, chasing shadows among trees and questions among shadows. Savannah searched for more answers—something of worth to take back to her uncle—but she carried the mission with such determination, it was impossible not to catch her passion. She was bent on discovering where that atonement tree on her mother's map was. It seemed farfetched that a piece of timber on a child's map might align with the story of the woman in the woods or that anything might actually be buried beneath it, as the tale would have them believe. But after the scars marked in the walls of that cabin yesterday, the wall of Alastair's own imagination seemed to be shoving out into this wilderness, too.

The day after finding the cabin, Alastair and Savannah soaked their blistered feet in a blessedly cool stream after lunch. Supplies were running low. Mary and Will's friends had quickly grown tired of the "glorious expedition"—some of its mystique having washed away in a rainstorm the night before. They'd headed back down the mountain a few hours before, leaving only Savannah, her cousins, and Alastair to press on.

"What say you?" Wilbur whipped a thin branch through the air, addressing the somber crowd. "One more day to conquer the wilds?" His enthusiasm was admirable, but not enough to rally the spirits of the others.

"Yes!" Savannah shot to her feet, sloshing water onto the rock she stood on. Her footprints were like her—deceptively delicate, surprisingly stalwart. Time after time over the course of the days, she'd impressed him with how quickly she'd become a part of this mountain. Rooting into it, traversing it as naturally as a breeze over the ferns.

"Maybe," Mary said, from where she lounged against a tree, eating a plump, dark berry. Wherever Savannah's cousin had plucked the berry from along the journey, she hadn't cared to share her bounty.

Mary made to pop the last berry in her mouth, but froze halfway, catching the longing gaze on Savannah's face. Mary held up the glistening purple berry. "Surely you approve, Savannah. You said yourself the woman in the woods spent her days gathering berries with her father."

Savannah swallowed, mouth watering. "Uncle," she said quietly. "It was her uncle."

"Quite right." Mary brought the berry to her lips, closed her eyes in rapture as she devoured it.

"We've only got enough food for half a day more." Alastair hated to be the bearer of bad news and deeply felt Savannah's disappointment when her face fell. But she masked it quickly, rallying.

"Half a day," she said. "Anything can happen in half a day." She said it with such hope and conviction, he almost believed her—despite the growing suspicion that they were chasing after a fairy tale.

"Very well," Mary said. "A few more hours, then. I'm game for even more, after all those berries." Mary had surprised Alastair with the spark of interest she'd shown when Savannah had revealed to her their discovery yesterday afternoon. There was a gentling in her after Savannah took her cousin by the hand and showed her around the clearing and cabin while the others explored near a waterfall. A vague but unmistakable spark as she shuffled through the papers and beheld the crumpled British uniforms. The journal, in particular, had held her interest, and she'd turned its pages with almost a reverence.

Will, on the other hand, had been positively uncontainable in his excitement. *"See? Told you the wailing waif was real. And that uniform! Who wants to wager it belonged to the man who saw her in the woods when she buried that old box? I bet the uncle caught him and did him in. Or maybe her uncle WAS the man who saw her. Or . . .*" His conjectures had gone on and on as they'd tromped through the woods searching for the fabled tree itself.

His guesses grew more farfetched as they carried on, but a few more hours found them spent. Even Will's sense of adventure dulled as the sun sank below the treetops. Their shadows stretched long, their movements slow, and Mary leaned wanly against a scraggly tree, her paling face hinting that the climbing altitude did not agree with her constitution. It was with good reason that the Hinterwood up here was rarely visited, and Mary was proof of that.

Savannah noticed, too, for she paused on the opposite side of a patch of ferns. The unfurling green in every hue stood between her and Alastair, looking for all the world like her skirt was woven of ferns. Like she was a part of this place, and it of her. Her cheeks touched with pink, dark eyes wide with anticipation and urgency, it was as though she was born for this.

But as her gaze settled upon her cousin, concern swept over those features. Alastair could feel how torn she was, glancing away into the darkening wood, and back. The pull into the mysterious beyond was strong, and yet as she closed her eyes and inhaled, she seemed to school her thoughts away from the call of it, and onto her cousin.

"Come," she said, emerging from behind the bank of ferns. She reached her hand out to Mary, whose eyes were shadowed and tired. "Let's get you home."

Mary snatched her hand away, narrowing her eyes as if she did not trust this gesture. But as she did, her body went entirely limp.

"Mary!" Savannah dove to catch her, just in time to ease her fall to the ground. Alastair and Wilbur rushed to them, and as they neared, Mary's limbs began to seize. Alastair's pulse hammered in his ears. Savannah flung her long braid out of the way, leaning close to steady Mary's convulsing arms. As she took hold of those hands, Mary's fingers clenched, then unclenched—and Alastair caught hold when he saw what they bore.

Stains. Deep purple, marking her fingertips like ink. "What's this?"

Savannah laid Mary's head in her lap, and while stroking hair from her cousin's forehead, leaned in to look. She shook her head, at a loss, until sudden remembrance stopped her. "She—was eating berries earlier."

"What kind of berries?" Alastair's stomach sank, raking his own memory with the question. If this was what he thought . . .

"Blueberries. At least I thought—but I didn't see them closely."

Mary's convulsions slowed, and Alastair checked her other hand and the inside of Mary's mouth. All splotched deep purple-black.

"This is the work of inkberries. Poison," he muttered, and regretted speaking the word aloud when Savannah's face went ashen. He swallowed, meeting those dark eyes, where desperation lived as she threaded her fingers in between her cousin's. "We need to get her back down the mountain."

9

The days that followed clouded together in Savannah's mind. Nights plagued her with waking dreams of Will and Alastair supporting Mary in her limp state, her arms barely hanging on around their necks, as they stumbled down the mountain. Of Savannah cradling Mary against herself after her stomach had purged itself once again of the poison's workings. Of feeling helpless to make it all better, to undo the harm.

They'd made it back to Everlea Island, tucked Mary safe into her bed in the grand house, where a heavy hush curtained them all for days as they waited and prayed for the poison to leave Mary's body. It was no quiet battle. Seizures and convulsions marched to the rhythm of a much-too-fast heartbeat. The doctor had been to see her several times, advising them to stay the course and let Mary's body do its work. They were too late for ipecac once they'd gotten her home, but time seemed to be offering a slow, tentative cure. Three days in, he seemed more hopeful than concerned, and they all began to breathe easier. Her case was grave, the doctor said, and though none of them could say just how much she'd consumed of the inkberries, it was more than enough to do great ill to her petite body.

Savannah had taken to the kitchen, reaching into her memory

to bake a batch of charcoal biscuits to help soothe the battle waging inside of Mary. And as she worked late into the evening, the view from the kitchen window reached across the bay to where one Alastair Bliss lived, in an old family home called Sailor's Rest. It wasn't the house—all white and clapboard in the old captain's house style—that caught her attention. It was the steady glow that came from within the shingled boathouse to the left, and the silhouette of the man working within.

Every day as the week wore on he came to check on them, and though she knew his work in the mountains was calling him, he did not set foot from this harbor while things remained unsettled at Everlea. He came, always bearing firewood. At this rate, he was liable to fill the whole island with it by week's end. But it was what he knew to do, something he could do, and Savannah keenly felt the gift of it. She'd help him stack it on the wraparound porch, and then wordlessly, they'd slip away for a walk around the small island.

This was her hour of solace each day. A place where somehow she belonged, right in the thick of not belonging. A comfortable silence to dwell in alongside a heart that understood hers. Or an unexpected warmth, him reaching out to take her hand as they crossed a brook. Or—one night—her place of confession, where her torment spilled out onto listening ears.

How could Savannah have been so naïve? To think that somehow, by her tagging along on her cousins' expedition, she might be able to help keep them—what? Safe? Like she'd thought she could keep her mother safe from the fever that took her life?

These were the questions that tumbled out, caught securely in Alastair's quiet strength. His answer had been simple: "I may not know much," he'd said. "But I have a feeling no matter how mixed up the problem is, the answer's almost always the most simple thing hiding beneath all our worries. That if we scale it back and look for the simplest truth—there lies the thing to do."

It was these words that sent her back into Everlea Estate when all she wanted to do was hide away. *"Scale it back. There lies the thing to do,"* Alastair had said. And all Savannah knew to do . . . was be here. She borrowed Alastair's book—*Rob Roy*—to read aloud when Mary was wakeful. She brought out Mama's deep red skein of yarn and the afghan she'd never had a chance to finish, and knit away the silent hours, weaving prayers for this family into every stitch.

She might not be able to undo the harm done, but she would not leave Mary's side. The least she could do was tend the once-upon-a-time friend who had been so dear to her heart in their youth. As her cousin slept, layers of curated sophistication gave way to glimpses of that child. Her face clear and unassuming in its rest, slow breaths lifting the crisp white sheets around her chest like a baptism of second chances.

Mary's own mother, Savannah's aunt Fern, ventured into the upstairs room a few times a day. She'd clasp her daughter's hand and close her eyes, lingering in the silence before slipping back out under some cloud. Savannah couldn't help feeling that her own presence here made her aunt feel less welcome. Or perhaps she couldn't bear to be in the same room as the niece who, in some ways, was responsible for all of this. Prolonging their time on the mountain, and for what? To chase a fable? She couldn't blame her.

"Stay," she said softly the next time Aunt Fern stood to depart. "I'll go." Savannah stood from her place in the corner.

Aunt Fern's green eyes looked tired, dark circles beneath them, as she let them rest on her niece. "No need for that," she said at last, lowering herself back to the chair at Mary's side. Her voice was somber as she stroked Mary's hand. Mary stirred, her eyes fluttering open briefly before succumbing to sleep once more. Her episodes had become more seldom, which was a good sign that the poison's effects were waning at last.

"You remind me of her, you know." Aunt Fern's voice took on a wistful air. At first Savannah thought she was talking to Mary, but it was her that her aunt's eyes settled on. Sad eyes, with a faraway look. Slowly, Savannah tucked her dress out of the way and settled back into the creaking chair.

"I remind you of Mary?" The thought brought a small smile. Mary was leagues more captivating than Savannah and her homespun ways.

"You remind me of your mother," Aunt Fern said. This, Savannah had not expected. No one had mentioned her mother once, not since Savannah's arrival, making her feel all the more the pariah.

She leaned forward, biting her lip and hoping Aunt Fern might say more. It stoked a comfort so warm around her homesick heart to hear those simple words.

"She was always the one getting up an adventure," Aunt Fern said at last. "Turning the old abandoned railcar behind the mountain into a hospital for wounded forest creatures. Selling pinecone garlands in the town square to raise enough money to end the Spanish-American War . . ." Was that a smile? The memories seemed to weave inside her aunt, pulling threads of magic from her childhood memories. "A castle in the forest." This last one spoken so low Savannah wasn't sure she'd heard right. "She filled life with . . . *life*."

Savannah pursed her lips, her pulse quickening. She recalled the picture Mama always kept at her bedside, of the two sisters sitting on a fallen log, holding hands, their pale eyes hiding mirth for the camera. Savannah reminded her aunt of that girl?

"I . . . know she cherished those times with you, Aunt Fern."

Fern's face fell somber again. "Yes, well. They came to a close all too soon, I'm afraid."

Savannah inched forward on her chair. "Can I ask why?"

Fern shook her head thoughtfully. "Who can say? I went off and found myself a real castle. That's what your mother called our home in Newport. And she . . ."

Disgraced the family. Married beneath her. Raised a wild-hearted daughter who has no business in society. Savannah braced herself for any of these.

"She went off and lived that magic right into her grown-up life." Aunt Fern raised her gaze to meet Savannah's earnestly for the first time. "I asked her once, in our letters, why she'd given it all up—the inheritance up here waiting for her, the riches. She could've sold it, afforded you all your own estate."

"What did she say?" Savannah slipped her hand into her apron pocket, where that childhood map met her fingers with odd comfort.

"She said she left the riches for the treasure."

Closing her eyes, Savannah saw that golden sand sprinkling from her mother's palm, illuminated by sinking sunlight.

"It was you," Fern said. "You were her treasure. You, and your father."

A hot tear dashed down Savannah's cheek, and as she brushed it away she wished for the thousandth time she'd gone for the doctor sooner. Known more what to do to help her mother. "I—" Words choked in her burning throat. "I'm sorry, Aunt Fern. I should have done more." Words that longed to spill but trembled to do so crept over the dam and rushed over the fall. "It's my fault she's gone. And Daddy, too, with his broken heart after she—"

Fern rose, her silk swishing as she tentatively crossed the room and laid a cool hand on Savannah's shoulder. Warmth did not come naturally to her, and Savannah felt the monumental effort it took for this woman to pull Savannah close, until her head rested at her aunt's side.

"We weren't as close as we'd have liked." Her stilted words

climbed out from some hidden place. "But I know just what your mama would say to that. She'd say that the good Lord knows what He's about. His number of days for us might not be what we thought, or even what we hoped. But nothing can stamp out His great purpose in every last one of those days. And for your mama . . . it was time for Him to come gather up His beloved and bring her safely home."

Savannah's soul, coiled up somewhere tight inside, began to unfurl at those words. "Do you believe that, Aunt Fern?" She could hear her mama say the words, feel the light of them slip in with hope.

The woman gave a sad smile. "I've not thought in a long time about what I believe. Perhaps it's time I did so." Mary inhaled deep and slow from a peaceful rest on the bed, a motherly affection crossing Fern's face. "Someday, Savannah Mae, when you have children of your own, don't let them repeat our mistakes. I pray they'll be as close as your mother and I once were, and when the trials of life come, it will only bring them closer. Not drive them apart." She patted Savannah's shoulder, then took a small step back.

"Now, I've seen you with that map." She nodded at Savannah's apron. "Let's have a look, shall we? I might just remember a thing or two about it."

Savannah slipped it from her pocket, unfolding it and handing it, hand trembling ever so slightly, to her aunt. There was something deep hanging on this moment.

Her aunt took it like it was a treasure, a sheen in her eyes. "Oh," she breathed. "The days your mother and I spent gallivanting through those woods." Her smile froze as she drew the paper nearer. "I'd nearly forgotten about that tree," she said.

Everything in Savannah stood at attention. "You know that tree?"

"No one could forget that tree," she said.

Savannah's pulse skittered. She recalled her uncle's words. *"Bring me one solid reason not to sell . . ."*

"The story Mama used to tell. About the woman in the woods, planting the sapling. Is it the same tree?"

Sadness crept into Aunt Fern's countenance. "That is a story passed down to us from our father, and his father before him, for so many generations," she said. "There's no telling what's truth and what's fable in it, now."

She knew something. The struggle of whether to share it shone from her eyes.

"In the story, the king's tree disappeared." Savannah gently invited more explanation. "Do you know—or rather, does the story say where it went?"

"That, my dear, is a legend too sad for remembrance." She sighed deeply, her eyes shifting to Mary, watching her own daughter's breaths come steadily after the scare she'd given them all. "But they say that the man who built that cabin"—she tapped the castle in the woods on the map—"was a wounded soul."

Savannah thought to the man's stash of liberty papers, the hints that he had been involved in events that shaped the country she now lived in. Such fierce determination that would have taken . . . and yet there had seemed a hidden tenderness, too. "In the cabin, there was a sketch of him with a young girl," she said.

Aunt Fern nodded. "His niece. Lissette. She was his ward, having lost her own family. They say they were inseparable . . . but the night the tree disappeared, something broke between them. She wanted the tree to save the soldiers stranded in the harbor below. And he . . . he saw his chance for vengeance."

No. That cobwebbed cabin, the light gilding a story lived over a century ago—it had promised such hope. Castle in the woods, Atonement Tree—these were the makings of a story of redemption. Not vengeance.

And yet . . . there had been the crumpled garments of Red-coat uniforms hidden in the closet. Was that not also a sign of vengeance taken?

Her aunt continued. "They say he cut that tree down and burned it right up. That he'd been taking the king's trees for decades out of spite, building his own home with it. A royal residence, right up there on our mountain . . . and nobody knew."

"So, the British soldiers on the stranded boat . . . they perished?" She recalled Alastair's account of the *Gaspee*. No mast, no way to escape, should anyone set their sights on the ship as a target.

"That, we do not know," she said. "They say the whole story is buried in that box beneath the sapling. Which would be . . ." She paused, calculating. "One hundred fifty-one years ago, now." She laughed. "Not a sapling any longer. She planted it to atone for the one burned, or so the story goes. But no one has found any proof of it being real—not even me and your mother."

"But the map." Savannah pointed at the sketched tree, where the *n* on *atonement* was scratched in backward in a way that burrowed her mother's fanciful imaginings deeper into Savannah's heart.

Aunt Fern's serious eyes lightened. "Oh, we scoured that mountain for that tree. This"—she traced the tree on the map—"was our best guess. Even so, we never found it. That part of the mountain is Hinterwood; the growth is thick there. Like another world."

"So there's a possibility the tree is there."

"Anything is possible." The corners of Aunt Fern's lips turned up, just barely. "Though this rendition of the map would make it quite a feat to find," she laughed, stroking the lines drawn by a child. "You have your uncle's map, too, yes?"

Savannah did, and watched with bated breath as her aunt

took pen to paper, marking a path upon the official map that set Savannah's mind spinning.

In a haze, she offered a stunned thank-you to her aunt. Fern was settled in again at Mary's side, and Mary, eyes fluttering into consciousness again, gave Savannah's hand a squeeze.

"Go on," her cousin said. "You'd better go find that tree."

"But I can't leave you—" Savannah started to protest, and Mary lifted a hand to stop her.

"If you think I'm going to let this wretched poisoning be for nothing . . ." She trailed off, her cheeks tinged pink, the first sign of color in days. "Besides—" She pulled her other hand out from the folds of her dressing gown. "This old relic isn't at home here. Best take it back to its homeland."

She held out a dark volume, and there was no mistaking the Patriot's journal. Savannah looked to her cousin, a question in her eyes.

To which Mary rolled her own eyes. "Oh, don't be so surprised. What's a girl to do if there's a mystery afoot? I had to know more, and that seemed the only account. There were a few words in there that I wanted to know more about." Mary broke her gaze, thrusting the journal at Savannah and fingering her sleeve. "Something about . . . forgiveness." These last words were mumbled, her tone softer. But just like that, her gaze snapped back, direct and alive as ever. "Anyhow. Get up that mountain, will you? And maybe—read that old thing." She twirled her finger at the journal. "Or don't. See if I care."

Savannah gave a soft laugh. Her cousin clearly did care. She hadn't expected this, that a skeleton of a bridge could be constructed in the dregs of that broken room. So many dashed hopes between the three women present within, yet it felt like a gathering place. God's hand moving and weaving, stitching these unlikely hearts to one another.

"Alright," she said. In her heart, she was already flying. Not toward the mountain, but toward the man whose roots ran deep into it.

As her feet fell softly down the corridor to deliver her to that man, a voice sounded from the office.

"Savannah Mae Thorpe," it said. Uncle Albert's voice, oddly uneven beneath its polished surface. "There's been a change of plans."

10

He what?" Angry heat coursed through Alastair. The cool near-November air did nothing to curb the injustice.

Savannah nodded gravely from where she stood in a scattering of curled-up pine shavings in the boathouse. "Uncle Albert says he has no choice but to sell the land, no matter what."

"But it's *not* his choice. It's your land."

"Technically, yes. But legally . . . he can." She twisted the striped fabric of her dress in her hand. "None of it makes sense. It's Monday. He's never here on Mondays. He was pacing that office. His fingers wouldn't stay still; he kept rifling through those stock papers, pointing out plots that would go first. Starting with the island."

Alastair froze in his own pacing. "The island is . . . yours?" That house they'd been so gracious to "let her come live in," as she put it. It . . . belonged to her?

"Apparently so. Something's not right, Alastair. He's never like this. He's always intense, but today he was like a barely contained force."

Alastair cringed. Memories blown back to a time when he'd been no different, the whims of the stock market plunging him into places he did not know he had in him.

"He was almost . . ." Savannah's voice trailed off in search of a word.

"Desperate."

"Yes," she said. "How did you know?"

The memory of it slammed him hard. "Sometimes a man recognizes a place he's been." He left it at that, thinking maybe she'd let it go. That he wouldn't have to tell her. But she turned a tin bucket upside down and sat, waiting. Listening.

"I . . . had a piece of land," he said. "Right up with yours, on Birchdown Mountain. I bought it when your uncle began to sell off your aunt's plots of land. My father was so proud. He said to save it for something remarkable, that I'd know it when it came. When your uncle blew into town boasting of his stocks, what he was doing with the money from his wife's land profits after they'd sold . . ." He shook his head. "I plunged in too hard, too fast. A lot of people go about it wisely, but . . ." He looked at his listener, dreading the judgment he might see there. Or worse—disappointment. She, at least, had the good sense to fight for her land.

But he saw only kindness there, curved around her fathoms-deep eyes.

"I was too hasty. I sold half my plot of land. Put everything I had into a shipping stock. One that was promised to defy all expectations and deliver riches." He looked through the open door, toward the old Bliss house, Sailor's Rest. "I wanted to get the home place up to speed for my parents. They work hard, have a farm a county over, and they deserve to know this place will be here as a refuge for them whenever they need it. But—I was too headstrong. Lost all the money, and then some. That desperation you describe in your uncle . . . that was me. I was consumed by it."

He waited for her to speak. To pronounce a verdict or walk out. But all she said was, "Shipping?"

He nodded. She stood from her stool, walking over to where he'd been working on a canoe, lathing long coils of wood up and away from these planks of a tree that would someday traverse waves. She ran her hand along the sweetly spiced wood. The action was simple, but somehow felt like a burying of his transgressions, a benediction upon this new way of life.

"A business you're still in, I see." She dipped her head toward the canoe.

His laugh was dry, ironic. He picked up a piece of sandpaper, and started in on the hull of the canoe. "I hope so. It's what I want to do," he said. "Build boats. It feels . . . good, somehow, to pull wood from that earth, to use it and create life from it rather than gamble it all away on a pipe dream. If I'm blessed with children one day, I promise they won't have to learn that lesson as I did. I'll teach them the trade, should they want it." His sanding grew fiercer. "And I'll tell them what my father told me—to save the land that's left for something remarkable."

Savannah stilled his hand, letting her fingers linger upon his. The sandpaper was rough beneath his palm, her touch soft atop it. Flushing at her action, she removed her hand quickly and fidgeted until she spotted a torn corner of sandpaper upon the desk, snatched it up, and began smoothing the boat alongside him.

"They'll recognize remarkable when they see it," she said, her movements slowing. "They'll be witnessing it every day." And the way her eyes locked onto his, everything in him wanted to stand taller, stronger, to be the remarkable man she seemed to be telling him he was.

"But, Alastair." The wind gusted in from the harbor, pushing her skirt around her ankles and her hair into her face. It looked like it might blow her slight form right into him—and his arms tensed, readying to catch her.

But she turned instead, facing into that wind. "Something is off about *all* of it. Aunt Fern's story of the Patriot . . . Uncle Albert's desperation to sell . . . none of it adds up."

The wind brushed past her cheeks, bringing the pink of adventure to them. "There's only one place to go."

11

The wind raked over the mountain and down over Ansel Harbor, digging in like there was treasure at its core. And perhaps there was.

"It's blowing something fierce," Alastair said, drawing up beside her in the boathouse door. Surprise and comfort collided at the sound of his voice. He said that like he was speaking to one who meant to go out in it.

Which he was.

"I think I've got to climb that mountain, Mr. Bliss."

The wind whipped her dark hair around and as she turned to face him, he brushed a tendril of it back, studying her.

"It'll be dark by the time you reach that spot," he said. He'd seen the place her aunt had marked. They had been close, before. So close. And even so, you'll have to hurry to reach it by night.

She nodded, hoping the warmth she felt beneath his gaze did not show.

"And you'll need tools," he said, never taking his focus from her. "A shovel, for starters."

She flicked her eyes to the corner of the boathouse, where tools leaned like friendly volunteers. "If only I knew someone who might lend me one. . . ."

His smile was warm. "If only."

"And if only I might be able to persuade that someone to come, too."

That smile, the curves around his mouth, gentled into something more serious.

"You're a savvy one, you know that?"

"Savvy Mae," she murmured. "That's what my dad used to call me." A genuine smile at the name she hadn't heard in so long. "Well, I don't know how savvy I am, but if you're of a mind to, Mr. Bliss, I do believe there's a mountain calling us."

Alastair had been right; it was almost dark by the time they reached the Hinterwood. The fury of the wind was fierce, Savannah's hands chafing from holding fast to trunks and branches along the way. She didn't know which drove her more: the need to save her land by whatever means she could . . . or the thirst for truth. This story that echoed her own heart's longing for forgiveness.

"This is it," Alastair shouted above the wind. He held the map out and beckoned her close; she being the one with the kerosene lantern. Together, leaning over the paper mottled and creased from the rough journey up, they drew their heads together over the plot of land that was to hold the Atonement Tree.

"There," Alastair said, pointing to a stand of aspens whose last clinging leaves quivered. "That's where my land ends . . ."

Savannah consulted the map again. "And mine begins." She spun slowly in a circle, willing the light of the kerosene farther than it would go. Shadows craned and stretched, choking out this vestige of hope she held. Turning her eyes upward, she began to search for a giant of a tree. Leagues above the rest, if it was truly old growth. But everywhere she looked, the sky met the treetops far too soon.

"Maybe we're going about this all wrong," Savannah said.

"Do you think we're looking in the wrong spot?" Alastair narrowed his eyes to see better in the darkness.

"I don't know. I just keep thinking about that cabin. Those arrows, being all scattered about, at every height, no rhyme or reason." And the transgression of them, covered over with needlework spelling out grace itself.

"Every height," Alastair repeated her words.

She lowered her lantern closer to the ground and began circling the plot of land again, weaving in and out of white aspen trunks. "Anything could have happened up here in all the years since the woman planted that sapling," she said. "Fire . . ."

Alastair looked around. "There aren't any signs of fire."

"Flood . . ."

"The water would have rushed down from so high up. I don't think it would have had the force to take down a tree so old; not at this height."

She drew her eyebrows together in thought, and just as she was about to speak the word *wind*, the force itself pummeled her with such force she stumbled straight back into Alastair. "W-wind," she said, breathless.

It howled through the branches, chasing away the last of the twilight, and the last of her hope. "It's no use," she said. "We're on a wild-goose chase if there ever was one. Who's to say the sapling from the story ever even took root and grew? If it even ever existed."

One look into Alastair's face, and she knew he hadn't heard her. He was standing, eyes wide, staring at something.

Without moving his gaze, he reached down and twined his fingers with hers. "What do you make of that?" he asked.

And there, looming dark and tangled before them, just beyond the wildwood wall of aspens, was a giant of a jagged stump. Sprawling roots tangled their way into the ground atop an eroding slope, beckoning them close.

Hand in hand, Savannah extending the lantern before them, they answered that call. Savannah couldn't help but wonder, as she placed her feet among moss and fern, if she were retracing the very steps of the young woman so desperate to make things right.

Close enough to touch it now, she laid her hands upon the moss-covered bark. Even in its death, green life dwelled here. The stump was high—taller than her, taller almost than Alastair's stretching height—and its break was rough. If the wind howled on this peak like this often, it was no wonder the giant had fallen.

Rounding its great width, they followed the tree's storied limbs to where the rest of it lay, overgrown and reaching. Years, it must have lain here. All in pieces—some great, some small. Some shards that had long since worked themselves down into the soil, to become again a part of it.

Partway up the length of the scattered trunk, Savannah paused. Something knotty marked its surface. Not the deep gauge of the arrow from the story, but the outgrowth of such a scar. Gnarled from its years—but unmistakable in its three rigid lines.

"The arrow," she said, and bent to set the lantern beside it. Her fingers traced this mark made so long ago by hands convinced they were stained with the blood of innocent sailors. A desperate cry for atonement.

"Amazing," Alastair said, and stooped to examine it. "So it's true, then."

"Something is true," Savannah said. "Let's find out what."

It must have been hours they spent, digging around the aged roots of the stump. How something so old and long fallen could still hold such strength, she did not know. But though every muscle ached and her eyes stung from the ceaseless beat of the wind, it gave her hope. That these roots, so strong, might yet be guarding the truth.

The moon was high and full by the time they'd circled nearly the whole skirt of roots, digging wherever they could.

"It's no use," Savannah said. The air was calming now, at last . . . perhaps to match their waning stores of energy. "We'll have to come back. Bring more tools, dig deeper—" With this, she plowed her shovel in one last time—and the hollow *thud* that sounded burrowed straight into her stomach.

Alastair was at her side in a moment. "What was that?"

Something coiled up inside her, renewing her excitement. Another shovel fall, this one deep but gentle, and she felt something give beneath its leverage.

The next moments were a blur of shovels and soil, moss and sticks, palms immersed in this crypt of history until at last— together, they pulled out a boxy shape. Wooden and simple, and with tendrils of roots still wrapped around it like they meant to guard it to the last.

Earth fell away from it as they set it on solid ground. A gentle brush-off of clinging soil revealed splotched letters on one side. Worn black letters that appeared to say *INE TEA*.

"Fine tea?" It wouldn't be tea, buried here all these years though. Certainly not.

"Go ahead," Alastair said. "Open it."

His urging matched that of her heart, but she couldn't make her fingers do her bidding. It was a heady thing, touching something that had not been touched or seen by another soul for over a hundred years. And its contents could seal the legend of the woman in the woods as a tragedy. Heaviness descended upon the moment, along with a hush. Only crickets sounded, slowing their song to the chill of the night.

With a deep breath and a prayer, she slid the top from its rails.

Lantern light scattered across just two things within the tin-lined space. Pulling the first out, she beheld a small painting of a man proud in uniform, grave in expression. The uniform of a Redcoat. His face was somber yet alive, as if tightly reined passion lived within. On either side of him, each with a hand on his shoulder, stood two handsome boys. Dark eyes like the older man, and such respect for him, too.

"I know this face," Savannah said. "It's our Patriot." Her mind flew to the closeted uniform. The one she'd been so sure meant he had taken a British soldier's life, when all along—*he* had been the British soldier?

Alastair slid his hand behind hers, helping to hold the framed picture. "You're right," he said. "But—why would someone loyal to the crown sabotage the king's trees? Build a cabin of lumber meant for masts?"

"And why would he have all of those revolutionary artifacts in his cabin? The papers, the flags . . . the feather." She'd been certain it was from one of the headdresses the Sons of Liberty donned when they dumped the famed chests of tea overboard in Boston. She shook her head. "I don't know. Maybe this will tell us." She reached in and pulled out the second item. A scroll of paper, tied with a bit of twine. Worn and brittle, the string snapped open at Savannah's gentle touch, and she unrolled the paper with care, making sure it did not do the same.

The writing was splotched on the aged paper, but with some work, she could make out the lines of the slanted script.

"'Good Father, forgive my uncle. He knows not what he does. A father blinded by the loss of his two sons who gave themselves for their once-beloved England. By the loss of his own land, when England forbade him to cross over new-drawn boundaries here. He sees no way but vengeance. I meant only to help, to send this tree as a boon to the sailors below . . . and instead, I've played a part in their end. Leading to the tree's destruction by my uncle, when I had been so certain he would help.

"'I plant, therefore, this new one to take its place. May the years tend it long after I am able to, and may it be used for good, and not evil. May it lead to life, not death. May it unite, not divide. May it, in the way of your own great Atonement Tree, bring light from darkness, through you, O Lord. Please'"—Savannah's throat burned as she read the two words that had ushered them into this story to begin with—"'forgive me.'" Even the crickets were hushed now, this moment feeling hallowed as they witnessed this unheard prayer, sitting on the ground once watered with the woman's tears.

"So the sailors never did make it," Alastair said. His voice was grave. She shook her head.

"It can't be," she said. The ache in her chest bloomed, rooting deeper.

Alastair laid a hand upon her arm. Maybe it was silly of her to so deeply feel the loss of people whom she would never know. But there had been so much hope buried just beneath the surface in her mother's map, in that cabin—and something in her longed for redemption to break the surface. For those in the past—and for herself, too.

"We'll keep looking," Alastair said. "There must be letters, accounts—something from history that would shed more light on this. We may be wrong."

Accounts. When he spoke the word, a vision of Mary flashed across her memory. Giving over the old journal. *"That seemed the only account,"* she'd said. *"Read that old thing."* In her haste after discovering Uncle Albert's plans, she'd failed to do so.

She scrambled over damp earth to where her satchel lay and pulled out the Patriot's journal. Flipping through, by the low light and the aged text, it was almost impossible to read. A few things were clear—handwritten notes about the time and place for dumping the tea overboard in Boston. A sketch of two young boys, their faces fresh and full of wonder. And the last thing written in the journal:

My Savior's blood can wash me white again.

The words from the framed embroidery, which covered over

the carved arrows in the cabin. It was followed by a proclamation, which she read aloud.

"'No young men shall perish this night. I have seen one so young, her courage and faith buried deep in the ground. It smites me. She tells me these sailors are sons, too. Like mine, only they still have a chance. May it be so, and may the tide of this sad life change this night. We shall bring forth a mast. They shall have life.'"

Savannah's heart was in her throat, thinking of it. The nameless woodsman who witnessed the young woman's act of atonement . . . was Lissette's very own uncle. And she, in her youth and courage, changed his heart from vengeance to life.

If this was possible, if such a thing could happen . . . then surely this tree could, as the young woman had prayed, be used for good.

12

When the mountain released them back unto the world at dawn, Alastair watched Savannah crowned with the first light of day. It was as if they were reborn. Both of them holding this tale in their hearts, and she holding a tea chest in her hands. One that had likely born the current of the Atlantic, if it had indeed been part of the Boston Tea Party.

Whether or not that was true, he didn't know. He hoped so, for her sake. It might fetch a tidy sum as an artifact, to help resolve her struggle with her uncle.

But as it happened, she had other plans.

They arrived back at Everlea to find a man in ruins. Albert Hapley, renowned Wall Street banker, hanging his head low on this dark day, following the collapse of a prominent company he'd funneled his fortune into. One he had tried—and failed—to prop up with further investment from funds he had "planned to procure."

"Ruined," he said, a man in a trance. "I'm ruined. We're ruined. Selling trees will never save us now. We're—" He tried to form the word *bankrupt*, but could not get it out. "We've lost more than we could ever regain through selling land. We're too late, Savannah Mae Thorpe."

Alastair watched as Savannah knelt before her uncle, gathered up his hands in hers, still caked with soil beneath her fingernails.

"Take it," she said, and her voice was pure and earnest. "Take the island, take the house. Please. It's yours. Sell it, or keep it. May it be a home for your family, or provide a home if you sell it to another. There is hope, Uncle."

She spoke those last words with such conviction, he looked as if even he might believe her. And well he might, for she'd dug it up with her own two hands, just hours before, finding it in the tale of another uncle and niece.

A noise sounded on the stairs. Mary hugged a dressing gown to herself, eyes wide. As she descended, Savannah approached her, wrapped her hands around her cousin's, and leaned in to whisper something. Mary's face showed a succession of fear slipping quickly into a foreign sort of peace. She nodded, and Savannah cast a look over her shoulder at Alastair. One that asked him to follow her.

Out in the morning, her dress muddied and her worn old boots making her half an inch taller and the events of the night washing her complexion with a bright freshness, he was captivated. Together they made their way through the golden-leafed curtains of the weeping birches and down to the shore.

"Savannah . . ." he began, not knowing what to say. He felt like they were standing on some great precipice together—right in this tale that redeemed the past but left the future wide open. And he did not want that future to be without her. "You . . . just gave away your home," he said. "Where will you go?"

He had an idea or two bursting to get out, a home across the harbor longing for the spark of life she would bring. But he could not ask that of her. Not yet. . . . Could he?

She did not seem troubled by the question, peace cloaking her like a shawl as the sea sparkled before her.

"I guess you could sell that land," Alastair said, dropping

his gaze to the rocky beach beneath their feet. Kicking a stone. What was he thinking? She was an heiress to a lumber empire. And he a simple lumberjack. Plying his hand at building boats, a dream for a far-off someday. She could sell that land and take herself anywhere in the world she wanted to go.

"No," she said, the word soft as she turned to face him. "That land . . . it's a place to be saved. If it's ever sold, it's going to be for something that makes a difference. Something monumental. Besides . . ." She brushed a streak of dried soil from her dress, held the grains of sand in her palm and let the sun sparkle over them. "I've got all the riches in the world, right here."

She slipped her hand into his, and together they climbed back up from the sea, into a story waiting to be lived.

EPILOGUE

The forest awakened with spring. Boisterous footsteps pounding upon it, laughter burrowing into the roots as they twisted into soil. Two worlds about to collide. The young woman flew through the woods, the swishing of her skirt tempered by the steady swing of a picnic basket through the crisp air.

There, at the edge of the Hinterwood, the foursome broke into a clearing. The air was alive here, right in the middle of the Bliss family land. For when Savannah and Alastair had wed five years before, all boundaries and parcels had melded together, right along with their hearts. And now the living, breathing joining of the two of them scampered around in the form of two wild boys, both four years old and bursting with adventure.

"Come, boys," Savannah said, and Alastair pulled out the *INE TEA* box. This holder of stories past, ready to embrace stories future. "We have something to tell you."

The pair scrambled down from a mound of boulders. Settled in on the picnic blanket with hearty helpings of hazelnut pie, their eyes grew as round as the pie plate when their mother began the tale. "There once was a woman who lived in a castle," she said. "Right up here in the woods of Maine. At least—to *her*, it was grander than any castle she could imagine. . . ."

The story went on, as it did every spring. All the pieces in place, gathered from the box, the journal, the letters she and Alastair had tracked down in the months following their discovery of the Atonement Tree. The account of one embittered British admiral who had joined up with a group of New England Patriots after the loss of his sons and his land. The darker ways that particular group began to operate over the years, seeking blood more than prisoners. The way he'd sent word to that band of Patriots when a ship became stranded—and then attempted to thwart the ship's only chance of timely escape, by burning the single pine that would have been tall enough to provide a mast before their attackers arrived. How he, in a letter to a cousin after all was said and done, gave account to the way his niece confronted him, dousing the fire and pleading with him not to let these men come to ruin, not to let their blood stain his hands and add to his sorrow. *I thought their deaths would be retribution. Payment for my own sons' deaths on behalf of a king and country that betrayed me after all we'd sacrificed,* he'd written. *She, messenger of the Almighty that night, broke light into my darkness by putting out that fire. Back to the tree's clearing she went, convinced I would not change my course. I followed to retrieve her—and heard her read her written prayer before she buried it. She pleaded forgiveness, but it was I who needed forgiving.*

Savannah proceeded with the tale of a scheme surrendered, the horse he'd hitched the log to, the mast the men were supplied with, whose very top was burned, marked with a story of near catastrophe. It was a legend that had been passed down, changed over time, turned from heart to heart until at last it had reached Savannah's young ears, down in the sands of Georgia, finally to be brought home and discovered in its true form.

"Now, what's inside here"—she leaned in, patting the wooden box as her words wound magic around the secret—"is the next part of the story. The very best bit. Because that part is up to you."

This was Alastair's cue to slide open that old box. The one that the history of a nation hinged upon. But instead of unrest and vengeance, it now housed hope, hewn straight from the Atonement Tree.

Savannah picked up a pad of paper and fanned its blank pages as if it were the greatest treasure in all the world. "This is made from the pulp of that tree." She pointed over to the jagged stump, the one standing watch and seeming, she liked to say, rather pleased with the whole scene. "On these papers, you may draw your maps. Write your stories. Confide your greatest hopes or most daring deeds. Whatever you use it for, you have one great responsibility, my boys."

By this time, Robert and Roy were growing antsy. With maple syrup from the pie running through their veins and adventure soaring in their souls, they could hardly keep still.

Here, Alastair stepped in and sat cross-legged between them, draping one arm around each of his young warriors. "Listen, boys. This is important."

And like magic, they stilled. Alastair Campbell MacGregor Bliss always had that effect on his young ones, for whom he longed to leave a legacy of courage. Leading with few words, changing their lives with his example.

Savannah's heart brimmed to overflowing and she leaned in, recalling the prayer of the woman in the woods. "This may seem like just paper, but you must vow to use it for good, and not evil. Let what you write upon it lead to life, not death. May it unite, not divide. May it, in the way of our God, bring light from darkness."

They were solemn as soldiers, then, and the way they looked at each other and nodded like she'd just knighted them both, imprinted on her heart.

"Shake on it," Alastair said, gripping their little-boy hands each in a hearty handshake before springing up to chase them around the clearing as they shrieked in delight. She watched on, awash with joy. Sliding the wooden box closed around its paper treasure, a deep settling came over her. An impression that such men—her three brave ones—were intended for great things. That though it might cost her greatly, it might fill her heart more than she could ever imagine. And that come what may, there would be light in the darkness.

AUTHOR'S NOTE

The poem hanging on the cabin's wall was one I came across by chance, when searching for embroidered samplers from the 1700s. The words are from a beautifully stitched piece by Jane Atkinson, dated about 1780, and as of this writing, housed in the Museum of Fine Arts in Boston. Though every effort has been made to trace the poem's origins, sometimes history tucks these details just out of our sight. So whether it was Ms. Atkinson herself who penned the rhyme or someone else entirely—my thanks to them, all those years ago, for putting such lovely words to the truth that "the mercies of the Almighty still are more."

The New England woods and waves were indeed home to events of great import leading up to and during the revolution. You'll find nods to many of the true stories within this one fabled one, from the King's Broad Arrow and the Pine Tree Rebellion to the *Gaspee* Attack, the Sons of Liberty and the Boston Tea Party, Paul Revere's printed engraving of Benjamin Franklin's "Join or Die" phrase, and Thomas Paine's *Common Sense*— these are breadcrumbs on a trail of a very rich and storied history. And while yes, those ancient white pines were coveted for masts of the British ships, the particular story alluded to for this tale is just that: a story. One I hope you have enjoyed, and one I hope echoes with redemption.

And I'll let you in on a secret, good reader. That tale of redemption does not end here. The land, the pad of paper, and the wood of the Atonement Tree, the legacy of courage that Alastair dreamed of giving to his someday-family, and the bravery of the twin boys you saw adventuring in the epilogue . . . their story has just begun. To join them on the rest of their journey, may I invite you into the pages of *Whose Waves These Are*? I promise, you haven't seen the last of this tree, nor the last of the goodness and light that Lissette knelt and prayed for on the forest floor that night so long ago.

ABOUT THE AUTHORS

Kristi Ann Hunter graduated from Georgia Tech with a degree in computer science but always knew she wanted to write. Kristi is an RWA Rita Award–winning author and a finalist for the Christy Award and the Georgia Romance Writers Maggie Award for Excellence. She lives with her husband and three children in Georgia. Find her online at www.kristiannhunter.com.

Elizabeth Camden is the author of 11 historical novels and two historical novellas and has been honored with both the RITA Award and the Christy Award. With a master's in history and a master's in library science, she is a research librarian by day and scribbles away on her next novel by night. She lives with her husband in Florida. Learn more at www.elizabethcamden.com.

Amanda Dykes is a drinker of tea, dweller of redemption, and spinner of hope-filled tales who spends most days chasing wonder and words with her family. Give her a rainy day, a candle to read by, an obscure corner of history to dig in, and she'll be happy for hours. She's a former English teacher, and her novella *Bespoke: A Tiny Christmas Tale* was met with critical acclaim from *Publishers Weekly*, *Readers' Favorite*, and more. *Whose Waves These Are* is her debut novel. Readers can connect with her online at www.amandadykes.com.

Books by Kristi Ann Hunter

HAWTHORNE HOUSE

A Lady of Esteem: A HAWTHORNE HOUSE *Novella*
A Noble Masquerade
An Elegant Façade
An Uncommon Courtship
An Inconvenient Beauty

HAVEN MANOR

A Search for Refuge: A HAVEN MANOR *Novella*
A Defense of Honor
Legacy of Love: A HAVEN MANOR *Novella from* The
Christmas Heirloom Novella Collection
A Return of Devotion

Books by Elizabeth Camden

HOPE AND GLORY SERIES
The Spice King

The Lady of Bolton Hill
The Rose of Winslow Street
Against the Tide
Into the Whirlwind
With Every Breath
Beyond All Dreams
Toward the Sunrise: An Until the Dawn *Novella*
Until the Dawn
Summer of Dreams: A From This Moment *Novella*
From This Moment
To the Farthest Shores
A Dangerous Legacy
A Daring Venture
A Desperate Hope

Books by Amanda Dykes

Whose Waves These Are
Up from the Sea: A Whose Waves These Are *Novella*

Sign Up for the Authors' Newsletters!

Keep up to date with latest news on book releases and events by signing up for their email lists at:

kristiannhunter.com

elizabethcamden.com

amandadykes.com

More from the Authors

Daphne Blakemoor was happy living in seclusion. But when ownership of the estate where she works passes to William, Marquis of Chemsford, her quiet life is threatened. William also seeks a refuge from his past, but when an undeniable family connection is revealed, can they find the courage to face their deepest wounds and forge a new path for the future?

A Return of Devotion by Kristi Ann Hunter
HAVEN MANOR #2
kristiannhunter.com

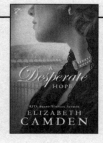

A female accountant in 1908, Eloise Drake thought she'd put her past behind her. Then her new job lands her in the path of the man who broke her heart. Alex Duval, mayor of a doomed town, can't believe his eyes when he sees Eloise as part of the entourage that's come to wipe his town off the map. Can he convince her to help him—and give him another chance?

A Desperate Hope by Elizabeth Camden
elizabethcamden.com

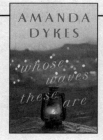

In the wake of WWII, a grieving fisherman submits a poem to a local newspaper asking readers to send rocks in honor of loved ones to create something life-giving—but the building halts when tragedy strikes. Decades later, Annie returns to the coastal Maine town where stone ruins spark her curiosity and her search for answers faces a battle against time.

Whose Waves These Are by Amanda Dykes
amandadykes.com

BETHANYHOUSE

More Novella Collections

Three of Christian historical fiction's beloved authors come together in this romantic and humorous collection of novellas featuring prequels to their latest series. All for Love includes Mary Connealy's "The Boden Birthright," Kristi Ann Hunter's "A Lady of Esteem," and Jen Turano's "At Your Request." These sweet love stories will touch your heart!

All for Love
by Mary Connealy, Kristi Ann Hunter, and Jen Turano

Take a journey across America and through time in this collection from some of Christian fiction's top historical romance writers! Includes Karen Witemeyer's "Worth the Wait: A LADIES OF HARPER'S STATION Novella," Jody Hedlund's "An Awakened Heart: An ORPHAN TRAIN Novella," and Elizabeth Camden's "Toward the Sunrise: An Until the Dawn Novella."

All My Tomorrows
by Karen Witemeyer, Jody Hedlund, and Elizabeth Camden

The path to love is filled with twists and turns in these stories of entangled romance with a touch of humor from four top historical romance novelists! Includes Karen Witemeyer's "The Love Knot," Mary Connealy's "The Tangled Ties That Bind," Regina Jennings's "Bound and Determined," and Melissa Jagears's "Tied and True."

Hearts Entwined
by Karen Witemeyer, Mary Connealy, Regina Jennings, and Melissa Jagears

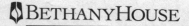